FAMILY SECRETS 3 – PROPHETIC DESTINIES

NANCY PETREY

Energion Publications
Gonzalez, Florida
2022

ISBN: 978-1-63199-845-4
eISBN: 978-1-63199-846-1
Library of Congress Control Number: 2022947622

Energion Publications
P. O. Box 841
Gonzalez, Florida 32560
pubs@energion.com
energion.com

Praise for Family Secrets 3 – Prophetic Destinies

Family Secrets 3 – Prophetic Destinies is a story about a group of young people who are all, in one way or another, intertwined in the American Jewish Community. It is about their Jewish heritage, their struggles, their desire to "make aliyah" to Israel, and also about the particular way Yeshua lays a claim to each of their lives. Nancy Petrey develops a very readable and engaging story about the personal losses, challenges, and successes of the characters' lives. Her understanding of the issues surrounding Jewish culture and Israel is superb, and even those who have a grasp of these issues may be surprised at how much they learn by the close of the book. The musically inclined will be thrilled by the way the book uses music, ranging all the way from Handel's *Messiah* to modern hymns, as stage setting and strategic backdrops for events as they unfold. It reminds us all of how great a role music plays in bringing the mind and the spirit into harmony with each other. In short, if you love Israel, and you love Yeshua, you will love this book.

~~ Ron Smith, agricultural missionary in Haiti for 22 years, where he learned Haitian Creole and began a translation of the Bible in 2013. This year, 2022, the Haitian Creole translation will be uploaded to the YouVersion Bible App. Ron also speaks Spanish and French. He serves on the Board of Directors of the Good Shepherd Ministries in Haiti, an educational outreach to 1700 school children.

Family Secrets 3 – Prophetic Destinies is more than a novel. It is the story of young lives committed to Christ who discover their Jewish heritage. It is insight into Jewish customs, language, and the yearning of Jewish people to make aliyah to their homeland. It offers biblical instruction in life's ups and downs and is a book of praise, prayer and acknowledgment of God in every aspect of life. It is a book of worship and beautiful music and enjoying the presence of an Almighty God. Finally, it is a book of an adventure-filled life for those of us who put our faith and trust in Yeshua. Nancy Petrey, because of her love for Israel and Yeshua, has written another book that has taken me on a wonderful journey. Readers should be prepared to laugh, cry, reflect, and learn along the way.

~~ Sue Smith, wife of Ron Smith, from Lakeland, Florida. Sue has an Elementary Education degree and is a retired Registered Nurse. She and Ron are active in their Florida Church in the winter and their North Carolina Church in the summer. They do team teaching, write Study Guides for their church groups, and are active in their community's Bible Study Group. They also partner with Harry Fowler Ministries and distribute the Bible Book Marks with the plan of salvation.

♥ ♥ ♥ ♥ ♥

Praise for Family Secrets 2 – Double Destinies

Having been blessed by Nancy Petrey's first novel, *Family Secrets – Divine Destinies*, I was eager to read her sequel to it, *Family Secrets 2 – Double Destinies*. I found the sequel to be an even greater blessing. The captivating plot of this delightful romance novel kept me eager to learn what would happen next.... Very cleverly Nancy uses the dialogue to teach Christians about their Jewish roots, the meaning of Yiddish words and traditions that help us understand Christian values. Lovers of music will be blessed by the way the author uses her extensive knowledge of music to enrich this enthralling love story. If you want to get lost in a book filled with suspense, conflict, tenderness, joy and inspiring examples of the power of prayer, I heartily recommend this book! It is a book you will commend to your friends.

~~ Walter Albritton, Assistant Pastor of New Walk of Life Church, Montgomery, Alabama, Pastor of United Methodist churches for 70 years, author of 20 books.

Family Secrets 2 - Double Destinies is first a love story, but it carries the reader on a journey of many dimensions. Two college couples (both engaged to be married) drive the story and deal with the temptations of young love, conviction and life calling, Christian and Jewish heritage. Life is mostly smooth sailing, but conflict interrupts with themes of rape, demon possession, dangerous "friends," and a terrorist assault.

~~ Randall Murphree, Editor of The Stand magazine, American Family Association

You will be surprised at the sweet, southern love story of two college couples who are planning a double wedding and then find themselves the next minute thrown headfirst into an international adventure! Although this book is a fictional love story, Nancy Petrey weaved an astonishingly accurate and historical amount of facts, including the Holy Scriptures, throughout the entire book. It is an educational experience for the reader, yet very exciting.... The pages just flew by, and I could not put it down.... I found it very inspiring, and when I finished the book, I wanted to know more. I felt the urge to jump into a Bible Study on Jewish Roots.... I would wholeheartedly recommend this book to anyone who likes love stories, intrigue, and lots of adventure! This book, very importantly, will give you a better understanding of Jewish culture and history.

~~ Janice Horowitz Bell, Jewish friend, businesswoman, and Bible teacher, Elba, Alabama

Family Secrets 2, the sequel, picks up where the first novel, *Family Secrets*, left off. Gloria, Jeff, Sarah, and Pete continue their adventure, as family intrigue comes to life, and the pieces of the puzzle come together. There is a sense of adventure and drama as you read each page. Danger, miracles, repentance and healing are captivating as the novel unfolds. Romance, challenges and mysteries are revealed along the journey of these two couples from friendship to matrimony. Faith overcomes evil through divine intervention. But what sums it up best is found on page 101 - 'Little is much when God is in it.' That theme resonates throughout this novel. Both entertaining and educational, this is yet another great writing by Nancy Petrey.

~~ Richard Street, international businessman, Chicago

Loved it!!! A page turner, couldn't put it down...

Once again, Nancy Petrey has used her God-given talents to create a second beautiful novel, *Family Secrets 2 - Double Destinies*, the sequel to *Family Secrets - Divine Destinies*. Nancy captures the imagination through a heartwarming Southern Love Story, woven with fast paced adventure and mystery, God Incidences, and so much more. I love how Nancy incorporates The Word, Truth, into the story and plants a desire in your heart to research the Jewish roots of our Faith. I enthusiastically encourage you to read and enjoy both together and be blessed. May you have "ears to hear and a heart to understand" all that is written. "To whom much is given, much is required." (pg. 106) Thanks for all the talents you share with your enthusiastic audiences.

~~ Penny Spencer, co-author with Rev. Kevin Spencer, *Understanding Our Roots: the Forgotten Stories and Promises of Our Hebraic Heritage*, Castle Rock, Colorado

DEDICATION

It is a joy to dedicate this third novel of the Family Secrets trilogy to my son Jim — James Curtis Petrey, Jr. Because of his inspiration and his willingness to review my writing, this trilogy has come to be. He has given me invaluable feedback on all three novels, and I heeded his suggestions for interesting plot lines. Curtis, my deceased husband, used to read everything I wrote. It is almost like Jim is following in his footsteps, being "the wind beneath my wings."

Jim himself has a talent for writing. He was the class poet of his high school graduating class and was on the staff of the literary magazine, *Sabre*. Many of his poems were published in this anthology of poetry. He continues his writing in blog fashion and on social media as an analyst of current events and as a commentator on sports and music. He is an amazing storehouse of historical facts.

Thank you, Jim, for taking this journey with me. Our conversations have always been rich, but talking about my books has added a lot to our times together. I love you, son.

ACKNOWLEDGEMENTS

In order for me to write this book about Jewish people making aliyah (immigrating to Israel), I needed to do a lot of research on the internet and draw from books in my library. However, the most helpful sources were friends in Israel. Roy and Mary Kendall, who have lived in Jerusalem for 32 years, were gracious to answer my many questions and advise me. They have a ministry called "School of Worship (SOW)," which has developed into a multi-faceted, non-profit organization with Roy and Mary ministering to people around the world in deep-level worship and in understanding God's heart and purposes for Israel. Roy is an ordained minister and leads worship from the piano. My husband and I first met them on a mission trip to Jerusalem in 1996, and I have visited with them since then on my subsequent trips to Israel. There is no better example of hospitality than that of Roy and Mary Kendall.

Another great source for information was Pamela Suran. She and her husband Shmuel made aliyah in the 1970s. I first met Pamela in March 2002, when she was a tour guide for the Passover Prayer Convocation and Outreach Conference, hosted by Lars and Harriet Enarson, who have a worldwide prayer ministry, The Watchman International. Then in September 2003, my Jewish friend, Janice Bell, and I were privileged to have Pamela give us a private three day tour of Jerusalem. In 2004 she and Shmuel visited the Bells in Elba, Alabama. They spoke in both Janice's church and my church. Besides being a licensed tour guide, Pamela is an artist and has created art for calendars from Israel and has done other important artistic projects for buildings in Jerusalem. She and Shmuel have a ministry called Chazon Yerushalayim (Vision of Jerusalem). In their early days they launched several Messianic Jews in outstanding ministries of their own. Pamela gave me invaluable information and advice about many subjects in my book.

I am always grateful for my publishers from Energion Publications, Henry and Jody Neufeld. This book will be the eighth book they have published for me. Their work is of the highest quality, and it is a joy working with them through the publishing process.

It has been a delight to get to know my endorsers, Ron and Sue Smith. On their way to his board meeting close by, they visited me in Petrey. Sue has read my first two novels and has given me positive reviews. She and Ron both read this third novel and have graciously endorsed it. Ron's love for music and his experiences in Israel brought a richness to our conversation. He and Sue are making a big contribution to God's kingdom through their missionary work in Haiti, his translation of the Bible into Haitian Creole, and in other projects.

Randall Murphree, the Editor of American Family Association's magazine, *The Stand*, endorsed my first two novels and included his reviews in the magazine, for which I am deeply grateful. But he has gone a step further and critiqued every word of this third novel, offering valuable corrections. He will also write a review for the December issue of *The Stand*. Randall is a former long-time judge for the Christy Awards for excellence in Christian fiction, so his input is quite an honor for me. On a personal basis, Curtis and I have served with him on the team of several Emmaus Walks. And when Curtis attended board meetings at AFA, it was always a joy to be with him and all the AFA family.

I thank the people who have undergirded me with prayer during this writing project, most notably, Debra Little and Holly Shelton, as well as my email and Facebook prayer partners. Those who have made comments on my Facebook posts, encouraging me to write this third book of the Christian romance series, are deserving of thanks, too. And, of course, my son, Jim Petrey, has helped me immeasurably by reviewing each chapter, making comments and corrections. His help has made all the difference.

Finally, I give praise and glory to my heavenly Father, my Savior and Messiah Yeshua, and the Holy Spirit, who has surely poured ideas into my head and heart each time I have sat down to type. He has amazed me. I pray He is glorified, His Word spread, and that people will come into His kingdom because of this book. Hallelujah!

TABLE OF CONTENTS

CAST OF CHARACTERS

JEFF MENDELSSOHN QUENTIN, JR. – Mississippi State University (MSU) student in Senior year, studying business and managing Quentin Wholesale Grocery Distribution Center of the Golden Triangle in Starkville, Mississippi, husband of Gloria Sondheim

GLORIA SONDHEIM QUENTIN – MSU student in Senior year, studying piano and voice, wife of Jeff

PETE CARSON – MSU student in Senior year, studying criminal justice and working as a private investigator, husband of Sarah Zipporah Bernstein

SARAH BERNSTEIN CARSON – MSU student in Senior year, studying accounting and working for Quentin Distribution Center, wife of Pete Carson

"DROR" (BENYAMIN, JR.) MIZRACHI – MSU graduate student in History of the U.S. South, an Israeli from Tel Aviv, Hebrew teacher for Jeff, Gloria, Pete, and Sarah

GRACE THOMAS – MSU student in Senior year, studying interior design, a leader at the Baptist Student Union (BSU) and special friend of Gloria Quentin

PASTOR JEFF "Goeff" JAMES – pastor of Adaton Baptist Church and friend to the Quentins and Carsons

CELESTE JAMES – wife of Pastor James, aunt of Dror Mizrachi, sister of Devorah Mizrachi, and daughter of Susannah Goldberg

MISS LIZZIE – leader of a prayer "swat team" (Della, Ruby, Lena, and Pearl) at Adaton Baptist Church

WALTER AND JENNY SESSIONS – MSU students and friends of Jeff, Gloria, Pete, and Sarah

SUSANNAH GOLDBERG – mother of Celeste James and Devorah Mizrachi, grandmother of Dror

LARS AND ELSA CARSON – parents of Pete Carson, from Columbus, Mississippi, owners of Carson Travel Agency

ELINOR CARSON – Pete's younger sister, high school graduate

JULIE ROLLINS – friend of Elinor Carson

JOSEPHINE AND NATHAN BROWN – neighbors of Susannah Goldberg in Jackson, Mississippi

MRS. DONALDSON – mother of Sally Donaldson, high school friend of Celeste and Deborah Gold, in Jackson, Mississippi

JEFFREY MENDELSSOHN QUENTIN, SR. AND LEAH COHEN QUENTIN – Jeff's parents from Tupelo, Mississippi

ALVIN AND SYLVIA SONDHEIM – Gloria's parents from Long Island, New York

SAM AND ANNA SONDHEIM – parents of Alvin, grandparents of Gloria, and citizens of Katzrin, Israel on the Golan Heights

MRS. BIANCA PAGANI – Gloria's piano teacher at MSU

EDSEL GRUBER – concert manager of Gloria and Dror from New York City

DR. SALOMON ROTHSCHILD – doctor in Tel Aviv

SHIRA SHAPIRO – nurse to Dr. Rothschild and neighbor of the Mizrachi family, a Messianic Jew

INTRODUCTION

I t has been a delight to write this third novel in the Family Secrets trilogy. The first book, *Family Secrets – Divine Destinies,* was started in September 1997. Two years before, the Lord had called me to be a Mizpah for Israel (a watchman and a witness), and I had diligently pursued that calling of teaching the church about her Jewish roots, beginning in the church which my husband Curtis pastored in Columbus, Mississippi. I shared information about ministries in Israel, organized Israel prayer groups, studied Hebrew, taught Israel awareness classes, spoke in other churches, and led mission trips to Israel.

I pondered how I could reach more people and get the Jewish roots message across, and the idea came to me to write a fictional story with Jewish characters. I would make it a Christian romance novel set in Starkville, Mississippi, on the Mississippi State University campus. That was in 1997. It was fun writing, but I came to a point where other things had priority, and I stopped. In 2002, I picked it up and resumed writing but got bogged down a second time. My son Jim visited me in Petrey in April 2021. The subject came up about a novel he was writing. That brought to mind the manuscript I had stored in a file drawer. I decided to read my dormant novel to see if the story was any good. With new eyes, I saw its possibilities and determined to finish it and get it published. It had been 19 years since I last tried and only had 19 chapters written.

I sat down at the typewriter on April 17, 2021, and in 34 days I had completed the first draft! The narrative had flowed from my fingertips. There were many "God-incidences" along the way, and I was sure the Holy Spirit was inspiring me. My publisher released *Family Secrets – Divine Destinies* on August 2, 2021.

Many people insisted I write a sequel. I started writing on August 27th, and by the end of October, in less than two months, it was completed. *Family Secrets 2 – Double Destinies* was published in time for Valentine's Day 2022.

Some of my customers commented I should write yet another novel. I recalled that my son Jim had commented during the writing of my first novel that I would eventually write a trilogy. He was prophetic! However, writing a book is a lot of work, and I did not want to write a third book in so short a time. Just to be sure though, I prayed, "God, if you want me to write another book, making a trilogy, please give me a clear sign that I can't mistake."

Not long after I asked Him, I was traveling from Huntsville to Lynchburg, TN, with my brother and his wife. I sat in the back seat with my phone and was reading comments on my Facebook posts. I saw the comment from a friend, saying that I should write another sequel, making a **trilogy**. At that very moment I looked to the side of the road, and there was a building with a **SIGN** on the side of it with only one word – **TRILOGY!!** God was gracious to give me a **literal sign!** He made sure I got the message by drawing my attention to that sign again on our way back to Huntsville later in the day.

In obedience I began to write this book, *Family Secrets 3 – Prophetic Destinies*. As in the writing of the first two books, the Holy Spirit arranged God-incidences along the way to encourage me to continue. I know these three books were His assignment for me, and I pray He will use them for His purposes in many lives.

The main characters of all three novels are two college couples. In the second book, the couples continue their ministry together that began in the first book, and there is a double wedding at the end. They make two trips to Israel, one in each book. This third book centers on their plans to move to Israel after graduation from college. A third major character is introduced, an Israeli, who gets involved with the two couples, teaching them Hebrew. Music plays a big part in all three books. In books two and three, there are exciting performances in concerts presented in Europe and in Israel. This third novel includes a search for family roots, missing persons, a dread disease, violent attacks, and many supernatural occurrences, such as dreams, visions and spiritual gifts. There are page-turning twists and turns in the plot.

Besides romance and Scripture lessons, the third all-encompassing ingredient in the trilogy is **prayer**. The four main characters constantly acknowledge their dependence on the Lord and seek His will in prayer. They can see His orchestration of their lives, and their most fervent prayer is to glorify Him. All three books are entertaining, but also educational and historical. Just as Jesus used fictional parables to get His teaching across, I have used Christian romance fiction for the same purpose. And my prayer is that God will be glorified, and lives will be changed.

Shalom v'ahava (peace and love),
Nancy Petrey

FIRST
ANNIVERSARY

STARKVILLE, MISSISSIPPI
SUNDAY, JUNE 13, 1999

"I see they have sparkling grape juice on the menu. Perfect! We can toast our first year of marriage, 360 days of marital bliss!" exclaimed Pete, as he pulled Sarah closer to him in the booth at Harvey's Restaurant.

"Whaaat? Only 360 days? Gloria and I have had three hundred and sixty-TWO days of marital bliss!" grinned Jeff, as he also pulled his bride closer.

Gloria and Sarah looked at each other in surprise, winked, and poked their husbands in the ribs. "Sarah, I will not betray your confidence, if you won't betray mine," laughed Gloria. "I'm so glad you forgave Pete that time. I had a harder time than you did, forgiving Jeff."

Sarah replied, "I've learned that marriage is not for sissies. It's surely no bed of roses. You have to work at it. If I were not a believer, it would have been curtains for Pete after the first month. Oy vey! Of course, I would never have considered divorce, but I did think about murder!" Sarah covered her mouth to keep from laughing.

"Sarah! It is so out of character for you to say a thing like that. Babe, how could you even think such a horrible thing?" Pete teased, "You know I am the ideal husband, catering to your every whim."

"Well, bro, this is an eye-opening conversation. I guess I might as well air out our dirty laundry, too. One time Gloria locked me out of the apartment! Can you believe she would do that to such a perfect husband?" Jeff feigned deep sorrow.

"I am calling a truce, men," declared Gloria. "We are supposed to be celebrating our first year of marriage. How about we recount the many times we have been the model Christian couples? It was 362 days for Jeff and me, and, Pete, it was 360 days for you and Sarah. Isn't that what you said?"

Jeff looked at Pete. "I don't know about you and Sarah, but at the end of those big arguments Gloria and I had, it was worth all the grief to make up. Ooh! My wife is unsurpassed in loving her man and binding up his wounds."

"Yep, making up after an argument is truly marital bliss. Makes you want to have another argument," laughed Pete.

"Don't you guys think we better say a little prayer before the waiter comes?" asked Sarah. "Glad you think so. Let's join hands." The laughter died down as Sarah prayed and gave thanks for their first year of marriage. "HaShem, thank You for bringing us together with our spouses. Please fulfill Your purposes in our marriages and our ministry together. Help us to always forgive and to make our spouses happy and fulfilled, and help us to bring You pleasure. In the name of Yeshua." Everyone added, "Amen."

Gloria remembered something. "Here's a P.S. to your prayer, Sarah -- Dear Yeshua, thank you for our ministry together of teaching the Jewish Roots class at Adaton and helping us complete it today on our first anniversary of marriage. We have already seen the fruit. Show us how to go forward with the class and bring in even more fruit for you, dear Lord and Savior. Amen."

The waiter patiently waited until the prayer was over. All four ordered filet mignon steaks, baked potatoes and salad, with sweet iced tea and sparkling grape juice.

Jeff had an idea. "I know we see each other every day in our duplex apartments, and we don't need updating on our marriage journey. But I would like to suggest that our celebration tonight begin with a stroll down memory lane, as the old folks say. First, let's share memories from the time we first met, then our trip to Israel for Hanukkah, our engagement experiences, our honeymoon trip to Israel, and this past year of happenings in school, in church, in our jobs, and in our families."

"Honey, aren't you hungry? How can we talk about all of that and have time to eat? I say we each pick one or two highlights of the past year of marriage, not going back to when we first met. That would take hours, and Harvey's would have to kick us out to close up!" Gloria had big 'puppy dog' eyes, looking lovingly at Jeff.

Pete eagerly began, "Okay, I will go first. I want to tell y'all about something that happened this past year that I have never shared with anybody." He paused to let his words sink in, observing Sarah's surprised expression. "Yes, honey, it has to do with you, my beloved wife." All were very attentive.

"Well, after we got back from our honeymoon in Israel, I reported to my job. I really like working as a private investigator for the tri-county area – Starkville, Columbus, and West Point. Secrecy is one of the requirements of any investigation, but now I can share this particular story because it was finally resolved, and the people concerned want it made public. You know them."

Gloria, Jeff, and Sarah gasped. "Hurry, Pete, and tell it fast before our food gets here," urged Gloria.

"Okay. I will cut to the chase. Walter…"

"Walter Sessions?" chorused the three. "Oh, no. Was Walter in trouble? Or Jenny?" queried Jeff.

"Every one of you be quiet, and let me tell it. Yes, Walter and Jenny approached me. They hired me to set up surveillance for Jenny after she received a threatening note, stuck under her windshield wipers. It was a warning not to testify in court against Nasir and Omar."

Sarah began to tremble. "Pete, how could you hide this from me? If they would threaten Jenny, then that means that I could be a target also. As you all know, I WAS the target that day at Adaton Baptist when it was my time to teach the Jewish Roots lesson. The knife Nasir threw hit Jenny, but it was meant for ME!"

Gloria interrupted. "Oh, what a day of miracles! Our guys uncovered the plot of those terrorists and were prepared to foil it. Jenny repented. She and Walter fell in love. Her lesbian lifestyle was over, and Sarah got a new friend."

Sarah grinned. "Well, I know the note could not have come from Nasir and Omar because they are in prison. The day that Pete and I visited them was another miracle of God. After we left them with our gift of a New Testament and a sweet roll, I had a knowing in my heart that HaShem would eventually draw them to believe in Yeshua and be saved. I could feel the anointing of the Holy Spirit as we talked to them. I believe that it must be one of their Muslim friends in the terrorist network who is threatening Jenny. Oh, wait. Pete, you said the situation was resolved. Please forgive me for interrupting. We will be quiet. Just tell it quick before our food gets here."

Pete resumed, "It's hard to believe that Nasir and Omar's terrorist network did not bail them out. They instructed Nasir and Omar to have their public defender waive the right to a speedy trial. They were afraid that in a trial Nasir and Omar would reveal the names of those in the network. Sarah, I had to keep this from you, because I knew you would press me to go back to the jail to visit. I had to lie and say they were brought to trial and transferred to Parchman Penitentiary to serve their sentences. I wanted to be absolutely sure that they posed no threat to you. Also, you did not need to know that their terrorist friends had been visiting them."

"I forgive you, honey. So keep talking," pressed Sarah.

"When Jenny got the note, she and Walter prayed hard to know what to do. Besides hiring me, they decided to go to the Oktibbeha County Jail and visit Nasir and Omar. If you only knew how hard it has been to keep this good news from you, Sarah, and also from you, Jeff and Gloria. The minute Nasir and Omar saw Jenny, they cried out and asked her to forgive them! Jenny said they broke down and sobbed, confessing their ignorance and wickedness. They showed her the New Testaments you gave them, Sarah. As they turned the pages, Jenny and Walter could see they had underlined a lot of verses that indicated God's promises to forgive sins and give new life."

Jeff was close to tears, but Gloria and Sarah let the tears flow freely. "Oh, Sarah and Pete, this is our destiny as couples and friends to bear fruit for God's kingdom. I am so proud of you!" exclaimed Gloria.

The waiter came with their food, set everything before the couples, and then quickly withdrew. He could see there was an important conversation going on, not small talk.

Pete opened the sparkling grape juice, poured into each glass, and held his glass up to make a toast. "I will tell you the rest of the story later. Right now I want to acknowledge our heavenly Matchmaker and thank Him for giving us a glorious life for our first year of marriage. Sarah Bernstein Carson, you have surpassed my greatest expectations and fulfilled my wildest dreams for an ideal wife in every dimension. Let us drink to our Life together forever! L'Chaim!"

"L'Chaim!" echoed Sarah, Jeff, and Gloria.

"And then let us kiss!" laughed Pete. Sarah only sipped the juice and then fell into Pete's arms for a deep, satisfying kiss.

Jeff held his glass aloft, looked passionately at his gorgeous wife, and made his toast. "Gloria Sondheim Quentin, I am more in love with you now than when I loved you at first sight in the library twenty months and twenty-three days ago. Because of you,

I love the Lord with all my heart, and I thank Him for the gift of you as my wife. To our Life together forever! L'Chaim!"

The others repeated "L'Chaim!" Gloria and Jeff quickly drank the juice, leaned into the corner of the booth and then smothered each other with kisses.

The waiter had alerted his co-workers that these couples were celebrating their first anniversary of marriage. After the meal was over and the table cleared, the waiters marched to their booth. They sang "Happy anniversary" loudly and clapped enthusiastically as they presented a white cake topped with a lighted candle. Hot coffee was poured into each cup.

The conversation during dinner had been more like small talk. Afterward, they lingered over the cake and coffee, and Pete resumed his story. "When I questioned Nasir and Omar about the visits from their Muslim friends in the terror network, Omar said, 'For the first time I could see hate and fear in the eyes of our so-called friends. They were full of threats, but, amazingly, I felt no fear at all. Nasir said he didn't either. To put it plainly, Nasir and I had already made the decision to believe in Jesus and to follow Him. We turned into different people. We were not terrorists any more, and we didn't hate Jews any more. It was a Jew who gave us the book that opened our eyes. We both talked about how we loved that girl Sarah. And we like you, too, Pete. And we know now that Jesus is Jewish, and His real Hebrew name is Yeshua. He is not "Issa," and he is not only a prophet, as Islam teaches.'"

Jeff had to know. "So, what will they say when they are finally brought to trial? Will they reveal the names of the other terrorists? Is Jenny still at risk? What about Sarah?"

"These are good questions. I had a chance to talk to the public defender, and he said he is NOT going to bring them to trial. After Jenny told him she was not going to press charges, and all the people at Adaton Baptist had refused to testify, he arranged a private hearing before the Judge. The Judge was impressed with Nasir and Omar and sentenced them to three years as suggested by the sheriff.

He is allowing them to remain in the Oktibbeha County Jail. He understands the danger of a public trial for Nasir and Omar, and he knows they are not terrorists themselves, not any more. Actually, it seems God is showing them favor, because they have a lot more freedom in the jail than any of the other inmates. In Parchman they would not be as safe because there are plenty of terrorists inside the penitentiary. I have advised Walter and Jenny not to visit them again because the terrorists will be watching them. I talked to the campus police, and they are patrolling around the Sessions Manor regularly, as well as around our duplex."

Sarah spoke up. "Remember that verse and the song Gloria taught us? "The name of the Lord is a strong tower. The righteous run into it, and they are safe." That's Proverbs 18:10. Also, another verse that builds my faith is found in Joel 2:32, Romans 10:13, and Acts 2:21 – "Whoever calls on the name of the Lord shall be saved." Three times in Scripture that promise is made! I believe it. I won't live in fear. If terrorists threaten me, I will cry out to HaShem, and He will save me."

"Atta girl! **My** girl. Well, who else wants to share a highlight of our first year of marriage?"

Gloria dived in with her usual ebullient manner. "Holy Rollers, let us not forget why we are called that. We have been preparing ourselves this past year to do some holy rolling in Israel by learning the steps of aliyah[1] and learning to speak Hebrew. Although I have thoroughly enjoyed my school work, especially learning piano pedagogy from Mrs. Pagani and vocal performance from Mr. Menotti, and also teaching the Jewish Roots class at Adaton and learning to cook for Jeff, the greatest highlight of the year has been, and will continue to be, our preparation for aliyah!"

"You bet, dear wife. I have enjoyed hearing you read your book to me, *Shock Absorption: A Survival Guide for Living in Israel.*[2] And you have taught Pete, Sarah, and me some fine Hebrew." Jeff turned Gloria's face toward him. "Ani ohev otakh rabbah, Gloria. Aht yafah. Ooh! Hallelujah!"

A good-looking young man at the next table stood up, walked over to their table and congratulated them. "Mazel tov!" He turned to Gloria. "I couldn't help overhearing. You and your friends know what your husband said, but for the benefit of others in hearing distance, let me translate." After repeating the Hebrew, he translated: "'I love you very much. You are beautiful! Ooh! Praise the Lord!' I have to agree." Gloria blushed.

Jeff stood up and shook the stranger's hand. "Thank you for translating that. I'm glad I got it right. My name is Jeff Quentin. My wife is Gloria, and our friends here are Pete and Sarah Carson. I guess you heard me say that we have been studying Hebrew together. How did **you** know what those words meant? Your Hebrew sounds different from ours."

The young man introduced himself. "I am Dror Mizrachi from Israel. I am a graduate student at Mississippi State University. Forgive me for listening to your conversation. I am delighted that you plan to make aliyah. I would love to hear all about it. Another thing is that I am willing to offer my services as a Hebrew language teacher and prepare you for aliyah, both for a small fee. I know something about making aliyah, because I did it myself."

The Holy Rollers felt inspired to respond in unison, "Toda rabbah! Thank you very much!" They looked at each other, their faces filled with wonder.

"Name your price, Dror," said Pete, eagerly.

"I suggest we meet in the chapel tomorrow night. It's always empty. I just finished teaching a six-week course of economics there to a friend and found it to be the ideal place for learning. Make it seven o'clock. I will present a course of study for the four of you," suggested Dror.

The friends broke out laughing. Jeff explained, "Well, you found our hideout! That place is like holy ground to us because Gloria and I also met there to study economics. And it is the place we met Sarah, too. Then later, all four of us met there to forge our ministry together."

Sarah had to add something. "In the past, I did some serious praying at the chapel. Dror, I hope you are open to beginning our study with prayer. Our Holy Roller group doesn't do anything without HaShem's guidance and power."

Dror looked a little sheepish at first but then managed a confident smile. "Yes, you may lead us in prayer before we start. Bring notebooks, pens, and any Hebrew dictionaries you may have. If you have books on aliyah, bring them, too. We will map out a course together, and I promise my fee will be reasonable."

Gloria reached out and shook Dror's hand. "You are an answer to my prayers. I can't thank you enough. We will see you promptly at seven o'clock tomorrow night at the chapel." The others shook Dror's hand and expressed appreciation for his willingness to teach them. He returned to his table.

Pete leaned in and whispered, "As if you wives didn't notice, that dude is tall, dark, and handsome. At least he isn't as tall as me, and you like my blond hair better than his curly black hair, don't you, Sarah?"

"Oh, Pete, you know how smitten I am with you. I guarantee you, he is no competition, even if he speaks perfect Hebrew!" Sarah reached out for Pete's hand and squeezed it.

Jeff looked at Gloria. "Honey, do you think you can resist his charm when he has to get right up in your face to show you how to roll your Rs?"

Gloria laughed out loud. "Jeff Quentin, when I made my marriage vows, I meant every word. Besides that, you are the only one who can *rev my engine!*"

Pete put his finger to his lips. "Be quiet, y'all. I hope he didn't hear us. Now I think it's time to close this meeting of the Holy Rollers and continue to celebrate our anniversary, as we return to our apartments and resume our year-long honeymoon!" The others enthusiastically agreed. Their romantic feelings had not diminished with marriage. On the contrary, the fire of love had only flamed brighter.

CHAPTER TWO

HEBREW CLASS
WITH ISRAELI
TEACHER

G loria and Jeff arrived early at the chapel, turned the lights to the brightest setting, and sat down on the first pew. "Jeff, the four of us agreed spontaneously last night at Harvey's to meet with this Israeli guy, but we don't know the first thing about him. We should have prayed first," worried Gloria.

"Yeah, honey, I thought about that as I was falling asleep last night, and I offered up a prayer that this would be a productive meeting and help us get on a fast track to learning Hebrew and preparing for aliyah. I felt God's peace. When I looked over at you, I saw you were fast asleep. Sorry we didn't pray together. I was soon out like a light. But when I woke up this morning, the first thought that struck me is that we must ask Dror to tell us all about himself before we start our Hebrew lesson."

"Absolutely, Jeff. However, we need to pray together first and then ask Dror to talk about himself. Hey, here come Sarah and Pete, right on time. Maybe we can have a quick prayer before Dror gets here. I have a feeling he is not a believer, so let's go ahead. Being in one accord is essential."

"Right, babe." Jeff called out, "Pete and Sarah, come down here, and let's have prayer before Dror arrives, okay?"

Gloria reached out her hands, and they made a circle. Jeff led out in prayer. "Heavenly Father, God of Abraham, Isaac, and Jacob, and the God and Father of our Lord Jesus Christ, we acknowledge

You in this study group tonight. We ask for Your Presence. Fill us anew with Your Holy Spirit. Quicken our minds and hearts to receive knowledge of Your sacred language, Hebrew. Please help Dror to guide us in the best way so we will be prepared for aliyah and will fulfill Your purposes in the Holy Land. In Yeshua's name. Amen." The others joined in with loud amens.

Dror walked down the aisle, an amused look on his face. "Well, we are all here. I am willing to devote two hours to our first session if you are. What would you consider to be a reasonable fee for my services, perhaps $10 an hour from each of you?"

Pete replied, "I think I can speak for all of us. And I say yes, that's a reasonable fee." Pete reached in his pocket and handed Dror $40 for Sarah and him. Jeff held out $40 for Gloria and him.

"Okay, the mundane is over. Now let us get to the magnificent," chuckled Dror.

Gloria intervened. "We are eager to learn from you, a Hebrew speaker from Israel. What could be better? We do anticipate that our experience in this class will be magnificent, but we have a request. Before we begin, we must know something about you, why you are here at the university, and when you made aliyah, how long you lived in Israel, and if you plan to go back. If there's anything else you want to tell us, we are all ears," smiled Gloria.

Dror flashed a dazzling smile at Gloria and answered, "This will be brief, but as we continue the lessons, I will tell you more of my life, and perhaps next week you can tell me about your lives, especially why you want to make aliyah. Okay, I made aliyah from Columbus, Mississippi, with my parents in 1987. We live in Tel Aviv. I got a degree from Hebrew University in Jerusalem in history and then did my three years of duty in the Israeli Defense Force. Last year I enrolled at Mississippi State to pursue a master's degree in the History of the U.S. South. I have been writing articles for the Journal of the Southern Jewish Historical Society. My passion is to discover my Jewish roots in the South. Does that surprise you?"

"Oh, my!" Sarah exclaimed. "As they say here, 'You are lighting my fire.'"

Gloria blurted out, "We teach a Jewish Roots class every Sunday. And we are passionate about this subject, too. I think it's a different subject from yours, however. Our lessons are on the Jewish roots of the **church**. But even if it's not the same as your Jewish roots passion, we still want to invite you to come to our class. We meet every Sunday at ten a.m. at Adaton Baptist, a small church outside Starkville. Will you come?"

Pete could see the uneasiness in Dror. It seemed that a shade had come down over his eyes, and he was withdrawn. Being a peace-maker by nature, Pete tried to smooth things over with another invitation. "Dror, we also attend the synagogue in Columbus occasionally. If you haven't made a visit yet, it would be fun for you to go with us. My wife Sarah has an Orthodox Jewish background, and she educated the rest of us about Judaism when we first attended B'Nai Israel Temple back in 1997."

Jeff *stepped up to the plate* with another conciliatory statement. "I think it's great that you are a writer for the Southern Jewish Historical Society. My mother, Leah Quentin, has attended some of their meetings with her Columbus friend, Delia Green. Pete is from Columbus. I am from Tupelo, and both our wives are from New York. I might as well tell you this, too, and then you probably want to get started teaching us. Gloria's grandparents made aliyah a few months ago!"

Dror's expression now lightened considerably, and he assumed authority. "Okay, students, I am on a time clock at $10 an hour," he chuckled. "I am glad we are getting acquainted, but I suggest in the future we study first and then afterward have *fellowship,* as you call it. Get comfortable and be ready to write. I have my little portable board and marker. You can copy the print letters I write on the board and also look at the study sheets. We will start with pronouns. You know English, and you even know a few sentences and phrases in Hebrew, but soon you will be able to speak, read, and write Ivrit. That's the word for Hebrew."

Dror handed out sheets. "This sheet of pronouns is the very same one that is used in the ulpan in Israel. You may already know that *olim*, new immigrants, must attend this Hebrew school, *ulpan*, five days a week, five hours a day, for five months."

Gloria interrupted. "Oh, I love all those fives. The number for 'grace' is 5. And that is what I'm depending on to learn Hebrew, God's grace."

"You got that right, babe." agreed Jeff. "Hey, Dror, if we have to go to the ulpan school after we get there, is it still important to study Hebrew now?"

"Yes, it is, Jeff. Having an Israeli to teach you will get you much closer to becoming fluent in the language. The hard part is having conversations in Hebrew. I plan to teach you that, too."

"Oh, glory!" exclaimed Sarah. "That is what I really look forward to. My parents made aliyah, and I want to be able to talk intelligibly with the people they knew in Israel before they were killed."

Dror was taken aback. "Oh, let me offer my condolences. I have known quite a few people, students and even neighbors, who had untimely deaths in Tel Aviv and Jerusalem. I trust your parents' death was not a result of Palestinian terrorism."

Pete put his arm around Sarah's shoulders. He could sense a wave of sorrow engulfing her, and he answered for her. "Yes, Professor Nathan and Naomi Bernstein were killed by a suicide bomber after he boarded their bus in Jerusalem in August of 1997. They had lived in Katzrin since 1995."

Dror's face registered genuine empathy toward Sarah. "Well, you are very brave, as are all of you, including Gloria's grandparents, to not let that violence stop you from moving to your ancient Jewish homeland. If only Jews around the world could be persuaded that they are actually safer in Israel than in their home countries, where anti-Semitism is now increasing daily."

Dror quickly regained his composure and moved to the white-board. "Let us begin with the most popular Hebrew word, 'shalom.'"

"See it at the top of the page, third word from the right. Of course, you already know that Hebrew and other Semitic languages are read from right to left. Indeed, Hebrew books are read from what you would consider the back and read to the front. Now copy down the word *shalom* as you watch me form the letters on the board. We will learn to write every letter of the Hebrew 'alephbet,' which corresponds to your English 'alphabet.' Before you go tonight I will give you a sheet of the 22 letters of the alephbet[3] in print form, and you can practice writing them. Also, please memorize them. There are different letters used as word endings for four of these letters."

Gloria's excitement was growing by leaps and bounds. "Jeff and I have already been practicing writing the letters, using a book we have. I have an extra copy and want to give it to you. It's a devotional book. Each day's devotion is based on a Hebrew letter." Gloria pulled the book out of her purse. "Here it is, *Messiah and His Hebrew Alphabet* by Dick Mills and David Michael.[4] Pete and Sarah, I have another copy back at the apartment I can give you, too. Jeff and I love it!"

Dror reluctantly took the book and quickly resumed his teaching. "First off, you must learn the Hebrew pronunciation for vowels. In the Hebrew transliteration, the vowel A is pronounced AH as in 'father.' E is pronounced EH or A, as in 'pet' or 'hey.' I is pronounced E as in 'submarine.' O is pronounced as a 'long O' as in 'home.' U is pronounced OO, as in 'super.' Got it?"

"Okay, write 'shalom' just as I do. I'm sure you know it means 'peace,' but it is also used for 'hello' and 'goodbye.' The other two words at the top of the page, reading right to left, are 'shiur rishon,' meaning 'lesson first.' The adjective follows the noun in Hebrew. Of course, in English it is 'first lesson.' Next line - start at the right side and see the first pronoun, pronounced 'a-TA,' meaning 'you.' The woman is pointing to the man, indicating this pronoun is masculine. Keep reading and see the man and woman both pointing to themselves, indicating the pronoun is 'I,' which is 'a-NI' and is both masculine and feminine. The next pronoun is the feminine word for 'you,' which is 'AT.' I will give you time to write all these on your paper."

Jeff felt so proud of himself. "I have to commend Gloria for introducing this to me. I have already learned these pronouns, especially so I can properly say 'I love you' in Hebrew. You heard me in the restaurant."

Dror seemed unimpressed. "Well, let us go on to just two more pronouns, 'he' and 'she.' The Hebrew letters you see there are pronounced 'hu' for the English 'he.' And the Hebrew letters 'hi' mean 'she' in English. Copy those on your blank sheet, looking at the study sheet or watching me write it on the board. Hurry now. You have some more copying to do. Look at the sentences on the bottom half of the sheet. I have provided the English translation for you. Notice that 'Shalom' as a greeting is the same as saying 'Hi' or 'Hello.' Also, notice the spelling of the names for Joseph, Ron, Rena, Susannah, Don and Dena. There are no Js in Hebrew, so the pronunciation for 'Joseph' is 'Yosef.' And there is one more pronoun I want you to know for this first lesson, the word for 'who.' It is pronounced 'mi.'"

Sarah broke out into laughter. "I have been keeping quiet, because I never want anyone to think I am a know-it-all. But I will let you in on a little secret. I learned all this at Yeshiva University in New York. *He* is *hoo; she* is *he,* and *who* is *me*! Hebrew is crazy! He is hoo – she is he – and who is me! Got that, everybody?" Sarah couldn't stop laughing, and soon everybody but Dror got tickled, and the laughter went on and on.

Dror finally called the class to order. "Okay. I concede. These pronouns are pretty funny for English speakers. Let's finish the lesson in this way. I will read a sentence, and you will parrot me. We will do it first in Hebrew and then in English, going down the page. Use expression, guys. Let's go – 'Shalom! Ani Yosef.' Now English: 'Hi! I am Joseph.'" Dror waited, listening to hear if they were pronouncing the Hebrew correctly. "Next line: 'Mi hu?' 'Who is he?'"

Sarah started to laugh again. "Me hoo? Who is he?" Then she turned it around, "Who is he? Me hoo?" Dror lost control of the class again, as Sarah kept repeating, and the others gleefully mimicked her.

Clapping his hands, Dror admonished, "Oh, I see you are getting the hang of it, but not as adults!" The laughter immediately stopped. "Now I will teach you how to roll your Rs and get your accents right. And remember, if the word has two syllables, the accent is on the second syllable. With three syllables, the accent varies." Dror led them in drills all the way through the study sheet. Then the lesson was over.

"I can't believe it is already nine o'clock. I loved it, Dror. You are an excellent teacher," applauded Jeff. The others heartily joined in the applause.

Gloria reached in her purse and pulled out a camera. "Tonight is historic, people. I must have a picture. But how are we going to get all five of us in it?"

Dror took the camera. "I can take a picture of you four next to the whiteboard with 'Shalom!' written in Hebrew. That will get the job done, okay?"

"No way." Pete intervened. "We have to have **you** with us. Hey, wait, I see some people sitting on the back row. I didn't realize there was anyone in here. Maybe one of them will take our picture. I will go see." Pete walked to the back and got a surprise. "Oh, great! It's y'all, Gary and Priscilla. I thought we were alone. Please forgive us for taking over the place with our Hebrew class."

"Don't worry, bro. We just slipped in here for a little good night kiss before Priscilla has to get back to the dorm. We blotted y'all out," laughed Gary.

"Well, I have a favor to ask. Will you take a picture of us with our teacher?"

"Sure thing. I know Priscilla will want a copy of it. After I kissed her, she looked up and made a comment about him. She said, 'That man is drop-dead gorgeous!' Do I need to tell you how that took the wind out of my sails? Arghh! But I will do it. I will get my own copy so I can throw darts at that man. Priscilla and I are engaged, for heaven's sake!"

Gloria was elated to see Gary and Priscilla. "Great, Pete! I see you enlisted Gary to take our picture. Let's get it done, Gary. Then you and Priscilla can come over to our apartment for a little sharing time with the four of us."

Pete introduced Gary and Priscilla to Dror, and Gary took the camera. Five shots were taken, which included the group, the two couples, and two shots of Dror alone. As the couples were about to leave, Gloria said, "Dror, I think we need to get your contact info in case we get a ministry date and have to miss a lesson." Dror, Pete, and Jeff exchanged their business cards. The students all thanked Dror and vowed they would study and return the next Monday night for lesson two.

CHAPTER THREE

GOD LOOKS ON THE HEART

"Come into our humble abode," said Gloria to Gary and Priscilla as she unlocked the apartment. "It just so happened that I did a little house cleaning Friday. Sarah was too busy doing books for Jeff, so she put off cleaning their apartment till tomorrow. That means that Jeff and I have the privilege of being hosts. I have even baked a pie."

"She sure did," boasted Jeff. "That's one of the perks to being the manager of the Golden Triangle distribution point for Dad's grocery company. I can break open a case of Fisher's shelled pecans, share with the employees, and bring some home. My wife has learned to make a mean pecan pie, I'm tellin' ya."

"Yeah, and Sarah can make a mean sweet potato casserole with a sweet pecan topping," bragged Pete. "That's not all she's good at either." Pete reached over and hugged his smiling wife.

Jeff loved being a business executive. "Well, one thing I know about Sarah is that she is a hard-working and accurate bookkeeper. My income has grown over the past months, and she is in line for a raise."

This was good news to Sarah, and she thanked Jeff in advance. With help from Jeff, Gloria soon had the pie and coffee ready to serve. She basked in the compliments as everyone experienced her delicious dessert.

Gary was the first to begin serious conversation. "I think I have seen this man Dror in my history class. I will pay more attention to him the next time I go to class. He sits in the back and has his head down most of the time, reading and taking notes, it appears. After hearing Priscilla's comment, something tells me I better size up the competition." His nervous laugh bothered Priscilla.

"Now, Gary, I only have eyes for you. You know that," reassured Priscilla. "I simply stated the obvious tonight. The guy is very handsome on the outside, but it's more important what he's like on the inside. Nobody can match you, honey, for strength of character and a loving heart." Priscilla squeezed her fiancé's hand.

Jeff saw an opportunity to stress God's viewpoint of external appearance. "I think the Holy Spirit has shown me some things about our looks. But first, I want to say that all three of you ladies are beautiful externally. Gloria, with her dark brown hair, big brown eyes, white teeth, perfect nose, and great figure, certainly caught my attention the first time I saw her. But my heart was not moved. It was only when she burst out in song unexpectedly that I saw the beauty of her inner being and was knocked off my feet! It wasn't long before I discovered her beauty secret, and it was Jesus living inside her." Jeff looked over at Gloria, and she was wiping her eyes.

Gloria responded, "I have to say something, guys. I mean 'y'all.' Sorry, but I still struggle with exchanging my New York accent for the southern drawl of a southern belle. Anyway, I must tell you that when I first saw Jeff in the library that night, I was blown away. Maybe my appearance didn't affect him so much, but his appearance certainly affected me. I had already planned to witness to someone about Jesus, but I didn't know it would be such a handsome guy as Jeff. Actually, I thought we looked a lot alike. He was a male version of me in coloring. When he stood up, I could see he wasn't but a few inches taller than me, but oh, those muscles and powerful physique." Gloria looked at Jeff. He was blushing.

Pete felt for Jeff. He knew men didn't like to be publicly complimented in that way, that it was embarrassing. He would turn the attention away from Jeff. "Okay, I admit it. Dror Mizrachi is what Priscilla said. I'm not gonna say it. But he doesn't have the muscles you and me have, Gary!"

"And no one, I mean no one, has such a stunning head of hair as you do, my handsome husband," interjected Sarah. "A natural blonde male is a prize in any culture, and you, Pete, are the 'grand prize' for me. Not only that, but your six-foot, seven-inch height makes my heart race. I am the most secure wife there could be. You have plenty of muscles, too, and you make me feel protected."

"Don't you love this mutual admiration society?" chuckled Pete. "Thanks, babe. I am lapping up that positive PR. As for you, dear wife, you have the slimmest figure of any girl on campus. I love your long, silky dark brown hair, your smooth olive complexion, and despite what you believe, I think your Jewish nose is perfect! Your beautiful smile sets my feet a-dancin'."

Jeff realized he had sparked this embarrassing conversation, so he needed to hurry up and share what the Spirit showed him and bring closure to this topic. Gary and Priscilla's accolades could wait. "Okay, it's good that none of us is lacking in the area of physical appearance, but let's keep in mind that each person is God's work of art, whether they are attractive or ugly, whether they are smart or ignorant, and whether they are well-formed or handicapped. Ya know, one day, if we don't die young, we are all going to be old and wrinkled, and we may look ugly on the outside. This is what the Spirit showed me the other day. When Samuel the prophet went to the house of Jesse, as God directed him, to anoint one of his sons as the King of Israel, he almost anointed the wrong man because of his good looks. "But Yahweh said to Samuel, 'Do not look at his appearance or at his physical stature, because I have refused him. For Yahweh does not see as man sees; for man looks at the outward appearance, but Yahweh looks at the heart.'⁵ And you know the story. God's pick was the shepherd boy David, who was outside looking after the sheep. He had not been called to the house for Samuel's inspection. Evidently, his father didn't think he was a candidate for king."

A song came up in Gloria's mind. Unbidden, she softly sang: "'But when others see a shepherd boy, God may see a king. Even though your life seems filled with ordinary things, in just a moment He can touch you, and everything will change. When others see a shepherd boy, God may see a king.' Oh, y'all, I love that song. It touches my heart. I can't remember all the lyrics, but it ends this way: 'Well it wasn't the oldest. It wasn't the strongest chosen on that day. And yet the giants fell, and nations trembled, when they stood in his way. Then the chorus again: But when others see a shepherd boy, God may see a king. Even though your life seems filled with ordinary things, in just a moment He can touch you, and everything will change. When others see a shepherd boy, God may see a king.'"[6]

Sarah was crying. "We need to pray right now, while the Spirit is moving. Gloria has brought us into the throne room of God with that beautiful song. Dror is on my heart. Yes, he is handsome. Yes, he is smart. Yes, he is likely a good person. But he is not born again. The Spirit inside me has let me know that. Let's pray for this man until we see our prayers answered."

They all stood up and made a circle, holding hands. Priscilla hesitantly offered, "I want to lead the prayer for Dror. But also, I want the Lord to change me, so I see others the way He sees them." Tearfully, she began, "Dear loving Father. Thank You for bringing us together tonight for Your purposes. Maybe You are looking at us sort of like midwives to help You birth Dror into Your kingdom. We don't know much about him, but we offer him up in prayer and ask that You save his soul. In Jesus' name."

Gloria continued the prayer. "Father, you are showing me that our common interest in Jewish roots is the highway to his heart. He is searching. Please help him find out about his family roots in the course of his job with the Southern Jewish Historical Society. Please reunite him with family members unknown to him. Most of all, Lord, help him accept Your invitation to believe in Yeshua as his Messiah and have eternal life. Help him to realize his need for forgiveness and cry out to be saved."

Jeff closed the prayer. "Lord, give us wisdom in our relationship with Dror as our teacher. Help us move on to real friendship, and cause him to accept our invitation to our Jewish roots class and attendance at the worship service. In the mighty name of Yeshua HaMashiach, we pray. Amen."

Gary hugged Priscilla tight. "Hey, sweet girl, we gotta get goin.' I have an eight o'clock class in the morning. Hope I get some sleep tonight. I have the 'Holy Ghost chill bumps' from that prayer time. I am pumped! And it all started with your remark, Priscilla. So, I'm glad you said it after all." Gary and Priscilla had a good laugh and headed for the car.

"Wait, wait, wait, y'all!" Gloria pulled Gary and Priscilla back into the apartment. "I have a specific prayer request for Dror and for me. Please just agree with a loud amen. Let's pray: Almighty God, I think I hear you saying to call Dror on his cell phone. Thank You for nudging me to get his contact info tonight. You have put this urging in my heart to call and remind him about our Jewish Roots class. I am asking You to show me the exact time to call, so he will say yes. And then, Lord, I ask You to send Your angels to make sure he gets to the church on time and does not try to avoid coming. Make him think about how proud he is of keeping his word. Mmm… Lord, You had me pray that. Now I know You will answer. Thank You. Toda rabbah. In Yeshua's name. And the people said, 'Amen!'" The chorus of amens was so loud, the neighbors surely must have heard.

MISS LIZZIE'S QUESTION

ADATON BAPTIST CHURCH
JUNE 20, 1999

J eff drove right up to the front door of the church. Gloria, Pete, and Sarah got out, and he went to park his golden Ford Expedition SUV in the church yard. Oh, Lord, I feel unusually excited about our class and the worship service today. And it is satisfying to know that we have finished teaching the long outline, 'Why Jewish Roots?' that we began back in February of last year. It shouldn't have taken us so long, but we had to minister in other churches on some Sundays. Thanks, Lord, for using us to spread Your message. And, Lord, I can't stop praising You for helping us lead our church friends on a tour of Israel last Christmas. Brother James preaches with more anointing than ever, and his sermons are filled with things he learned in our class and in Israel. Glory! Father, what I myself have learned has made a big difference in the few sermons I have preached since then, too. I just want to sit here praising You before I go inside. I have one main request. Please get Dror here today, and touch his heart. You have made our Holy Roller group fruitful, and let Dror be some of the fruit. Please put the words in Gloria's mouth as she teaches us today. Oh, I better get myself inside. In Yeshua's name. Amen.

The classroom was packed when Jeff walked in. He could tell that Gloria was relieved he was finally there. He sat down at the "teacher's table" with Pete and Sarah. Gloria was standing at the lectern. She only had her Bible, no extra materials, but he refused to worry. Gloria had already told him not to be concerned, that she had a special teaching. His eyes swept over the room. He leaned over and whispered to Pete, "Dror's not in the room. Have you seen him?" Pete shook his head. "Well, I don't see Pastor either. He must be outside, waiting for Dror to arrive."

Gloria welcomed everyone. "Shalom, haverim! Boker tov!"

The class gave their usual response. "Ken, shalom v' boker tov, haverim v'moreh." Then she asked if there was anyone who was new to the class and didn't understand the Hebrew words.

From the back corner of the room a man raised his hand and stood up. He quickly answered with a broad grin, "Ken. Ani Dror Mizrachi min Yisrael. Ani hadash. Ani mevin Ivrit."

The class broke out in applause. There was a general uproar at this surprising development.

Pastor James came in the door, smiling big, and escorted Dror to the front. They stood beside Gloria. She extended her hand to Dror. "Baruch haba, Dror!" Dror flashed his brilliant smile.

Miss Lizzie stood up from the front row. With great authority, she made a request. "I love Hebrew, but I am a slow learner, and I demand that you translate every word in English. Right now."

Everyone laughed and chorused loudly, "KEN!"

Gloria put out her hand to Dror, indicating that he answer Miss Lizzie's request. She whispered to him that Miss Lizzie was a pillar of the church and a powerful prayer warrior.

The class became quiet as Dror walked over to Miss Lizzie and bowed to her. "Miss Lizzie, they told me your name and your position of influence, and I am your servant. I will be glad to assist you, as well as the whole class, in learning Hebrew. So, here is what has been said." Miss Lizzie smiled, nodded to Dror, and sat down. The pastor went to the back of the room.

Gloria stood aside, as Dror came to the lectern. "Your teacher Gloria said, 'Hello, friends! Good morning!' The class answered,

'Yes, hello and good morning, friends and teacher.' When Gloria asked if there was anyone new in the class, I introduced myself, saying 'Yes. I am Dror Mizrachi from Israel. I am new. I understand Hebrew." Gloria said to me, 'Welcome, Dror!' Let me say to Gloria and to the class that I think you are learning Hebrew very well, and I commend your talented teacher." He winked at Gloria. The class applauded. Dror went over to the teacher table to shake hands, then returned to his seat.

Gloria was blushing but obviously elated. "We are honored to have Dror Mizrachi here today. Last Sunday night, your teachers met him at Harvey's, and we have enlisted him to give the four of us Hebrew lessons every week. He will help get us ready to make aliyah next year." The class applauded louder than ever. "As is our custom, let us begin the class with prayer. But today, before we pray, we will sing God's commandment to pray for the peace of Jerusalem from the words of King David in Psalm 122:6. You all did so well the last time we sang this. Even though a Hebrew speaker from Israel is in the room, let us make a special effort to direct our song and prayer, not to our guest for his approval, but to our Messiah, our Lord and Savior Yeshua. When He was on earth He spoke and sang in Hebrew. It is to Him we make this musical offering. Here we go:

'Shalu shalom Yerushalayim, (4 times), Shalom, shalom (3 times), Shalu shalom Yerushalayim. Pray for the peace of Jerusalem (3 times), Jerusalem shall live in peace. Shalom, shalom (3 times), Jerusalem shall live in peace'"[7]

"Now let us pray." Gloria could feel the strong presence of the Holy Spirit, as she depended on Him to pray through her. "Heavenly Father, God of Abraham, Isaac, and Jacob, and God and Father of our Lord Yeshua HaMashiach, we come to You today with hearts overflowing. We are deeply grateful to you for the milestone you have helped us achieve, the completion of our course, 'Why Jewish Roots?' And we are doubly grateful that You opened the doors and led us on our trip to Israel last Christmas. I know, according to Your Word, that our Gentile friends here in the church, believers in

Messiah Yeshua, are heirs with us Jews of Your promises to Abraham because You adopted them into the commonwealth of Israel.[8] We are experiencing the oneness of Jew and Gentile in the Kehilah, the body of Messiah, that You prayed for, Yeshua. Thank You! Now show us how to pray effectively for Your heart's desire, that all Israel be saved![9] Amen." The class echoed "Amen."

Gloria held up the course outline of Why Jewish Roots? "Friends, I hope you will refer to this outline and notes to remind you of the 1. Benefits, 2. Responsibilities, and 3. Results of loving your Jewish roots. We ended last Sunday with the final result of the whole church embracing its Jewish roots – the return of the Messiah! You may have already guessed it. We teachers will have another outline to give you next week on this glorious topic, 'The Second Coming of Messiah.' As homework, I urge you to read Matthew 24, and reread Romans 11. We will also be exploring Luke 21, Mark 13, and Zechariah 12-14, if you want to read more. But for the rest of the class period I would like us to explore the meaning of the Hebrew word shalom. If we are to pray effectively for the peace of Jerusalem, we need to know more about the meaning of shalom. And in the next lessons we will be learning more about Jerusalem, which is the 'city of the Great King,'[10] and the city to which Yeshua will be returning."

Jeff couldn't help but notice that Dror was squirming in his seat. He began to earnestly intercede that Dror would not block out what Gloria was saying. He whispered to Pete, asking that he and Sarah would join him in that silent prayer.

Gloria drew a deep breath and opened her mouth, trusting God to fill it.[11] "Dror is teaching us that shalom is used as a greeting in Israel for 'hello, hi, and goodbye.' Jeff and I also found out when we first went to Israel that a common greeting on Friday evening after the sun goes down, beginning the Sabbath, is 'Shalom, shalom.' That means 'Perfect peace.' But there is a deeper meaning for peace, not just the absence of conflict or war. The full meaning of shalom from the Strong's Concordance is this: 'Completeness, wholeness, peace, health, welfare, safety, soundness, tranquility, prosperity, perfectness, fullness, rest, harmony, the absence of agitation or discord.'" The class members were writing furiously in their notebooks.

Gloria continued, "I found this in my Spirit-Filled Life Bible,[12] in a box insert by Nahum 1:15, explaining that shalom is 'the wholeness that the entire human race seeks. It occurs about 250 times in the Old Testament.... In Isaiah 53:5, the chastisement necessary to bring us shalom was upon the suffering Messiah. The angels understood at His birth that Jesus was to be the great peace-bringer, as they called out, 'Glory to God in the highest; and on earth peace, good will toward men!' (Luke 2: 14-17; compare Isaiah 9:7)." Gloria lifted her head from the Bible to see if she could read Dror's expression. She paused a few minutes for this explanation of shalom to sink in.

Miss Lizzie stood. "We are getting in deep here, and I don't want to miss what the Lord is showing us. I think He is telling me that we should ask Dror Mizrachi to come to the front and read the verses Gloria just mentioned and give us understanding from the viewpoint of one who lives in Israel."

Gloria was flabbergasted and couldn't speak for a few moments. The class turned around to look at Dror in his seat. The Holy Rollers were sending up lightning prayers that God would be in total charge. They knew Miss Lizzie rarely missed the voice of the Spirit.

Dror stood up, while Gloria still remained speechless. He replied to the church matriarch, "Miss Lizzie. How could I refuse you? I would be delighted to read and try to explain the verses from your Old Testament, which is the same as the Tanakh, my Bible. Unfortunately, it is back in my room." The class sensed something important was happening.

Sarah stood, "Dror, I have my Tanakh right here," and she held it out to him as he walked forward. She even had it turned to Nahum 1:15.

"Toda, Sarah," said Dror as he took it, walked up to the lectern beside Gloria, and began to read, "'Behold, on the mountains the feet of him who brings good tidings, who proclaims peace! O Judah, keep your appointed feasts. Perform your vows, for the wicked one shall no more pass through you. He is utterly cut off.' The prophet Nahum is predicting the defeat of the wicked city of Nineveh. But it appears that he is quoting Isaiah in an earlier prophecy, found in chapter 52, verse 7. I will read it to you: 'How beautiful upon the mountains are the feet of him who brings good news, who proclaims peace, who brings glad tidings of good things, who proclaims salvation, who says to Zion, Your God reigns!' In this case the prophet Isaiah is predicting the overthrow of Babylon. The ruler Darius will decree restoration to Zion." Dror closed the Tanakh and began to walk back to his chair.

The class broke out into applause. Jeff stood and urged Dror to come back to the front and continue to read. "Dror, that was wonderful. We all feel honored that you are sharing not only your knowledge of Hebrew with us but your knowledge of the Scripture. Would you now please read and explain Isaiah 9:7?"

Gloria smiled at Dror. "Yes, please do continue in Isaiah. But I would like for you to read the preceding verse also."

Dror came back to the front. His face betrayed his angry thoughts. He impatiently turned to the place and began to read, "For unto us a Child is born, unto us a Son is given; and the government will be upon His shoulder. And His name will be called Wonderful, Counselor, Mighty God, Everlasting Father, Prince of Peace. Of the increase of His government and peace there will be no end, upon the throne of David and over His kingdom, to order it and establish it with judgment and justice from that time forward, even forever. The zeal of the Lord of hosts will perform this." Dror walked over to the teacher's table, gave Sarah her Tanakh, and went back to his seat.

Miss Lizzie stood and looked back at Dror. "Aren't you going to tell us that Isaiah is prophesying about the Messiah to be born, that He is the Prince of Peace, and He will reign over Israel? Surely you have heard the famous oratorio, Handel's Messiah, that sets this passage to music along with verses from all over the Tanakh, as you call it."

Pete saw red flags. He knew they couldn't get Dror saved right here in front of the class. It seemed like a gauntlet had been thrown at his feet by Miss Lizzie. He had to do something, but he didn't know what. He felt like Dror was now swimming away from the bait, and they may have lost their only chance to catch him. Pete noticed that no one was saying anything. It was a truly embarrassing moment. He had to do something. Help, God! Intervene and bring a solution. Draw Dror to Yourself. Only You can do it.

Gloria shuffled her outline. "Well, I think it's time to end the class and give us extra time for fellowship before the worship service. Our heads and hearts are full of God's Word. He has planted it in us, and it will accomplish what He pleases, and it will prosper in the thing for which He sent it.[13] I will close in prayer and end by speaking the Aaronic blessing over you. I love each and every one of you. Let's pray. Dear God, You are our Abba. You long for Your children to sit on Your knee. We need you for everything – for wisdom, for strength, for comfort, for courage. We need to feel Your presence, Your love. We ask You to forgive us for any way in which we have offended You or hurt others. Cleanse us anew by the blood of Jesus. Thank You. Please bless our class and especially guide us in the new study of the coming of our Messiah. Thank You for the blessing you gave us today in having Dror visit our class. He helped our understanding of Your Word. This we pray in Yeshua's name. Amen."

Gloria unzipped her purse and pulled out her tallit. She put it over her head, held her hands high over the class and blessed them: "Yevarechecha Adonai ve'yishmerecha. Yaer Adonai, panav elecha, v' chunecha. Yisaw Adonai, panav elecha, ve' yasem, lecha shalom. The Lord bless you and keep you; the Lord make His face shine upon you and be gracious unto you. The Lord lift up His countenance upon you and give you peace. Amen."[14]

Gloria could see that Dror was leaving. She made a beeline for him and asked him to sit back down for a few minutes. He reluctantly took his seat again, and she sat beside him. "Dror, let me say again how much I appreciate your coming to our class today. Everyone was really taken with you. You made a good contribution, and I learned from you. I hope I didn't butcher the Hebrew blessing, and I won't mind if you correct me. I am probably doing it all wrong." Gloria was almost out of breath, trying her best to make amends. She knew Dror was offended by Miss Lizzie's question.

"Well, actually, I was pleasantly surprised. I will be glad to help you polish it up at our next Hebrew lesson."

Miss Lizzie sat on the other side of Dror and extended her hand to him. "Mr. Mizrachi, I am being taken to the woodshed for how I treated you just now. I want to ask you to forgive my obstreperous behavior in putting you on the spot with that uncalled-for question." She was near tears and squeezed Dror's hand. Her facial repentance of sorrow was genuine.

Dror broke out into a big smile. "Oh, Miss Lizzie, you are the sweetest matriarch I have ever met. Everyone knows us young whippersnappers have to be kept in line. But I have no idea what you mean by being taken to the woodshed!"

Jeff, Pete, and Sarah had gathered around and heard the conversation. They all broke into laughter, including Gloria. Miss Lizzie got out a Kleenex and wiped her eyes. "Young man, the Lord has to chastise me sometimes. That's what I meant about the woodshed. Spiritually speaking, I have already felt the lash!"

Dror put his arm around Miss Lizzie and lovingly replied, "Yes, I certainly do forgive you for putting me on the spot. I have had enough experiences with Christians that I take it with a grain of salt when they try to convert me. Somehow, it bothered me today more than usual. I must confess that my Hebrew students here have really impressed me with the genuineness of their faith, and I respect them. As I have been told, it is your bounden duty to try to make me see Jesus as the Messiah."

Jeff breathed a sigh of relief. "I am so glad we are having this conversation. Now the cards are on the table, as the saying goes. More than anything, all of us **do** want to see you come to faith in Yeshua as the Messiah, or MaShiach, as you say in Hebrew. But I promise we are not going to gang up on you, and I ask that you continue to teach us."

Sarah interjected, "Yes, and we want you as a friend. Friends help each other. You are helping us learn Hebrew and prepare for aliyah, and **we** are stoking the fires of your faith to help you grow in Bible knowledge." Pete squeezed Sarah's hand and drew her close to him.

Miss Lizzie regained her fiery spirit. "Young man, I have a gift for you. I don't think I am overstepping my authority this time. It is the least I can do to show my respect and love for you. Here is a New Testament. You can do whatever you want to do with it – throw it away or put it in the drawer or read it. It's yours. Now I am out of the woodshed. Whew!" She wiped her forehead as if she were wiping sweat off her brow and chuckled.

Dror hugged Miss Lizzie, and they stood up. He said his good-byes and headed for the door. Pete was sure he planned to go back to the campus and skip the worship service. The others saw him leaving, and with a sad look of resignation, they continued conversation with the class members crowded around them.

Just as Dror grabbed the doorknob, the door opened. It was Celeste, the pastor's wife. Dror was face to face with her. "Aunt Celeste!" he blurted out. Celeste put her finger to her lips and ignored his greeting, going straight to Gloria. She hoped the others had not heard.

"Holy Rollers, I want to invite you to dinner today. The pastor and I would feel so honored if you would come immediately after church is over." She turned around to face Dror. "And that includes you, too, Mr. Mizrachi. All you have to do is walk next door."

CHAPTER FIVE

REUNITED AT LONG LAST

"I love your home, Celeste. It is so kind of you to invite us for lunch today, or as Jeff would have me say in Southern, 'dinner.'" Gloria laughed. "Oh, my! I see your table is about to collapse under the weight of so many dishes. How did you find time to prepare all this and have it ready at the end of church, since you are in charge of the nursery?"

In her humble manner, Celeste explained that the class members had been planning this for the completion of the course, *Why Jewish Roots?* "Your class brought the food, and I had very little to do. They love you all so much. Also, they not only brought the food, but they took up a collection and bought the four of you some gifts in gratitude for all you have taught them. I will present them to you after the meal."

Pastor James ushered everyone into the dining room and indicated the seating order. "Thank you. Celeste, for helping me honor our staff. That is what I am calling you four from now on, 'our staff.' What you have done for Adaton is a gift from God. You have freely volunteered your service with no thought of recompense. And Dror, the class brought a gift for you, too. Miss Lizzie made sure you were not left out."

Dror was shocked. "Oh, that is very generous of you, but this food and fellowship would have been sufficient as a gift. I thoroughly enjoyed being in the class this morning. The members made me feel very welcome. Today was perhaps only one of three Christian meetings I have attended. And I must say, Pastor, you delivered a good message in the assembly, and the music was enjoyable. I was glad to be sitting by Gloria during the music time. What an amazing voice!" He looked at Gloria admiringly.

Jeff wasn't too excited about this handsome guy sitting by his wife and complimenting her. Unfortunately, before being seated, he stood beside him, and it was obvious that Dror towered over him in height. He could feel the tentacles of jealousy trying to invade his heart. *Lord, I bless my enemy, and I ask you to bless him, too. I refuse to be jealous of him. Help me, Lord, to live by what I said the other night, that outward appearance is not what matters to You, but having a clean, contrite spirit is what You honor. Oh, Lord, please create in me a clean heart, and renew a right spirit in me.* Jeff felt Gloria squeeze his hand under the table. She must have sensed his jealousy, he thought.

Gloria responded, "Thank you, Dror. I simply love to sing and have always loved it, but my singing voice was nothing to write home about until I had a personal encounter with the Messiah." She looked up at him to see his reaction.

Pete came to the rescue of Dror who looked like a fish out of water. "Yes, Gloria was a singing sensation in Europe last year. Sarah and I were in Hungary searching for our Jewish roots and were there to hear Gloria perform in Budapest. I thought the audience would never stop clapping!"

Pastor looked at Dror. "Hey, we don't want this food to get cold. Dror, please say the blessing for us, first in Hebrew and then in English, if you don't mind."

Dror was happy to comply. He prayed reverently, "Baruch Ata, Adonai Eloheynu, Melech HaOlam, hamotzi lechem min haaretz. Blessed art Thou, O Lord our God, King of the Universe, who brings forth bread from the earth." Everyone said Amen.

Gloria couldn't help but think about Jesus being the Bread of Life and how much Dror needed Him. She would be patient. He could only believe if God drew him. But she had a strong feeling that it had already begun to happen. Joy flooded her soul at the thought.

The conversation flowed as the seven diners hungrily sampled almost every dish on the table. Celeste kept running back and forth to the kitchen with pitchers of tea and water. The time passed quickly, and Pastor helped her clear the table and bring out many sweet dishes and hot coffee. Jeff decided to try various desserts and bypass the pecan pie, for a change. Sarah picked out the blueberry cheesecake pie. Gloria got a big slice of apple pie. Celeste dashed to the kitchen with the pie and brought it back with a glob of ice cream on the top. Gloria thanked her and wondered how she read her mind. Pete served himself a small bowl of jello with whipped topping. Dror didn't want the dessert. He put his napkin on the table and sat back in his chair with a satisfied look. Everybody looked at him. *What self-control,* thought Jeff. *So that's how he has such a flat stomach and a lean physique.* Jeff ate a few more bites of the three desserts on his plate, and then pushed it away.

Celeste saw that everyone had finished and stood up. "Jeff, will you help me bring the gifts out? But first we need to clear the table again."

Pastor stood, and so did Jeff. Celeste laughed. "Honey, since we have two Jeffs here, would you mind letting us call you 'Joff,' the shortened form of the British name spelled G-O-E-F-F that your parents gave you?"

Pastor sighed, "Okay, but let me explain to our guests that I changed my name to Jeff a long time ago. **Why** my mother insisted I be named Goeffrey, I don't know. Goeff is a little better, but please only call me that when Jeff Quentin is around!"

Celeste put her arm around her meek husband. "Yes, Goeff, I promise. You are a dear. Now let's go get the gifts."

Pastor came in with two large gifts, and he handed them out to the couples. "Dror, my wife said to send you to the den for your gift. There is something about it that requires a long explanation. Just go down the hall to the end and turn right."

The two couples thought that was strange, but they would go ahead and unwrap their gifts. Dror had no idea what was happening, but he was glad he would get to talk to his Aunt Celeste in private. As soon as he entered the den, Celeste hugged him tightly. "Oh, Dror! Yes, I am your aunt, and my stomach has been churning with butterflies ever since I saw your face. I could talk to you for hours, but I can't do it now. Jeff, or rather Goeff, has no idea about my past. He doesn't even know I am Jewish. You must tell me all about your mother Deborah and her life in Israel. I love her so much. How can we get together in secret? Quick, we don't have much time. Give me your phone number, and I will give you mine."

"This is wonderful! When you opened the door to our class, I instantly knew you as my Aunt Celeste, even though I had not seen you since I was eleven years old. So many happy memories of my childhood in Mississippi flashed before me in that moment. I came to Mississippi to search for my family roots last year and enrolled at Mississippi State University as a graduate student in history. I have a side job, writing articles for the Southern Jewish Historical Society. I know my father's parents well, but I know nothing about my mother's parents. Please tell me about them. I don't even know if they are still alive, and I don't know why my mother never mentions them. I want to know everything."

Celeste was crying, and Dror encircled her in his arms. Drying her eyes, she said, "I will tell you later, but now we need to open your present here and let me give you instructions."

Dror tore into the beautifully wrapped box tied with shiny blue ribbon and drew out an expensive-looking tallit. His jaw dropped when he unfolded the blue-striped, gold-flecked prayer shawl. Celeste took it out of his hands, draped it around his shoulders, and took him to the nearest mirror. Sensing that Dror was a worldly person, she was silently praying that he would accept the gift and truly appreciate it. He seemed to be at a loss for words. Tears welled up in his eyes.

With faltering speech, Dror said, "For some reason, Mother hasn't wanted me to wear one of these. She and Dad don't seem to have any religion. We have gone to the synagogue on occasion, and we do have Passover at home, but, otherwise, we could be considered 'secular Israelis.'"

Celeste knew they would talk later, but now she had to give Miss Lizzie's instructions to Dror. *Oh, too late. Here come my husband and his 'staff.'* Putting on a cheerful demeanor, she said, "Come on in. I was almost through with the instructions. It was to be done in private, but maybe Miss Lizzie won't mind if I tell them to Dror in front of you all. It's probably Miss Lizzie's reasoning about not letting the left hand know what the right hand is doing."

Sarah gasped. "Oh, what a glorious gift! My tallit is similar, but this one is surely the finest to be had. It shows how much Miss Lizzie loves you, Dror."

Celeste looked at Dror with pride. "Well, let me discharge my duty. Dror, I am to tell you to put this on in the morning when you say the Shema. She especially requested that you remain silent for several minutes and wait for the Almighty to speak to you in your spirit. She has made a sacrifice to part with this treasure because it is her deceased husband's tallit. He wore it as he prayed every morning and night. Miss Lizzie said he told her he had always wanted to be Jewish like His Savior was. His favorite story about Jesus was when the woman who had the issue of blood touched the fringe of His tallit and was healed.[15] Miss Lizzie may not have wanted me to tell it, but she said she and her prayer ladies anointed the tallit with fragrant oil and prayed that you would feel the arms of the Lord around you every time you put it on."

Dror was touched by this extravagant gift. He felt nothing but respect for Miss Lizzie now. He expressed his deep gratitude and asked for his donor's address, so he could write her a thank you note.

Gloria felt chill bumps on her arms and knew the Lord's presence was filling the room. "Dror, the Pastor can tell you how important Miss Lizzie's *swat team* is to the church and to him personally. And the Holy Rollers can tell you how these women organized the most magnificent double wedding in history! The main activity they have is fervent intercessory prayer. When those ladies pray, things happen!"

Pete spoke up. "Sarah and I love our gift. Our class members are very thoughtful. These movie DVDs and music CDs will provide just the relaxation we need after we go through our busy days and clear away the supper dishes each night. They were wise to understand that young people need good, wholesome entertainment. I can't wait to thank them next Sunday."

Jeff was next. "You are right, Pete. They seemed to know just what kind of gifts to give us. The illustrated book of the Land of Israel and the City of Jerusalem hits the spot with us. We do have some picture books and maps, but nothing we have compares with this awesome book. And it has the history since Abraham up to the 50ᵗʰ birthday of Jerusalem in 1998 scattered in paragraphs beside the pictures throughout the book. Wow!"

"Yes, wow! I love it!" exclaimed Gloria.

Dror was the first to say his goodbyes. "I look forward to seeing *the church staff* tomorrow night at the chapel at 7:00 o'clock for our Hebrew lesson. I better go now. Goeff and Celeste, this was one of the most enjoyable experiences I have ever had with Christians. The meal was stellar, and I loved the conversation and the outstanding gift. Let me add that the Jewish Roots class was an eye-opener, and the worship service was a blessing. Toda rabbah. Shalom."

CHAPTER SIX

TAKING INVENTORY

PETE AND SARAH'S APARTMENT
AFTER MONDAY NIGHT CLASS

"**B**ruchim HaBayim! Welcome to our home!" Pete unlocked the door and ushered everyone into the living room. Pete and Jeff settled into the recliners. Sarah went to the kitchen, and Gloria followed her. "Oh, Sarah, I love this fragrance. Is it vanilla or what?" asked Gloria.

"I'm glad you like it. I have various scented candles, but vanilla is my favorite. I have some strawberry shortcake in the fridge. Help me serve it, please. The coffee is ready because I put it on timer."

The four got settled around the coffee table, quickly finished the dessert and coffee, and then leaned back in their chairs. No one spoke for about five minutes. Jeff suggested they have silent prayer, and he would close it. The Holy Rollers rarely met without praying first. After they prayed, peace pervaded the room.

Sarah wanted to talk about their class. "Fellow students, I think we all did well tonight, and Dror was superb. The way he had us making conversation in pairs was fun. The new phrases are fun, too, and we are getting them down pat. But verbs are the hardest thing. Besides pronouns and nouns having gender, so do the verbs. Another strange thing in Hebrew is the word order in sentences, with the verb taking the lead, whereas in English the subject noun or pronoun most always comes first. And all verbs are built from a three-letter root. It took all I could do to keep from blurting out that Hebrew is a sacred language, and God is three-in-one, the Trinity. He is Father, Son, and Spirit. It's no wonder that the verbs in God's language, Hebrew, reveal Him that way. But if I had indulged myself like that, Dror would have been scandalized. He would think I had blasphemed, because Jews who don't know Yeshua think that we worship three gods! Ouch!"

Gloria wanted to advise them. "Remember, people, that we have to be salt and light around unbelievers. Any time we can plant a little seed in an unbeliever, we have to be brave and do it. God gave me the courage to ask Dror if he had had time to look at the devotional book I gave him, and you heard what he said. He had scanned through it and was pleasantly surprised that the author used both the Jewish and the Christian definitions of each Hebrew letter. He liked that plenty of verses from the Tanakh were used. Of course, he expected the New Testament to be quoted a lot. But he said he happened to catch a historical caveat that was in error about a false Messiah, Simeon Bar Kokba, leader of the final Jewish revolt against Rome in A.D. 135, who was killed by Emperor Hadrian. Let me read it to you in my copy of the book: 'Nearly 580,000 Jews perished while leaning on this man who called himself the *Star out of Jacob*, mentioned in Numbers 24:17. But prior to this, of those people who had heeded Jesus' explicit instructions in Luke 21:20-22 concerning when to flee from Jerusalem, not one lost his life!'"[16]

Pete confessed, "Thanks, Gloria, for reminding us what he said. I'm sorry to say I lost my concentration and quit listening. But that's a big thing. Now he knows that Jesus' warning was real, and lives were saved. His prophecy came true. And I remember what you taught us in the Jewish Roots class about Emperor Hadrian after the revolt. He plowed under the temple mount and built a temple to his god and renamed the city after himself, Aelia Capitolina. He also changed the name of Israel to Syria Palestina after the Philistines to further erase any trace of Jewishness from the land. Then later the name was changed to Palestine. You said that all the maps in the back of the Bible are wrong because they are titled Palestine, not Israel, as it was named in Jesus' day."

"Bravo, sweet man!" cheered Sarah. "You are smart, my love, to remember all that. And also, I remember what I learned from Papa Sam in his Hanukkah teaching about the Maccabees, linking Daniel's prophecy to Jesus' prophecy in Matthew 24. When believers saw the Romans surrounding Jerusalem, they were to flee to the mountains in Judea. Around 66 A.D. it happened, and they fled to Pella. The Romans burned down Jerusalem in A.D. 70. Goodness, our learning is being reinforced over and over. But, Lord, You have got to help me keep these two Jewish revolts straight, the first one in 66-70 and the last one in 135 A.D."

Gloria continued, "You are right, Sarah. I see now that the author of this devotional book is mixing up the two Jewish revolts. In this book the author says 1,500 people who heeded Jesus' warning were saved, as opposed to 580,000 who were killed because they trusted in Bar Kokba, a false Messiah. There are two things wrong here. Jesus' warning in Matthew 24 would be fulfilled in A.D. 70, not in 135. And, secondly, I have read elsewhere that it was 63,000 Jewish believers,[17] not 1,500, who were saved. Oh, my. I am glad Dror called this to my attention. Could it be that Dror understands that the author is mixing up the two revolts, like I am now seeing it? Oh, Lord, I see what You are doing. You are setting up another conversation with Dror in which I can be a seed-sower again. Toda rabbah, Lord."

"Go for it, girl. God works in mysterious ways for sure. But I want to change the subject. Y'all have strained my brain! Let's take inventory, guys," suggested Jeff.

"Girls, too?" laughed Gloria.

"You know what I mean, sweetheart. I will start, and then we can each share. First, we are seniors at Mississippi State University. We got married a year ago, and this is our last year of college. We have said all along that we would make aliyah after we graduate. It will be here before we know it. I suggest we project a timeline. It has popped into my head that our second anniversary date, June 13, 2000, could be the time of our departure. Since we are taking some courses this summer, we will have a light class load for the fall and spring, giving us time to pack, make sure of our destination in Israel, and apply for jobs there. Do y'all agree with this overall plan?"

Gloria was excited. "Jeff, you know that God made us one when we married, and this proves that oneness. I have had the exact same thoughts." She reached over and hugged Jeff.

Pete laughed. "Hey, ya'll aren't the only ones who are enjoying that oneness. Sarah and I have already had this conversation, and it is our plan, too. Obviously, the Holy Rollers are going to roll into Israel a year from now. God knew all along this would be our divine destiny."

Sarah had to add, "Yes, and our double destinies. I want to bring into the conversation a discussion about our Jewish family members, my sister Chaya, my brother-in-law Max, my other siblings, and both your parents, Jeff and Gloria. Also, Gloria, I want to know all about Papa Sam and Mama Anna's phone calls and letters since they made aliyah last fall."

Gloria replied, "Papa Sam and Mama Anna said, 'Come on in! The water is fine!' They love living in Katzrin. If we decide to live on the Golan Heights with them, we will have a ready-made church family and eager friends to introduce us to life there and to Israel in general. What could be more perfect? But, Sarah, you may want to live in Jerusalem, since your older brother Abe and his family live there. Then there are other wonderful towns, especially in the Galilee. I think we should make this a priority in prayer, the place where we put down roots."

"You're right, Gloria," said Jeff. "We will have to go to ulpan as soon as we arrive. I guess they have these schools all over Israel. I read that Katzrin has a lot of immigrants, or I meant to say *olim*. Okay, let's move on to another subject. I had a serious talk with my parents a month ago and told them that God had called Gloria and me to move to Israel. I acknowledged how heart-wrenching it would be to be separated from them, especially since I am their only child. But I did encourage them to think about doing the same thing later on. Dad knows I won't be able to continue to manage Jeffrey M. Quentin Wholesale Grocery Distribution Center in the Golden Triangle. I have already found the perfect person to take my place, Walter Sessions."

"What? Walter?" Pete was surprised. "Did he agree? What did Jenny think about it? It does sound like a good thing for them though. Walter will have his master's degree in business and his thesis written by then. I bet your dad will make it financially worthwhile."

Sarah filled them in. "They have been living on Walter's inheritance, but Jenny opened a seamstress shop, and she is extremely busy and making good money. Her mother came down and stayed for two weeks to help her get it started."

"Aww, how neat," Gloria responded. "What a miraculous work the Lord has done in Jenny. And I love it how you and she have such a great friendship now, Sarah. God is truly in the life-changing business. And when I see Walter and Jenny sitting in church, I see how much in love they are. I think the Lord told me they would be having a baby before long."

Jeff became alarmed. "Uh oh! I want to go on record about my view of babies and fatherhood. It's right at the top of the chart. But I have asked the Lord to hold off on creating a baby for us until **after** we get settled in Israel."

"Guys, can you believe that Sarah and I discussed this on the night before we had our double wedding? We prayed the same as you did, Jeff." Gloria squeezed Jeff's hand.

Pete reached over and hugged Sarah. "If that's the way you want it, babe, I will adjust my prayers. You know I come from a big family, and I hope we have lots of little Carsons. But I am willing to wait until we are settled in the Promised Land. Okay, now we are of one accord. Hey, aren't we the Holy Rollers?"

Everything got quiet. The couples sensed their conversation was shifting to dangerous territory. Gloria spoke softly. "Dror called me this morning. He wants to take piano lessons from me."

Jeff heard alarm bells in his spirit. "I say no! He is not trustworthy. I have seen him looking at you with a hungry expression, Gloria."

Gloria expected Jeff's reaction. She continued softly, "I waited to tell you, Jeff, until Pete and Sarah were here, so they could help you be more objective about this. According to what Dror said, he is genuinely interested in learning to play the piano. He studied music at Hebrew University in Jerusalem, and he took voice lessons, as well as trumpet. I told him I was teaching Grace Thomas piano at the church on Thursday nights at 6:30, and he could come at 7:30. He was delighted and agreed to my fee of $15 an hour. Jeff, if you want to come with me, sit there, and listen, that is fine with me."

Pete knew he better not say what was in his mind, especially because Sarah was digging her fingernails into his hand. So he only said, "Well, it sounds harmless to me. Who knows, maybe Sarah and I both will take piano lessons. At a reduced fee, however." Pete got tickled at himself, but no one else thought it was funny.

Gloria continued, "Dror said he had a meeting with Pastor and Celeste at their house for dinner, I mean supper, at 5:30 that same night, so it was a good time for him."

Jeff sighed, "Okay, Gloria, but don't you sit too close to him on the piano, you hear me?"

"Of course, honey. You might remember what I did to the last man who sat too close to me on the piano in Budapest. I slapped him hard backstage!"

Everybody stood and did a group hug, laughing heartily. They knew the evening was over, and they all felt like some good plans had been made toward their goal of moving to Israel.

CHAPTER SEVEN

CONFESSION

HOME OF JEFF AND CELESTE JAMES
THURSDAY NIGHT

Dror appreciated the dinner invitation to the pastor's home, but he didn't see how Celeste and he would be able to talk alone. Nevertheless, he anticipated some warm Southern hospitality and was grateful. Pastor met him at the door. "Come in Dror. Celeste and I are so glad you accepted our invitation. We both want to get to know you better. You have made a wonderful impression on us, and also Miss Lizzie instructed us to wine and dine you and to press you into church membership," he chuckled. "But you can be at ease. We certainly will not do that. There are no strings attached to our hospitality."

Dror flashed his brilliant smile. "I must say, Lady Fortune has smiled on me. Two meals in the same week at your home. If the fare tonight is half as good as Sunday's, my waistline might spread another inch." Dror reached out and hugged Celeste.

The table did not hold as many dishes as it did on Sunday, but there couldn't have been a better meal – roast beef and gravy, mashed potatoes, fresh white peas, tossed salad, cornbread, tea, and peach cobbler. After the meal Dror and Jeff poured on the compliments with expressions of satisfaction, patting their stomachs and leaning back in their chairs.

"I am delighted you enjoyed the food. To be honest, I enjoyed watching you eat," laughed Celeste. "I don't want to rush you, Dror, but I know you have a piano lesson at 7:30, and I have some serious things to say to both of you." Celeste looked at her husband with fear in her eyes.

Pastor suggested they go to the den to be more comfortable, but Celeste said, "No. I want us to remain at the table and talk face to face as I *open a can of worms*. I am not trying to be funny. On the contrary, I have a sad confession to make to Jeff, and, Dror, you need to hear it, too."

Pastor explained to Dror, "I overheard some of your conversation with Celeste in the den Sunday. When I wanted to know more, Celeste said that Deborah, her sister and your mother, is part of her story, so I suggested we have you over tonight. I have been on my knees, praying hard, to know how to respond to what I heard, that Celeste is Jewish. I have to know why she never told me. I am trying to understand why Celeste did not feel she could trust me with her past."

Then Jeff turned to Celeste, "Honey, you know I love you with all my being. Nothing you have done or will ever do will cause me to reject you or hurt you. Evidently, something must have happened to you and wounded you deeply, but not sharing these things has made the pain worse. Now go ahead and tell the whole story." Jeff tenderly patted her hand across the table.

"Okay, I will just tell you everything. Please don't interrupt me until I am finished. After I tell you the main facts, you can ask me questions. First, I am Jewish. You didn't know that, Jeff. Of course, Dror knows. Second, I got an abortion. Third, my father rejected me and put me out of the house. Dror, your mother Deborah, my sister, stood up to him and defended me. Mother didn't try to stop Father, but she cried really hard. I could see she didn't agree with Father's decision to banish **both** of us from their home. I cannot have children because the abortionist botched the procedure. I was raped, but Father didn't believe me."

Celeste hated to relive all this, but Jeff had a right to know, and Dror needed to know, too. "Let me go back further. I confided in my close friend Eva after about four months of my pregnancy. I was only fifteen. My parents had not noticed my weight gain, and I didn't have morning sickness. Eva was not Jewish, and she was not a Christian either. I liked her a lot, so I overlooked her immoral behavior, even though I myself was morally clean. She watched my stomach swelling more and more. One day she said, 'You should get an abortion. It's the only thing you can do. From what you have told me about your parents, I know they will not allow it. But if they let you live with them and give birth, they will take the baby away from you immediately and put it up for adoption.' I knew what she said was true. I loved my parents, but my father was rigid, proud, and domineering. My mother never stuck up for me and Deborah. She was afraid of him. I don't know, but something must have happened to Father to make him so unbending. I did love them both though. I have grieved all these years, not having seen them or even knowing if they are alive or dead." Jeff patted her hand again.

"I need to get through this. Let me go on. My friend Eva said, 'The best thing to do is let **me** take you to the clinic. I had to do it one time, and I'm glad I did. Nobody ever knew except my friend Joanie. She's had a secret abortion, too, so she won't tell on me. And I certainly won't tell on **you**.' Well, I shut down my conscience and followed Eva into the clinic. She was my spokesman and even filled out the papers for me. I was like a robot. They made me answer a few questions myself, and then they took me back to a room, explained what would happen, and left me. My conscience was still shut down, and my emotions were frozen. They called for me, and I obediently got up on the table. I blotted the noise coming from the machinery out of my mind. Then I did something I thought I would never do. I had been to church one time when I was a child, and I still remembered how the teacher said if we ever got in trouble to call on the name of Jesus. So I did it. In my mind, not out loud,

I yelled the name of Jesus and asked Him to help me and to forgive me! I knew I was doing wrong. The minute I said His name in my mind, my conscience came awake! And oh, did it hurt. If only I knew then what I know now, it wouldn't have taken me so long to let Jesus heal me of that hurt. But, to be honest, I am certainly not completely free of it to this day. And I made the stupid decision to keep all this hidden from you, Jeff. I am so sorry."

Celeste had avoided Jeff's eyes, but now she examined his face. He was crying. Then she let the tears fall. They stood and faced each other. Jeff reached out and took her in his arms, and she sobbed and sobbed, drinking in the very real comfort of her husband as well as the comfort of the Holy Spirit.

Dror was in anguish. He realized his mother knew all about this, and both she and Celeste had been painfully rejected instead of being loved and comforted. Something inside him began to open up.

Celeste sat back down, dried her eyes, and said, "Oh, Jeff, you were like Jesus holding and comforting me just now. I thought I had been cleansed of all my rejection, self-hate and guilt, and Jesus had forgiven me, but right now it is REAL! It is REAL! And what you have said in your sermons is so true. The devil has tried to rob me all these years. There's no telling how many hours I have put in, taking care of other people's children in the nursery, trying to make up for what I did. But now, I feel free, yes, so free! I will probably keep looking after children, but I don't have to any more. Jesus loves me. As you have preached, Jeff, He doesn't even remember my sin. Oh, glory! And Dror, thank you, thank you, thank you, for blurting out 'Aunt Celeste' last Sunday. If not for you, I would not be experiencing the freedom I am tasting now. I love you, nephew."

Dror was overcome with emotion. He was partly confused, partly sad, but partly happy. He knew it would take quite some time to process all that had just happened. But he had to say something. They were looking at him. "Aunt Celeste, I rejoice with you and your husband for your victory over your past and your suffering. I can't wait to tell my mother."

"Dror, I know you are eager to hear what happened after both your mother and I were cast out of our home. I am guessing Deborah has not told you any of this, because you were not yet born."

"That's right, Aunt Celeste. I was hoping to find my grandparents and you, so I could be filled in on that time in our family history."

"It's a long story, but I will summarize it quickly, so you can make it to your piano lesson." She looked at her husband, "Jeff, again I ask you to forgive me for hiding all this from you."

"Of course, I forgive you. I want to see reconciliation occur with your parents, if they are still alive," answered Jeff. "We have some more time before Dror's piano lesson. Go on, Celeste. Finish the story. I hope there is enough time to also tell how you met me."

"Okay. We lived in Jackson, Mississippi. Deborah was 17 and was about to graduate from high school. She had been working at a department store, and she became friends with another clerk, Sally, who was a Catholic. The day Father pushed Deborah and me out of the house we got in Deborah's car and drove over to Sally's house. They had a huge house, really a mansion, and there were five bedrooms. When Sally heard our story, she said her mom would gladly let us live there until we decided what we would do or until our parents took us back. Sure enough, Mrs. Donaldson had a heart of gold, took us in, and treated us as her daughters. When her husband got to know us, he was glad to treat us that way, too."

"Deborah got me a janitorial job in the department store, so we had a pretty good life there. We tried numerous times to talk to our parents but did not succeed. They didn't answer the phone or open the door. We accepted Sally's invitation to her church, and we made new friends. After Deborah graduated, and then I graduated in two more years, both of us moved to Columbus and entered as freshmen at Mississippi University for Women. I had a full scholarship, and Deborah got a student loan. We got part-time jobs at Dillard's. Life was good. We had already shortened our last name, Goldberg, to Gold, hoping it didn't sound Jewish. We didn't want anything to do with that religion. In our minds, Judaism had made our father mean. I felt like he would have stoned me, had we lived in Bible days. Okay, I will hurry up. Sorry to be giving so many details."

Dror and Pastor agreed they wanted all the details.

"Deborah met your dad, Dror, at a friend's party. She knew he was Jewish by his last name, but he was not religious at all. Regardless, she couldn't help falling in love with him, and they were soon married. You were born the next year. Oh, I have to ask you why you call yourself Dror? You are 'Little Ben' to me. Your parents named you Benjamin Mizrachi, Jr."

"I renamed myself Dror after I became a teenager in Israel. Mother and Dad didn't bat an eye. I just wanted to be macho and have an Israeli name. It means 'freedom,' and there are many famous Israelis named Dror. Sorry I sound so juvenile. And Mom changed her name to Devorah, with a V, and Dad pronounces his name 'Benyameen,' which means 'son of my right hand.' As you know that is the name of our Prime Minister, Benyamin Netanyahu."

"That is interesting. I like all your names. Well, let me continue my story. Deborah and Benjamin bought a little house. Benjamin commuted to Mississippi State and got his degree in business. His father was a generous and wealthy man, so your grandparents helped support them. Deborah kept taking courses and working at Dillard's until she graduated. I did a lot of babysitting for them." Celeste smiled at Dror.

"Yes, Aunt Celeste, I remember. You were indulgent and let me do things my mother would never allow. I really loved you." Dror looked at his watch. "Could I have a second installment on your story, Aunt Celeste? I can't miss my first piano lesson, but later I really would like to hear all about how you met the Pastor. When we meet again, I can also tell you what our life was like in Israel after we made aliyah in 1987."

Dror walked to the door, turned around, and hugged Celeste tightly. He allowed the Pastor to give him a bear hug. Looking at his watch again, he thanked his hosts profusely, and stepped outside.

CHAPTER EIGHT

UNUSUAL PIANO LESSON

Gloria spotted Dror coming in the sanctuary and called out to him, "Come down front, Dror. I am running a little behind. If you don't mind, just take a seat on the front pew and enjoy the piano artistry of my talented pupil, Grace Thomas. Her lesson will end in about ten minutes."

Dror sat down and listened. The music became a soothing lullaby to him as he got comfortable in the front pew. In minutes he was fast asleep.

"Dror! Wake up. It's time for your lesson." Gloria was standing over Dror with Grace by her side.

Dror sat upright and got his composure. Then he stood. In a sleepy voice, he boomed out, "Oh! Please forgive me. I am very embarrassed. I apologize to you, Miss Thomas. Your playing was lovely and so soothing, it quickly sent me to dreamland. I didn't know how exhausted I was, but, as it turns out, your beautiful song cured it. I feel fit as a fiddle now." Dror smiled broadly as he bowed and kissed Grace's hand.

Gloria was amused and decided not to interrupt the conversation that ensued between Dror and Grace. She could see Grace was flustered and a little bashful.

"Well, I am not used to having an audience, and I feel especially honored to have a distinguished Israeli listening to me play, even if I did put you to sleep," laughed Grace.

Gloria made a formal introduction of Dror to Grace and then insisted that Grace remain for a while as she began Dror's first lesson. Having looked around and realized that Jeff wasn't there, she felt it would not be wise to be alone with Dror. "Okay, Dror, we better get started, so I won't get home late. Jeff said he would worry about me being out in the country after dark and driving back, but I intend to give you the full hour that you are paying for."

"That won't ever be a problem, Gloria. I can follow you in my car. Well, let the lesson begin. My goal is to be a virtuoso in three months!" Dror laughed.

Grace sat down and observed the interactions of the teacher with the student, marveling that Gloria could be so business-like with this extremely handsome man. She decided to pray that Gloria would not be tempted to betray Jeff, but she was already confident that her friend would never do that. As for herself, she didn't think the Lord would mind if she feasted her eyes on Dror and fantasized just a wee bit about being his girlfriend. As she listened, suddenly she realized that Dror was already proficient at the keyboard. It was amazing that Gloria could seem so unmoved. She had asked him to demonstrate what he already knew about piano music, since he had told her he had some lessons at Hebrew University and also played the trumpet and could read music.

Gloria was amazed at Dror's playing. He had just launched into Chopin's "Minute Waltz" and played it by memory, only missing a few notes. *Oh, my goodness! He is good. Why did he ask me for lessons, when he can already play? Lord, please reveal to me what is happening. Is this a strategy of the devil, some of his "wiles" to draw me away from my commitment to You and also to Jeff? So far my carnal nature has not responded to Dror's good looks and now his musical ability. Help, Lord! Show me what to say, how to teach Dror, and what is going on. Maybe it is a test from You but a temptation from the devil. You are my Keeper. I will not fall. I will remain true to You and to Jeff,* Gloria vehemently prayed. *In Yeshua's name. Amen.*

Dror finished his piece and looked at Gloria. "Well, what do you think? I know I made a few mistakes, but overall, what do you prescribe?"

"Dror, that was beautiful. I am puzzled why you want me to teach you. What is the real reason?"

Dror hesitated a few minutes. "Okay, if you really want to know, I will tell you, but I am afraid I may shock you with my answer. I love economics and business. I love history. But I also love music. I dated a girl at Hebrew University who was majoring in music. I started going to concerts with her. I went to her voice recitals. Of course, I enjoyed hearing her sing, but I was impressed with her accompanist. He was excellent, and she was dependent on him. Without him, she wouldn't have done so well. He made her look good. Maybe I got jealous, I don't know. Anyway, I signed up for piano lessons, and I worked really hard, because I fell in love with this girl. I wanted to replace the other guy as her accompanist. My piano teacher said I had an amazing aptitude for piano. She could hardly believe I had never had a lesson before I started with her. Okay, here is the embarrassing part. The girl I had given my heart to took it and ripped it in pieces. Now get this, she had fallen in love with her accompanist. It sounds like a soap opera, doesn't it? I became angry and bitter and vowed I would never give my heart to anyone again. Not only that, but I would keep practicing piano and become an exceptional accompanist."

Gloria felt such compassion for this man who had now exposed his wounded heart to her. "Dror, as you told your story, the Lord spoke to me and said that He has already reserved someone for you, someone who has never loved or been loved by any man. She will give you her whole heart, and you can trust her. God will use her to heal your wounded heart. You will love her, and together you will make beautiful music." *Was that really You, Lord? If it was, please let this hope take root in Dror tonight.*

Dror was moved but was determined not to show it. "Gloria, you are a sweet person, but I have to be honest. I don't really believe what you said. However, I won't reject it entirely. You can see I am skeptical. And why I have told you all this, I don't know. Be sure to tell it all to Jeff, because it doesn't seem right to have a heart-to-heart conversation with his wife and he not know about it. And while I am spilling my guts, I might as well admit that I have had the idea of stealing you away from Jeff the same way Ginna was stolen away from me. I feel totally rotten about it now. I don't have any religion, but still I know I need you and Jeff to forgive me. Now I've said it. Whew! What a day this has been. Two heart-to-heart talks in one day."

Gloria was taken aback and was speechless. Dror was looking at her. She knew the so-called piano lesson was over, and she could hardly wait to get home. Yes, she would tell all of this to Jeff. But Dror was waiting for her to say something. All the feeling of God's presence had gone, but she would open her mouth and, by faith, believe God would put the words there. "Dror, you can trust me to never speak of this to anyone but Jeff, as you requested. Yes, I forgive you, and I know Jeff will, too. I don't think we better continue the piano lessons though. However, I am still all in with the Hebrew lessons. The Lord has taught me that when He forgives, He also forgets. And that's the way it will be with Jeff and me. We are going to be praying for you. If you still want to take piano lessons, I can probably get Mrs. Pagani, my teacher, to teach you. Now I better get on home. Good night."

As Gloria gathered up her piano books and her purse, she got her key out to lock up the church. Dror had already left when she was about to turn off the light. But something startled her. It was Grace. "What? Grace! Now you have fallen asleep. I forgot all about you. I did ask you to stay while I taught Dror, but then I forgot you were here. Oh, I'm sorry, but we need to leave now. Thank you for staying while I taught Dror."

"Gloria, please forgive me. I wasn't even sleepy when I sat down, but after Dror finished playing the piece for you, I started getting drowsy and was soon out like a light. Isn't that funny?'

No, it's not funny, thought Gloria. *I hope she didn't hear that confession from Dror. Oh, my goodness. You didn't let her hear it, did You, Lord? Now I see. You put her to sleep. So now only Jeff and I will know Dror's secret sorrow. We can pray for him. The good thing is Jeff will be free of jealousy. We can both love Dror with Your love, Lord. I do believe You gave that prophecy to me for Dror. Please fulfill it soon.*

CHAPTER NINE

WHY DID YOU MAKE ALIYAH?

Jeff was sitting in his recliner, reading his Bible, when Gloria walked in. "Well, little wife, how did it go tonight? I'm sorry I couldn't make it. I gave myself a talking-to about standing strong in my belief that you would not betray me, and you would not fall in love with that handsome piano student. Now all I have to do is to see if my trust in you is merited. I can make an evaluation by holding you in my arms and smooching a while." Jeff reached out to Gloria and pulled her down on his lap. She had been praying hard on the way home that Jeff would take in her revelations about Dror and respond with unwavering trust in her. She welcomed this moment, and passion rose up within her.

"Oh, honey, wow! I needed that," responded Gloria to Jeff's amorous behavior. "Did I pass the test?"

"Hmmm. Well, yes you did. Before I planted my lips on yours, I looked to see if your lipstick had been even slightly smeared," laughed Jeff. "You looked innocent as a lamb to me. But now your lipstick is all over your face and all over mine! Oh, how I love you, Gloria. I just can't get enough of you. You are not only gorgeous, but there is goodness in you."

Gloria pulled a tissue out of the Kleenex box on the coffee table, cleaned off hers and Jeff's faces, and then leaned in for another delicious kiss from her beloved. "This demonstration of your trust, Jeff, is perfect timing because of what I must share with you. As for seeing goodness in me, don't forget what Jesus said when He was told that same thing, 'There is no one good but God.'[18] But we know He IS good, because He IS God. Furthermore, all believers should have goodness in them because goodness is a fruit of the Spirit.[19] Voila!"

"Yes, voila, there it is, my bride." agreed Jeff. "Now curiosity is getting the better of me. Hurry up and tell me what you want to share."

"I'll not sugar-coat it. I will tell you the worst thing he said before I tell you the rest of it. He said he wanted to steal me away from you."

Jeff felt like a bombshell had been dropped in the middle of the room. "Blast that guy! He is my enemy after all. I have been feeling like this for a while, but in prayer God helped me to diffuse my anger and obey Yeshua's command to love our enemies and pray for them, to bless them. I had gotten victory over my jealousy, and now you tell me this! I am angry, and I say that's normal. I don't think God disapproves of my anger in this case." Jeff struggled to have self-control.

"Oh, Jeff, maybe I was wrong to blurt out the worst part of what Dror said tonight before telling you why he said it. Please forgive me, honey. Maybe I missed God on how to share with you, or maybe He wanted to test you. And He already tested me tonight. I am happy to report I passed the test. Jeff, you can trust me, you can. I love you with all my heart, and I could never love another man the way I love you. Keep trusting me. I will tell you the rest, and your anger will turn to pity for Dror. He really does need our prayers and encouragement. We can learn a lot from him, and I thank God for sending him to us. We need the Hebrew lessons and his story of his own aliyah, as well as the subject of aliyah in general. And he needs us. I have the strongest feeling that it won't be long until He trusts Yeshua as his Messiah." Gloria cupped Jeff's face in her hands, looked deep into his eyes, and lavished him with kisses until neither of them could breathe.

"Hey, stop, stop, babe! I trust you. I trust you. But I am going to clobber you, if you don't hurry up and tell me every detail of what happened tonight. My anger is completely gone, and peace is flooding my soul."

Gloria grinned and proceeded to recount the entire evening, including Grace and her falling asleep.

Jeff was on the edge of his seat. "I would have never guessed in a million years that all this happened to Dror. It's amazing, but now I feel love and compassion for this guy. And I agree. He is soon going to be our brother in Christ," exclaimed Jeff. "I can't wait for us to share all this with Pete and Sarah… Hmm. I just had a 'God idea.' Let's get the Holy Rollers together and have a meeting with Dror to hear his story of aliyah and tell him what our hopes and dreams are. We can meet at the Quentin Distribution Center, sort of neutral ground. I say we first ask Pete and Sarah about this and then call and ask Dror if he would meet us there Saturday night. The meeting room is perfect for our purposes. There is a big conference table, but not too big, and we could gather around it, spreading out materials and our Bibles. And it would be a conference, wouldn't it?"

Gloria was elated. "By all means. I have wanted to get us on the same page about aliyah for a long time. I have been studying it a lot, and I request that you let me teach what the Scripture says about it. But Dror should go first and tell about his own experience. Is that the right agenda, Mr. CEO?"

Jeff was glowing. "I agree wholeheartedly, babe. Since you are the CEO's wife, I ask you to make the calls and set it all up." Gloria high-fived the company boss.

JEFFREY M. QUENTIN WHOLESALE GROCERY DISTRIBUTION CENTER
After Shabbat, Saturday, June 26

As Dror drove up to the building, he was impressed. The Holy Rollers were already there and welcomed him. Jeff gave him a tour of the building. He pointed out his office and Sarah's office. "I don't spend much time in here because of attending classes and being at home for most of my meals. Gloria and I sometimes study here just for a change of scenery. Then we have that comfy couch over there when we need to rest or have a little intimacy. As for Sarah, she's not here much, but when she is, Pete drops her off and stops by later to check on her. There is a couch in her office, too." Both Gloria and Sarah were blushing.

Dror laughed. "Well, does any work go on concerning grocery distribution?"

Jeff was quick to answer. "God has supplied me with three strong and dependable guys. They are all Christians, have a great work ethic, and maintain the shipping department like a well-oiled machine. They keep the trucks in tip-top shape and handle all the drivers to everyone's satisfaction. I don't do much except for staying in contact with companies and supplying their needs. Dad was here for a month, showing me how it's done, and I have just continued on as he modeled. Well, that's enough about this facility. We need to get started on learning about aliyah. Everyone be seated."

"I am calling this meeting of the Holy Rollers to order to discuss the important subject of aliyah," declared Jeff. "Welcome, Dror, to our inner circle." Everyone laughed. "We already agreed before you got here that we want to hear your story of aliyah. You can have the floor. Tell us why you made aliyah."

Dror looked at Gloria and Jeff's faces as their eyes riveted on his. He couldn't detect anything negative, even though he knew Gloria had told her husband all about his motives in asking her for piano lessons. He marveled at their ability to forgive him so easily. *These people are like none I have ever met. Their faith in God is obvious and seems to influence every area of their lives. I don't believe the Messiah has come yet, and they have got to be wrong in believing that Jesus is the Messiah. But I still admire them for acting on what they believe. And maybe their reasons for making aliyah are similar to my parents' reasons. I can't wait to find out.* He coughed. "Okay, I know you are paying me for Hebrew lessons, but this information on aliyah is free."

"Hey, Professor," quipped Pete. "I feel like you are our friend besides being our teacher. Let's don't talk about money. What is happening here tonight is not a business meeting, but a time of sharing and fellowship. Sarah even prepared a snack for us later."

"Well, that's very nice, Sarah. Yes, Pete, I had already planned to simply share with you that part of my history. My parents, Ben-yamin and Devorah Mizrachi, moved from Columbus to Jackson when I was about ten years old. Mother's childhood home was there, and she wanted to make another effort to connect with her parents, especially to let them know they had a grandchild, me. They had a plan – the three of us would attend the same synagogue my grandparents attended when my mother and her sister Celeste were growing up."

Gloria interrupted. "Wait. Your aunt's name was Celeste? That doesn't sound like a Jewish name. Of course, you know our pastor's wife is named that."

Dror had not planned to reveal Celeste's story. "I'm sorry, guys. It is her story to tell in her own time. But I will say your pastor's wife is my aunt. I know that shocks you. It shocked me, too, when I saw her that day at the church. I still remembered her after not being in contact for over twelve years. But please, let me go on, because we will be here all night, if I include her in my story of making aliyah."

"Amazing! We have a God of surprises. Everything that has happened to us since we gave our lives to Yeshua is nothing short of divine orchestration by our sovereign God," declared Sarah. "Okay,

Dror, we will sit on our curiosity and give you free rein in what you share with us. Go ahead."

"My dad was willing to leave his parents in Columbus to move us to Jackson. Growing up, his family life was a happy one. He knew my mother did not have a happy childhood, and he saw that the longer she was alienated from her parents – my grandparents – the more discontented she became. Mom and Dad love each other very much. My dad didn't mind selling his business, uprooting, and moving, if it would make my mom happy. Anyway, we moved, bought a house, and I started to school. Dad found a job and advanced up the ladder, so to speak. He was financially successful. We began going to the synagogue. But my grandparents were not there. Mom drove out to the place she lived as a child and teenager. She was shocked that the lot was vacant. Her house was not there! She was filled with despair."

"Oh, Dror, that is so sad," sympathized Sarah.

"Mother had an idea. She would make friends with some of the older members of the synagogue and question them. Surely someone would know what happened to Isaac and Susannah Goldberg. Making inquiries, she found that a woman in her 70s, Rena Rabin, had known the Goldbergs. Rena told Mom that when Isaac and Susannah attended Shabbat services, she sat beside them, and Susannah Goldberg soon became her friend. One day Mom met with Rena in her home and found out some shocking things. Mom told us, 'Through an acquaintance named Flora who lived in our neighborhood, Rena had learned that the Goldbergs were targeted by a gang in Jackson. They persecuted them and called them names like 'Christ killers' and 'dirty Jews.' Also, they painted graffiti on their car and sidewalk. Flora told Rena that Mr. Goldberg was stubborn and would not report it to the police. One night when they were in bed, they smelled smoke. Their house was on fire! They grabbed their robes and a few things at hand and ran outside. It looked like Mr. Goldberg had lost his mind, Flora said, because he ran back into the house. He collapsed in the flames. A neighbor was able to pull his body outside, but this brave man was badly burned. He was a Christian and had tried many times to befriend the Goldbergs, but to no avail. Before my father died, Flora said she saw the man leaning over him. She heard the man praying. My father lifted himself up and grasped the collar of his neighbor, trying to tell him something. Flora told Rena that Father raised his hand up, and there was a smile on his face when he breathed his last!"

Everyone fell silent, in awe of this story, which was sorrowful but had a dim ray of hope. Dror had never shared this before, and it suddenly dawned on him that family secrets and secrets in his own life, long buried, were now being brought to light. He sat there a few more minutes, pondering why these secrets were being exposed and why they were being exposed to these new friends.

"I will continue. After the fire, my grandmother never went back to the synagogue, but she did call Mrs. Rabin a few times. Then they lost touch with each other. I know you are wondering when I will get to the part about aliyah. Soon, I promise. Mother told us she knew she would never see her father again, but she felt duty bound to search for her mother. Unfortunately, Mrs. Rabin could give her no help because she didn't know what happened to Susannah Goldberg."

Sarah felt like everyone needed a break. The air was heavy. "People, I say it's time to have some picker-uppers. We have Cokes, Mountain Dew, and Dr. Pepper in the fridge. I recommend caffeine, but we do have Sprite. And I have some chips and dip plus homemade brownies. Stay seated, please, except for Pete. Honey, I would like for you to fill their drink orders, and I will be back in just a few minutes with the snacks."

After about twenty minutes of snacking and light conversation, Dror resumed his life history. "There's just a little more to tell. I won't give details, but about this time both Mom, Dad, and I got our first taste of anti-Semitism in Jackson with name-calling, pranks, and Mom's loss of job status. This went on several months. Each night at supper we had more bad news to share. I became fearful in school and couldn't concentrate. My grades went down. Finally, Dad had enough and called a family council. He said, 'Family, we are going to move to Israel! I have been studying up on it. It's called *making aliyah*. That's a Hebrew word meaning *going up*. You have heard it in the synagogue when someone steps up on the bemah to say a blessing over the Torah and read from it. It is said these laymen have 'received an aliyah,' but they pronounce it 'aleeya.' Back in Bible times the word meant going up to Jerusalem. The pilgrims would actually climb the mountain up to Jerusalem, which had a high elevation."

Gloria broke out singing, *"Let's go up to Zion, let's go up to Zion. Let's go up to Zion, the City of our God. And we'll sing Hallelujah, sing Hallelujah, sing Hallelujah! There's joy in the Lord!"* Everyone clapped. "I can't wait to teach on this in class. Two more songs come to mind, and the words are from Psalm 48 and Isaiah 40. Oh, my, I am about to burst with joy! I will be teaching you this soon."

Gloria surely knows how to lift our spirits, Dror thought. *I need to get to the point here. It's getting late.* "Thanks, Gloria. Anyway, after Dad explained a little more about making aliyah, Mother said, 'Benjamin, I want to go as soon as possible. Benjamin Junior and I are depending on you to set it all up for us. I want out of here! I am tired of being looked down on and even being persecuted simply for being Jewish. I want to immigrate to our very own Jewish nation, Israel. I will try to get Celeste to go with us, but she probably will say no. She has met someone and fallen in love. Oh, the wonderful thing about it is there's a chance that my mother is already there. Do you think she made aliyah after my father died? She wasn't too old to uproot, and it doesn't seem she had any reason to stay here. It would have given her a fresh start. Before we leave, I will keep searching for her here, but if I can't find her, I will look for her in Israel. I am excited!' I had not seen Mom this happy in a long time, and it was contagious. Dad and I became just as excited as Mom. He didn't waste time. Everything fell into place so quickly. We got help from members of the synagogue, and we departed on

September 11, 1987. There is much more to tell, but we can meet again. After all, you have a year to plan this."

Jeff said, "We can't thank you enough, Dror, for sharing your life with us. We can learn a lot from you, and we value your knowledge of aliyah. We know God sent you to us." Jeff shook Dror's hand, and so did Pete. Gloria and Sarah gave him a quick hug, and he thanked them for the hospitality and friendship.

Dror was turning to go out the door, but Gloria was sure the Lord had spoken to her while Dror was sharing. She silently prayed that he would accept her invitation. "Before you leave, Dror, I want to remind you of our Jewish Roots class in the morning. I know I said we would begin a study on the second coming of the Messiah, but I believe the Lord wants you to tell the class a little bit about the anti-Semitic persecution that preceded your family's move to Israel. Actually, I have failed to get that study outline ready for the second coming anyway, so we can change our schedule. The Lord is pouring into my mind Scripture passages about His drawing the chosen people back to their Land. It's all in my heart and mind, and I am eager to teach the class after you share for about fifteen minutes. Will you do it?"

Sarah was relieved she wouldn't have to teach the following Sunday according to their rotation plan. Gloria hadn't given her the material anyway, so she urged Dror to do it. Pete and Jeff also agreed that Dror and Gloria should have the class time.

Dror reluctantly accepted. "Okay, I will do it. I had already promised Grace Thomas I would be there and attend church with her. Thanks for giving me her number, Gloria. I went ahead and asked her to have lunch with me after church." Dror smiled broadly. "Well, see you tomorrow, guys."

CHAPTER TEN

FULFILLMENT
OF PROPHECY

The classroom was packed. Word had gotten around that Dror would be sharing his personal story. Grace and Dror sat on the front row. Jeff, Pete, and Sarah were at the teacher's table. Gloria stood at the front of the class. "Boker tov, talmidim. Good morning, students. We have a treat today. Dror Mizrachi from Israel is going to share his story of moving to Israel from Jackson, Mississippi. First, I have a new song for you on this subject of aliyah, and then we will pray before Dror speaks." The class broke out in applause.

"I will sing the song for you today, and next Sunday we will sing it all together – 'Up to Jerusalem' by Paul Wilbur.[20] *I was glad when they said to me, Come to the House of the Lord. Standing here in Your gates again, Up to Jerusalem, Up to Jerusalem, Up to Jerusalem. Jerusalem, peace, Adonai Sar Shalom. Blessing be yours, God's peace within your walls….*'" When the song picked up tempo and volume, the class began to clap in rhythm. It was obvious everyone loved it. Gloria could feel God's pleasure. "Now let's pray – Thank You, Father, for bringing Dror Mizrachi to us all the way from Israel, Your Holy Land. I pray that You will recall to his mind things about his life that You want him to share. Guard him from the enemy as he exposes the work of the evil one and shows how You use even Satan's attacks in order to fulfill the prophecies of Your Holy Word. We give You glory and honor and praise for Your grand plan of redemption that has unfolded in the Holy Land and is still unfolding in our time. In the mighty name of Yeshua HaMashiach, amen."

Grace reached over and squeezed Dror's hand as he rose from his seat and came to the front. "Haverim and talmidim, friends and students, it is a pleasure to be a part of your class. Thank you for making me feel so welcome. I am eager to hear Gloria's teaching on aliyah that will follow my story, so this will be short."

The class was spellbound as Dror described the devilish slurs and pranks in elementary school that occurred quite often in the short time he and his parents lived in Jackson. Sympathy welled up in their hearts, and tears coursed down Grace's cheeks. Dror admitted that he wished he had not been born Jewish, but he received such comfort from his parents when he reported these things to them. They assured him that he was part of the chosen people of God. At home his parents would reveal some of the attacks at work they had endured. His mother would tell what little she knew about the Exodus to him, and she declared that just as the Israelites in Egypt were freed from their bondage, so would they be freed one day. She told him that the Holocaust was a horrible price to pay for the birthing of their nation Israel, but now it was a refuge for Jews everywhere.

One of the youth raised her hand. Dror let her speak. She said, "We are studying about the Holocaust in my history class. Our teacher said he was planning a trip for the class to see the Holocaust Memorial Museum in Washington, D.C. I plan to go."

"Yes, it is inspiring and historically accurate, but also very depressing. I visited it recently. The evil the Nazis did is so gruesome it's hard to imagine, and the Holocaust survivors who can attest to it are dying out. Thank goodness this museum and Yad VaShem in Jerusalem give proof of the horrors of the Holocaust. Hatred of the Jews has never stopped, and some even deny that the Holocaust happened at all."

Pastor James spoke up from the back. "I want to plan a trip for this class to see the museum in Washington."

"That's a worthwhile trip for your church, Pastor. I would also recommend The National Museum of American Jewish Military. You can view a video series of American Jewish GIs who liberated concentration camps in the Holocaust. Well, let me resume my story. As my parents talked about Israel, I had a burning desire to move there. Justice was too slow in coming for the Jews in America, I thought, even though it was Jewish people who had contributed so much to the 'good life' that all Americans have enjoyed. Dad told me to be proud of being Jewish and gave me a book about Jewish achievements in every field. I was floored. I studied that book and memorized names and achievements. I had never been more proud of being Jewish. One night at supper Dad made an announcement. He said, 'We are moving to Israel!' Mom and I cheered."

Gloria felt like this was a good ending to Dror's talk. He could share again in another class. She thanked him, and the class applauded. Gloria had never been more fired up. "Class, please open your Bibles to Acts 3:21. I will read it. 'For He (Jesus) must remain in heaven until the time for the final restoration of all things, as God promised long ago through His holy prophets' (NLT). Class, I don't know about you, but I want that 'final restoration of all things' to hurry up, so Jesus will come back from heaven to earth. And there is nothing that fires me up more than to see prophecy being fulfilled. It is important that we study about aliyah before we begin our course on the Second Coming of Messiah because it is a big part of the 'final restoration of all things' and must take place before Jesus returns. Waves of aliyah have increased since Israel gained its independence in 1949. This 'restoration' is taking place in modern times, and I want you to write down these verses and the historical fulfillment of God's prophecies. Turn to Jeremiah 16: 14-16. 'But the time is coming,' says Yahweh, 'when people who are taking an oath will no longer say, 'As surely as Yahweh lives, who rescued the people of Israel from the land of Egypt.' Instead, they will say, 'As surely as Yahweh lives, who brought the people of Israel back to their own land from the land of the north and from all the countries to which he had exiled them.' For I will bring them back to this land that I gave their ancestors. But now I am sending for many fishermen who will catch them, says Yahweh. I am sending for hunters who will hunt them down in the mountains, hills, and caves.'" Gloria gave the class time to let this sink in. "What is being prophesied by Jeremiah in these verses is a second Exodus, unlike the one from Egypt, which was an exodus from only one country. He says the Israelites will be brought back from the land of the north and from all countries. This is what is happening in our day! It gets me so excited!"

Dror raised his hand. "Pardon me, but I think the prophet is referring to the exiles returning from Babylon in 537 B.C."

Gloria explained, "Well, Babylon isn't really to the north of Israel. It is due east. The return, the aliyah that Jeremiah referred to, is from Russia, as well as from 'all the countries' where God had scattered them. I think these historical facts will prove it to you. Get ready to write. In May of 1949, Operation Magic Carpet brought 45,000 Jews from Yemen to Israel in 380 flights! Immigrants that year totaled 250,000 and cost $3,000 each to absorb, a staggering cost of $700,000 to the fledgling government of the new State of Israel. This was clearly a miracle of provision by the God of Israel." Gloria looked at Dror. He was nodding his head and smiling at her. Of course, being a student of history, he would already know about the things Gloria was teaching.

"Class, I have three more examples of mass aliyah during our lifetime. Write this down, and please forgive me for not having already printed out this information: In 1985, Operation Moses, a covert evacuation of Jews from Sudan during a famine, brought 8,000 Ethiopian Jews to Israel in 30 flights. A mass immigration of Jews from the Soviet Union began in 1989. But here is the most spectacular aliyah – on May 24, 1991, in a covert military airlift Operation Solomon brought over 14,200 Ethiopian Jews to Israel in just 36 hours. It took 41 flights, and seven babies were born on the way! U.S. President H. W. Bush gave major assistance. The operation set a world record for a single-flight passenger load when an El Al 747 plane carried 1,122 passengers to Israel. These Jews were snatched from death in famine and civil war. I was only 13 at the time, but I remember my parents showing me the newspaper headlines. They said I should know about this, that it was a miracle of God. It caused me to wonder why it was important and why my parents made such a big deal out of it. Well, I see now that it was a big deal. Wow!"

Grace Thomas raised her hand. "Besides the mass immigration from Russia, you have just given us three examples of the fulfillment of Jeremiah's prophecy, one from Yemen and two from Ethiopia. Death because of famine and civil war were reasons the Jews in those countries wanted to get out. You used the words, 'covert operation,' which must indicate that the escape of the Jews could have been stopped by their hostile governments. But God made sure they arrived in the Promised Land. And it makes me proud that our government assisted the airlift in 1991. And the Jews making aliyah from Russia were certainly fleeing that oppressive government."

"You are absolutely right, Grace, and you are very observant. That leads me to explain the rest of Jeremiah's prophecy. God said He would send fishers to catch them and hunters to hunt them down. God wanted His people to return. He was the one who scattered them, and He had promised many times to gather them back to their own land – 'He who scattered Israel will gather him, and keep him as a shepherd does his flock' (Jer. 31:10). This is the way He would gather them - He would send fishers first, people to urge them and assist them, so they could actually do it – make aliyah. If they wouldn't listen or respond to His offer to bring them to the Promised Land, He would have to send the hunters. Hitler fits the description of a ruthless hunter."

79

Sarah had to speak. "I am so glad that the Holy Rollers have not needed fishers to catch us or hunters to hunt us down. We are making aliyah willingly, and we can already see that HaShem is getting us ready to make the move. Pete and I talk about it all the time. Please, everyone, pray for us to hear the voice of the Spirit and obey. We know HaShem has a purpose for us to live in Israel. We can see His hand at work. He has already sent us a Hebrew teacher, Dror Mizrachi, and the experience of his parents and him making aliyah gives him insider information we need."

Dror replied, "Thank you, Gloria, for bringing out the Jeremiah prophecy. It looks like my family didn't respond to the fishers, if indeed there were any. But one thing I know is the hunters came around in the form of anti-Semites who harassed us in various ways. They made us want to leave and go to the Promised Land. I can tell you for a fact that Israel is the most secure country in the world. We are surrounded by hostile countries and terrorist groups, but we feel safe, and our military and intelligence people know how to protect us."

Pastor James came to the front. "Class, I know each one of us feels that God has blessed us with our Jewish teachers. And I don't want to leave Pete out. He is a Gentile like all of us. In Hebrew he's a 'goy.' And this goy has been a blessing also. Just recently the Lord has pointed out to me that we Gentile Christians, we 'goyim,' should show our gratitude not only for these Jewish believers among us, but for our Jewish heritage – the Messiah, the Apostles, the Scriptures, and the original Church, which are all Jewish. I was reading in Isaiah, and a verse jumped out at me, looking like it was written in gold. Let me read it to you: 'Thus says the Lord Yahweh: 'Behold, I will lift up my hand to the nations, and raise my signal to the peoples; and they shall bring your sons in their arms, and your daughters shall be carried on their shoulders.'[21] The Spirit immediately explained it to me: God will use the Gentiles, or goyim, indicated by the word nations, to bring His chosen people home to Him in the land of Israel. That means Christian churches should support in prayer and finances the work of aliyah. Our church council will be meeting soon, and one of the things we will bring up is figuring out how we can act on this verse."

Jeff stood up. "Pastor, that is more than generous of you. And there is no doubt we can use your prayers. In what Gloria just taught we can see that Satan opposes God's plan to bring His people home to Israel. He sends the hunters to persecute them and try to stop them. But God only uses that to wake them up to understand they need to go to their Jewish homeland to be safe. Yes, all of you, please remember us in your prayers."

Pastor continued, "I have a request of Gloria, which will help me fulfill my plan of support for your aliyah. Gloria, I want you to sing that beautiful song in our worship service next Sunday, the one you opened our class with today."

"Oh, yes, I would love to do it, Pastor. Thank you for asking me. The lyrics of the song, 'Up to Jerusalem,' come from Psalm 122, and we have already learned the sixth verse of that Psalm in the song, 'Shalu Shalom Yerushalayim, Pray for the Peace of Jerusalem.' I tell you what, talmidim, let's end our class today by singing it again, and then I will lead us in prayer for Pastor's plan for our church to assist in aliyah."

CHAPTER ELEVEN

A BORN
ACCOMPANIST

MUSIC REHEARSAL AT ADATON
THURDAY NIGHT

Gloria was playing the piano and singing when she heard the sanctuary door open. "Come on in, Grace. Oh, I see you brought Dror with you. Erev tov, Dror and Grace. Well, Grace, come on up here, and let's see how you do as my accompanist for next Sunday. I didn't have time to order an accompaniment CD, and I don't want to sit at the piano and play for myself. I think it is much more effective to stand and sing. That helps me to connect with the congregation more easily, and Pastor James hopes I can impart the vision of aliyah to them through this song. I love the melody, rhythm, and, of course, the words of 'Up to Jerusalem.'"

Grace looked worried. "Gloria, I hope I don't disappoint you. I promise I have practiced a lot, but I keep stumbling on the rhythm. The CD is a big help. I bring my CD player to the practice room, put the sheet music you gave me on the piano, and then try to play along with the CD. Since Sunday I have probably practiced it at least twenty times. I pray you can sing to my accompaniment."

"Don't worry, Grace. I have already been praying about it. You just follow me, even if you stumble. Keep going. No one at the worship service will be able to tell whether you play it right or not. Well, let's get started. I have my copy, so give me the introduction and keep going just as it is written, okay?"

Gloria's confidence in Grace began to fade after the third try. Grace was so nervous, and now she was crying. "Gloria, I just can't do it! Please play for yourself. You have performed that way before, and everyone loved it. Dror and I will sit out here and listen. It will be wonderful."

After Gloria performed it, Grace and Dror applauded, but Gloria wasn't satisfied. She didn't feel anointed by the Spirit, as she usually was. *What do you want me to do, Lord? Should I ask Dror to accompany me? Surely he wouldn't be able to play it right without any practice, and I don't want to take up his time with another rehearsal. Father, this is important, as You know. Pastor James is counting on me. He has heard from You about supporting aliyah, and my song will be a catalyst for his message.*

Dror had come up on the stage and was standing by the piano when Gloria lifted her head. "Sorry to interrupt your prayer, but I want to offer myself as your accompanist. Grace has heard me play and is urging me to do it for you. I have been with her in the practice room, so I have heard the song enough times to almost play it by memory!"

The minute Gloria saw the expression on Dror's face, she knew the Lord sent him. "Oh, Dror, what a brave thing to do. This little church is always packed lately, and I don't want to put you on the spot. They may not know much about music, but if you and I bomb out, they will lose confidence in Pastor for asking me to sing. And I might not be asked again."

Dror got tickled and started to laugh. "You think it will be a big *balaGAN? Yihiyeh b'SEDer, yaldah!* We must show some *CHUTSpa!*" Gloria started to laugh.

"You think I don't know what you said, don't you? Well, I do! You aren't the only source I have for learning Hebrew, you vain thing," teased Gloria.

Grace stood up. "Y'all quit making all those inside jokes. I demand you translate."

"My sweet little dove. Don't fly away. I will tell you, and also you may join our Hebrew class anytime you wish. It's on Monday nights in the chapel at 7:00 for two hours. For you, beautiful girl, I will waive the fee." Dror poured it on thick, flashing his trademark smile.

Gloria could see that Grace was melting in her seat, soaking up Dror's charm. And then the prophecy she made to Dror came to her mind. *Lord, is Grace the one you intend for Dror? Your thoughts are not our thoughts, neither are our ways Your ways, but Yours are so much higher.*[22] *I love to see You at work. Please have Your way concerning this song. I request that You supernaturally equip Dror to play the accompaniment beautifully. In Yeshua's name. Amen.*

"Well, what did you say, Dror?" asked Grace.

"I said to Gloria, 'You think it will be a big confusion. It will be all right, girl. We must show some cheeky nerve!" Now it was Grace's turn to laugh.

"Go ahead and play the accompaniment, Dror," urged Grace. "I heard you play it in the practice room. If it's good, I will reward you with a big kiss." The minute she said it, Grace blushed.

Dror mimicked a concert pianist as he pantomimed throwing the tails of his tuxedo behind him, sitting down and adjusting the bench. He raised his fingers above the keyboard with a flourish, then brought them down forcefully to play the introduction. Liberace could not have been more flamboyant.

Gloria got tickled and could hardly sing. But after the first few words, she lost herself in the words and music of the dynamic song. She was following the Divine Conductor, and her heart throbbed with excitement as if singing and dancing in the golden city of Jerusalem. Her body moved to the music, and her voice soared on heavenly wings to the heights of emotion. It was like the day she stood behind the pulpit to report on their trip to Israel. She had a vision of the Garden Tomb, and she **became** Mary Magdalene for a few minutes. She didn't want it to end, and now she had that same feeling. She was standing there reverently after the last note was sung, when Grace came running on to the stage.

Grace threw her arms around Dror and kissed him full on the lips, as he lifted her off her feet and swung her around the stage, embracing her tightly. When Dror let her go, she went over to Gloria and hugged her fiercely. "Oh, Gloria, I was transported to heaven with your beautiful singing and Dror's magnificent playing. I don't see how more practice would make it any better. This was meant to happen. The only part I played was bringing Dror here tonight. He is a born accompanist. It was made evident just now. And Gloria, I have heard you sing many times, but tonight was more glorious than ever. The Holy Spirit set you on fire!"

Gloria came out of her reverie. "I have to agree with what you said about Dror. I am going to call Mrs. Pagani tonight and insist that she attend our church next Sunday. When she hears Dror play, she will surely agree to give him piano lessons. One of her colleagues, Arturo Zappala, who accompanied me on the concert stages of Vienna, Budapest, and Prague last year, is no better than you are, Dror. It must be supernatural!"

♥ ♥ ♥ ♥ ♥

HARVEY'S RESTAURANT
SUNDAY AFTER CHURCH

Jeff chose a big table at the back of the restaurant for their gathering. They had arrived at 12:45, and most of the tables had already been taken. Thankfully, this one was in the least noisy part of the room. Here they would be able to hear each other. He knew this was important to Gloria. He pulled out the chairs for Gloria and Mrs. Pagani. Dror seated Grace. Jeff said, "Dror, in case you are wondering, Pete and Sarah were invited but felt they should accept Walter and Jenny's invitation for lunch at Sessions Manor. And, of course, Gloria and I were invited there, too, but Gloria had already made a prior engagement for us to meet with you, Mrs. Pagani. This concerns our planning to move to Israel, as well as a request for your help for our friend and professor, Dror Mizrachi." Dror grinned at Jeff's choice of words – professor, indeed.

"Oh, young man, as the saying goes, 'You blew me away!'" responded Mrs. Pagani. "I want you to tell me all about your training. I know a little something about the caliber of music students coming out of Hebrew University. Surely, you were a prize pupil of some piano teacher there."

As Dror was trying to process such a nice compliment, Gloria took up the conversation. "Mrs. Pagani, I really appreciate your coming to Adaton today to hear Dror play the piano. I knew you would be impressed. But before we discuss Dror's musical future, I ask you to give me your honest opinion about my singing. Do you think my voice teacher, Mr. Menotti, would have approved of my singing style today? I understand he is not a church-going person, and he may think this type music is inferior."

"Oh, my child, you underestimate Mr. Menotti. He is well aware of your penchant for Christian music. He knows you can develop the ability on your own to successfully conquer that field of music. But he wants you to have the best classical education he can give you. He knows many doors will be open to you that way, just as proved to be the case last year in Europe. As for me, your singing combined with that exciting message from your pastor 'warmed the cockles of my heart!'"

"Mrs. Pagani, you are a dear. Now I will get down to business. Would you be able to squeeze Dror into your schedule as a piano student?"

Mrs. Pagani looked over at Dror and made some quick calculations in her mind. "Mr. Mizrachi, I have a full student load, but I will make room for you. Come by my studio – Gloria will tell you how to locate me – at 3:00 tomorrow afternoon, and we will discuss your background, your goals, my expectations, and the time slot and fees. How does that sound?"

Grace squeezed Dror's hand. He smiled broadly at Mrs. Pagani. "I cannot thank you enough, Mrs. Pagani. Gloria sings your praises, and I feel confident you can make me a virtuoso pianist in short order. The music faculty at Hebrew University will hardly recognize me when I return to Jerusalem as a candidate for an accompanist position. I will see you tomorrow. I have some piano books from my teacher at Hebrew University from which you can judge my level of development and prescribe the course I must take going forward. I am deeply grateful to you. Gloria probably told you I am pursuing a master's degree in history, and I have a side job, too. But I can assure you, I will do the practicing you require of me gladly."

The waiter brought the food. His timing seemed to coincide with the celebration of a life-changing moment in Dror's dreams and goals. The conversation flowed freely. Jeff could see that these music people had a special camaraderie, but he refused to feel like an outsider. "At least I can carry a tune, according to Gloria," Jeff laughed. "But to change the subject a little, let me ask you what you thought of Pastor James' message today, Mrs. Pagani."

"Well, Jeff, I must say it was a brand new Bible story to me. But I haven't attended very many church services, so the story may be well-known to all of you." They assured her that they also were not familiar with the story. "He certainly did make his point, however. The takeaway for me was that when God says something will happen in the future, it will happen. This type thing should answer the doubts of the skeptics. Jeff, if you don't mind, please summarize the story again. I want to remember it."

"I will try, Mrs. Pagani. Let me see… Without a Bible in front of me, I'll do the best I can. Okay, there was a prophet who came to Bethel to an idolatrous altar on the high place. King Jereboam of Israel – that's the 10 northern tribes – was standing there, burning incense. The old prophet said that one day a child named Josiah would become King of Judah, and he would sacrifice the idolatrous priests on that altar, and men's bones would be burned on it. The prophet said God would give a sign to verify the prophecy – the altar would be split apart, and the ashes would pour out. King Jereboam was angry, stretched out his hand, and said, 'Arrest him!'

88

His hand withered, and the altar was split apart! Jereboam got the message. And he begged the prophet to restore his hand.[23] Now here is the exciting part: Centuries later, when Josiah became King of Judah, he cleansed the land of pagan altars at the high places. He went to the altar at Bethel which King Jereboam had made. Josiah burned the altar and crushed it to powder and burned a wooden idol. He took the priests' bones out of the tombs on the mountain and burned them on the altar. Then he looked and saw a gravestone. When he asked whose it was, the men of the city told him it was the tomb of the prophet who came from Judah and proclaimed the very things that King Josiah had just done against the altar of Bethel![24] Wow!"

Grace got carried away as the full import of this fulfilled prophecy shook her. "Fulfilled prophecy! And to think, this is only one prophecy God inspired many, many years before it was fulfilled. I have been told that Jesus fulfilled over 300 prophecies in the details of His birth, His three years of ministry on the earth, and in His death, burial, and resurrection! And the thrilling thing is that there are more prophecies to be fulfilled in His **second** coming!"

Mrs. Pagani was straining to understand what Grace said, as well as the meaning of the story about King Josiah. Dror's face seemed to have a shade drawn over it. Gloria was overcome by the Holy Spirit and had to share. "To God there is no time. He lives in eternity. He can see the end from the beginning. The thing I learned just a short time after I was born again is that God has a plan for my life and for every life. Listen to this verse: 'We are God's workmanship, created in Christ Jesus for good works, which He has before ordained that we should walk in them,' Ephesians 2:10. In other words, the good works we will do after we are saved have already been planned by Him. It's a matter of us seeking God's will, and we will step right into His plan. Voila!"

Jeff was reminded of a favorite verse. "Listen to this, since you used the word *step*, Gloria. 'The steps of a good man are ordered by the Lord, and He delights in his way. Though he fall, he will not be utterly cast down, for the Lord upholds him by His hand,' Psalm 37: 23-24. Now that's comforting, isn't it?"

Gloria looked up at her man adoringly. "But, honey, you said the steps of a good man are ordered by the Lord. But what about a good woman?"

"I am a literalist, little woman," teased Jeff. But for **you**, my very feminine wife, I will concede and let you in on the promise." Gloria strongly elbowed Jeff in the ribs. Dror joined in the laughter, and the shade went up on his countenance.

Grace had never spoken out so much before, but she felt a fire burning in her. "I love this conversation. I can actually feel my faith growing. Here is another verse I have recently memorized. The last few words really grab me. 'God saved us and called us with a holy calling, not according to our works, but according to His own purpose and grace which were given to us in Christ Jesus before time began.' 2 Timothy 1:9. Ooh! Did you get that? Not only did God have a plan for our lives before we were born, but He formed this plan before time began! I can't fathom it. Gloria and Jeff, you Holy Rollers keep saying you have a 'double destiny.' That truth was evident in your double wedding, but you also have a **prophetic destiny**. I know you four are constantly seeking God's will in your plans for aliyah. Well, I believe God has already orchestrated the whole thing. Just go with the flow, and let the Holy Spirit lead."

Gloria's heart filled with gratitude for her friend Grace. Not only had she played the most important role in Gloria's being born again, but Grace continued to be her cheerleader ever since then. "Thanks, Grace, for putting the exclamation point on Pastor's sermon today. After telling the story about the old prophet, King Jereboam, and King Josiah, he showed us how the return of the Jews back to their ancient homeland is a fulfillment of some 700 prophecies in the Old Testament. And thanks for pointing out that all the prophecies about the first coming of the Messiah have been fulfilled in Yeshua. This conversation has certainly been very 'meaty,' and how appropriate to have discussed these things over a delicious meal. I know the Bible says to 'desire the pure milk of the Word as newborn babies,'[25] but it also says, 'solid food belongs to those who are mature.'[26] I marvel at how we have grown in our faith. God is maturing us. What a blessing that He has stored so much Scripture in our minds in a very short time."

Dror had been squirming in his seat. His dearth of Bible knowledge was hitting him hard. He realized that if he continued interacting with Grace, as well as his Hebrew students, he had to grow up fast. Suddenly it occurred to him that maybe Grace would teach him. He really had feelings for her, and there was no doubt she adored him, Bible ignorance and all.

Mrs. Pagani had been struck by the term 'prophetic destiny' and the wonderful thought that God has a plan for each life. "I have really enjoyed this time with you young people. It has been rich. And it has got me to thinking, 'What is my prophetic destiny?'"

Grace had to share. "Gloria, do you remember what I said last Thursday night about Dror being a 'born accompanist'? What has been said here makes me realize that God had it planned for him all along, even 'before time began,' as the Scripture says. It's Dror's prophetic destiny, among other things, to become a piano accompanist. I have no doubt he will be that virtuoso he has dreamed of."

Mrs. Pagani longed for her afternoon nap. "Well, I must leave you now. I look forward to seeing you tomorrow in my office, Dror. Who knows, part of your prophetic destiny may be as a student of mine. Now that is an ego-builder!" She laughed at herself. Jeff pulled the chair back for Mrs. Pagani. She went over to Gloria and kissed her cheek, then said goodbyes to each of them.

CHAPTER TWELVE

OBSTACLES TO ALIYAH

QUENTIN DISTRIBUTION CENTER
SATURDAY NIGHT, JULY 10

"**T**here is 'trouble in River City!'" bemoaned Gloria as the Holy Rollers seated themselves around the conference table in Quentin Distribution Center. "I guess we could have met in our apartment, but I feel the need of meeting in a location devoted to business and making decisions. "I have news that I haven't even told Jeff yet, so this is 'hot off the wire.' Papa Sam called me today with awful news. He and Mama Anna are in danger of being deported from Israel! He asked for prayer."

"Oh, no!" chorused Jeff, Pete, and Sarah. They were sitting on the edge of their seats, waiting for Gloria to explain.

"He told me stuff I didn't know. I had thought that their aliyah process went off without a hitch. Not so. Well, they had all their documents in order, proving they were bona fide Jews. They had a statement of endorsement from the Rabbi of their synagogue in Chicago and all the other papers they needed for Israeli citizenship. Remember it was last fall they immigrated. They were happily settled in Katzrin, attending the kehilat regularly, and having fellowship with Rabbi Leonard and Miriam Katz. But one day when they got their mail and opened a letter from the Ministry of the Interior, they were devastated. They had to go to Jerusalem and meet with Minister Eli Rabinowitz. When he asked them point blank if they believed that Yeshua was the Messiah, Papa Sam said their dream of living out their lives in Israel went up in smoke! The government thinks that any Jew who believes Jesus is the Messiah is no longer a Jew, but he is a Christian. And, of course, citizenship is only open to Jews and not to people of another religion. Oh, it breaks my heart. What are **we** going to do? And also, how can Papa Sam and Mama Anna stay in the land as non-Jews, according to the government's view of them?"

"I guess the Minister of the Interior checked up on the Olive Tree Congregation in Chicago and discovered it is a Messianic Jewish congregation. Is that how they found out?" asked Jeff.

"Yes, that's what happened. Does anybody have any ideas about ways we can make aliyah without denying Jesus?"

Pete said, "I have been doing some research on the internet concerning myself being a Gentile with a Jewish wife. I found out that until 1996, just three years ago, the Gentile spouse of a Jew was given permanent residency automatically. But now it can be as long as five years for a Gentile spouse to be given permanent residency and become a naturalized citizen. Well, from what you have told us about your grandparents, Gloria, I see we have another hurdle to jump. Israel will not consider Sarah to be Jewish if they know she believes in Yeshua, making her a Christian or non-Jew in their eyes. Of course, we all know it makes her more Jewish than ever. That's the blindness that Paul talks about in Romans 11, and God Himself did it. He blinded the Jews as part of His plan for the Gentiles to receive the gospel. It's not hopeless though, because the day is coming when they will 'see Him whom they pierced' and repent.[27] In the meantime, that blindness is putting a monkey wrench in our plans to make aliyah."

Sarah had been thinking. "Holy Rollers, it looks like we need to reestablish our relationship with B'Nai Israel temple in Columbus. Hopefully, the Rabbi there will give us a certificate of endorsement. Hey, it is possible, because they meet on Friday nights, when

94

Shabbat begins, as you know. We don't have to exchange church attendance for synagogue attendance. We can do both."

Gloria smiled. Hope filled her heart, until she realized the dilemma of her grandparents. "That is certainly an option, Sarah. But listen to this. Papa Sam said the viewpoint of the Ministry of the Interior in regard to Jews who believe in Jesus is that they are enemies because they do missionary work, trying to 'steal Jewish souls.' Accepting Messianic Jews as immigrants would be in direct opposition to the Zionist purpose of a Jewish state. They fear that we would turn a sizable part of the population into Christians."

Pete interrupted. "Let me tell you what else I found on the internet. This could be another obstacle. We can apply for our work permits at the Ministry of the Interior online, but the site is in Hebrew. And the advice from another site is that it's doubtful you can even get a work permit if you don't know Hebrew. A work permit is the first step to applying for jobs in Israel. At least we can do all of this online, but knowing Hebrew is a must. Although Dror has been instructing us well, I can see that I need to put in a lot more study time. And this will take time away from my job and classes on campus, not to mention my home life. I want my honeymoon to continue with Sarah. Y'all can see how frustrated I feel, and I'm sure you do, too. I say we pray."

"Yes, Pete," agreed Gloria. "And we must intercede fervently for Papa Sam and Mama Anna not to be deported."

The two couples fell to their knees, and Jeff led them in heart-felt prayer for Gloria's grandparents and for the clearing away of all obstacles to their prophetic destinies in Israel. They arose from their knees, invigorated to continue preparing for aliyah. Jeff exhorted them to realize their God was mighty. He parted the Red Sea for the Israelites to cross over into their Promised Land. He would also 'part the waters' of the Atlantic Ocean to give them safe passage to Zion and full acceptance as a part of the Chosen People. Everyone agreed that the obstacles were formidable, but they declared that 'nothing is too difficult'[28] for Yahweh and the 'Captain of their salvation,'[29] Yeshua HaMashiach.

Gloria looked at Pete. "I am glad you have found out things we need to know on the internet. I myself have been researching places in Israel to live. At my piano lesson this week Mrs. Pagani said she had been communicating with the music department at Hebrew University to find out what jobs are available for graduate music students. She assumed I would seek a master's degree in music there, although I never said that. Actually, it is her desire, not mine. But when Dror came for his lesson Monday, he and Mrs. Pagani talked about the demand for piano accompanists for individual students who were willing to pay the cost, especially at The Academy of Music and Dance on the Givat Ram campus. So, I have been praying about it. If God can use me in music at the University, I am willing. Of course, Dror would have priority over me, but maybe the demand is great enough that I could be a paid accompanist also. This is what I am getting at – if I did get the job, that would mean residing in Jerusalem or very close by. We couldn't live in Katzrin because it is a long way from Jerusalem. Another thing Jeff and I have talked about is that it's possible he can get a paid job with the Bridges for Peace Food Bank in Jerusalem. He found out they have positions available. Most of the positions are volunteer, but some executive positions pay fairly well. And it's what he knows about, food."

"Hey, we **all** know about food!" laughed Pete. "But I see what you mean. That's a double reason for living in Jerusalem. As far as Sarah and me, she has family there. And I have been looking on the internet for a security personnel position and found some promising leads. Considering the increase in suicide bombings, lots of restaurants and shopping malls are beefing up their security detail. These jobs are dangerous, but they pay very well. Sarah has reluctantly agreed for me to seek this type job. I can narrow down my search to Jerusalem, if that's where you and Jeff are going to live."

"Here's something else I am praying about. I want you all to help me pray. Finding an apartment in the Old City would be so exciting, I think, especially considering all the history attached to it," said Gloria. "You do remember our touring it on our honeymoon, don't you? And we went back there with the Adaton group last Christmas. Both times we went inside Christ Church. I got just enough from the tour guide to whet my curiosity, but now I have looked it up on the internet and found out all its history. They have guesthouses, but there are also a few available apartments for permanent residents. I've got goosebumps, just thinking about living there! I have written a little history of the Old City and also of Christ Church. Let me read it to you. I can make copies, if you wish:

"The Old City is a .35 square mile walled area within the modern city of Jerusalem. Until the 1860s this was the entire city of Jerusalem. It is divided into the Christian Quarter, the Muslim Quarter, the Jewish Quarter, and the Armenian Quarter. Following the 1948 Israeli War of Independence, the Old City was occupied by Jordan.

During the Six Days War of 1967, Israel won back the Old City and the rest of East Jerusalem. That gave the Jews control of Israel's holiest site, the Temple Mount, for the first time in 2,000 years! Here is the way it happened, taken from an original recording of the voices of the Israeli soldiers as they entered the Old City on June 7, 1967:

> 'The Temple Mount is in our hands. The Temple Mount is in our hands. All forces stop firing! The time is 10:20, the 7th of June. At this moment we are passing through the Lion's Gate. I am at present under the shadow of the gate. And again we are going out to the sunny street. Lion's gate. We are in the Old City. We are in the Old City. The soldiers are standing very close to the walls. We are marching now on the Via Dolorosa. Do you understand this? The Old City, we are again within the Old City. Al Aksa Mosque. Under the ruling of the mandate we could not enter here. One moment. Straight ahead is the wailing wall. Hurrah! Hurrah! Hurrah! Hurrah! It is hard to express in words our feelings.'[30]

(General Rabbi Shlomo Goren, chief chaplain of the IDF, sounded the shofar at the Western Wall to signify its liberation. This caused a great celebration of the Jews all over the world!)'

"Wow! The Old City is quite an historic place. Likewise, Christ Church is also a historic place. I will continue to read: 'It is the oldest Protestant church in the Middle East, and it was built to evangelize the Jewish people. Its founding bishop in 1842 was an Anglican Jew, Michael Solomon Alexander.' I wish the Ministry of the Interior would respect this history, the fact that a recognized JEW was the founding bishop of a Christian church!"

"'Inside the church, you can see that the building has more similarity to a synagogue than to a church, with Jewish symbols and Hebrew script everywhere, including the Hebrew words of Jesus. It is the only church in the Old City that fully acknowledges in symbol and architecture the Jewish roots of Christianity. It came to be known as the 'Jewish Protestant Church.' It was Bishop Alexander's belief that a Hebraic understanding of Jesus, the New Testament and Christianity's Jewish roots was vital for churches in the west.' And just to think, we may possibly be living right there in the guesthouses of Christ Church in the Old City. Glory to God, I say!"

The Holy Rollers held a long discussion that went on for an hour about the obstacles to aliyah as believers in Yeshua, about living in Jerusalem, and about getting jobs. One concrete action emerged, and that was to contact Dror for a meeting. They hoped that he could enlist his parents in Israel to help in their quest to surmount the obstacles to aliyah. In the meantime, each one would continue to pray for God's guidance, as well as search the internet on three subjects – aliyah for believers, jobs, and housing. At the very end of the meeting Gloria insisted they stop and pray again for her grandparents, that they would find a way to stay in the Land without compromising their faith in Yeshua.

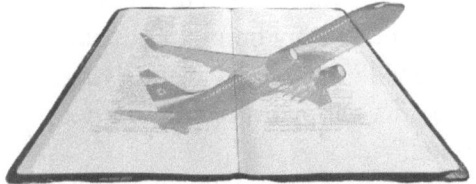

CHAPTER THIRTEEN

NEXT BEST THING

Jeff shook Gloria awake. It was four o'clock in the morning. "Honey, wake up. Wake up! I just had a dream. You gotta hear this. God answered my prayer. I know He did."

Gloria turned over, rubbed her eyes, and slowly sat up in bed. A big smile spread across her face as she viewed Jeff's disheveled appearance transformed by an aura of light. He was almost hyperventilating he was so excited, and she had never seen a wider grin on his face. Groggily, she responded, "Husband and head of the Holy Rollers, out with it. I am all ears, even though I am half asleep. Before you say a word, I have to tell you I love you with every fiber of my being. You are the most wonderful and most handsome man on the planet. Now tell me, but I have to hug you first, my love."

She's right. Love comes first, and I have never loved my adorable wife more than I do this minute. Jeff took a deep breath, calmed down, lifted his bride out of the bed, and carried her to the living room. They sat together on the sofa and passionately embraced. "Gloria, remember we got down on our knees by the bed last night and prayed for God to solve our problems related to aliyah. I know He gave the answer in my dream. Here it is. My father was sitting in a chair in his office. I could see Yeshua standing behind him, holding His hands over Dad, as if He were imparting knowledge to him and also blessing him. Dad got out of the chair and picked up the phone on his desk. Then a map of Israel appeared on the desk with a big Star of David over Jerusalem, and the map was glowing. Dad wrote something on his notepad, while he talked on the phone. Then he walked outside where an airplane was waiting for him. It was a big cargo plane, and trucks were loading crates into the back of it. A huge sign in red letters was painted on the side of the plane – FOOD! The scene switched to my home in Tupelo. My mother had come outside. She looked up to see the plane flying overhead, and she waved to it. She had a happy expression on her face. Then the dream suddenly ended."

Jeff and Gloria were silent for several minutes. Gloria softly said to Jeff, "I think the Lord gave me the interpretation of your dream. Yes, it is an answer to our prayers. The Lord has told me that your dad is going to make you a proposition, and He wants you to say, 'Yes, Dad, I will do it, no matter how hard it is.' Wait… Jeff, did I just prophesy to you?"

"Babe, I have always been taken aback at how you say stuff like that, and later it comes true. So, that's what it is, prophecy, huh? Well, Grace has already told us that we have prophetic destinies, and that fits right in for one of us to be a prophet. Oh, babe! You may be a real prophet, or should I say 'prophetess?'"

"Jeff, don't be so surprised. Haven't we already learned that from our study of Acts at the Baptist Student Union? Remember in the second chapter how Peter stood up and quoted the prophet Joel in his explanation of the supernatural things that had just happened to the 120 believers in Jerusalem on the Day of Pentecost? He preached, 'And it shall come to pass in the last days, says God, that I will pour out of My Spirit on all flesh; your sons and your daughters shall prophesy, your young men shall see visions, your old men shall dream dreams.'"[31]

"So you are telling me I am an old man?" Jeff grabbed Gloria and began to tickle her until she screamed.

"Okay, okay, young man, let me go! I confess you are the man of my dreams, a young man that I want to grow old with." Gloria sat on Jeff's lap and melted in his arms.

"Gloria, let's get serious. My dream indicates that Dad is going to set up a food industry, or at least a food distribution business in Israel, and he wants me to run it. Maybe we can get a work visa in Israel instead of making aliyah, and our belief in Yeshua won't be an issue. Would you be willing to give up on citizenship and settle for a yearly renewable work visa?"

"Jeff, you know that I only want to do what Yeshua wants us to do. I believe He is saying that there is much more to what your dad will tell you. I also know that you are eager to pick up the phone and call right now, but you must not. I sense that Mr. Jeffrey is working things out before he tells you about it. That means you must be patient, and so must I. In the meantime, I am going to pursue getting a scholarship to the Jerusalem Academy of Music and Dance in Givat Ram which is part of Hebrew University. Mrs. Pagani told me about it. She has a colleague there and is making an effort to get me a scholarship, and maybe I can get an accompanist job, too. When we meet with Dror, we can ask him about that strategy for living in Israel without making aliyah. Mrs. Pagani has assigned me some piano pieces that I could play in an audition. They are very difficult, but she assures me this display of my skill and talent will make me a 'shoo-in!'"

"So you would be a 'shoo-in,' huh? Well, guess what just popped up in my mind? It's a song titled 'Shoo-Fly Pie and Apple Pan Dowdy!' When I was growing up, I loved to hear Jetty in the kitchen singing that song. I only remember part of it." Jeff begins to sing, '*Shoo-Fly Pie and Apple Pan Dowdy, makes your eyes pop out, your tummy say 'Howdy.' Shoo-Fly Pie and Apple Pan Dowdy, I never get enough of that wonderful stuff.'*'[32] Gloria laughed. "Well, don't laugh. Pie is a serious subject to me, little chef. Didn't I hear you say that you were going to make a pie for our meeting with Dror tonight? I hope you are fixing apple pie with ice cream. I know that's your favorite, babe."

"As a matter of fact, that's just what I am going to do. Did you have a vision of it? That's what young men have who are baptized in the Holy Spirit – visions!" Gloria started to tickle Jeff, but he won the tickling match, and soon they were rolling on the floor laughing.

♥ ♥ ♥ ♥ ♥

"Get the door, Jeff," Gloria called out from the kitchen. "I am getting the coffee ready."

Jeff greeted Pete and Sarah from next door, and Dror drove up at the same time. "Come on in, Ivrit Professor and talmidim. Gloria and I welcome you to our humble abode."

Pete laughed. "You said that the last time we met over here. So, after all the newly-wed spats, it is still a 'humble abode'?"

"You better believe it, bro. I have had to eat 'humble pie' many times. Gloria is always right. Speaking of pie, she has got us fixed up. I hope you like apple pie with ice cream and hot coffee. She should be coming out of the kitchen with it right about now." Jeff went to the kitchen to help Gloria bring out the refreshments.

The camaraderie between the five young people was enjoyed to the fullest. The conversation was in a light mode as the pie and coffee, including second servings, were consumed. Jeff was eager to begin their discussion. "The meeting of the Holy Rollers with our distinguished guest is now in session. As president, I am calling us to order."

Gloria quickly backed Jeff's authority as she explained, "Remember the first time we 'rolled' together, Pete and Sarah? It was Jeff who named us the 'Holy Rollers,' so it is only fitting that he is our president."

Sarah wanted to keep things serious. "You are absolutely right, Gloria. I concur, and I know I can speak for Pete, too. He concurs." She smiled at Pete.

Jeff directed the meeting. "Dror, please tell us what you know about making aliyah, the actual mechanics of it for regular Jews. If you know anything about Messianic Jews making aliyah, that is our main concern. As you know, we four met Saturday night and discussed the obstacles caused by our belief in Yeshua as the Messiah. Gloria told us that her grandparents who made aliyah last fall have been found out as believers in Yeshua, and they are threatened with deportation. We will never deny our Lord, so that is not an option. Also, we will not sneak in. But we are looking for ways to live in the land and get a work permit. Gloria is seeking a music scholarship, for instance. I think the Lord has shown Gloria and me that I may be able to get a work visa, renewable yearly. Now take the floor, and tell us what you know."

Dror processed this information for a few minutes. "Well, the next best thing to making aliyah and obtaining citizenship is to do the two things you just named. It is amazing that I talked to my mother Devorah only yesterday, and in our conversation she shared with me about the difficulties of making aliyah for Messianic Jews. She herself does not believe in Jesus, but she has neighbors that do, and they have become close friends. It has been a learning experience for Ima."[33]

The couples gasped. "From the horse's mouth, so to speak!" exclaimed Gloria. "Oh, Dror, you are a Godsend. Your mother's neighbors have first-hand information. I'll tell you what – if this isn't a big God-incidence, I don't know what is." Everyone agreed. "Tell us everything, everything, Dror."

"Okay, I am the professor, as you say, Jeff. So you can make notes. I am going to start at the beginning of this whole matter of making aliyah. Ready? Here we go. Under the 1950 Law of Return, anyone born to a Jewish mother or converted to Judaism was qualified for citizenship. In 1970 an additional qualifying phrase was added – '... and who is not a member of another religion and did not voluntarily change his religion.' This addition was needed because of the highly-publicized case of Brother Daniel, a Jewish Carmelite monk, a Christian, who sought citizenship. He was denied. Then later there was another famous case brought by Messianic Jews. They fought it out in court for over seven-and-a-half years, but lost. The high court verdict came down on December 25, 1989. They were Gary and Shirley Beresford who had come to Israel from South Africa and Zimbabwe in 1986. They kept living in the Land and getting their visas renewed as they fought the court decision. Many Messianic Jews rallied around them and helped them financially and in other ways. The court decision was all over the newspapers, and some of the Messianic Jews were worried about their own status as citizens. The Ministry of the Interior stepped up their efforts to keep Messianic Jews out of the country, fearing them as missionaries of Christianity and a threat to Israel of no longer being a Jewish State. They began to ask all applicants if they believed in Jesus. If they said yes, they were denied entry."

Sarah was becoming more and more agitated. "Well, what happened? Were the Beresfords deported?"

Dror answered, "Ima said the last her neighbors knew, their visas expired in 1993." Everyone groaned. "Here's the thing – the Israeli public did not agree with the court's decision. There was this Dahaf Survey of Israeli Jewish Public Opinion Concerning Messianic Jewish Aliyah in 1988. It was like America's Gallup Poll. And get this – 61% of the Israeli Jewish public would allow a Jew who believed in Jesus to make aliyah![34] It turns out that the secular Jews in Israel were allies of Messianic Jews because of their belief in civil rights. Ima's neighbors said, 'We are Israel's *refuseniks*. We would have died as Jews in Auschwitz, so why can't we live as Jews in Israel?'"[35]

Pete's anger was getting hotter and hotter. "In my search on the internet I have discovered something incredible! The Israeli government will accept a Jew of any religion or even an atheist to become a citizen. This includes Jews who believe in yoga, Hare Krishna, Hinduism, Confucianism, New Age, Satanism, Bahaism, and many other religious expressions. These people are considered Jews, while Jews who embrace Yeshua, a Jew from birth who lived and died as a Jew, are ostracized and condemned!"[36]

"Well, Pete, wasn't Yeshua ostracized and literally condemned by the Jewish leaders in Israel? This is a modern replay," declared Gloria. "Multitudes of the common people loved Him and followed Him, but their religious leaders were jealous of Yeshua. After He raised Lazarus from the dead, they said, 'What shall we do? For this Man works many signs. If we let Him alone like this, everyone will believe in Him, and the Romans will come and take away both our place and nation.'[37] Do you see the similarities?"

Dror was getting uncomfortable with the direction of the discussion. He stood up. "I want to thank you for changing our class meeting from the chapel to your apartment, Gloria and Jeff. Your hospitality was wonderful, including the pie and coffee. I really can't stay for our usual two hours, but I am not charging you anyway. In fact, I was going to cancel our class, because Grace and I have plans. However, I am so glad I was able to pass on to you what I learned from my mother. I can see your dilemma. Remember, the next best thing to making aliyah is to get scholarships and work visas. I will help you, Gloria, in your pursuit of a master's degree in music and perhaps concert performances." He flashed his brilliant smile and headed to the door.

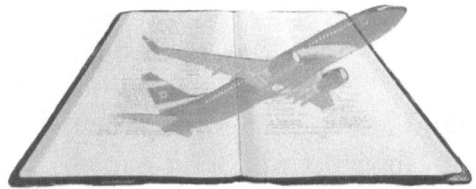

CHAPTER FOURTEEN

THE FAVOR OF
THE LORD

SESSIONS MANOR
JULY 21, 1999

Walter and Jenny Sessions welcomed their friends at the front door and ushered them into the dining room. Jenny reached out and hugged Sarah first. "This is truly a blessing that all four of you can be here tonight. Walter and I knew you never miss the Baptist Student Union Bible study, but it meets so early that you could still have dinner with us afterward. Let's go right to the table. I bet you are hungry."

Jenny indicated that Sarah should sit next to her with Pete beside her. Walter took Jeff and Gloria on the other side of the long table to sit next to him. The crystal, china, and silver sparkled, arranged on six lace place mats. Large platters of food had shining silver covers. Walter said, "Let's bow our heads for the blessing. Dear Lord, we are so honored to have our dearest friends here tonight. We all love You and thank You for giving us salvation through Your Son and our Savior, Jesus Christ. It is You who brought us together, and it is You who gave me my beautiful wife Jenny. Thank You for prospering us and for creating such delicious food. In the name of Yeshua, amen."

"I hope you like what Walter and I prepared – fried chicken, black-eyed peas, green beans, mashed potatoes, tossed salad, homemade rolls, and later a surprise dessert," announced Jenny, chuckling. "We have so much to talk about tonight. Walter and I agreed we should waste no time in having our dinner, so we can then go to the living room and have conversation for as long as you can stay."

Walter added, "I will remove these covers, and you can dig in, friends."

Gloria laughed. "I hope you didn't hear my stomach growling. The Bible study was excellent, but my thoughts kept going to food, and I wondered what we would have for dinner. You have more than met my expectations, Jenny and Walter. I had already heard from Jeff that you, Walter, had taught Jenny to cook, and now she is a better chef than you." Gloria got two pieces of chicken, two rolls, and a big serving of mashed potatoes.

Sarah kept complimenting Walter and Jenny on the beauty of their home. "Oh, I love this house. I didn't think you could make a former fraternity house a real home, but you have. Your choice of colors, the furnishings, the rugs, and the wall and table décor all make your house look like it came right off the pages of *Better Homes and Gardens*. Of course, it's obvious that you made the drapes, didn't you, Jenny?"

"Yes, I did. Mother came and stayed a while to help me decorate the house and to open my seamstress shop. Thanks for coming by the shop, Sarah, and you, too, Gloria."

Pete was practically *inhaling* the food on his plate. "Mmm, this chicken is deelishus! Y'all should open a bed and breakfast in part of your sprawling mansion. Walter, I want to see the rest of your house, especially your study. I'm sure you have one, and you probably spend a lot of time in it. Well, the four of us have finished our junior year, and you finished your senior year. You are working on your master's degree in business now, right?"

"That's right. After I get that degree and write my thesis, I will be looking for a job. Jenny and I don't want to wait around to add to our family," Walter boasted.

"Well, Walter, I know I have made hints about it, but right now I am coming out boldly and making you an official offer to take over my job as manager of Quentin Distribution Center next June," Jeff blurted out. "Will you do it?"

"Yes, Jeff, you did mention that possibility. I have already been praying about it in case you made an official offer, and the Lord has given me the green light. I can't thank you enough. The timing is perfect, because my inheritance will be almost used up by then. I don't want Jenny to have to support us!" Jeff and Walter stood up and extended their hands in a strong handshake. Applause went up from the rest.

Pete interrupted, "I hate to bring up a negative subject in the midst of this happy news, but I am duty bound as a P.I. to ask this question. Jenny, have you had any more threats from Nasir and Omar's former terrorist associates?"

Walter reached over to hold Jenny's hand. "I will answer for Jenny. Friends, you can rest assured that Jenny has not had any more threats whatsoever from those evil people. We know how to put on the armor of God, and we pray together every night and plead the blood of Jesus over us and everything that belongs to us. The Holy Spirit has chased every trace of fear out of our hearts. We are standing in faith for God's promised protection." Walter and Jenny smiled big, and their friends applauded once again.

Everyone was wiping their mouths with the beautiful lace napkins, when Jenny stood up. "I see we made record time in consuming mine and Walter's culinary efforts, which makes me think the food was good. Let's be seated in the living room. Walter and I will bring out the surprise dessert. Take your napkins with you, please."

Sarah hugged Jenny. "Yes, the food was over the top! Thank you so much."

About five minutes after the two couples were seated, Walter and Jenny rolled the dessert cart into the living room. Gloria, Jeff, Sarah, and Pete gasped when they saw the very tall cake covered lavishly with strawberries and whipped cream on a cut glass pedestal. It was lit up by blazing sparklers placed around the edges of the cart and one on top of the cake. After blowing out the sparklers Jenny cut the cake, making big servings on china plates with silver dessert forks. Walter handed out lap trays and headed to the kitchen to bring out cups and saucers. Jenny got the coffee and poured it.

Everyone expressed amazement at the idea of decorating with sparklers. Jenny grinned. "It was my idea, and Walter made sure this was done with flair."

Gloria responded, "Walter and Jenny, I have something to tell you. When you rolled out that cake with sparklers on it, the Lord whispered to me that He was about to give you a little 'sparkler' to begin your family. He must mean that your baby will soon be on the way!"

Jenny looked at Walter and laughed. "Walter and I have talked about it, and we both hope you are right, Gloria." Good wishes erupted again from the guests.

Pete was getting impatient. "Hey, guys, I am salivating over this exquisite dessert. I say every man for himself!" He was the first one to finish, and then he collected the trays and dishes. Walter helped him. Soon everyone was sitting back in their chairs, completely satisfied and raving over such an outstanding dinner.

Gloria timidly ventured to open the conversation. "Friends, I am about to burst with some good news. I have been holding it back until just the right moment. This is something to really praise God about. First, Walter and Jenny, I have to give you the background. As you already know, my grandparents made aliyah last fall, and they have been living in Katzrin, up in the Golan Heights, and loving it. Less than two weeks ago I got a phone call from them, saying they were threatened with deportation by the Ministry of the Interior. They had to go for an interview in Jerusalem. Their kehilah – Hebrew for church – went into overdrive praying and fasting for them. And Jeff, Sarah, Pete, and I were praying hard, too. Papa Sam and Mama Anna had put down roots in that town of Katzrin, and they knew HaShem planted them there. They could not move."

Jeff felt slighted. "Gloria, what is the good news? You didn't tell me."

Gloria clasped Jeff's hand and looked at him adoringly. "It was only today that Papa Sam called me, and there was no opportunity to tell you because of our tight schedule. The Lord showed me that tonight in the company of our close friends was the time to share His glorious work."

Jeff relaxed, and Gloria resumed, "Papa Sam called me today about this happy development. I will start by saying that he is an excellent Bible teacher. The Holy Spirit – he calls Him the Ruach HaKodesh – opened the door for him to teach the Torah to his neighbors. It started with one old couple, who live right next to them, and in only a few weeks, three other couples began attending the study at their house. Remember, Holy Rollers, when we led Adaton on a tour last December that we took them to Katzrin, and we visited Papa Sam and Mama Anna on the day they were getting ready for their Torah study. Mama Anna, bless her sweet heart, always has snacks and a special dessert for the people. Each week they prepare their house with prayer, anointing all the chairs with fragrant oil and calling the names of the dear people who would sit and listen to the Word of God. Papa Sam told me today that the Sondheim name has become known all over the city. God has given them such **favor** with everyone, young and old, rich and poor, educated or not, religious or not. Papa Sam and Mama Anna have developed the habit of walking in different parts of the city and praying over every building and every person they see. The day they received the threatening letter from Minister Eli Rabinowitz of the Ministry of the Interior was the same day they would have the Torah study that night. After praying about it, Papa Sam said they felt the Spirit was saying to read the letter at the meeting and ask their friends to join them in prayer that God would do a miracle and allow them to stay in the Land. Well, the friends were just as upset as my grandparents, especially one couple. They were outraged. All of them are *olim* – that means *immigrants*. There is a large population of olim in Katzrin. Several had experienced problems when they made aliyah and were very sympathetic. Papa Sam said the news spread fast in the city, and their phone rang off the hook in the coming days."

Sarah's heart was racing. "Oh, Gloria, please don't draw out the story. I see you are smiling, so the outcome must be good. Please hurry up and tell us what happened."

Gloria smiled even bigger. "My friends and my husband, I am happy to report to you that the miracle they had prayed for happened!" Cheers and hallelujahs went up. "I know you want to know how God worked. Papa Sam broke down and cried, trying to get the words out. He indicated that this type thing was brand new in Israel's history, but, strangely enough, it did not appear in the newspapers. Okay, here is the end of the story – the members of the Torah study started a campaign to keep my grandparents in Katzrin, secure with their citizenship papers. On the day they were to meet with Minister Eli Rabinowitz, about fifty citizens from Katzrin accompanied Papa Sam and Mama Anna to the government building in Jerusalem. There were few chairs, so the people stood closely around them. They waited until Rabinowitz announced that the Sondheims were disqualified to make aliyah and be Israeli citizens because of their belief in Jesus as the Messiah. At that very moment, the supporters raised their voices in protest, shouting one loud 'NO!' Then their spokesman, the mayor of Katzrin, voiced the reason for their protest." Gloria took a deep breath.

Walter responded, "If you are going to tell us that all these people had now come to faith in Yeshua, I am going to faint dead away!"

Gloria laughed. "No, they remain blinded to Yeshua as their Messiah, but God does work in mysterious ways, as we have always heard. To continue, the mayor began a testimony of his association with the Sondheims, and one by one, each of the group gave his or her testimony of how nothing but good had come from Sam and Anna Sondheim living among them. Stories were told of physical healings, of the healing of broken marriages, of delinquent children returning home, of logjams in community development being cleared away, of financial miracles, and on and on. The minister's eyes got bigger and bigger. His aides who were standing at the edges of the room responded emotionally. Then the mayor made a final statement. While I was on the phone I wrote it down in shorthand. Let me read it: 'Mr. Rabinowitz, let me assure you that neither Sam nor Anna have asked us to believe in Jesus as the Messiah. Our knowledge of Scripture has grown by leaps and bounds, and they have not used the Brit Hadasha in their teaching. We know you are a rabbi, and each of our group can tell you that we have memorized large portions of the Torah, the Prophets, and the Psalms. We have never been happier. But best of all, these two wonderful people have loved us unconditionally, and they have taught us how to love each other.'"

Jenny spoke up. "I don't see how they could understand Scripture without the Holy Spirit, and I don't see how they could really love each other without our Savior Jesus. We know He is the Messiah, but they still don't know He is their Messiah, Gloria?"

"Papa Sam said that the Lord told him to 'prepare the way' like John the Baptist did. He is laying the foundation in the Torah for their salvation yet to come. He and Mama Anna have claimed each and every soul for Yeshua. They are positive that the Spirit is already drawing them. Well, here's the outcome. It appeared to Papa Sam that Mr. Rabinowitz became so flustered, he just wanted to get all of them out of the building as quickly as possible. He took a big stamp and slammed it down on the official citizenship papers of both my grandparents, weakly saying, 'Granted.' He looked around at his aides and said, 'Please help these people out.'"

Jeff, Pete, Sarah, Walter, and Jenny stood up and applauded, shouting, "A miracle! A miracle!"

Jeff asked, "But why didn't it make the newspaper headlines?"

"Papa Sam expected Minister Rabinowitz to cover it up, as he had acted illegally and was embarrassed. I told the group to be very quiet as they got in their vehicles and not to speak to anyone, urging them to pray earnestly that this potentially inflammatory news would die peacefully. He knew that the security of all Jewish believers was at stake if this story came out in the papers."

Pete shook his head. If I had heard this from anyone else, Gloria, I would not have believed it! That calls to mind our prayer that God will 'part the waters' for us like He did for the Israelites crossing the Red Sea. God surely did give your grandparents **favor**, didn't He?"

"Indeed He did, Pete." exclaimed Gloria. "I loved the Bible study at BSU tonight. There are so many promises of God on this topic, His giving us the **favor** of man. Let's share what we learned. We have got to claim these promises for our prophetic destiny in moving to Israel. I will start us off in Proverbs 3: 3-4. 'Let not mercy and truth forsake you; bind them around your neck, write them on the tablet of your heart, and so find favor and high esteem in the sight of God and man.' Favor is an invisible thing, of course, but Solomon's figurative description is so neat. And it truly fits what Papa Sam and Mama Anna experienced."

Walter added, "I wish I had been at BSU tonight. Jenny and I hardly ever miss, but we knew you would share with us. And after all, we had to prepare your culinary delights. Anyway, I do have a verse to share that has been a blessing to me, Psalm 90:17 from the NIV. I have used it in prayer while studying for my business courses – 'May the favor of the Lord our God rest on us; establish the work of our hands for us - yes, establish the work of our hands.'"

"Thanks, Walter. I am going to start praying that, too, as I work on my piano pieces for a scholarship audition at Hebrew University Academy of Music and Dance. Praise the Lord! Dear Yeshua, please establish the work of my hands on the piano."

Pete declared, "I have hope now. Y'all know what a hot temper I have, and I have been breathing fire about our obstacles to aliyah.

But hearing what has happened to your grandparents, Gloria, has greatly encouraged me. I like that verse we studied tonight at BSU, Psalm 30:5, and I claim it for myself and all of us: 'For His anger is but for a moment, His favor is for life; weeping may endure for a night, but joy comes in the morning.'"

Sarah drew close to Pete and squeezed his hand. "My love, that verse is talking about God's anger, not yours. Maybe God has been angry at you for complaining so much. Nevertheless, I can envision Him giving you His favor and transforming you from sorrow to joy." Pete nuzzled Sarah's neck and sighed, deeply contented.

Gloria began to sing and put her whole heart into it. "It is morning, it is morning in my heart. Jesus made the gloomy shadows all depart. Songs of gladness now I sing. For since Jesus is my King, it is morning, it is morning in my heart!'[38] I couldn't help it, y'all. When a song bubbles up in me, I just have to sing it. This one comes from my experience as a twelve-year-old in the Methodist church back home. Well, it's getting late. Jeff and I better go. Thanks again, Walter and Jenny, for a glorious evening."

CHAPTER FIFTEEN

MISSING PERSONS

Jeff and Pete held the doors of Jeff's Ford open for their wives. Pete looked at his watch. "Hey, I thought it was bedtime, but it's only ten o'clock. None of us has an early class. I have an idea. Y'all come over to our apartment, and let's play cards."

Jeff was quick to reply. "Thanks, bro, for the invitation, but Gloria and I have plans. I am forming a new organization, and we are doing research for it."

"And what would the name of this new organization be?"

"It's the Fellowship for the Advancement of Romantic Marriages. I will let you know when our schedule allows for playing cards."

"Oh! So that's it. Well, bro, this is a huge coincidence. Sarah and I are also doing research for the same organization. Membership is closed to just Sarah and me, however." Pete put his hand over his mouth to keep from laughing.

Gloria elbowed Jeff sharply in the ribs. "Okay, lover boy. I am going to put you in the doghouse if you don't quit joking this way."

"And Pete can join Jeff in the doghouse!" Sarah laughed.

Pete's cell phone rang. "I see the number, and it's Mom or Dad. Gotta take this.... Hello, that you, Dad? .... Whaaaat? ... NO! ... Can I bring Jeff? ... Well, give me forty minutes to get there. I will pack some clothes."

Sarah panicked. "What's wrong, Pete?"

"Speed up, Jeff. I've got to go to Columbus. My sister Elinor is missing!"

Jeff, Gloria, and Sarah expressed horror. "I'll drive you, Pete. What about the girls? Can they go with us?" asked Jeff.

"I can't think straight, buddy. I guess it's okay. We will need all the prayer backup we can get. But what about your job, Jeff? At least we don't have classes. I know you are going with me, Sarah."

"Maybe we better take two vehicles," suggested Gloria. "You and Sarah go ahead of us. Jeff and I will follow. Okay?"

"We may be staying overnight, so we better take some totes or small suitcases because Dad said they have alerted the police in Jackson. I have no idea why, but Dad said to hurry, and he will tell me everything."

♥ ♥ ♥ ♥ ♥

CARSONS' HOME
COLUMBUS, MS

Elsa and Lars Carson met their son at the door. "Oh, Pete, we knew you would come right away. We hoped you would bring Sarah and also Jeff and Gloria. Oh, here come Jeff and Gloria," said Mr. Carson. "My tendency is to rush right out and drive to Jackson, but Elsa urged me to give you the details of Elinor's disappearance first and then have prayer before we head to Jackson. Pete, this is your expertise, doing detective work. Combined with the guidance of the Holy Spirit, I am confident Elinor will be found quickly. Sit down, all of you."

"Children, would you like some coffee?" offered Elsa. No one wanted anything. Elsa's eyes were so red it was evident she had been crying. Sarah wrapped her arms around her and comforted her.

Lars continued, "Elinor and her best friend, Julie Rollins, went to Jackson to a rush party at Millsaps College. They left Sunday afternoon in Julie's car, planning to spend three nights with Julie's aunt and uncle, Gus and Adoline Rollins, in Jackson. They wanted to tour the campus on Monday. The rush party was last night. They

118

were supposed to be back in Columbus this afternoon or early evening. About 10:00 o'clock tonight we got a call from Margaret Rollins, Julie's mother. She said Gus and Adoline had just called to say that Elinor and Julie are missing! When Elsa asked why they had not notified them sooner, Margaret said that Gus and Adoline were allowing them to sleep late. Finally, at noon, they knocked on the bedroom door. They went in and saw no sign of them! They immediately called the college and got the name of a contact person for the sorority having the rush party. A girl named Liza said that Elinor and Julie had left the sorority house last night sometime after 11:30. When Adoline insisted the girl tell her every detail she could remember about Elinor and Julie, she reluctantly admitted that the girls appeared to be intoxicated. They had slurred speech and couldn't walk a straight line! When Margaret said that, Elsa lost it!" Lars broke down and cried.

Pete comforted his dad, and Sarah continued to comfort Elsa, as she cried harder. "Dad, why did it take so long for Adoline to call Margaret?"

Lars tried to hide his anger. "She explained to Margaret that she and Gus wanted to pursue every possibility of the girls' where-abouts, before they called and upset them. Personally, I think Gus and Adoline didn't take it as seriously as they should have. Oh, Lord, please forgive me for my anger."

"Believe me, I understand, Dad," Pete responded. "You said on the phone that the Jackson police had been contacted. I guess you or Gus filed a missing person's report. What are Julie's parents going to do?"

"Jesse and Margaret have already left for Jackson, son. Jesse knows the Millsaps president, and he is meeting them at the police station. Jesse and Margaret are alumni of Millsaps, which is a Methodist college. They attend First United Methodist Church here. Julie was sold on Millsaps, and she convinced Elinor they should both enroll. I had no idea our daughter would drink alcohol. I hope this was the first time. I am devastated! Maybe they had a wreck, and the car is in a ditch, and it is not visible from the highway."

"Lars, don't let your imagination run away with you," urged Elsa. "We have got to pray right now. We need the Lord's direction."

Pete knew he should lead the prayer. All six of them got on their knees, lifted their hands to heaven and implored the Lord to bring Elinor and Julie home safely. "El Shaddai, our Mighty God, protect Elinor and Julie wherever they are. I claim Your promise that not a hair of their heads will be harmed. If anyone is attempting to hurt them, push their enemies back. Give each one of us supernatural wisdom. Guide us, and guide the police to the right location, and restore those girls back to their families. I pray in the matchless name of Yeshua our Messiah and King, Comforter and Guide." Everyone said "amen."

♥ ♥ ♥ ♥ ♥

JACKSON POLICE STATION

When they arrived at the police station at 2:00 in the morning, they saw Julie's parents and her aunt and uncle sitting in the far corner with a distinguished-looking man, whom they soon learned was the president of Millsaps College. Introductions were made, and the details of the missing persons case were shared by Gus Rollins. The officer at the desk came over and led the group back to a private room.

"My name is Sergeant Callahan, and I will brief you on what we have found out so far. We have patrolled the streets going out from the Kappa Delta Sorority at Millsaps, looking for Julie Rollins' car. The description we have is a 1995 bronze color Toyota with slightly damaged left fender. We patrolled the route the girls would have taken to get back to your house, Mr. and Mrs. Rollins, and also the routes to some of the bars in town. So far, we haven't found the car or the girls. All our policemen have pictures you gave us, and they know the clothes they were wearing and their height and approximate weight. The chief just came in a few minutes ago, and he wants to talk with you."

Margaret Rollins was angry. "What? They looked for them in bars? My daughter does not drink! I think the police need to talk to some of the people at the party. It is possible that Julie and Elinor were going to a shopping mall that stays open late. They may have told someone before they left. Anyway, do we know the time of night they left the party?"

Jesse Rollins tried to calm his wife. "Honey, they know what they're doing. Try to be patient. Remember that Adoline told us she found out that they left the party sometime after 11:30 last night."

Sergeant Callahan assured the group that the people at the party had been questioned, but no new information was forthcoming.

The Carsons and the Quentins were offering up silent prayers, as they held hands. They felt God's strength, and peace slowly began to fill them. The police chief walked in. There was fear in his eyes, Gloria noticed.

"Thank you for coming tonight. My name is Chief Braun. I want you all to take a deep breath. I am about to tell you some things that may greatly upset you, but these are things you need to know. You need to be prepared in your minds and your emotions. Remember that clarity of thought is imperative in a situation like this. None of you will benefit if you let anger or unreasoning grief control you. Hope is the strongest thing we officers can give you. We have seen success in this type of investigation in many cases. I assure you I have put my best men on this search, and I will not withhold anything from you. You will hear from me every step of the way. Have you heard what I said?"

"Okay, chief, we hear you. I am steeling myself to be able to accept what you are about to tell us. Please continue," Lars answered.

"I will say the ugly words right now. I am talking about sex-trafficking. Wait, don't interrupt me. Of course, we don't know that is what happened to your girls, but it is a real possibility, because we have been on the trail of a sex and labor trafficking ring in Jackson, going all the way to New Orleans. After seeing pictures of your daughters and noting their beauty and age, I have to say that they are the types that these evil people target. Okay, now I have put it all out there. I have to give you some warnings. If any of you begin to search for these degenerates on your own and attempt to rescue your daughters, you could be killed. We have seen this happen. You people have got to believe that we know what we are doing. Any interference from you could not only get you killed, but it could jeopardize the lives of these girls." The chief went around the room and shook each one's hand warmly and looked into their eyes with confidence. He then nodded to Dr. Gene Messick Hanson, president of Millsaps College, and stood back in a corner of the room.

Dr. Hanson stood up. "Chief Braun has contacted the FBI and was assured they would send Special Agent Michelle Sherwood to head the investigation. She happens to be a friend of mine and my wife. Chief Braun got a phone call from her, saying she would be here shortly."

Everyone in the room was tense, but the Holy Rollers and the Carsons were bombarding heaven with their silent prayers. In about thirty minutes, the door opened, and in walked the FBI agent. She was greeted by Chief Braun and Dr. Hanson, who introduced her to the group. Agent Sherwood walked around the room, extending her hand to each person, as Dr. Hanson pointed out the parents, a sibling, aunt and uncle, and friends. At that moment the door opened, and in walked Pete's brother and his wife, Britt and Camille Carson. Britt introduced himself to the agent, giving his job profile in the security forces at Columbus Air Force Base. Agent Sherwood expressed gratitude that he had come and that Pete also had training in security as a private investigator. Then she asked everyone to be seated as she presented the problem of sex trafficking in the Jackson area.

"Friends and family of Julie Rollins and Elinor Carson, this is what we are facing: 'In Mississippi, the geography and the interstate highways make Jackson a stopping-off point for the sex trade, which is highly portable. Midway between Memphis and New Orleans on the north-south axis, and Atlanta and Dallas on the east-west route, traffickers – pimps - shuttle their wares between sports and music events looking for buyers. Jackson is the hub for the Southeast, and they're bringing people from Atlanta, the Northeast down through here going toward Texas or from the Northwest going toward Florida. Sexual slavery can happen to youngsters raised in 'good' homes just as easily as it does to those from 'bad' or poor circumstances. All it takes is a naive girl looking for a little affection. The predators look for pretty kids whom they can easily flatter.'"[39] Gasps went up from Jesse, Margaret, Lars, and Elsa.

Elsa raised her hand. "Let me say right now that these girls have been raised by Christian parents and have been in church all their lives. In both their homes, they have received plenty of love and affection. I believe Elinor and Julie, although immature, have a strong sense of right and wrong and would not be enticed by unsavory characters. They have been taught to avoid strange places and strange people. My strong feeling is that they may have been kidnapped, or they perhaps lost their way and had a car accident and have not been found yet." Elsa was anxiously wringing her hands.

Pete knew his time had come to speak up. "I can corroborate everything my mother said. Agent Sherwood, you need to know that as a private investigator, I have had training in the area of sex trafficking. I want to offer my services and urge you to consider calling on me. I will give you my contact info, and my brother Britt can give you his."

The FBI agent smiled and thanked Pete and Britt but did not give any indication that they were needed. Dr. Hanson escorted her from the room, and the meeting was officially closed. As the Rollins family filed out, the Carsons and Quentins remained. They first prayed for God's guidance, then made decisions about their participation the next day in finding the girls. Gloria and Sarah would ask Dr. Hanson to get them an appointment with the Kappa Delta sorority. They wanted to question the girls further and walk around the perimeter of the sorority house. Pete and Jeff would drive around the area and also visit malls and department stores. Lars, Elsa, Britt, and Camille would go to Millsaps campus, in case the girls had gone back there after the party. Perhaps they could find the cafeteria or another hang-out type building that had been open for business late, and they could question people. Then if these efforts were fruitless, they would spend another night at the motel and travel home on Friday.

N one of the Carsons, Quentins, or Rollinses turned up new evidence in Elinor and Julie's missing person cases. On Friday, the Holy Rollers headed back to MSU, with Jeff and Pete in Pete's Chevy and Gloria and Sarah in Jeff's Ford. Lars and Elsa traveled back to Columbus with Britt and Camille.

Pete and Jeff were in deep thought for an hour after they left Jackson. Finally, Pete said, "In my mind I've been going over the chapters on sex trafficking in one of the text books from my criminal justice class, Jeff. To find Elinor, I have got to think like one of those kidnappers or pimps would think. If the girls were taken by some big operators in a sex-trafficking ring, just where would they go, also taking into consideration what the FBI agent said about sports and music events? Well, not far from Jackson on a major highway is a big city filled with gambling casinos, Vicksburg. That seems like as much of a lucrative site for selling sex as a sports or music event."

"Hey, wait a minute, Pete. Did you say Vicksburg? That is strange. Last night I dreamed about a place with casinos. It may not be significant, because our motel window was looking out on some flashing neon lights, and it took me a while to get to sleep. And you know how casinos are lit up. But I do remember in my dream the name on a sign identifying the city. Hey, this is significant. The name was Vicksburg!"

"Bro, when you said that name, I got goose bumps. Maybe they were Holy Ghost goose bumps. Whoa! Should we turn around and take that major highway out of Jackson going west to Vicksburg? It's Interstate 20. But what about Gloria and Sarah? They are way up ahead of us."

"I think we should do it. I see a restaurant up ahead. Just pull in there. I will call Gloria and tell them to come back and meet us at the restaurant," urged Jeff.

Pete pulled in to the parking lot, and in about fifteen minutes, Gloria and Sarah pulled up. Gloria got out of the SUV, holding her cellphone to her ear. "We've got a lead! We've got a lead!" yelled Gloria. "I am so excited. The Lord is definitely on this case. I don't want to take time to go inside the restaurant. This can't wait. Jeff and Pete, come on over and get in the Ford."

"It was awkward to have a phone conversation while I was driving, but I managed to hear every word Pastor James said. He said he and Celeste were in bed sleeping last night, when suddenly she began screaming, 'I want my mama! I want my mama! They have had her too long, too long! I will rescue her, I will do it! She hates gambling. I will bring her home with me.' Pastor James shook her awake. He talked to her soothingly and quoted Scripture to her. She finally came to her senses. What she said has something to do with Elinor and Julie, because when Pastor James told me, I had this burning sensation all over my body. It's so weird. I felt fear and awful shame engulf me." Gloria started shaking. Jeff hugged her tight, and she calmed down.

"Tell us, babe. What did Miss Celeste say to Pastor?" Jeff asked.

"She said in the dream she was in a place that was dark, but on the outside it was lit up with bright neon signs. Then she realized the people were gambling in the dark at roulette wheels, slot machines, and card games. There were mostly men running the games, but then she saw women on the stairs, dressed in bright colored dresses, women like you see in saloons in the old western movies. She saw men coming to the stairs, and the women would lead them up to the second story. They were laughing, a wicked laughter. But there was one woman who had on a nicer dress, and she was trying to hide behind the staircase. Then an evil-looking man took a whip and drove her upstairs! Miss Celeste said, 'I ran up the stairs and opened every door, but I could not find her. It was my mother. I had to rescue her!' Why did Pastor James call me and tell me this? Why? Is Miss Celeste's mother in danger? I've never heard her mention her mother. We haven't had time to tell them that Elinor and Julie could possibly have fallen prey to sex traffickers. Her dream was about her mother evidently having the same fate. Oh, Jeff, could Elinor and Julie be in a place like that, a gambling casino? Pastor assured me that Adaton is praying. He said they called a special prayer meeting Wednesday night after we contacted him. He said Miss Lizzie and her prayer warriors came, and Miss Lizzie spoke before they started praying. She said for everyone to ask God for dreams and visions that would lead the police right to the place where Elinor and Julie are!"

"This is awesome!" exclaimed Jeff. "Miss Lizzie was certainly led by the Holy Spirit in asking the church to pray for dreams and visions. God answered her. He gave me a dream last night, too, and it was also about a gambling casino. I saw the brightly-lit sign, 'Vicksburg.' That place is full of riverboat casinos. So, Miss Celeste and I both had dreams about gambling casinos. That can't be a co-incidence. Pete and I called you to meet us here because we feel led to turn around and go to Vicksburg, and we want you girls to go with us. And now you tell us this!"

Gloria and Sarah were excited. "Why do we ever doubt that God will answer our prayers? Yes, Miss Lizzie and her ladies are powerful in prayer, but besides them and all of Adaton, there are probably hundreds of people praying. I know the First Baptist Church in Columbus is praying. Also, Britt and Camille's church is praying. WE are praying. Everything that happens after we pray is significant. These two dreams mean something. Oh, forgive me, I forgot to tell you that Pastor James and Miss Celeste want us to have dinner with them tomorrow night. Also, Dror and Grace have been invited."

"My goodness, two dreams in one night. I wish God would give **me** a dream," complained Pete. "First Jeff, and then Miss Celeste."

The presence of the Holy Spirit was keenly felt as Jeff continued to talk about his dream. "For sure, my dream was significant. God is confirming it because of its similarity to Miss Celeste's dream. And this popped into my mind – about Joseph in Egypt. Remember when he interpreted the Pharaoh's two dreams about the seven years of plenty, followed by the seven years of famine in Egypt? Pharaoh's first dream was about lean cows eating up fat cows. His second dream was about withered heads of grain eating up fully-formed heads of grain. Joseph said, 'And the dream was repeated to Pharaoh twice because the thing is established by God, and God will shortly bring it to pass.'[40] That leads me to believe that Elinor and Julie are shortly going to be rescued because God is showing us he has established it. But I am still stumped. What in the world does Miss Celeste's dream mean? Is her mother being held in a casino? Dreams aren't always literal, so probably her dream is symbolic of something else." Jeff was shaking his head.

"None of us know yet, Jeff," answered Gloria. "But it is obvious to me that we are going to find out tomorrow night at their house. I can smell victory in the air. I say we praise the Lord!"

"But aren't we going to travel to Vicksburg? It's plain as the nose on your face that we should do that," Pete pleaded. "I don't want some grimy loser pawing over my sister another day. There's no time to lose."

"Honey, I feel for you," comforted Sarah. "But when we forge ahead on our own, we can mess up God's timing. There are so many factors involved here. Maybe the FBI is exploring the possibility of Vicksburg even as we speak. They have weapons and experience and know how to do the rescue without our girls getting hurt. I've been thinking. Since the car hasn't been found yet, there must not have been a wreck. At least they are alive and not physically injured. If kidnappers have taken over the Toyota, maybe it will be sighted and lead the authorities right to the place where Elinor and Julie are. I don't think it will hurt, however, if you call Chief Braun and tell him you have reason to believe the girls are being held at one of the Vicksburg casinos. He may tell you they have already searched there. Whatever. But there is one thing I am sure of. The Lord is directing us to have dinner with Pastor and Miss Celeste tomorrow night. I say we chill and hold our horses until we see them."

"Wiser words were never spoken, dear Sarah," encouraged Gloria. "I was thinking the exact same thing. God's ways are not our ways, and His timing is extremely important. We must keep our faith and trust Him. He loves Elinor and Julie more than any of us. Those dreams were given by Him, and He will continue to direct us, even if it seems weird to us."

CHAPTER SEVENTEEN

RESCUE

HOME OF PASTOR AND CELESTE JAMES
SATURDAY, EARLY EVENING, JULY 17

"Celeste and I are so glad you all could come tonight. Here are some ground rules, young people. Since we have two Jeffs here, please remember to call me Goeff. I know you want to show respect and say 'Pastor,' but tonight we are simply brothers and sisters in Christ, okay? We have a lot to talk about, so let's get the meal over with fast. But, honey, I don't mean your gourmet cooking isn't to be savored and lingered over. However, time is of the essence in light of Elinor and Julie's disappearance. Let's be seated at the table – Jeff at the far end, then Gloria, Sarah, and Pete on the right side; Grace, Dror, and Celeste on the left side, and me at this end. Jeff, please lead us in the blessing."

"First, on behalf of Pete and Sarah, my wife, and friends, I must say that we are extremely grateful for the prayers of the church and the support offered us by you, Goeff and Miss Celeste. Let's pray. Dear God of Abraham, Isaac, and Jacob, and the God and Father of our Lord Yeshua, we praise and honor You for hearing our many prayers and already showing us how You are answering them. Thank You for protecting Elinor and Julie wherever they are. We claim Your promise that not a hair of their heads will be harmed, and You are delivering them from evil. And thank You for the food Miss Celeste has prepared and for the love of this godly couple. Please guide our conversation. In Yeshua's name. Amen."

The simple meal of chicken casserole, fruit salad, rolls, and tea was quickly consumed and words of gratitude expressed to Celeste. She said they would have cake and coffee later and led them back to the den where the chairs were arranged in a tight circle.

Celeste began the conversation. "Goeff and I have been much in prayer concerning Elinor and Julie's disappearance. In fact it was after our prayer meeting Wednesday night that I became emotionally involved, although I have not met either one of them. Goeff can tell you I began to cry when we got home that night, and I asked him to pray again with me about the girls. I didn't want any entertainment or snacks. I only wanted to read the Bible and search for a word from God about their rescue. I say 'rescue,' but no one has told me what they need to be rescued from. They have been missing three days, and every hour that passes makes me increasingly anxious for their safety. It was about ten o'clock when we went to bed that night. I know Goeff called and told you, Gloria, that I woke him up in the middle of the night, having had a bad dream. You Holy Rollers know all about that, but Dror and Grace, you haven't heard it. Here is what happened. I was screaming. Goeff, tell them what I said."

Pastor clasped his wife's trembling hand. "Celeste yelled out, 'I want my mama! I want my mama! They have had her too long, too long! I will rescue her, I will do it! She hates gambling. I will bring her home with me.' After I finally got her awake, she described the dream. You tell them, honey."

"I can see it in my mind's eye now. I hate what I saw. I was inside a dark building, but on the outside it was lit up with bright neon signs. In this large room people were gambling at roulette wheels, slot machines, and card games. There were mostly men running the games, but then I saw women on the stairs, dressed in bright colored dresses, women like you see in saloons in the old western movies. There were men coming to the stairs, and the women would lead them up to the second story. All of them were laughing. It sounded so wicked. But there was one woman who had on a nicer dress, and she was trying to hide behind the staircase. Then an evil-looking man took a whip and drove her upstairs! I panicked and ran up the stairs and opened every door, but I could not find her. One door was locked, and I beat on it so hard until I collapsed on the floor! My mother was in that room! I had to rescue her!"

Celeste looked imploringly into the eyes of the young people. "I stopped thinking about Elinor and Julie and started thinking about my mother. I haven't seen her since I was a teenager. I never found out what happened to her. It hit me hard Wednesday night after that bad dream when I realized that Susannah Goldberg is a missing person, too. Pete, you are a private investigator. I will pay you any amount of money if you can find my mother."

Celeste began to cry and was inconsolable. The young people looked at her incredulously. Pastor James took her in his arms and tried to calm her. "Celeste, our main purpose for meeting tonight is to help Pete find **his** loved one, his sister. Yes, we planned to talk about your mother, too, but these girls are so young, and they have their whole lives ahead of them. Finding them is Pete's first priority. Then he surely will help you find your mother, but you also have to consider that she may not be alive. You told me it has been at least 27 years since you saw her. She is around 65 years old, you said, if she is still living."

Pete was shaken, but he wanted to give words of hope to the pastor's wife. "Miss Celeste, I am your man. I will definitely help you find your mother. But, as Goeff stated, we must find those girls first."

Jeff could hold back no longer. "Goeff and Celeste, the more I have heard tonight, the more convinced I have become that Mrs. Susannah Goldberg and Elinor Carson and Julie Rollins are being held hostage at the same place. Putting together your dream and a dream I had Thursday night, as well as Pete's calculation about the place, I will be bold and come right out and say it: All three of them are hidden away in a casino in Vicksburg, Mississippi. And yes, this involves sex trafficking!"

Dror, Grace, Goeff, and Celeste were aghast! Dror said, "This is crazy! And I am not believing it until you give me enough real reasons to make your weird conclusions plausible. And, by the way, this is my grandmother you are talking about. I have never met her, but my mother and her sister, my Aunt Celeste, remember her well and love her. Mom even had a slight hope that she may have gone to Israel and would be living there. I saw just now you all were amazed to hear my grandmother's last name, Goldberg, which means she is Jewish, and so is her daughter, my Aunt Celeste. She has reasons for having kept this a secret, but I think she is ready to tell her story, but at a later time. I see her nodding. Yes, that is her wish."

Pastor stood up. "We've had enough bombshells dropped tonight that all our minds are blown. Thank goodness I can quote God's Word and claim His promise here and now – 'For God has not given us a spirit of fear, but of love, and of power, and of a sound mind.' 2 Timothy 1:7." He made everyone quote it two more times, until peace filled the room. "Now, young people, we are going back to the dining room table, and we are going to have some delicious cake and coffee. All the confusion is about to be cleared up. Dror, I am asking you to begin the story of your family, which was a revelation to me when you shared it right at this table. You also shared some of your story with our Jewish Roots class."

Gloria added, "And Dror met with the Holy Rollers one night and told us even more about his family that has a bearing on what has happened. Please share that, too, Dror. I know Grace has probably not heard any of this, and you, Goeff, have not heard it either."

"Shall I start before or after the dessert, Goeff?"

Pastor was quick to answer. "I am on the edge of my seat. But wait till we bring the cake and coffee. Then begin any time you wish. You could even talk between bites!" Everyone laughed, and the somber mood vanished.

The dessert was finished off in silence. Then Dror began. "My parents, Benyamin and Devorah Mizrachi, moved from Columbus to Jackson when I was about ten years old. Mother's childhood home was there, and she wanted to make another effort to connect with her parents, especially to let them know they had a grandchild, me. They had a plan – the three of us would attend the same synagogue my grandparents had attended. My dad was willing to leave his parents in Columbus to move us to Jackson. Growing up, his family life was a happy one. He knew my mother did not have a happy childhood, and he saw that the longer she was alienated from her parents – my grandparents – the more discontented she became. Mom and Dad love each other very much. My dad didn't mind selling his business, uprooting, and moving if it would make my mom happy. Anyway, we moved, bought a house, and I started to school. Dad found a job and advanced up the ladder, so to speak. He was financially successful. We began going to the synagogue. But my grandparents were not there. Mom drove out to the place she lived as a child and teenager. She was shocked that the lot was vacant. Her house was not there!"

"Dror, I had no idea about this sad part of your history. I am so sorry." Grace patted Dror's hand.

"Mother had an idea. She would make friends with some of the older members of the synagogue and question them. Surely someone would know what happened to Isaac and Susannah Goldberg. Her persistence paid off. She found a woman in her 70s, Rena Rabin, who had known them. Rena told Mom that when Isaac and Susannah attended Shabbat services, she sat beside them, and Susannah, although much younger, soon became her friend. One day Mom visited Rena at her residence. I will never forget that night when she returned home. She told Dad and me the whole story. Rena was told by an acquaintance named Flora who lived in the Goldbergs' neighborhood, that the Goldbergs were targeted by a gang in Jackson. They persecuted them, calling them names like 'Christ killers' and 'dirty Jews.' They also painted graffiti on their car and sidewalk. Flora said my grandfather was stubborn and would not report it to the police. One night when they were in bed, they smelled smoke. Their house was on fire! They grabbed their robes and a few things at hand and ran outside. It looked like Mr. Goldberg had lost his mind. He ran back into the house and collapsed in the flames. A Christian neighbor was able to pull his body outside, but this brave man was badly burned. For a long time he had tried without success to befriend the couple, according to Flora. She said the man was seen leaning over him and praying. Mr. Goldberg lifted himself up and grasped the collar of his neighbor, trying to tell him something. Then he raised his hand up, and there was a smile on his face when he breathed his last! My mother was devastated to hear how her father died, but at the same time, she was given hope by the description of his peaceful end. Mom said Mrs. Rabin looked so glad that she had preserved this memory, so she could tell the Goldbergs' daughter."

Pete couldn't help but interrupt. "Did your mother search the newspaper archives to look for this news story about a fire?"

"That's a good question. I guess she didn't think of that. My mom met a few more times with Mrs. Rabin, hoping to stir up the memories of this elderly woman, but all she said was that she talked to Susannah on the phone a few times, but Susannah never came back to the synagogue. Mom gave up looking at that point."

"Let's go back to what you said, Jeff," urged Pete. "Your dream about seeing the lights of a casino and a sign with 'Vicksburg' written on it seems to match Miss Celeste's dream about a casino where her mother was being held. I have studied the subject of sex trafficking and know some of the strategies of the pimps. What I learned was corroborated by the FBI agent that talked to us at the Jackson police station. She said that Jackson is the hub for the southeast, and they're bringing people from Atlanta, the northeast, going down through Jackson toward Texas or from the northwest going toward Florida. Vicksburg is on the route going west from Jackson. If you are employing me, Miss Celeste, I can do the investigation independent of the FBI, and I can look for my sister at the same time. Jeff and I will come up with a plan of action. How does that sound?"

Celeste's face brightened. "Oh, yes, please do it. But one thing puzzles me. If my mother was abducted by sex traffickers at some point in her life, why would they need her at her current age of 65?"

"My wheels have been turning about that very thing, Miss Celeste. If she is in that casino, it may be for another reason. Is it possible your mother could have gotten in with the wrong people after your father died, and maybe she became an entertainer? The casinos have stage shows, you know. Maybe she is only an employee, although your dream indicates otherwise. I don't want to insult you and imply that your mother became like the prodigal son, but we have to consider it. And what about her parents? I know you checked with them."

"No, Pete, at that time they had been dead for several years, both from cancer, about a year apart. But what you said about Mother becoming an entertainer is something to consider. Let me say this. I dearly loved my father, but he abused my mother, as well as my sister Deborah, Dror's mother, and also me. It wasn't physical, but it was mental abuse. Some people would call him a religious fanatic. None of us could please him. We all became victims, especially my mother. She would not dare cross him. It seemed she could not have an opinion of her own or do anything without his permission. There is one thing she loved to do, but she had to do it secretly. And that was dancing. I've been thinking about it – if she ever got out from under Father's thumb, she would spread her wings and fly. She would go to a dance studio and learn all the dances and have the time of her life. When you mentioned that Mother might be in that casino as an entertainer, it sort of rang my bell. Yes, it is possible she did get in with the wrong people to carry out her desire to dance. I could see how easy it would be to victimize her. But it's too horrible to think about, that she could have been entertaining in awful places all these years!" Celeste began to cry again.

Pete looked down at his vibrating cell phone. He was getting a call, and the display showed "Lars Carson." He went back to the den and answered it. "Dad? We're here at Pastor and Mrs. James' house. Just finished dinner. What's up?"

Lar's voice was full of excitement. "Son, she's home!! Elinor's home!!! She is okay, and so is Julie. We are celebrating. The Jackson police chief drove them here, and another officer followed them on Julie's car. You won't believe it, but Dr. Hanson, President of Millsaps College, and his friend, FBI Agent Sherwood, came in another police car. Jesse and Margaret are here, too. Son, can you and Sarah come? None of us will be going to bed any time soon. We are so excited! There's a lot to tell. Bring Jeff and Gloria with you, and come!" As soon as Pete said yes, Lars hung up.

Pete ran back to the dining room, rejoicing. "Elinor's home! Elinor's home, and she's okay! Julie, too. Dad just called and wants Sarah and me to come right now. They are celebrating. The big wig law enforcement people came, including the Millsaps President. Dad only wanted to hear me say I'd come, and he hung up. So, that's all I know. Jeff and Gloria, he said for y'all to come, too. Oh, glory! I'm about to bust a gasket! Holy Rollers, let's go!"

A loud cheer went up, with squealing, jumping, clapping, and hugging going on the next few minutes. Pastor James yelled, "On your knees, everybody! God answered our prayers. You Holy Rollers, don't move another inch until we all get down on our knees and praise and thank our awesome God." Everyone was out of breath, but they fell to their knees, even Dror. "Lead out, Pete," commanded Pastor.

Pete began to pray with great emotion, "Heavenly Father, thank You, thank You, thank You! You heard and You answered. Oh, how good You are. We lift up Elinor and Julie to Your throne of grace and ask that You heal them of whatever trauma they experienced and restore them better than new. Please reward the police and the FBI and everyone who worked on the case." Pete paused to catch his breath. "And Father, we petition You for a miracle. Please let Miss Celeste and Miss Deborah's mother be found, too. If You want to use Jeff and me to go forward in finding her and bringing her to Miss Celeste, equip us and guide us. We ask all this in the glorious name of our Lord Jesus Christ." Loud amens came from everyone, including Dror.

As the Holy Rollers were leaving, Gloria said, "Pastor, please call Miss Lizzie right now and thank her for us. I know it wasn't only her prayers and the prayers of her 'swat team' that brought about the girls' rescue, but the Spirit told me He had used them mightily!"

CHAPTER EIGHTEEN

DELIVERED FROM THE HAND OF THE WICKED

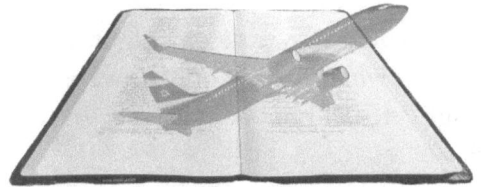

Pete drove into his parents' driveway and parked beside Julie's Toyota. Further up the driveway he identified her parents' car, as well as Melvin, Edwin, and Britt's vehicles. No police cars were in sight. "Y'all, it looks like all my family is here, but everybody else has left except Julie and her parents. Aw shucks! I wanted to grill the officers about their successful rescue. Well, at least we can talk to Elinor and Julie. I can't wait to hug my little sister's neck and see how she looks. She better not have any signs of abuse, or I will hunt down those evil people to the ends of the earth, if that's what it takes!"

Sarah grabbed hold of his hands and squeezed hard. "Pete, you calm down right now. You look like a dragon, breathing fire. 'It's not by might, nor by power, but by My Spirit, says the Lord.'[41] You know that you can't do one thing without God's power. When we walk in that house, I want you to exude peace, not anger. The girls need to be bathed in peace. We want to be a healing balm to them, honey."

Gloria felt the Spirit prompting her to speak. "Listen to your wife, Pete. The Lord is speaking through her. And I have a verse for you also from James 1: 19-20 – 'So then, my beloved brethren, let every man be swift to hear, slow to speak, slow to wrath; for the wrath of man does not produce the righteousness of God.' And I can tell you from experience that God gave me this verse to cure my anger, way back when I was only thirteen."

"Ready, Pete? Let's go inside," said Jeff. "You suffer from anger, and I suffer from impatience." The car doors swung open. Pete was greeted at the door by Elinor.

"Oh, big brother, I really needed you last Wednesday night. I kept saying to myself, 'Pete would know what to do. If only he were here.'" Elinor gave him a warm hug. Pete held her at a distance in the entry hall and looked her over.

"Elinor, you look beautiful! Maybe I don't have to go beat up on anybody after all. Let me hug you tight. I can see it won't hurt you. I love you, little sister." Pete swept her off her feet.

Sarah, Gloria, and Jeff were standing in line to love on Elinor. They kept repeating, "Thank God you are safe."

Lars and Elsa, Margaret and Jesse, and Julie Rollins were standing in the hall with big smiles on their faces to see the same joyful reunion they had experienced not long before.

"Come on in, children," invited Elsa. "Let's sit down and share this miracle of God. We have already heard from Elinor and Julie, but I know you four are anxious to hear their story. Chief Braun, Dr. Hanson, Agent Sherwood, and the other officer had to get on back to Jackson. I know it is not customary for these law enforcement people to deliver the missing persons to your door in another city, but we got special treatment. Dr. Hanson has more influence than I realized. He also felt partly responsible this happened in the first place. He was bending over backwards to make things right. In fact, he is offering both Elinor and Julie a scholarship to attend Millsaps College!"

Jesse Rollins said, "I know it's an old cliché, but God surely does work in mysterious ways."

"I'll go first," insisted Julie. "I'm the one that got the invitation to the Kappa Delta rush party from my friend Lori Cushman. Of course, I invited Elinor to go with me. It was a nice party, and they made a big fuss over us, the same as all the other potential candidates for their sorority. Being a Methodist college, I was surprised that one table was full of beer cans and wine bottles. At least there was not any hard liquor, or so I thought. Elinor and I have never even tasted a beer, and the only time we have had wine was with our parents present at a special dinner. Elinor told me that she had decided to be a teetotaler. I had not really made up my mind, but if Elinor wasn't going to drink, neither was I. So we ate the sandwiches, petits fours, cookies, all sorts of hors d'oeuvres, and helped ourselves to the delicious punch."

"I want to tell part of it, Julie," said Elinor. "I was having a ball. After we stood around the refreshment tables a while, we sat down and had conversation. A girl named Alicia kept bringing us refills on our punch. The group began to pop jokes, and we joined in with our own jokes. It was hilarious. Julie and I got to laughing so hard we had to run to the bathroom! When we started back to the couch, Julie stumbled. I tried to help her up, and then I fell down. We just sat in the floor and started laughing. I said, 'Julie, it's time for us to leave. We are getting too silly, and we've laughed so hard, I can hardly walk straight.' So we said goodbye to the girls standing around, made sure we thanked Lori Cushman for inviting us, and left."

"Okay, I will continue the story," said Julie. "When we left there I got disoriented and wasn't sure which street to take to get home. I didn't say anything to Elinor for a while, thinking I would figure it out. About ten minutes later I noticed the gas gauge, and it was almost on empty. I confessed to Elinor that I was lost, and we were about to run out of gas. We started looking for a gas station but couldn't find one that was open. By now it was after midnight. At that point we got really scared. Stupid us! We weren't thinking straight. We should have called Uncle Gus to come get us. We pulled over and sat there, trying to decide what to do. I guess I had too much pride to call Uncle Gus, especially since it was so late. Then I saw a big sign pointing to I-20 and decided to gamble that we had enough gas to make it."

"What Julie is not telling you," Elinor interrupted, "is that we were drunk! We were so naïve that we didn't figure out the punch was spiked. Now we realized it and got sober fast. Julie followed the sign's direction, and we soon saw an all-night gas station just up ahead. However, at that moment the car sputtered and stopped! We would have to walk to that station, get a can with gas, come back, put it in the gas tank, and drive to the station to get filled up. That's what we set out to do. A scroungy-looking guy walked out of the station and said he would be glad to help us. He filled up a can, put it in his truck, and told us he would drive us back to the car, so we wouldn't have to walk. Now y'all, this is where it gets scary. I hate having to relive this, but you need to know."

"Let me tell this part, Elinor. It's more painful for you than for me. We reluctantly got in his old truck, but that guy did not take us back to our car. He got on the interstate and started driving west. We both screamed and demanded he turn around and take us back. He said, 'You girls be quiet. I have a nervous disorder, and when I get screamed at, sometimes I go off my rocker and do bad things. I just got out of the state hospital for choking a pretty girl like y'all. She didn't die, or I wouldn't be here. They let me out after I had good behavior for a year. Anyway, we are just going to drive down the highway about 50 minutes to Vicksburg. I have a thing for gambling, and we are going to have a little recreation. Then I will drive you back to your car. That's not so bad, is it?' Then he leered at us with a wicked grin!"

Elinor was tensing up. "Well, there is something good that came out of this ordeal. I learned how to pray. Never in my life have I prayed so hard for God to rescue us. And I kept asking Him for wisdom. What should I do? How could Julie and I escape? Bible verses I memorized as a child came into my mind, and I said them under my breath over and over. Julie looked at me like I was crazy. Then she realized I was praying, and she squeezed my hand and began silently praying herself. Okay, here's the bad part. This guy's name was Oliver. We finally arrived at the gambling place in

Vicksburg. There were dozens of casinos, all lit up with neon signs, some blinking. The one he took us to had a big hotel attached to it. I saw the sign 'Rainbow Casino.' Before we got out of the truck, he tied our hands behind our backs with rope. Then he pulled a sharp knife out of his pocket and warned us to keep our mouths shut. He took us around back. There were no street lights in the back. He had a key to the casino. He unlocked the door and pushed us inside. Then a light came on, and we saw a mean-looking, greasy-haired man sitting in a corner, whittling on a piece of wood. Oliver said, 'Hey, Carlos, this haul should be worth twice what you been paying me. These two are pure, like angels. They are top dollar. So pay up. I gotta get back to the station. Who knows but what I may have more cargo for you this very night.' Then he began to laugh, and it sounded demonic." Elinor shuddered. She couldn't go on.

Lars spoke up. "Girls, would you like to take a break and have something to eat?"

"No, Dad. I want to get through this. Julie, you go on with the story."

"We really got an education about sex trafficking these last few days. I had never even heard there was such a thing. Well, Carlos paid Oliver, and he left. We didn't know what would happen to my car, but that was the least of our worries. Carlos took us up several stories in the hotel and unlocked one of the rooms. He said, "We got girls in rooms on the other side of the casino, too, but 'Madame Susie' lives in this one. She will take good care of you. She's gonna make you look real purty, and then you are going to work in the casino. The good news is you will make new friends, purty like y'all, and you can learn from them how to do your work. It will be somethin' you ain't never did before, but it will be fun. Ha! Ha! Ha!' Then he left and locked the door. Madame Susie showed us around. There were about six or eight other girls in the suite of rooms. The common area was large and had multiple love seats and tables. The kitchen was overflowing with large platters of snack foods and drinks, including hard liquor. The five bedrooms had large closets with gaudy gowns, and there were two king-size beds in each room. The dressing tables had lots of garish jewelry. Madame Susie had a private room. She assigned us a room together. Then she took us to the common room and gave us and another new girl a briefing on what was expected of us." Julie lowered her head in shame. "All the girls were in the common room, and everyone was fidgeting. They had heard it before, I guess, but it was the first time for the new girl and Elinor and me. What Madame Susie said was hard to bear, and we wanted to get to the end of it, so we didn't interrupt."

"I'll talk now," said Elinor. "The briefing was the most shocking thing I have ever heard. Neither Julie nor I understood the terminology used in describing the strategy to get customers in the casino. I quickly realized what a sheltered life I had led, and Julie, too. After about five minutes into the briefing, I felt sick to my stomach. I told Madame Susie I had to hurry to the bathroom. Julie was right behind me. We threw up and then grabbed each other and cried. Fear engulfed us! We couldn't go back out there. We stayed in the bedroom and hoped they wouldn't come get us. After about ten minutes, Madame Susie quietly knocked on the door. I opened the door. She came over and sat on the bed beside us. She didn't speak for a few minutes, but just looked at us. Her eyes were full of love, and tears were about to spill out. We didn't know what to think. But we took a chance and decided to trust her. Then she talked to us almost like we were her babies. She said, 'I see you girls have never known a man, and you don't even know the first thing about sex. I am going to step out on a limb and help you. It may cause me to be thrown out of here, which would mean no more income and not even a place to live. But what have I ever sacrificed for another person? You remind me of my two daughters, and you are just about their ages when I last saw them. My husband threw them out of the house, and I didn't do one thing about it! I have hated myself ever since. But now I see it's time to be unselfish, and I am going to get y'all out of here!' When she said that, both of us instantly knew she wasn't in this sex trade of her own free will. She was being forced to do this demeaning job. I couldn't help myself, but I reached up and put my arms around her neck, hugged her, and thanked her."

Jeff and Gloria and Pete and Sarah looked at each other and gasped. "You said this woman had two daughters your age that were thrown out of their house by their father?" asked Pete.

"Yes, that's what she said," answered Julie. "Then I knew why she was having mercy on us. I hugged her neck, too. Madame Susie was probably 60-something years old, but she was quite beautiful underneath all the gobs of makeup. Knowing how she must have been used and abused for probably years and years, I began to think of wanting her freedom as much as I wanted mine. In my heart I determined that we would not leave there unless she went with us. And suddenly it came to me. We had one weapon for getting out of that evil place of gambling and sex trafficking, and it was prayer. When Elinor and I were in the truck, silently praying, I felt God's presence for the first time in my life. I was supposed to be saved, but really I didn't care about Jesus or the things of God until that moment. I knew I needed Him, and I just had a feeling deep inside that if we would ask and believe, He would get us out of there, all three of us."

"Julie was braver than me. She told Madame Susie and me to get down on our knees. She was going to lead us in prayer. Madame Susie wouldn't do it at first. She said, 'I hate religion. My husband was full of it. He didn't believe our daughter when she confessed that she got an abortion because she had been raped. She needed comfort, not condemnation. But religion made my husband so hateful. A few years later he died when our house burned up, and I had nowhere to turn."

Pete interrupted again. "Elinor, are you sure she said her father died in a house fire? I will tell you later why this shocks me."

"Yes, Pete. She also said, 'My parents were no longer living. I had to make a life for myself somehow. I chose to take dancing lessons and get into entertainment. At first I got some gigs in nightclubs and was able to support myself. But what happened to you girls happened to me about ten years ago when I was 55. I was abducted by sex traffickers. I have been in several big cities over the years. Thankfully, the pimps have used me mostly to groom the young girls, since I was too old to attract buyers. Their name for women like me is 'the bottom.' I guess we are the lowest of the low. At the beginning, however, the pimps sold me when they ran out of young girls.' Finally, Julie convinced Madame Susie that prayer might work, and it was worth a try. What did she have to lose? She got on her knees with us, and Julie prayed her heart out. She was bold as a lion! Then I started praying, and something happened – we all were knocked flat on the floor!"

Gloria interrupted. "You mean you were slain in the Spirit?"

Elinor looked puzzled. "Well, here we are, alive. No, it didn't kill us, but it had to be the Spirit of God. I don't know how long we lay there, but when we came to, Madame Susie was acting so scared, and she was sobbing. She started confessing some awful sins, mostly of hate and rage and neglect of her daughters. Then she began to plead like a little child for God to forgive her. She promised over and over she would serve Him if He would forgive her."

Pete and Jeff gave each other knowing looks. Pete said, "Elinor, we know who that lady is! She has been a missing person just like y'all. We have got to go to that casino and get her out of there. Wait a minute. Julie said she vowed not to leave her in that place when you both got free. We don't want to rush your narrative, but please tell us why y'all left her and all about the rescue. Was it several policemen or FBI agents or what? How did they do it?"

Jeff agreed. "Yes, you girls tell us the details of the rescue, everything!"

Sarah had her Tanach open. "Wait, you guys. I've got to share some Scripture. Listen to this. God's Word fits every occasion, and this verse is what He did tonight. 'Let those who love the Lord hate evil, for He guards the lives of his faithful ones and delivers them from the hand of the wicked.'"[42]

Julie said, "Yes, He did it! I kept praying over and over, 'Lord deliver us from evil, deliver us from evil.'"

"God really did answer out prayers!" shouted Elinor. "From now on I am putting Jesus first in my life."

CHAPTER NINETEEN

FAMILY SECRET REVEALED

The Holy Rollers got the full story of the rescue by the FBI and police from Elinor and Julie. Then they quickly excused themselves to return to Pastor and Mrs. James' home. Before they heard the rescue part of the story Pete had called the pastor and told him to hold Dror and Grace there. The Holy Rollers had exciting news to tell them about Dror's grandmother and Miss Celeste's mother.

About a half hour later Pastor greeted them and ushered them into the den where Celeste, Dror, and Grace were anxiously waiting to hear the good news. Pete sat forward in his seat and began to repeat what they had just heard from his sister and her friend about their kidnapping and then their rescue from the Rainbow Casino in Vicksburg. He asked Gloria to tell the beginning of the story, but he took over the narrative at the point where Madame Susie vowed to get them out of that place. He spoke slowly so that Dror and Miss Celeste could take it all in and be convinced, just as he was, that Madame Susie was indeed Susannah Goldberg, their mother and grandmother. Many tissues were used from the Kleenex box placed near Celeste, as she experienced the full gamut of emotion from grief and horror to joy and excitement. Dror was wondering how his mother would feel when he called her.

Pete said, "Pastor, as we drove over here, the four of us made a plan. Tomorrow, instead of preaching at Adaton as you are prepared

151

to do, we ask you to allow Jeff to take your place in the pulpit. Gloria has agreed to go ahead with our Jewish Roots class, but I want to take Sarah with me to Jackson. Grace, we hope you will assist Gloria in the class. Also, I want you, Pastor, and Miss Celeste, as well as Dror, to come with me and Sarah. We are going to set Susannah Goldberg free! I have already called the Jackson Police Department, and Chief Braun said he would meet us at 10:30 in the morning. Dror and Pastor and Miss Celeste, do you agree with this plan? We need to be on the road to Jackson by 8:00 a.m." All of them, including Grace, agreed.

"Wait, wait!" exclaimed Celeste. "You haven't told us yet why my mother was not rescued at the same time Elinor and Julie were. I heard you say Julie vowed in her heart to get Madame Susie out of there."

"Okay, I got ahead of myself," Pete apologized. "I'll tell you what happened. It happened so fast, Elinor said, that they almost forgot about Madame Susie. Then Julie remembered, as they were being whisked away by the police, and said she had to go back. They said no, but she broke free and found Madame Susie in her bedroom where she had retreated when the police came in. Julie said, 'Come on right this minute! Don't stop for anything! The police said we could get killed if we don't run!' Then Madame Susie started crying. She said, 'I can't. I don't have anywhere to go. I don't have enough money. And I've got to help another young girl who was just brought in yesterday.' She pushed Julie out the door and locked it. Julie ran as fast as she could. The policeman was so mad. He jerked her out the back door and roughly pushed her in the police car with Elinor. Then he gunned the accelerator to the floor, Julie said."

"Oh, so close! She was so close to being rescued!" cried Celeste. "Why didn't she run when she had the chance? She could be free and start a new life! Wait... I think I know. She had no idea that there IS a place for her to live, a place where she will be provided for. It must be a foreign concept to her that she has love and happiness waiting for her. She couldn't know that she has a family who will meet her needs."

Pastor took his wife in his arms. "Remember, darling, that you didn't know that either until you met me."

Dror leaned closer to his aunt. "My mother said her sister met someone and fell in love. Aunt Celeste, you haven't told me that part of your story. Would you tell it to us now? It's only ten o'clock, and we aren't leaving for Jackson until 8:00 in the morning."

"Yes, Celeste, tell it. Your story glorifies God," said Pastor.

"Okay," Celeste agreed. "I will take up where Dror ended his story about him and his parents, Deborah and Benjamin, deciding to make aliyah. They asked me to go with them. There was nothing holding me in America. Yes, I had friends in Columbus, and I attended their church every now and then, but the only relative I knew about was Deborah. I was Jewish, so it made sense to make aliyah with them. But I had a feeling that this man I had met was worth staying for. He came in Dillard's one day, and I waited on him. He said he was trying to find the right fabric for a curtain in the Vacation Bible School program in his church. He had not been able to find it in Starkville. The more we talked, the more interested I became in him. It was fascinating to watch his face as he talked about his church. It took a while for me to realize that he was the pastor. That almost scared me off. Although I had become somewhat familiar with church life and the Christian jargon, I didn't know any church people that were excited about God. This man was literally glowing, and also he seemed genuinely interested in me. I was not about to reveal my Jewishness to him, but I thought I would find out his opinion of Jews. So I told him my sister and her husband really loved the nation of Israel, and they wanted me to go with them to visit. He was already glowing, but when I said that his face looked like fireworks! That removed the last of my reservations."

Pastor was blushing, and everyone broke into a cheer led by Jeff, "Pastor loves his Jewish roots! Pastor loves his Jewish roots!"

"Honey, you don't have to tell all the details," pleaded Pastor. "Shall I continue the story for you?" Celeste agreed.

"Here's the short version. When I saw Celeste, I thought I had encountered an angel. What a beauty, and she seemed like a really good person. I hoped she was a Christian, but I couldn't tell. I decided to risk it and ask her for a date. I was well aware of Paul's admonition to not be 'unequally yoked with unbelievers.'[43] She accepted, and my heart did a jig! We went to Harvey's. I ordered pork chops with sides and salad. I noticed she flinched when I first cut into the pork chop, but I didn't think anything about it. Looking back, now I understand, since Jews are conditioned from birth not to eat pork, an unclean animal. Oh well, that's not really important. Hey, I will try to hurry here. It's getting late."

Pete intervened. "Don't you dare hurry past this part, Pastor. I want to hear all the juicy, romantic stuff." He looked over at Sarah, as she rolled her eyes.

"Anyway, I learned on that first date that I loved that woman. I also learned that she was not saved. I wanted to hold her in my arms and kiss her so bad, I could hardly restrain myself. When I took her to her door that night, I reached out and clasped her hand with all the tenderness in my soul. I looked into her eyes, and she was looking into mine. Our eyes locked for about two minutes. It wasn't easy to get the words out, but I said, 'Celeste, will you let me pick you up tomorrow and take you to my church in Starkville?' Quickly I added, so as not to withhold anything from her: 'I will be preaching, of course, but I hope that won't make you say no.' She smiled so big, even laughed, and said, 'I would love to.'"

"You were like a shy little boy, and I couldn't resist you," Celeste said. "It was so refreshing to be in your presence after being around men who obviously had only one thing on their minds, sex. You made me feel safe, Jeff. Anyway, as I sat and listened to you preach, this yearning welled up inside me to know the same God you knew. He certainly had to be different from the God my father followed, a god with so many heartless prohibitions. At the end of the church service you gave a careful explanation of how to know your God, and it had to do with accepting the sacrifice of His Son on the cross to forgive sins and offer eternal life. Before I had time to really think of the ramifications of such a decision for a Jewish person who had been taught that Jesus was not the Messiah, I got out of my seat and walked to the front. A resolve built up in me to 'just do it!' A lady beside me did the same thing. I sort of followed her example. Then we got on our knees, and Jeff put his hands on our heads and prayed. It felt like surgery, like my old heart was taken out and a new heart put inside me. I looked up at Jeff, and his eyes were full of love. I made a decision right then I would not second-guess what I had done. I would proudly say I now believed in Jesus."

"And friends, I didn't waste any time," the pastor said. "After lunch when I took Celeste back to Columbus, I walked up on her porch. I took her in my arms and told her I loved her, and she was the only woman I had ever loved or ever would love. And I asked her to marry me!"

Jeff Quentin interrupted. "I am shocked, Pastor. You are such a fast worker. But you mean to tell me you didn't even kiss her before you proposed?" Everyone laughed.

"Hey, Buddy, let me tell my own story. I'm not finished. Yes, I 'laid one on her,' as you guys would say. Before Celeste came along I had probably stolen only two or three kisses in my lifetime. But I made up for lost time right then, and as you can see, she accepted my proposal. She kissed me back so forcefully, I nearly fell off the porch!" Laughter and joy permeated the room.

Eight people managed to have a huge group hug as well as individual hugs. Then the three couples said their good nights and again expressed appreciation for the dinner and all the fantastic conversation. Pastor and Celeste assured their young friends they would contact Miss Lizzie and the other leaders of the church before 8:00 in the morning and give them the good news of the girls' rescue and request their continuing prayers for the upcoming rescue of Celeste's mother.

CHAPTER TWENTY

BITTERSWEET
RESCUE

Pete and Sarah were about ready to leave their apartment and head over to the James' house, but they took a few minutes to go next door and pray with Jeff and Gloria. They told them that Pastor had volunteered to take his roomy van, since five of them, including Dror, were going to Jackson, and there would be six of them coming back.

Dror, Pete, and Sarah drove up to the James' house promptly at 7:50 a.m. Pastor and Pete took the front seats in the van with Dror behind the driver's seat. Celeste and Sarah took the back seat, and they were off at 8:00 o'clock. Pastor backed out of the driveway, and before anyone said a word, he began to pray, "El Shaddai, our Mighty God, You are the Lord of Hosts. You have innumerable angels doing your bidding. We thank You for assigning many angels to protect us as we travel. We love You, Lord. We thank You with all our hearts that Celeste and Dror are going to be reunited with their mother and grandmother this very day after long years of separation. Please prepare our hearts to love this abused woman, and heal her, Lord, of every wound. We also ask You to form the rescue plans in the minds of Chief Braun, his officers, and us men. Please keep everyone of us safe from harm. I claim Your promise that 'You will preserve us from all evil. You will preserve our souls. You will preserve our going out and our coming in from this time forth and even forevermore.'[44] Amen."

Everyone was lost in his own thoughts. After about thirty minutes Sarah tapped Dror on the shoulder. "Dror, have you talked to your mother in Israel yet? I have been praying that she will be able to handle this shocking story of what happened to her mother."

"Thanks for asking, Sarah. I've already told Aunt Celeste that I was able to get in touch with her after I got back to my apartment last night. Israel is eight hours ahead of us, so when I called Mom at midnight, she was having breakfast this morning and seemed to be in a good mood. She is always glad to hear from me. She put her phone on speaker, so my dad could hear, too. I gave her an abbreviated version of Elinor and Julie's predicament in being kidnapped and taken to the Vicksburg casino where they met Grandmother. I described what kind of job she had and told her what the girls learned from their conversation with her, about how she came to be in that place. I could hear Mom gasp and the sounds of my dad comforting her in the background. Then I told her why the girls couldn't get her to go with them when they were rescued by the police. Oy vey! Mom groaned so loud. But I quickly assured her we would be going to rescue her today and make her come with us. I said I was going to Jackson with Pastor and Aunt Celeste, and Elinor's brother Pete and his wife Sarah to the police station, and the police would rescue her, and we would bring Grandmother back to Starkville to live with Aunt Celeste and get her healed."

Pete said, "Dror and Pastor, I didn't tell you, but Chief Braun said he may need our help, because he is short-handed on Sunday." A spirit of anxiety swept through the vehicle.

♥ ♥ ♥ ♥ ♥

Chief Braun handed Pete a missing person form. "Okay, Pete, you fill out this form at the desk. Then we will talk," ordered Chief Braun. "Come on back with me, the rest of you. Pete, you come to the back room when you finish the form."

When all were in the room, Dror was the first to speak. "Chief Braun, I am the grandson of the missing person, Susannah Goldberg. I am willing to assist in the rescue if you need me. I have brought my gun. After graduating from high school in Israel, I served three years in the Israeli Defense Force. Not only am I in good physical shape, but I have experience in recovering Jewish soldiers held for ransom by Hezbollah, the Palestinian terror group in Lebanon."

Pete reacted, "Why didn't you tell us this before, Dror? I have heard that the IDF is probably the fourth best army in the world, although Israel is one of the smallest nations. We are honored to have you with us. And, Chief Braun, as a private investigator I also have my gun and know how to use it."

Chief Braun didn't seem to be impressed, but he thanked Dror and Pete for offering to help. "We need to get going. Sunday is a good day for this. The casinos are not busy, especially in the morning time. I have two deputies ready to follow us. None of our vehicles are marked, and we are not wearing our uniforms. You will be third in line, but remember, you are only our backup. I feel sure the Jackson Police represented by me and the two deputies can make the rescue."

"Before we leave, Chief, I would like to know how you knew Elinor and Julie were at the Rainbow Casino. Also, did you make any arrests?" Pete had to know.

"Okay, I'll tell you, but we need to hurry. One of our policemen was checking out every service station on I-20 that was anywhere near Millsaps College or the home of Gus and Adoline Rollins. This was Friday night, and it had been two days since the girls went missing. Sergeant Callahan noticed the back of a 1995 bronze Toyota in the garage of a Gulf service station on the interstate and figured it could be Julie Rollins' car. He made sure he wouldn't be seen, so he parked a little distance away. He was using an unmarked police car. After a few minutes, he saw a man come out of the service station, get in the car, and drive out on the interstate going west. Sergeant Callahan noticed there was a woman in the front seat. He followed the Toyota a distance behind. He radioed the station for help and said he was following a suspect in the kidnapping of Elinor and Julie. I and another deputy and also an FBI man drove out immediately and caught up with Sergeant Callahan. The suspect led us to the Rainbow Casino in Vicksburg. Sergeant Callahan parked at the back of the parking lot and waited. About thirty minutes later when the suspect came out the back door of the casino, the woman wasn't with him. Sergeant Callahan easily apprehended him and took him in custody. An FBI agent got in the Toyota and drove it back to Jackson. The deputy and I followed. We got the whole story from the suspect, Oliver Crawford, and we booked him."

Pete's wheels were turning. "I surely hope no one saw you."

"Yes, we were certain we weren't noticed. There were no street lights in that parking lot, and our police cars are very quiet. When Oliver gave us the directions to the upstairs rooms where the girls were, we didn't waste any time. We drove back to the casino. It was not our intention to make a lot of arrests, just to get Elinor and Julie out of there. And that's what we did about two hours later. However, we did arrest a man named Carlos Garcia. Because of that arrest, the gambling bosses know we may be back. That means this operation today is dangerous. Be prepared for anything."

As soon as he turned off the highway, Pastor drove his black van into the parking lot of the Rainbow Casino and parked at the edge of the lot in a secluded spot with trees. Celeste and Sarah had their heads bowed, praying earnestly. Pete and Dror had on bullet-proof vests, and their guns were at the ready. Chief Braun had warned them not to leave the van unless he called. Chief Braun and two deputies had come in two cars. They were about to exit their cars when a semi-truck pulled up close to the back door of the casino. In about ten minutes the back door opened, and two groups of girls carrying suitcases came out. The back of the semi opened up. A man got out and fixed a ramp for the girls to ascend into the truck. They crowded in, not uttering a sound. One very young girl was taken by another man around to the front and lifted up to the passenger seat, as ordered by the driver who apparently had claimed her for himself. The ramp was taken up inside the truck, and the back began to close. Chief Braun and his deputies drew their guns, and one deputy grabbed the man outside the truck. Chief Braun pointed his gun at the driver's head and said, "Halt! If you move an inch, I will blow your head off!"

Pete didn't wait for permission. His instincts said he better get that girl out of the front seat and quick. She could be hurt. He brandished his gun in the event another man was hiding in the front cab, and he ordered the girl to get out. The other deputy assisted her and quickly put her in his police car. Dror came out of the van and pointed his gun in the direction of the back door of the casino. He knew that a whole mob of goons could descend on them at any minute. He wasn't in charge, but he wished more policemen had come. Of course, no one anticipated a semi-truck driving up to take those girls to another location.

Chief Braun ordered the driver to find out if an older woman named Madame Susie was in the back of the truck. The truck was opened again for a search, but all the girls said, "She's not here."

Chief Braun had no choice but to call in the Vicksburg Police. He was sure they were accustomed to the scenario that had just unfolded. It took only twenty minutes for several cars of police to arrive at the scene along with vans sufficient to transport the girls. The driver was then ordered to park the semi. All three men were handcuffed and put in the Vicksburg police cars.

Dror went back to the van to wait for further instructions.

Pete got in the police car with the girl who identified herself as Angelina Blondell. "How long have you been here? Was Madame Susie your groomer?"

The girl was trembling. Pete guessed she was no more than 16 years old. "I just got here two days ago. Madame Susie took a liking to me. This morning she took me in her room to tell me all the ways I could avoid the worst parts of my job. Then she started crying and said she could have been rescued last night, but she turned it down. She regretted it. While I was in her room, the big boss came in and told her she would have to leave. He said we girls were going to another location, and they had a 'bottom' there. Madame Susie was out of a job. He handed her $100 and said 'Get out.' Then with great determination she said, 'At last I am leaving this horrible sex trade. I have a little money saved up. I am beginning to trust that God will help me start a new life.' That shocked me. I didn't think anybody in this place believed in God. Anyway, I helped her pack. She was going to have to walk somewhere, carrying her heavy suitcase. I started crying then and hugged her and told her I loved her."

Pete's heart dropped to his shoes. "How long ago was that?"

Angelina answered, "It could have been three or four hours ago."

Pete was thinking out loud. "I wonder if she tried to get a hotel room in Vicksburg. I have got to find her. Maybe she is planning on hitchhiking to Jackson where she used to live. That's what my gut tells me. Well, anyway, Angelina, you have been a big help. By the way, would you like to get away from here?"

"Oh, you mean it? You mean it? YES! I will pay you somehow if you take me to a bus to go back to my home in Jackson. I will even pay you with sex, if I have to!"

Pete could hardly believe how destitute this teenager was. He vowed he would make it his business to help her get started with a new life. "I am going to Jackson. I will ride with you in the deputy's car and take you home. How's that?"

Angelina hugged Pete so hard he started worrying what Sarah would think. "Angelina, stay here. I will be right back." Pete went and got Sarah, told her briefly about Angelina and asked her to sit with the girl in the deputy's car while he went to tell Pastor, Dror, and Celeste that Mrs. Goldberg was not there and why. He would get the deputy to lead Pastor's van back to Jackson. Every one of them was to be on the lookout for a woman with a suitcase, hitchhiking. They would stop at every restaurant along the way and look for her. She would at least need their restroom facilities. None of them knew what Susannah Goldberg looked like, even Celeste, since so many years had gone by. Angelina would be their primary "lookout."

CHAPTER TWENTY-ONE

THE SEARCH

"**D**eputy Sturgis, I want to thank you so much for going beyond the call of duty for me. I know we are still on the missing person case of Susannah Goldberg, and it is part of your job. But also, you helped me fulfill my promise to Angelina Blondell in returning her to her parents." Pete shook the officer's hand, and so did Sarah.

"You call on me any time. We policemen don't get to see joyful reunions very often and usually don't receive any thanks when we help make it happen. This was special to me, because my wife and I have a teenage girl, too. And since the case for Mrs. Goldberg is still open, maybe I will get involved again in a joyful reunion." Deputy Sturgis left them at the Jackson police station and drove off.

Pete and Sarah found Pastor and Miss Celeste and Dror relaxing in the back room of the station and plopped down on the loveseat next to them. Pastor's voice was sad. "Well, we had a fruitless search, as you know, but we checked out every possible place Mrs. Goldberg could have stopped between here and Vicksburg. While we were waiting on you two to arrive back at the station, I called Jeff and Gloria. I told them all that transpired at the casino and also about Angelina having been the last one to see Mrs. Goldberg, and that she gave us valuable information that points to her whereabouts. They were happy that Angelina was saved from possible harm by Pete's quick action and all the girls at the casino were

163

intercepted and saved from a life of sex trafficking. They rejoiced that the girls would be given a chance for a new life at a rehab place where Chief Braun had taken them. Jeff and Gloria, as well as Grace and the Adaton church, want all of you to know they have prayed and will continue to pray that our search be successful. They also requested that we stay in touch with Angelina. They are praying for her, too."

Pete took charge. "Okay, let's plan what we are going to do. From what Angelina said, we can deduce that Mrs. Goldberg was going to Jackson and start her life over with the help of God. That's a good thing. Now, let's think like she would think, given the information you shared with us, Dror, about your mother's search for her. Was it about eleven or twelve years ago?"

"Yes, it was. I can't get that image out of my mind, about their house burning down, and a neighbor pulling my grandfather out of the flames, as it was told to Mother. He had gone back inside and collapsed. It was a Christian neighbor, Mother said, and he prayed over him. My grandfather responded to that prayer, so the bystander said, lifted himself up, raised his hand, smiled, and died peacefully."

Pastor responded, "Just like the thief on the cross next to Jesus. That's what he did. After a life of crime, he looked to Jesus to save him, and Jesus assured him He would. At the last minute!"

Sarah added, "I am studying the gospels now, and that story has really gripped me. There were two thieves, one on either side of Jesus. One of them cursed Jesus, but the other one rebuked him and said Jesus didn't deserve His execution, but they did. Then this part really gets me – the thief said, 'Lord, remember me when You come into Your kingdom.' And Jesus said to him, 'Assuredly, I say to you, today you will be with Me in Paradise.'[45] How did the thief know that Jesus would be coming into His kingdom? He saw Jesus dying right there beside them. He was going to be dead. He didn't look like a King at all! The thief had no way of knowing that Jesus was going to be raised from the dead and after forty days go back to heaven and sit at the right hand of His Father, Almighty God. And yet the thief made that unusual request. He had faith. I can't get over it. Jesus was going to take him down into the bowels of the earth and get all those people from centuries before who had believed in Him, who had looked forward to the coming of the Messiah when they died, people like Abraham, Isaac, and Jacob and David and Isaiah and on and on and on. The thief would be with Jesus when He went to Paradise and snatched all those Torah saints up to take them with him to heaven. Oh, glory! I am about to have a shouting spell, as the Christians say."

Pete got so tickled at his sweet bride, he did shout. Everyone joined him, and it felt like their praises shook the jail!

Dror was having trouble taking in this joyful scene and processing the things Sarah said. "So even after all the abuse my grandmother, my mother, and you, Aunt Celeste, suffered at his hands, you think my grandfather, Isaac Goldberg, is in heaven now? That's hard for me to take in. It really is."

Celeste put her arm around her nephew. "Dror, I know how you feel. We are Jewish, and the New Testament is foreign to us, or rather, it used to be foreign to me. It seems almost scandalous that Jesus forgives even the worst sinners when they cry out for mercy. Oh, Dror, you have been coming to the Jewish Roots class for some time now, you are dating Grace regularly, a fine Christian girl, and you have heard Pastor preach many times. I know the seed of the gospel, the good news of salvation in Yeshua HaMashiach, has been planted in you. I wish you would accept Jesus as Savior and Messiah like I did that morning after I heard Jeff preach. I said to myself, 'Just do it!' And I am happy to say I have never looked back. More and more each day I know I have a personal Savior and Lord, Yeshua. In Judaism the hope is in a Messiah yet to come, but we Jewish believers and Christians know He has already come as the Lamb of God who takes away the sins of the world. We also know He is coming again as King. Just pray when you are alone, Dror. He will answer you."

Pete changed the subject. "Folks, we missed our lunch. I say we go book hotel rooms, rest a while, and then have dinner in a nice restaurant. We can go to bed early, get a good night's sleep and begin our search in the morning. I have some ideas. And I want to say by faith, 'We will find Susannah Goldberg tomorrow.'"

"Oh, yes, honey," Sarah agreed. "Do you realize we have been on the road since Wednesday night? This is the fifth day of traveling with the exception of Saturday. It's like the Jackson Police Department has become our 'home away from home.' I need time off and a good night's sleep."

"Right, Sarah. I can't miss any more days at work, and you can't either. In addition to that, we still need to show up in class. Thank goodness we are taking only two classes this summer."

Dror knocked on Pete and Sarah's door. "Boker tov, talmidim! Since we won't have Hebrew class tonight, I think we ought to speak as much Ivrit as we can today. Lecha, lecha! That means 'get going!' Slang is 'chop, chop!'" Dror was unusually cheerful.

"Good morning yourself. But also, savlanut, Professor, savlanut." answered Pete as he opened the door. "See, my wife and I are ready to play Sherlock Holmes today, so be patient, savlanut."

"Well, God wasn't patient with Abraham when He called him to leave home and set out for the Promised Land. He said, 'Lecha, lecha! Get going! In case you don't know, that is in Bereshit… oops! You know it as Genesis. It's chapter 12, verses 1-3, the call of Abraham." Dror loved to teach.

Pastor and Celeste walked out their door, suitcases in hand. The others got their suitcases and headed for the van. They quickly checked out of the hotel and drove to a nearby IHOP. After their lavish breakfast and a second cup of coffee, they were ready to go sleuthing. Pete had told Miss Celeste the night before that they were first going to the place she grew up, even though it was only a vacant lot. They would question people in the neighborhood. On the way they prayed that the Holy Spirit would lead them to the right house, and the right person would answer the doorbell. Celeste directed Pastor to the place. As they came in the driveway of the house across the street from the vacant lot they saw a colorful banner flowing from the doorpost. The words on it were "As for me and my house we will serve the Lord – Joshua 24:15." Celeste rang the bell, and an attractive gray-haired woman opened the door.

"Good morning. How can I help you?"

Celeste had a faint memory of this woman. "I am Celeste Gold James, and I used to live across the street from you. If you lived in this house at that time, then maybe you know or knew my parents, Isaac and Susannah Goldberg." Celeste studied the woman's face and saw that she was squinting at her and trying to recall if she knew this visitor.

"Oh, yes, I think I do remember you. You had a sister, didn't you? My name is Josephine Brown. My husband Nathan and I moved in this house when you and your sister were little children. Please come in, all of you." She smiled and showed them into the living room. "My husband is out in his workshop. Let me go get him. Please make yourselves comfortable."

Mr. Brown came in the room, wiping his sweaty face with his handkerchief. He extended his hand to each of them. "Welcome. My name is Nathan Brown. Please tell me all of your names." When he heard Celeste's middle name, Gold, his face lit up. "Oh, my, Celeste, it has been a very long time. You were only a child when I first knew you, and you were a teenager when I last saw you. I knew your parents, Isaac and Susannah Goldberg." Mr. Brown looked down, as memories flooded his mind.

Celeste didn't want to waste time. Silently, she lifted a prayer to God. *Oh, Lord, this is surreal. I thank You with all my heart for answering my prayers. I believe You have led us to the man who opened the gate of Heaven for my father right before he died! Put the words in my mouth now. Please let this miracle encounter lead us right to my mother.* "Mr. Brown, my sister Deborah ... by the way, Dror Mizrachi here is her son from Israel. I am Dror's aunt. He is looking for his grandmother, and I am looking for my mother, Susannah Goldberg. I changed my name to Gold, in case you are wondering. I am sorry I don't remember you, but I am thrilled that you remember **me** and especially my parents."

Nathan and Dror stood and shook hands. Dror repeated the story to Mr. Brown that his mother told him when she visited the synagogue and talked to Mrs. Rena Rabin. When he related the part about the house fire, Mr. Brown took over the conversation. His countenance glowed.

"Oh, glory! I praise the Lord that He is letting me see the fruit of my labor, as I see a pastor's wife and a fine young man from Israel sitting in my living room. Yes, I am the man who went back in the burning house and rescued your father, Mrs. James, and your grandfather, Mr. Mizrachi. I was highly privileged to pray for him as he lay dying from an apparent heart attack. I told him that Jesus was a Jew who kept the law perfectly, and He became the sin sacrifice that Isaiah described in the fifty-third chapter of his prophecy. I said that the thirty-nine stripes on his back that Jesus took from the Roman soldiers brought healing and salvation to all who would believe in Him as their Messiah. He was wounded by the nails in His hands and feet and the sword in His side. It was done for **our** transgressions, not His own. He was the sinless Lamb of God on the cross. Isaiah said, 'For the transgressions of my people, the Jews, He was stricken.' I raised my volume and said to Mr. Goldberg, 'He died for you and has forgiven you for your sins and offers eternal life to you if you will believe!' Mr. Goldberg smiled the biggest smile I had ever seen. He raised himself up and grabbed my collar and weakly said, 'I believe.' He lifted his hand, and then he drew his last breath."

Celeste was full of joy. Pete looked at his watch. He was rejoicing in his heart as much as Miss Celeste and Dror were, but they had come here primarily to find Susannah Goldberg, and he wanted to know where to search. "Mr. Brown, I can say on behalf of all of us that we are deeply grateful you saved Mr. Goldberg's life from the flames, and then you were the one to make sure he crossed over into heaven with a new, unending life." Praises and amens filled the room.

Celeste had many questions. "We are here to find my mother, and we can stay and search only one day. Can you tell us what happened from the time of my father's death up until you last saw her? Did you attend the funeral? Where did my mother go? I hope the car didn't burn up. I wonder if she had insurance and if she got a job to support herself."

Josephine Brown was glad she could finally carry out the request of her neighbor who had begged her to let her daughters know that some day they would meet again. "Yes, Mrs. James, we attended the funeral. I was shocked at the small attendance and that Susannah had so few friends. I knew she hardly ever came out of the house. I had wondered if she even knew how to drive. It seemed there was no help forthcoming, so I offered to drive her anywhere she needed to go. She asked me to take her to the bank the day after the fire and help her withdraw their money. Everything was burned up, so she didn't even have any identification! Bless Nathan's heart. He first notified the local synagogue, but no one offered to help, so he made the funeral arrangements himself. Susannah gave him part of the money. She remembered the name of their insurance company, so I took her there. Thank goodness, the man who identified himself as the Goldbergs' agent prepared the papers, though he apologized that the policy didn't pay much. Susannah was the sole beneficiary. He gave her a check for $10,000. It was the first time I had seen her smile since I knew her. That money seemed to give her hope that she would make it on her own. Fortunately, she could wear my clothes. We were the same size, so right after the fire, I gave her three outfits. It was so sad that she only had the nightgown she was wearing when the house burned. She wore the clothes I gave her until she could go shopping."

Celeste was sitting on the edge of her seat, trying to control her emotions. This was so hard to hear, and yet she understood that knowing the truth was, in effect, setting her free. "I am trying to picture it, Mrs. Brown. Her house was gone. Where could she lay her head? Right after the fire did she sleep in their car?"

"I offered her our guest bedroom for several weeks, until she could find an apartment to rent and a job. It's a good thing Nathan and I didn't have any children, or I would not have been able to give her so much of my time. Nathan and I urged her to go to church with us, since the synagogue had obviously no care for her or her husband, but she politely declined. I had to ask Susannah the reason the people of the synagogue did not come to her aid. She said that her husband was mentally ill and had alienated most of the people there. Well, that mystery was solved. But she did have one friend, an older lady named Rena Rabin, who was in poor health and didn't drive. Susannah talked on the phone to her a few times, but they soon lost touch with each other."

Mrs. Brown continued the story. "It appeared that Susannah didn't have any job skills. I helped her learn to drive, because she had to be independent and know her way around Jackson, whatever job she landed. One day we sat down right where we are sitting today, and I asked her, 'Susannah, what do you really want to do in life? Can you think of a job that would give you joy and would use the talents God has given you?' She didn't have to think long. She said, 'I want to dance for a living.' I was shocked. I said, 'Where in the world could you get a job dancing?' She quickly answered, 'I could be a dance teacher – after I learn all the dances, of course – and I could even be an entertainer!' She really became animated then. I said I would talk to Nathan, and maybe we could help her get started somehow. We prayed hard, because dancing was way beyond our life experiences."

Pete had an idea. "I think we need to find a dance studio nearby, a place like Arthur Murray Studios, where older people go to learn ballroom dancing. I wonder if there is one in Jackson. Maybe she took lessons there. What do you think, Mrs. Brown?"

"I really don't know. Not too long after that conversation, Susannah moved out. She had found a job as a clerk in a department store, and her pay was sufficient for her to rent a fairly nice apartment, she said. I don't know why, but she never called us to say where the apartment was. It broke our hearts that she never came back to visit."

"Oh, Mrs. Brown, I apologize for my mother. She was spiritually dead and obviously didn't know how to receive or give love. But I am sure that all the good seeds you and your husband deposited in her will one day bear fruit. Just like my father's salvation was a fruit of your husband's labor, my mother's salvation will be a fruit of your labor, Mrs. Brown. I just know it."

Nathan interrupted. "Honey, don't you remember the card we received several months after we last saw Susannah? It was a nice greeting card, a thank you note, and she wrote that she would never forget what we did for her. She assured us her job was going well. Enclosed were two $50 bills. She wrote that it was a small amount of money, not a sufficient thanks for our kind deeds, but she would send more later. There was no return address. The postmark was Shreveport, Louisiana. So that's all we know. Be assured that Josephine and I will be praying that you find Susannah, even today. We have seen God do miracles, so it's easy for us to believe. Please do come back and visit us and bring Susannah. I have never forgotten Isaac and her. Isaac was the first Jew, and the only one, that I ever led to the Lord. I felt it was a high honor. The Jews are God's chosen people. He will never turn His back on them."

CHAPTER TWENTY-TWO

REUNION!

As they drove away from the Browns' house, all gave thanks to God for the salvation of Celeste's father and the information they received that would help them find Celeste's mother. Sarah expressed sorrow that Mr. Goldberg had become confused about the beliefs of Judaism. She said, "My parents were loving people, and the Judaism they practiced is not the same as Mr. Goldberg's religion. My parents knew the Torah so well, that later in life it was not a huge leap of faith to believe in Yeshua as the Messiah, or at least that is what I think, not having talked to them about it. They gave me a good foundation in God's Word, but when I met the Living Word of God, Yeshua the Messiah, the emptiness in my heart was filled with love, joy, and peace. What a blessing to know that my parents found that, too, as Rabbi and Miriam Katz in Katzrin told us. When they died in the suicide bombing, they went straight to heaven to see Yeshua face to face and live with Him eternally."

Celeste got excited. "Oh, my goodness! The Lord has brought something to my mind from the time after Deborah and I had been banished from our house. Why am I just now remembering this? One day I was at my desk in math class, when a student came in the room and handed me a note from the principal's office. It said that someone wanted to speak to me and to come to the office. I went, but there was no one there except the secretary and the principal. They said a woman was looking for me and Deborah. She was in a hurry and wouldn't wait, but she got our address and said she would visit us after school. It didn't dawn on me that it was probably my mother! How could I have been so stupid? I made sure I went straight to Sally's house after school and called Deborah at her job to come home. The woman never came, and we forgot about it." Celeste pressed her husband on the arm. "It must be the Lord's timing that this memory has surfaced. At last I know where to look for Mother. Jeff, please let me guide you to the place." As Pastor drove, Celeste told her story. "Pete and Sarah, you haven't heard this, but I told it to Dror. After my father pushed us out of the house, Deborah and I went to live with a Catholic family. Our friend, Sally Donaldson, assured us that her mother would let us live there because they had five bedrooms, and also her mother worked with charities and had a big heart. We were amazed how rich they were and yet so humble and giving, Mr. Donaldson, too. Their house was a mansion. We went to church with them, but Deborah and I didn't believe that Jesus was the Messiah like they said he was. Anyway, we had a good life there for about three years. When I graduated from high school, we moved to Columbus and entered Mississippi University for Women, MUW. Deborah met Benjamin Mizrachi, and they married. I already told you how I met Jeff James and how I became a Christian."

Pastor was following the street signs as Celeste continued to direct him. "I see a big mansion up ahead. Is this it, Celeste?"

"Yes, it is. Oh, I'm getting chill bumps. It has been so long. After a few letters back and forth I quit communicating with Sally. I bet she is married now. We will probably only see her parents. I surely hope they are at home. All of you, stay in the van. I will go to the door."

As Celeste walked to the front door, Pastor led Pete, Sarah, and Dror in prayer. "Oh, Lord Jesus, please, please let the Donaldsons be home. And, Lord, do a miracle. Let Celeste's mother be on the other side of that door. We beseech You, in the matchless name of Jesus Christ, our Lord and Savior." Everyone said a loud amen.

Mrs. Donaldson opened the door. One quick look at Celeste, and she recognized her. "Celeste! Is it really you? Oh, my lovely 'adopted daughter,' come in, come in. I wish Sally were here." She saw the van in the driveway. "Please tell your friends to come inside." Reaching out for Celeste, Mrs. Donaldson hugged her tight. Celeste held on for a while, as good memories came to mind.

"It is so good to see you, Mrs. Donaldson. I must ask you something. We have been praying hard and have looked and looked for my mother, Susannah Goldberg. I have reason to believe she is looking for me and may have come here to visit you yesterday or earlier today. Please tell me she did." pleaded Celeste.

Mrs. Donaldson hesitated, but looking at Celeste's tear-stained face and distraught expression and hearing her anguished words, she could not carry out her mother's request. "Yes, Celeste, and she is here now. She insisted I tell her everything I could remember about you and Deborah, when you lived with us your last years of high school. But she made me promise if you came looking for her to turn you away until she gets settled in the city. Oh, I can't do it. I can't do it. Don't bring your friends in yet. I am going upstairs to get your mother."

Celeste prayed silently. As the two women came down the stairs, it appeared to Celeste that her mother was about to collapse, and Mrs. Donaldson was holding her up. Celeste hurried to the bottom of the stairs. "Oh, Mother, Mother, I love you, I love you, I love you! Thank God I have found you at last!" She wrapped her arms around her mother, holding her closely and sobbing.

Susannah struggled to control her emotions, a mixture of despair, guilt, and condemnation. She didn't want her daughter to see her like this. Her dress was too low cut. Her hair was dyed and too long. Her makeup and jewelry were too gaudy. But she couldn't let that hold her back. She knew if she turned her daughter away now, she may never have another chance to make things right. She remembered what she saw that night at the casino when she fell on the floor with the two sweet girls beside her. Recalling that vision gave her courage. Yes, it was now or never, she thought. Gently pushing her daughter away at arms' length, she said, "Celeste, let me look at you. It is really you! You are beautiful. I am so glad you found me. How did you get here?"

"Oh, Mother! My husband, Jeff James, drove me here. He's outside with another couple I have come to love, Pete and Sarah Carson. I will go get them. They will be almost as happy to see you as I am. They have searched for you and prayed many prayers for you. And, Mother, you have a grandson! It's Deborah's son, Dror. He came, too. Deborah married Benjamin Mizrachi in Columbus, and the three of them moved to Israel twelve years ago. Dror came back to search for his grandparents, for **you** and Father. He's a graduate student at Mississippi State University in Starkville, and my husband Jeff pastors a church there. I am a Christian pastor's wife. Mother, I know this is a lot to take in. Please sit down, and try to absorb it. I'm going outside to bring them in." Mrs. Donaldson helped Susannah to a chair and stood beside her, steadying her and gently stroking her hand.

When Celeste came out the front door of the house and started toward the van with smiles covering her face and a spring in her step, they knew their search was over, and a grand reunion was already taking place. Dror began shouting in Hebrew, "Toda rabbah, HaShem! Toda rabbah!" Pete and Sarah echoed him at the top of their lungs. Celeste motioned to them, and they were up the steps and into the living room in a flash.

The moment was so charged with emotion, that everyone tried to calm down, silently praying for the right words. Dror politely bowed in front of Susannah and knelt at her feet. Taking her trembling hands, he looked into her fearful face, as he searched for words to say. He knew his friends were praying for him. Cautiously, he began to speak. "Grandmother, I am your only grandchild, Benjamin Mizrachi Junior, nicknamed Dror. I live in Tel Aviv,

Israel. I came to America to find you, on behalf of my mother, Deborah Mizrachi, your daughter. As I look at you now, I can see the resemblance both to Aunt Celeste and Mother. You are pretty, just like they are. I rarely express love in words, but I have to say what I feel now – I love you, Grandmother." The others realized this young man had gone way out of his comfort zone, and now he was crying and was not ashamed.

Six happy people in the van soon passed the city limit sign of Jackson, Mississippi, going back to Starkville. They had so much to talk about and were stumbling over themselves to express what was in their hearts. Pastor and Dror were in the front seats, Celeste and Susannah in the seats behind them, and Pete and Sarah in the back seat.

Pete put in a call to Chief Braun to tell him the good news that Susannah Goldberg was no longer missing, and they were taking her back with them to Starkville. As the conversation lulled, Sarah leaned on Pete's shoulder and was soon asleep. There was such peace all around them. Susannah had agreed to go back to Starkville and make a new start, taking up residence with Jeff and Celeste. She didn't agree to attendance at church, at least not initially. Celeste discreetly handed Pete an envelope with $300 enclosed, a reward for finding her mother, but Pete refused it and said he would talk with her later about it.

Celeste knew in her heart that she was not to press her mother to talk about her past. It was enough that they were together, and she prayed silently that Susannah would be completely restored to health in every way. Then she got quite a surprise when Susannah looked at her and in a voice of wonder said, "I had a vision of Israel. I know it was Israel, because I have seen pictures of it, and I saw myself in the vision. I am not sure what it means. Maybe you can tell me."

"Oh, yes, maybe I can, Mother. Pete and Sarah are planning to move there, as well as their friends, Gloria and Jeff Quentin who are

Jewish, and so is Sarah. The four of them teach a Jewish Roots class in our church. Maybe you would like to attend," suggested Celeste.

Susannah stiffened up. "Oh, no, I don't want to get involved in church. I know I will be living in a Christian home. That will be enough for me to get used to after all the places I have lived." Shame covered her face.

Celeste would keep her vow to God not to put pressure on her mother, but she couldn't resist saying, "Well, I keep the nursery at church. I can always use some help. We have quite a few babies, and I am wearing myself out. Actually, young couples and college students make up the biggest part of our congregation."

Susannah remained quiet, but thoughtful. She knew her daughter was being kind, and she did not want to be difficult. She was eager to tell Celeste about her vision, but now was not the time, she knew.

Dror couldn't wait to get back to Starkville and call his mother with the good news. When he walked in his apartment, dialed his home number in Israel, and told his mother what happened, pandemonium broke out on the other end of the line. Deborah put Dror's dad on the phone, and he said, "Dror, your mission is accomplished. You found your savta. Return to Israel as soon as possible and bring Devorah's ima with you. I will send all the instructions for her to make aliyah."

Dror did not agree. "Abba, I must complete my master's degree in history, which I will have to rush to do by the end of May 2000. And I have fallen in love with a wonderful girl. It is my deep desire to marry her and bring her with me." His parents were overjoyed, until Dror told them she was a Christian.

CHAPTER TWENTY-THREE

THE NINTH
OF AV

Gloria was excited she had been asked to teach at the Baptist Student Union and could pick any subject, but it had to be Bible-related, of course. She chose the subject "Mourning on the Ninth of Av." This date on the Jewish or biblical calendar corresponded to sundown, Wednesday, July 21, going to sundown on Thursday, July 22, 1999, so her teaching would be on the exact day of their BSU meeting. How timely. She would combine the history of the Jewish nation with principles from Jesus' teaching. It was a hard subject, but it was relevant to Jeff, Sarah, Dror, Miss Celeste, Mrs. Goldberg, and her as Jews. Also Gentile believers needed to know it. Gloria was glad that Pastor was transferring Adaton's Wednesday night prayer service to the MSU campus to join the BSU meeting. It was a brilliant strategy because Susannah had already told them she wasn't ready to go inside a church building.

"Jeff, can you believe that Susannah Goldberg has agreed to attend tonight, only two days after moving in with her daughter and Pastor? I know God can do a quick work, but her willingness to come to a Bible study is putting my head in a spin." Gloria clapped her hands.

"I am looking forward to hearing what you will do with this subject, my beautiful wife. You are not only talented in music, but you are a gifted teacher. I am going to drink it in tonight, watching those luscious lips speak words of truth and love."

♥ ♥ ♥ ♥ ♥

Grace Thomas welcomed everyone to the BSU meeting and introduced the guests from Adaton Baptist Church. Word had leaked out over the campus about three teenagers and an older woman being rescued out of the sex trade from a gambling casino in Vicksburg, and some of the college students attending were a part of the rescue effort. The regular attendees looked around and saw many new faces. Every chair was taken.

As a few preliminaries were led by Grace, Gloria leaned over and whispered to Jeff, "Oh, my goodness. I hope these new people won't be disappointed that the program tonight is not about the rescue at the casino. But there is no way we can talk about that without mentioning Mrs. Goldberg, and how devastating it would be to her for people to find out she had been in the sex trade. At some future date it is possible she will want to tell her story publicly, but certainly not now. Jeff, please pray for me to be full of the Spirit as I speak. God knows what these college students, including us, need to hear, and He knows how to reach each one of them. There! I am not going to worry. But please pray." Jeff squeezed Gloria's hand firmly three times, code for "I love you."

Gloria began her message with a question. "Haven't we always heard it is darkest right before the dawn? Well from sunset tonight until sunset tomorrow is the anniversary of a tragic event that happened to the newborn nation of Israel in the Sinai desert over 3,400 years ago. The Israelites had come out of slavery in Egypt, led by Moses, on the way to the Promised Land, when the journey was halted by disobedience. Moses had sent a spy from each tribe of Israel to go and spy out the Land. Of the twelve spies, ten came back with a bad report, saying there were giants in the land, and the Israelites couldn't conquer them. Only two spies, Joshua and Caleb, said they could do it, that God had promised it. All the people, probably three million people, started crying and whining and wouldn't obey God to take the Land. So, regretfully, God had to judge them to wandering in the wilderness for forty years until all those disobedient people died out. The judgment happened on the ninth day of the fifth month on the biblical calendar, the month of Av. At sundown tonight is the beginning of the ninth of Av. The Jews still fast and mourn on this day."

A student in the back of the room raised his hand. "So, why make such a big fuss of remembering this day on the Jewish calendar every year and go into mourning? The Jews were always disobeying God. That's just the way they were. God even called them a 'stiff-necked people.'"

Gloria was actually glad this student with a low opinion of the Jews had asked this question. "You're right. Why the big deal? Well, it so happens that on this very day, the ninth of Av, there has been a string of tragedies in their history. Since I am Jewish, I can say it's my own history. God's judgment on that act of disobedience way back was the first one. Hold your hat. I am going to name the ones that have followed. Any of you who want this list, just ask me, and I will make you a copy. Ready to listen?

Both Jewish temples were destroyed on the ninth of Av – Solomon's temple in 586 B.C. and the second temple in A.D. 70, which was the result of the First Jewish Revolt.

The final battle of the Second Jewish Revolt (Bar Kochba) was lost at Betar on the ninth of Av, A.D. 135.

The First Crusade declared by Pope Urban II in 1096 resulted in 10,000 Jews massacred on the first day of the Crusade, the ninth of Av.

All Jews were expelled from England on this day in 1290. There were pogroms, confiscation of books and property at that time.

All Jews were expelled from France with great loss of property on this day in 1306.

The expulsion of Jews from Spain on the ninth of Av, 1492, came as a result of the Inquisition.

Hitler's 'Final Solution' began on August 2, 1941, which was the ninth of Av, and ended in the murder of six million Jews in the Holocaust.

The Jewish Community Center in Buenos Aires, Argentina, was car bombed on this day in 1994, the deadliest bombing in the country's history. Argentina has one of the largest populations of Jews outside Israel, 230,000.[46]

This is just the tip of the iceberg. The complete list is very, very long. It can't be coincidence that all these tragedies happened to the Jewish people on the same day, the ninth of Av. This verse from Isaiah 26:9 helps me make sense of it – 'When Your judgments are in the earth the people will learn righteousness.' How many times have you heard, 'I had to learn it the hard way'"?

Gloria observed the distressed looks of her audience. "I know you are beginning to wonder why this depressing subject is needed, and especially because it only affects the Jews. Hang on, and you will understand. You know the Book of Isaiah has a lot of judgments in the first half, but the second half of the book is filled with wonderful promises, beginning with Chapter 40. "Comfort, yes, comfort My people, says your God. Speak comfort to Jerusalem and cry out to her that her warfare is ended, her iniquity is pardoned! For she has received from the Lord's hand double for all her sins. A voice crying in the wilderness, 'Prepare the way of the Lord. Make straight in the desert a highway for our God.'"[47]

The same student raised his hand again. "I know those verses. They are about John the Baptist. He was announcing the coming of the Messiah."

"Yes, you are so right. Isaiah prophesied that the judgments on the Jews would end, and God would send them their Messiah to comfort them. When Jesus preached His Sermon on the Mount, He said, 'Blessed are they who mourn, for they shall be comforted.'[48] He was talking about people who are genuinely sorry for their sins. It gets very dark before the dawn, before the Bright and Morning Star comes, which Jesus calls Himself.[49] He comes to those who have been through horrible times, and they need His comfort. He said He would send the Holy Spirit, the Comforter, to His followers after He went back to heaven."

Grace Thomas raised her hand. "I think the Jewish people need comforting more than any other people group. It's hard to imagine why God's chosen people have had to go through such tragedies as happened on the ninth of Av. They have been hated down through the ages. And it reached a climax in the Holocaust! How much more could they take?"

"Thanks for pointing that out, Grace. But God had a plan to give His people a brand new start. He said, 'To you who fear My name, the sun of righteousness will arise with healing in His wings.'[50] Out of the ashes of the Holocaust the nation of Israel was reborn in 1948. At last these scattered people would have a place to put their roots down. There would be no more pogroms and no more being expelled from any country. And another thing Jesus said to suffering people like the victims of the Holocaust is, 'Come to Me, all of you who are weary and carry heavy burdens, and I will give you rest. Take my yoke upon you. Let me teach you, because I am humble and gentle at heart, and you will find rest for your souls. For my yoke is easy to bear, and the burden I give you is light.'"[51]

Someone raised her hand, an elderly woman, and the students turned to look at her. Gloria, Jeff, Pete, Sarah, Pastor, and Celeste, were shocked! It was Susannah Goldberg. Gloria prayed silently, *Help, Lord. Give me the right words more than ever now. Please comfort Mrs. Goldberg, please, Lord.*

Susannah stood. "What you said is important for me to understand, because my late husband was always saying, 'We must take the yoke of the law on us, no matter how hard it is to bear.' But you just said that the yoke of Jesus was easy, and it would give us rest. And while I am asking, I also want to mention that the Jewish people have special days of fasting and prayer about Solomon's temple being burned, the people taken captive to Babylon, and Jerusalem destroyed. My husband insisted we fast four different times, and one of them is on the ninth of Av. I don't want to disrespect God's law, but I have to say that being forced to do this made me hate being a Jew." Susannah sat down. Celeste squeezed her hand. Susannah was trembling and breathing hard, and Celeste could tell she was reliving that painful time in her past. She elbowed Pastor and indicated they needed to intercede for her.

Gloria smiled, "Ma'am, your personal experience has great relevance to this lesson. In my study of this subject I found that the Jewish leaders were faithful to keep these prayer and fasting times for many long years. In the Book of Zechariah, chapter 7, it says that the Jewish leaders went to Jerusalem to ask the priests, 'Should I weep in the fifth month and fast as I have done for so many years?' This was around 518 B.C., after the exiles had come back to rebuild the temple, and they were about half-way finished. Zechariah the prophet answered them, asking if they really did this for God or for themselves. He reminded them of their disobedience to God, and that is why He allowed the destruction of the temple and had to scatter them from His land. God had told them, 'Execute true justice, show mercy and compassion everyone to his brother. Do not oppress the widow or the fatherless, the alien or the poor. Let none of you plan evil in his heart against his brother.'[52] The prophet Isaiah in the 58th chapter says about the same thing. His message was that God hated their hypocrisy, thinking that their fasting would impress Him, when all the time they were ignoring needy people they were supposed to help – those wrongly imprisoned, their workers, the hungry, and the homeless. They even hid from their own relatives who needed help."[53] Gloria didn't understand why, but she felt like the Spirit was telling her to pause and let those words sink in.

Susannah leaned over and whispered to her daughter, "I need to leave now. This Bible lesson is dredging up my memories of the past. It's hurting me so bad. I am guilty of the same thing the Jews in that day did. I hid from you and Deborah. I wouldn't open the door, and I wouldn't answer the phone. Isaac told me not to let you back in the house, that you would defile it. How could I do such a thing? I was afraid of him, but I should have overcome my fear and done what was right. I have carried that burden all these long years."

Celeste didn't know what to do. Gloria surely was going to finish her lesson with words of hope, and her mother needed to hear them. Somehow, she had to keep her from leaving. She looked at her watch. "Oh, Mother, if I know Gloria, she will 'let the sun shine in' in just a few minutes. Like the song says, 'Open up your heart and let the sun shine in.' Please stay. Remember she started out by saying that it is darkest right before the dawn." She hugged her mother tight and kissed her on the cheek. Then she saw Susannah relax, and she sighed with relief.

Gloria noticed the whispered conversation between Celeste and her mother. She took it as a good sign but knew she must hurry to conclude the lesson on a note of victory. "Okay, we see that their fasting on the anniversary of the burning of the temple was not only futile, it was also sinful. God had never commanded it. The only mandatory day of fasting in His Word is on the Day of Atonement.[54] Maybe we can study about that sometime. But what I want to say about my own experience fits in here. I did something pretty bad when I was around twelve years old, and every year on the anniversary of that bad deed, I felt sad and begged God to forgive me. But two years ago I started to beg God's forgiveness, and He said, 'What sin? I don't remember that. Don't you believe that when you gave your life to Me and confessed your sins, that I cleansed you from all unrighteousness?' It was really God speaking to me because I found this verse: 'I, even I, am He who blots out your transgressions, for My own sake, and remembers your sins no more.'"[55] Gloria looked to see how Susannah might be responding to that good news. Sure enough, her countenance brightened some.

Pete spoke up. "Now, that is a verse I am going to memorize!" He looked around the room with a grin and said, "Can I get an amen?" The chorus of amens was punctuated with laughter.

"Well, I am ending the teaching with two more praiseworthy Bible verses, and all of us should memorize them, too. In fact, they are great songs, and if you get depressed, you can sing yourself happy. King David, the 'sweet Psalmist of Israel'"[56] was quite a musician, playing the harp, singing, and dancing, too. "Well, here I go. If you know it, join me in singing. It's from Psalm 30:11 – '*Thou hast turned my mourning into dancing for me. Thou has put off my sackcloth. Thou hast turned my mourning into dancing for me and girded me with gladness. To the end my glory may sing praise unto Thee and not be silent. Oh, Lord my God, I will give thanks unto Thee forever.*'" Gloria's voice was saturated with joy.

Pete was enjoying the teaching. He said, "I bet Job felt exactly the same as David did after all his suffering was over, and God restored his losses and gave him twice as much as he had before!"[57]

"Yes. Sometimes we have such great answers to prayer, it makes us want to shout or even dance. And guess what – I have a dance to teach you tonight. It is the national folk dance of Israel, and it's called the Hora. Some of you are thinking, 'I can't do that. Dancing is too worldly, and we shouldn't praise God that way.' My answer to you is to look at King David. If he danced in his worship of God, why can't we? His wife criticized him for dancing in public, and after that she was barren![58] But before we dance, let me give you the other verse that banishes sorrow and gives you joy in celebrating God's Word. This comes from the Book of Nehemiah. You remember that he was the one that God sent from Persia to Jerusalem to rebuild the walls. One day all the Jewish people gathered at the Water Gate, and Ezra read God's Word to them. They were distraught to hear the Law of Moses that they had broken, and they began to mourn, knowing they would be punished. But, surprise, surprise! I will read it to you: 'And Nehemiah, who was the governor, Ezra the priest and scribe, and the Levites who taught the people said to all the people, 'This day is holy to Yahweh your God; do not mourn nor weep.' For all the people wept, when they heard the words of the Law. Then he said to them, 'Go your way, eat the fat, drink the sweet, and send portions to those for whom nothing is prepared; for this day is holy to our Lord. Do not sorrow, for the joy of the Lord is your strength.'"[59] I need a few people to help me demonstrate this dance. My husband Jeff knows it, and so do Pete and Sarah. Also, my friend, Jane Jemison, who loves to dance, should come up here and help us. We will make a circle, and we will sing all three verses of 'The Joy of the Lord is My Strength.'"

Jeff, Pete, Sarah, and Jane came to the front, while Gloria taught everyone the additional verses to the song - "He heals the brokenhearted, and they cry no more," and "He gives me living water, and I thirst no more." Then, taking it very slowly, Gloria demonstrated the steps with the others following her. "People, after we sing and dance through the song, I want the rest of you to make more circles of about five to seven people. Of course, we will have to move the chairs to the sides of the room to make a dance floor in the center. Now, if you don't want to do this, it's okay. Just sing and clap your hands as we dancers whirl around."

Jeff craned his neck to see if anyone was leaving, but he could see that everyone seemed to be smiling and clapping and trying to sing, whether they were dancing or not. *Lord, I never would have believed it if I hadn't seen it with my own eyes. Thank You for giving us favor with our peers and for the joy I feel now. My Gloria is something else. Please make all of us as bold as she is. Oh, my, I see that Pastor, Miss Celeste, and Mrs. Goldberg have joined one circle, and they are having the time of their lives! What miraculous things You are doing in our midst, Father.*

After about fifteen more minutes of rejoicing, Jeff shouted above the cacophony, "Thank You, Lord, for turning our mourning into dancing. We bless You for taking our burdens, for healing us, for filling us with Your Spirit, and for making a way for us to express our joy because You have forgiven us for our sins, and You don't even remember them!" The dancers slowed down and gradually stood still with their heads bowed. Jeff continued with his prayer. "Heavenly Father, it feels so good to be comforted tonight, to know the presence of the Comforter. Thank You for teaching us that it is a holy thing to hear the Word of God, and we are not to weep or be sorrowful, for the joy of the Lord is our strength. You give us the power to walk in obedience to You and experience the abundant life Jesus promised. Help us not to forget that Jesus gives us an easy yoke and a light burden, and we can be obedient to Your commands through the power of the Holy Spirit. We pray in Jesus' name. And everybody said…" The room reverberated with the loudest Amen ever spoken there.

CHAPTER TWENTY-FOUR

A VISION

After Pastor, Celeste, and her mother returned home, Susannah pulled Celeste into the living room, saying "Sit down. We need to talk. Celeste, you know how uncomfortable I was tonight at the Bible study when Gloria was teaching from the Prophets about fasting. Was it okay when I stood up and said I hated being Jewish because your father made us keep laws like that, fasting four times every year to remember the temple being destroyed? Did it embarrass you?"

"Oh, no, Mother. I was glad you were interested in the subject. I told you I had hidden my Jewishness from Jeff until recently because I also have painful memories of Father treating us so strict. I blamed his religion, Judaism, and I hated being Jewish, too. Later, I found out he had a wrong interpretation of the Scriptures. He was causing himself pain, as well as you, Deborah, and me. Oh, Mother, your Isaac had a personal encounter with God right before he died. His chains dropped off, when his spirit rose up to heaven after the fire."

"How do you know that? You weren't there, and how do you know that there was a fire that destroyed our house?" Susannah's eyes looked wild.

"Your neighbors, Nathan and Josephine Brown, told me. That's how I know. Many years went by before Deborah went searching for you by attending your synagogue in Jackson. She found your friend, Rena Rabin, who told her about the fire and your neighbor, Nathan Brown, who pulled Father out of the flames. Mr. Brown prayed with Father, and Jesus saved him! And Mrs. Brown said she let you live with them a short while until you found a job and could get your own place. Oh, Mother, you must have had a horrible experience that night, seeing your house with all your belongings burn up and seeing Father have a heart attack and die."

Susannah began to cry, and it seemed she couldn't stop. Celeste reached out to comfort her. "Mother, if you want to tell me, I would like to know why you moved to Shreveport. Josephine Brown said you wrote them a nice thank you note and sent money, but there was no return address on the card, only the postmark of Shreveport. If you had rather not tell me, it's okay."

"Oh, yes, my darling daughter, I do want to tell you. I am ashamed of this part of my life, but I feel like I have to confess it in order to go forward. I worked as a clerk in a department store in Jackson, and at night I took dancing lessons and learned the main dances like the waltz, rhumba, tango, and even the modern dances. I learned tap dancing and ballet, which was my favorite. My teacher said I had a natural talent, and he would help me get a job in entertainment. He gave me the name of a man in Shreveport who hired dancers for floor shows in the big nightclubs. I won't go into detail, but that man hired me and assigned me to a dance captain in a nightclub. She and the choreographer were amazed that at my age I could do all the routines the young dancers did and even better. It was great fun for about ten years. I stayed clean and didn't date anyone or drink or do worldly things like the others did. I just wanted to dance. Everything was going well until this man followed me home to my apartment. He insisted I invite him in, but I said no, and I locked the door. He left and came back with another man. The two of them were able to get in my window, and they told me to pack my suitcase. They were going to take me to another nightclub where I could make more money and be the star performer. When I wouldn't go willingly, they forced me into their car. They kidnapped me! I did take part in the floor shows, but my costumes were vulgar, and men began to pressure me to go upstairs with them for sex. That was the beginning of the end for me, because I was trapped into becoming a part of the sex trade. That's enough to tell you, Celeste. I am so ashamed, so ashamed! I didn't want you and Deborah to know what I had become, so I never made an effort to contact you. Please forgive me for being such a horrible mother and for defiling myself."

Susannah convulsed with despairing sobs as Celeste cried with her and stroked her lovingly. "Mother, I don't need to forgive you. You were made to do those awful things against your will, and you were easy prey for the devil because of your isolation from our family who loves you. But after what you said happened to you that night in the casino when Elinor prayed, and the three of you were slain in the Spirit, I know God has cleansed you, according to His promise. I can hear Him saying this to you now – 'Come, let us reason together. Though your sins be as scarlet, they shall be as white as snow. Though they be red like crimson, they shall be as wool.' That's written in the Tanach.[60] Jesus paid the price for you to be free of your past, to know you are forgiven, and you are loved just like you are. I have experienced His salvation, so I know it's true. Jesus died for every sin in thought, word, and deed, for every person on the earth now and in the past and in the future, all in a moment of time on that cross in Jerusalem. He was the Lamb of God that Jews used to sacrifice at Passover, the Lamb of God who takes away the sins of the world. This is the verse you need to memorize, Mother – "For God so loved the world He gave His only begotten Son, that whosoever believes in Him should not perish but have everlasting life." I have a Bible for you with the New Testament in it, and that verse is found in the Book of John, who was one of Jesus' disciples. It is John 3:16. And it's bedrock truth."

"Well, I know so little, but I think I am beginning to believe. I can feel the love when I am around you and Jeff, and I could feel it strongly in that group of young people tonight. Yes, the love and the joy! I loved dancing the Hora. It was a good, clean dance, and it felt so right, a Jewish dance. I love your 'staff,' as Jeff calls them – Gloria and Jeff, Pete and Sarah. What lively, beautiful people they are. And I love my grandson Dror and Grace. Celeste, I think I will get up my courage and go to church on Sunday. Yes, something really did happen to me at the casino when Elinor prayed for us, and we went unconscious and fell to the floor. We didn't know how long we lay there. But when I came to, I knew I had been in the presence of God! Oh, Celeste, go get Jeff. I want him to hear this, too. I had a vision!"

Jeff was already listening at the door of the living room and praying as Susannah revealed her past. Celeste opened the door, and there he was with his finger on his lips, saying, "Shhh."

Celeste pretended she had walked to the den and brought Jeff back. "Okay, Mother, tell us what you saw in your vision."

Susannah became very animated, and her face lit up as she described her vision. "I was lying on the ground asleep. An angel came and woke me up and held out white garments for me to change into. Then a glowing ladder reaching to heaven appeared. The angel took my hand and climbed the ladder with me. At the top was the most beautiful Man I have ever seen. He had on a white robe, too, but it wasn't like mine. His shimmered like it was made out of diamonds, and there was a golden sash around his waist. His eyes were pure love, and I couldn't stop staring at Him. It was almost like drinking in the love as I looked into His eyes. I felt like He knew everything about my past, but He loved me anyway. Then I went into His arms, and as He held me close, I felt a soft rain drenching my body and making me clean like I had never been before. He pointed to a golden city in the distance, but He didn't take me there. The scene changed, and I was at the foot of some hills. The Man pushed me toward the tallest one and said 'Go up!' Then I saw some cute little deer scampering quickly up to the top of the hill. The Man pointed at my feet and said, 'Follow them.' His eyes were like fire, and I could not resist obeying Him.

I put my feet in the tracks of the deer, and up I went! When I got on the very top, I looked down, and I saw a beautiful Land. The Man did not tell me, but I just knew it was the Land of Israel. Then the scene changed again. I was on a stage dancing with other dancers. We were in a circle, and the audience was on its feet, singing and clapping in rhythm. Joy was flooding the auditorium. I remember the words I saw coming out of the Man's mouth. It was awesome to see the three-dimensional block letters in gold, spelling out the words that were waving in the air over the audience. He said, 'For you shall go out with joy, and be led out with peace; the mountains and the hills shall break forth into singing before you, and all the trees of the field shall clap their hands.'[61] That ended the vision, and I was back in the room with Elinor and Julie. The contrast between the vision and the reality of my sorry condition was almost too much for me to take. I cried my heart out for God to forgive me. I knew that He was my only hope."

Jeff was thinking about his role as Susannah's son-in-law, but now he had to be her pastor. "Susannah, is it okay if I call you that?"

"Surely. Something tells me I should call you 'Pastor,' and not 'son-in-law.' And is that okay with you?"

"Yes, I am your pastor." Jeff eagerly assumed his role as pastor, as a loving shepherd for his torn and tattered mother-in-law. "Susannah, God gave me the interpretation of your vision as you were telling it. It shows that God's presence has been with you during your life's journey, but He has never been closer to you more than when you were trapped in the sex trade. The angel climbing the ladder with you is reminiscent of Jacob's dream when he was on a journey to find a wife and stopped at night to sleep. He dreamed of a ladder from earth to heaven and angels going up and down on it. Scripture says, "Then Jacob awoke from his sleep and said, 'Surely Yahweh is in this place, and I did not know it.' And he was afraid and said, 'How awesome is this place! This is none other than the house of God, and this is the gate of heaven!'"[62]

Susannah seemed transfixed by what she was hearing. "I don't know what to say. The 'house of God,' the 'gate of heaven?' Oh, my! You mean my vision compares in some way with Jacob's experience?"

"Most definitely, Susannah. Celeste, please write down all these Scripture references for your mother to study later. Let me go on with the interpretation. Susannah, the Man you saw at the top of the ladder was Jesus. He is described as having eyes like fire and a gold sash around his chest. Celeste, write down Revelation 1: 13-14. The robe shining like diamonds is what His disciples – Peter, James and John – saw, when Jesus took them up on a mountain and was transfigured before their eyes. That is found in Matthew 17: 1-8 and also Luke 9: 28-36. This is the best part, I think. When Jesus held you in his arms, and you felt a cleansing rain, it reminds me of Mary Magdalene. She had been 'a woman of the streets,' but Jesus loved her and cast seven devils out of her. She never left him after that. And she was the very first person to see Him alive from the dead. Also, she was the first person He commanded to go and tell others that He was alive. Susannah, Jesus has given you a high honor in this comparison. I know you didn't see Mary Magdalene in your vision, but I think the Lord has told me that you are similar to her. Celeste, write down Luke 8:1-3 and Mark 16:9-10 and John 20:11-18."

"Pastor, my heart is beating so fast, I hope I don't die. I can hardly wait to get my new Bible and start reading all these Scriptures about my vision. Please go on, and tell me about the deer. I felt the most joy of all when I followed the deer up the mountain."

"This scene takes place at the very end of the book of Habakkuk, and there is an important lesson to learn from the way God created the feet of the deer, so they could swiftly flee from danger and surmount all obstacles before them. Their path was treacherous up the rocky landscape, but God gave them special feet to make their steps sure and enable them to reach their promised land. Since you are a dancer, Susannah, the Lord wants you to know that He is making your own feet like the feet of the deer. You should read the whole book of Habakkuk, the prophet. It is short and begins with the prophet's distress about the Babylonian army advancing on Jerusalem to destroy it. He questions God how He can let Jerusalem be destroyed by those more wicked than they. I marvel how God gave you a vision just like He did Habakkuk. He said for Habakkuk to keep watch. Here is God's answer: 'Write the vision and make it plain on tablets, that he may run who reads it. For the vision is yet for an appointed time; but at the end it will speak, and it will not lie. Though it tarries, wait for it; because it will surely come, it will not tarry.' Susannah, I think your vision is definitely going to come to pass. If I understand it correctly, you will be dancing in Jerusalem with great joy!"

Susannah jumped up and clapped like a little girl. "Oh, let it be so, HaShem!"

"But remember, you will have to watch and wait for the vision to come to pass. There will be times you will begin to doubt, but remind yourself that God has already shown it to you in the last part of your vision. There will be obstacles, but you are not to be discouraged. In the third chapter, Habakkuk makes a mighty declaration of faith that he will not be affected by what his eyes see, but he will only be moved by what God said. He had been told to live by faith. He would see the terrible judgments of God come on the nation for their idolatry, but he would need to remember the end result, a people brought to repentance and saved by His mighty hand. Here are the closing words: 'Though the fig tree may not blossom, nor fruit be on the vines; though the labor of the olive may fail, and the fields yield no food; though the flock may be cut off from the fold, and there be no herd in the stalls – Yet I will rejoice in Yahweh, I will joy in the God of my salvation. Yahweh God is my strength; He will make my feet like deer's feet, and He will make me walk on my high hills.' Verses 17-19."

"Honey, I love all these things you are saying and the Scriptures that confirm your interpretation. Now tell us what the Lord is telling you about the end of Mother's vision about the golden letters coming out of the mouth of Jesus when she was dancing on a stage. That verse, Isaiah 55:12, is so beautiful. How happy it is, and I can see Mother dancing to those words," said Celeste.

"Okay, now Susannah, that verse describes what is happening to you, and it is not future, but it is right now. You have been led by the Spirit of God to this very moment, and you have something to do in order for your vision to be fulfilled. Remember that God told Habakkuk to have faith. Well, that is what He is saying to you now, 'Have faith.' The words of Isaiah have a double meaning. The first meaning is that the Jewish exiles are returning to Jerusalem with great joy and peace. They have been freed from captivity. Yahweh has saved them! The second meaning is a description of you. 'For you, Susannah, shall go out with joy, and be led out with peace; the mountains and the hills shall break forth into singing before you, and all the trees of the field shall clap their hands.' Your dancing in Jerusalem will be received by the audience with clapping and singing. And who is the One who has set you free from captivity in the sex trade, from the bondage of sin, and from the hopelessness of your life? It is Jesus, the King of the Jews and the Savior of the world. He wants you, Susannah, to acknowledge Him as your own personal Savior and Lord, your Boss. Will you do it?"

"Yes, I will do it! His eyes are like fire. I must obey. He loves me. He has cleansed me. Celeste told me that I am as white as snow now. I am pure, because Jesus died for my sins. He loves me like He did Mary Magdalene. I want Him. What do I do, Pastor?"

"Let's get on our knees, and I will lead you in a prayer of repentance and faith. When you get up off your knees, you will be born again. You will be a new creation of God. Behold old things will have passed away, and all things will become new!"[63]

After Susannah invited Jesus to come into her heart, Pastor James had a new lamb in the fold, his own mother-in-law, and she was a sight to behold. Whereas before, she rarely smiled, now she would be smiling almost all her waking hours. Yes, she was brand new, and she was ready to share her story of deliverance so other captives could be set free. The first thing she did was to call Nathan and Josephine Brown, her neighbors in Jackson so many years ago. She told them she had been born again, and she thanked them profusely for all the love and care they showed both Isaac and her.

SUSANNAH GOING TO ISRAEL

Dror was amazed on Sunday that his grandmother was attending the Jewish Roots class, and he heard her say she would go to the worship service. It was Sarah's time to teach the class. Gloria had introduced a new unit on the Second Coming of Christ the Sunday before with Grace's assistance. She handed out the lesson notes, thanked Grace for helping her with the first lesson, and then introduced Sarah as teacher for the second lesson. Dror saw his grandmother taking notes. His aunt and Pastor were seated beside her to give her help in finding the Scripture references in her new Bible. Of course, Grace was busy taking notes and underlining verses in her Bible. Suddenly, he had a sinking feeling. He whispered to Grace, "I see that Sarah is using a lot of passages from the Tanach with which I am very familiar, but her quoting Jesus in the Brit Hadasha is making me uncomfortable. I need to talk to you later."

Grace smiled and whispered back, "I will be glad to talk to you about this subject."

"But I also have questions about aliyah for my grandmother. You know I am returning to Israel after this school year and planning to take Savta with me."

"Savta?"

"Yes, that's Hebrew for 'grandmother.' Do you mind if I ask her to come with you and me to my apartment after lunch?"

"Dror, I've never been to your apartment, of course, but with Mrs. Goldberg there, I will be happy to come," answered Grace. "And we better quit talking. I see Sarah staring at me."

Dror decided to get fast food after the service and take it to his apartment. His savta and Grace said that was fine with them. He told them to wait outside until he straightened up. It would only take five minutes, he promised.

"Welcome, Grandmother and Grace, to my bachelor's apartment. Before you say anything, I want you to understand that I always keep it clean and neat, but, unfortunately, I have let it go the last two weeks. As you know, my life has become a whirlwind of exciting exploits."

Grace laughed. "Would you believe your place is neater than mine?"

As they enjoyed their food at the table in the kitchen, Susannah kept up a steady stream of chatter. It was obvious she could hardly contain her joy.

"Grandmother, I am going to start calling you 'Savta,' which is Hebrew for 'grandmother,' because in only a few months you will be in Israel with me and 'Ima' and 'Abba,' Mom and Dad."

"Whaaat?" Susannah seemed to be in shock. "Oh, Dror, you are going to fulfill my vision so soon!"

"Savta, I don't understand. What vision?"

"I will tell you all about it later, except that in the vision I was in Israel. But I want you to talk now and say everything that is in your heart, Grandson."

"Well, as Gloria would say, that is for sure a 'God-incidence,' that you had a vision about being in Israel. My purpose in coming to Mississippi was to search for you, Savta, as well as to get my master's degree in History of the U.S. South. Then, if I found you, I planned to take you back with me to Israel. Well, I found you. Now we must get the ball rolling for you to make aliyah. Ima doesn't doubt that I will talk you into it, and she is so excited and is already painting and redecorating a bedroom for you. Abba is beginning to prepare your aliyah papers. He will be contacting you with questions, so he can fill out the forms."

Susannah was breathless. "Dror, in all the excitement I forgot I need to talk to Deborah. But, of course, I don't know how. You must call her right now and put me on the line. Oh, Deborah, my firstborn, I must talk to her. Yes, I want to go with you, Dror. I want to live with you in Israel."

Dror dialed the number. "Savta, it is before 9:30 p.m in Israel now, so I know Ima is awake.... Shalom, Ima. I have good news. Savta has agreed to accompany me to Israel in June. She wants to speak to you." Dror handed the phone to Susannah.

Susannah choked back the tears. "Hello, Deborah, my daughter. The first thing I want to say is 'I love you!' The next thing is 'Please forgive me for being such an awful mother and hiding from you after Isaac pushed you out of the house.' Let me go on to say that I love your son, my grandson. And all the people here in Starkville, Mississippi, are wonderful, wonderful. I am a changed person, and I can hardly wait to hold you and love you and make it up to you for all the years we have been separated. Just say you forgive me, please. Oh, please forgive me."

Dror and Grace watched Susannah's face light up with joy as she listened to her daughter's words, evidently words of love and forgiveness, welcoming her to live with them. Susannah replied with words of thanks and joyful expectation of spending the rest of her life in Israel with Deborah, Benjamin, and Dror.

Susannah handed the phone back to Dror for his closing of the conversation. She was smiling from ear to ear. "Oh, wait a minute. What about Celeste? I can't leave her behind."

Grace spoke up. "Mrs. Goldberg, I overheard Pastor and Miss Celeste talking about the likelihood that you would be going to Israel with Dror. Miss Celeste was assuring Pastor that her place was right here at Adaton with him, and she wasn't going to beg him to move to Israel. She said they could visit Israel twice a year and maybe stay for a month each time, but she would be happy here, and he should not worry about her feeling left behind. In fact, she said the Holy Spirit told her she must stay here, and He would fulfill all her desires."

Susannah sighed. "Thank you, Grace, for reassuring me. I know God is calling me to Israel. Yes, I will look forward to long visits with Celeste and Jeff in Israel every year. Dror, will you also bring me back to Starkville to visit Celeste and Jeff twice a year?"

"Savta, it will be my pleasure. You know I have to see Grace as often as I can. I have fallen in love with her." Grace reached for Dror's hand under the table and squeezed it.

Susannah wondered if she should try to intervene in this romance to hasten the relationship to its obvious conclusion. She began to talk to herself. *Old woman, what do you know about romance and true love? Nothing. And you hardly know your grandson and Grace. All you know is what you have observed between them. I wonder if Grace loves Dror. It looks like she does, but it won't hurt to ask.* "Grace, my grandson has admitted he loves you, but do you love him?"

"Yes, Mrs. Goldberg. I do love Dror. It happened the night I had finished my piano lesson with Gloria in the church and was waiting in the pew while Dror took his lesson. He and Gloria should not be left alone, I realized, so I stayed. My heart did flip-flops when Gloria introduced us. It may be trite to say, but I loved him at first sight." Dror reached out and hugged Grace close to him.

Susannah bit her tongue. She was about to say, "Then why don't you get married?" *Oh, thank You, Holy Spirit, for showing me the problem. Grace is a sincere believer, and Dror does not yet believe like she does that Jesus is the Messiah. He is a typical Jew who has been taught that Jesus is not the Messiah.*

Susannah felt the nudging of the Holy Spirit to give her testimony. "Children, I need to tell you how I first experienced love, and it wasn't from a man, at least not from a human. I may not even be alive today if Jesus Christ by His Spirit had not rescued me from a hopeless life of degradation. He pursued me. I didn't pursue Him. In fact, he knocked me out, and that's when I had the vision and knew He was real. He saved me. It was only four days ago that I got on my knees, and Pastor and Celeste led me in a prayer of salvation. I was born again! I am brand new, and I am walking in the marvelous life God planned for me even before I was born the first time. God was gracious to surround me with Christians and Jewish people who know He is the Messiah. I saw His hand at work in them. I wondered what this 'being saved' was all about, and I found out it was receiving eternal life through Yeshua – that's His real Hebrew name, and it means 'salvation.' Dror, you know that because you know Hebrew. I was told He would save me, and I thought, 'Save me from what?' The answer was 'Save me from hell!' I am not afraid to say it. Your grandfather was headed there until the moment before he died, and he said yes to Yeshua. I was headed there, too. Yeshua said, 'I am the Way, the Truth, and the Life. No one comes to the Father except by Me.' John 14:6."

Dror was moved by his grandmother's testimony, but he tried not to show it. Grace knew something was wrong, or maybe something was right, when she saw tears in Dror's eyes. "Are you okay, honey?"

"I have to say, your testimony, Savta, makes me emotional, knowing all the terrible things you have gone through for long years. I am thankful you have found peace, and you have found joy, too. I have my own beliefs, but it doesn't keep me from rejoicing with you. I do regret I never met my grandfather, but it is also good to know he died in peace, and you saw it happen."

"I am not quite finished. I want to say there was one more verse that cut me to the heart and propelled me to the decision to give my life to Jesus. It is John 3:16. Some people say that one verse sums up the New Testament. 'For God so loved the world that He gave His only begotten Son, that whosoever believes in Him should not perish but have everlasting life.'"

Grace could see that Dror was struggling. *Show him, Lord, show him how much You love him. Help him to throw off the shackles of the rabbis' teachings that Jesus is not the Messiah. Give me patience to wait and not interfere with Your work in him.*

CHAPTER TWENTY-SIX

AN IMPORTANT
LETTER

MONDAY, AUGUST 2, 1999

Gloria called Jeff at the office. "Jeff, come home right away. I have the most astounding news. I want to read you the letter that came today. Hurry, I am bursting with excitement."

Gloria read the letter over and over and kept looking out the window for Jeff's Ford to drive up. Finally, he arrived. "I hope you are not exaggerating. I was on a roll, getting all my work done. Honey, we are really making great profits for Dad's company, and he said he was giving me a raise. Now does my news match yours?"

"I don't think so, dear husband, but my news does involve future financial benefits. Sit down, and I will read this to you. It's from Edsel Gruber, and he has enclosed a concert program, 'Holiday Concert in Jerusalem.' Can you believe that I, Gloria Sondheim, am the featured performer?"

"Whoo! Mazel tov, my beautiful diva. But we gotta talk about your 'stage name.' I prefer Quentin. Anyway, get on with it. I am all ears," exclaimed Jeff.

"I can just picture my adorable Mr. Gruber, grinning broadly, as he wrote this. Well, here it is:

> *Dear Gloria, my protégé,*
>
> *You knew I was using every ounce of my influence as an American concert manager to get you on the music stage in Jerusalem,*

and my constant advocacy for you has paid off. Professor Giovanni Galante of Hebrew University Academy of Music and Dance is the program manager for the holiday season, which includes Hanukkah. On behalf of Hebrew University, he has accepted sponsorship of your concert after Hanukkah. It cannot take place at the University, however, because of a security lockdown. Each individual attendee would have to get a security clearance, and that would discourage most people from attending. But what looked like a bad thing has turned into a good thing! You will be performing at Binyenei Ha Uma in the Ussishkin Auditorium. My dear, that is the International Convention Centre. And it seats 3,000 people!

Mrs. Pagani told me that your school term is over on Friday, December 10th, and you will not be returning to school until January 3rd, so you will have time to perform in two concerts during the winter season. Israelis do not celebrate Christmas, of course, but they at least give it a nod in their holiday decorations and music programs. Hanukkah will be celebrated from December 3rd until the 11th, so I will get you and Jeff and Bianca tickets to fly out on the 12th or 13th after the traffic has cleared out and return on the 30th, if you can stay that long.

When I showed Galante pictures of you on the concert stages in Europe and also the newspaper articles, he was quite impressed and decided to let you be the sole performer, with the exception of a few numbers by an ensemble, the University Singers. I suggested to him that you could sing two or three arias from Handel's 'Messiah,' as well as a few secular Christmas songs. I reminded him of the throngs of Christian pilgrims to Bethlehem each year, and he agreed. The University is always in need of funds, so he became quite excited about having a large Christian audience, and he mentioned a ticket price. I am afraid he has set it too high, but he assured me that the local Israelis would flock to the concert along with the Christian tourists. He told me that Israelis in general, not the religious ones, are curious about Christmas.

I have enclosed a tentative concert program for your approval, but you may edit it any way you see fit. I am sure you will pray and get your answers from 'the man upstairs.' I am getting acquainted with Him in my church attendance and Bible reading. I have to admit that I also prayed before I contacted Galante. I can see you smiling as I write this, my American singing sensation.

As we go forward let us make all our communication through Bianca. She wants you in concert in Jerusalem, but her greater desire for you is that you obtain a piano scholarship to the Academy of Music and Dance on the Givat Ram campus. Through her colleague, a piano professor there, she is working very hard on it.

And, finally, I want to say that I only included one piano number for you, the "Hallelujah Chorus," accompanied by the University Choir and Orchestra, which will be the finale. Galante agreed with that. You and Bianca can make the final decision about any additional piano numbers, but your vocal solos will bring the heartiest applause.

Mazel tov, my songbird.
Sending heartfelt love,
Edsel Gruber

"Gloria, I am so happy for you. But it's a long time for me to be gone from the Distribution Center. I will have to call Walter and see if he can fill in for me. If I can't go, you would be fine with only Mrs. Pagani going with you, right?"

"Oh, Jeff, you are the wind beneath my wings. I need you. It will be a great opportunity for Walter to manage the company alone. And if he runs into any problems, he can call you."

"Honey, how can I not go when I look at your big, pleading brown eyes? Of course I will go. But if we are in Israel for two-and-a-half weeks, that is a very long time. Both our parents will be disappointed, not getting to spend the holidays with us."

"That's true, but we could spend Christmas with Papa Sam and Mama Anna in Katzrin. It will be be our two-year anniversary of our first trip to Israel at the very same place!" exclaimed Gloria.

"Oh, what memories. I will look forward to that. Also, that will give you plenty of time to sign up for courses at the University for the next summer or fall term. I know they will offer you a scholarship after they hear you sing and play at the concert. All the voice and piano teachers will compete with each other for you as their student. They will see that you are unflappable onstage."

"And what in the world does that mean, 'unflappable'?"

"It means nothing fazes you. People raising the roof with thunderous applause, throwing themselves at your feet, and throwing flowers on the stage will not go to your head. You will deflect all the glory to the Creator and Redeemer who gave you such fantastic musical talent! You passed the test in Europe, and I know you will pass the test in the Holy City. Worldly acclaim will not move you, my sweet, innocent Gloria."

"But isn't Jerusalem the place that Satan tempted Jesus to throw Himself down from the highest point of the temple to attract the praise of men?[64] If it was a temptation for Jesus who was perfect, then what makes you think that I will not succumb to the temptation?"

"I will tell you why. It's because the same Spirit that was inside Jesus that raised Him from the dead is the same Holy Spirit inside you, my love!"[65]

CHAPTER TWENTY-SEVEN

THANKSGIVING

"It's our two-year engagement anniversary, Mrs. Quentin. And you have never been more gorgeous or appealing to me. Your complexion is rosy, and you exude wholesomeness and health. Uh, hmm…. Oh, no, I just had an alarming thought. You aren't pregnant, are you, Gloria?"

Gloria's melodious laughter caused Jeff to draw her in his arms and cover her mouth quickly with his lips. "Don't say it, don't say it. We are moving to Israel in six and a half months. That will be so hard on you, babe. Please tell me you aren't pregnant, not yet. I want a baby, but not until we are settled in Zion, our Jewish homeland." Then Jeff covered her lips again before she could speak.

Gloria finally got loose and ran around the house, daring Jeff to catch her. "I won't tell you, husband, until you say, 'It's wonderful if you are pregnant now or any time.'"

Jeff caught her, sat her down on the sofa, and sighed. "Okay, you win. I accept your pregnancy. God knows what He is doing. It's all good, and I alone will do the packing and lifting of boxes, et cetera, et cetera."

Gloria laughed and laughed. "Who said I was pregnant? Certainly not me. Where did you ever get that idea?" Jeff hugged his teasing wife and tickled her until she yelled, "Stop!"

"You are gonna pay for this, Gloria. No more teasing about such a life-changing thing. I don't have the time to be a cardiac patient."

Gloria laughed some more and smothered her husband with kisses. "Yes, it's the second anniversary of our engagement, and we are both getting an awesome present. I heard from Mom and Dad today, and they are coming to Starkville to celebrate Thanksgiving with us, since I told them that your parents are coming. Isn't that great?"

"Well, my parents can drive over from Tupelo for the day, but your parents can't drive over from New York, so how long are they staying? Wait, I have an idea. I will call Mom and ask her to invite them. We can pick them up at the Golden Triangle Airport and drive to Tupelo. As you know, our house is big enough to accommodate all of us, and I'm sure we can stay two or three nights. It's time for your folks to find out what a good cook my mom is, as well as our maid Jetty. I know your father, a gold-star caterer, will be impressed."

"Honey, your plan sounds perfect to me. Please get the ball rolling. Speaking of rolling, I regret the Holy Rollers can't be together for Thanksgiving like we were in New York at my house, when you proposed and gave a ring to me. Sarah and Pete have their own Thanksgiving plans in Columbus at Pete's house. And it's so nice that they invited Dror and Grace."

♥ ♥ ♥ ♥ ♥

Leah Quentin opened wide the door and welcomed her Thanksgiving guests with Jeffrey at her side. "Baruch haba! Welcome. Come right in, Sylvia, Alvin, Gloria, and Jeff. Let us take your wraps. We can sit in the living room while Jeffrey and Jeff unload Jeff's Ford and take your suitcases upstairs. I am honored that you are staying three nights with us. As you said, Jeff, this gathering is very special for you and Gloria, being the second anniversary of your engagement to be married. And the 'scene of the crime' was at your house in New York, Sylvia and Alvin."

"Scene of the crime indeed," laughed Sylvia. "Their abrupt announcement immediately after they arrived at our house nearly gave me a heart attack! Jeff Quentin was a complete stranger to us, you understand. But later after dinner when Jeff knelt down and gave Gloria the sparkling engagement ring and made his emotional speech, I felt the greatest joy. And Leah, I have always wanted to visit Jeff's home and eat your good cooking. Gloria brags about it. But Alvin has sort of a 'wait and see' attitude."

Alvin hastened to correct what he perceived to be a false image of him as a caterer. "Now Sylvia, if my daughter, who has eaten the finest cuisine all her life, judges Mrs. Quentin to be an exceptional cook, then I am sure it is the truth. Now there!" Alvin laughed.

The friendly patter continued throughout supper with Leah receiving the accolades her husband and son fully expected. They poured it on so thick she blushed, but she didn't want to take all the credit. "Well, I am fortunate to have Jetty here for our meals this entire weekend. I do most of the cooking, but I could never have a holiday meal without Jetty. For tomorrow she will make two dishes I haven't mastered – the pone cornbread and her signature chocolate pie."

Jeff cheered. "Jetty, I can hardly wait." Jetty was all smiles as the family complimented her.

"Well, let us retire to the living room. Jeffrey has an announcement to make, and he is champing at the bit to trumpet it." Leah preceded her guests and indicated the seating.

As soon as everyone was comfortably settled on the sofas and chairs, Jeffrey set the stage for his announcement. "Well, son, how are your aliyah plans coming?" he asked. "Leah and I are happy for you and Gloria, as well as for Pete and Sarah, but we have been commiserating about our only child moving across the ocean. We can't bear to lose you and not be able to see our grandchildren when they are born. Of course, we know that we have the money to fly over there as often as we wish. But that is not the same thing as being within driving distance, or dare I say it, within walking distance and be able to see you weekly or even daily. Leah and I love Israel as much as you two."

Leah added, "Jeff, I will admit it. Jeffrey and I have been jealous. Hold your hat – we want to make aliyah, too, and we're going to do it!"

Gloria stared at the Quentins in wonder. "Oh, my goodness, you are? 'Yofi!'"

Leah grinned. "Gloria, don't think I am unaware of what you said. You said 'Great!' You see, Jeffrey and I have been studying Hebrew, and we are preparing ourselves. In fact we may go before you do. Tell them, honey."

"Okay, here is my proposition, Jeff and Gloria. I have already taken the initial steps to set up a food business in Jerusalem. I flew over there and began the process just two weeks ago. Jeff, I want you to manage it for me after I get it off the ground. Leah and I can live in Israel off the income from the Tupelo and Starkville offices. But you and Gloria need income."

Jeff and Gloria gasped. "Dad, this is not a big surprise to me. God gave me a dream about it several months ago. I wanted to call you then, but Gloria said I should wait until you got it all set up. I can hardly believe it. Gloria was right. She is a prophetess. In fact we have learned that all four of us Holy Rollers have a prophetic destiny in Israel. Oh, Dad, my heart is about to beat out of my chest!"

Gloria explained, "Here's the sad part. From our research and talking to Dror, we discovered that we may not be able to make aliyah and get an identity card and all the perks of citizenship. Jeff, Pete, and Sarah will have to get work visas for the first 30 days and work permits, which require renewal every year. I hope to get a music scholarship, preparing me for a music job. My A/2 student visa will be good for a year, and I will have to have it renewed annually. We won't be accepted as immigrants because we are Messianic Jews, believers in Jesus, which makes us non-Jews in the eyes of the government! They say we have converted to another religion,

Christianity, so we don't qualify to make aliyah. We will not lie and sneak in. We have made up our minds that we could never deny that we believe Yeshua is the Messiah. And they will ask that question. The four of us refuse to be downhearted though. We trust in our miracle-working God that He will make a way where there seems to be no way. And now, hearing your plans, Mr. Jeffrey, I see that God is answering our prayers through you and Miss Leah for steady income. Praise the Lord!"

Alvin spoke up. "Yes, we know all about that from Papa Sam and Mama Anna's situation. It is an absolute miracle that their citizenship hasn't been revoked. I have to say that Sylvia and I are having our eyes opened daily to the power of prayer."

Gloria looked at Jeff's parents. "Miss Leah, just how are you and Mr. Jeffrey going to qualify to make aliyah? Didn't I hear that you now believe that Yeshua is the Messiah?"

"Yes, yes, we do, Gloria. But, HaShem was looking ahead and kept us from being so public about it. Some time ago we made a decision to attend Temple B'Nai Israel right here in Tupelo. The makeup of the congregation goes from Orthodox Jews to Reform Jews. We faithfully attend the services. There is no resident rabbi, but we have a lay leader. We are in good standing there and have approached the visiting rabbi who leads our Passover service and asked him to endorse us for aliyah. He said he would be happy to do it!"

"Leah and I have more time to look into these things than you do, Jeff and Gloria. We are going to find out if you can make aliyah as a part of our family, not on your own. You will be our children and automatically get citizenship. I hope it works that way. We all need to covenant together to pray for that very thing," declared Jeffrey.

"Dad, since you will be on the ground in Israel with your food business, please do some inquiries on behalf of Pete and Sarah, too. You know that Sarah's brother, Abe Bernstein, lives in Jerusalem. He is an Orthodox Jew. Please find out if this will help to get them in. Sarah's father, Dr. Nathan Bernstein, had quite a reputation as a teacher of Jewish history at Yeshiva University in New York when they made aliyah. His wife Naomi was a beloved philanthropist. They had become believers in Yeshua not very long before they were killed by a suicide bombing in Jerusalem. It must have been in all the newspapers there. Perhaps the government will be sympathetic to Sarah's application for aliyah. Then Pete can be admitted as her spouse, I hope."

Alvin and Sylvia were taking everything in, looking at each other, and whispering. Alvin spoke. "I hear from my parents regularly. They are loving it in Katzrin on the Golan Heights. Don't forget that Papa Sam and I both have been successful in the food business. As I hear all you folks talking about taking off for Israel and becoming Israelis, for the first time Sylvia and I are considering making aliyah, too. Just as you, Mr. and Mrs. Quentin, are not openly identified as Messianic Jews, neither are we."

Gloria's eyes got big. She jumped out of her seat, praising the Lord, and then ran over to her parents and hugged them. "Mom and Dad, I wasn't completely sure, but I have been hoping and praying you would drive down a stake and say you believe in Jesus. What you just said is a declaration of faith in Him. Oh, what more could I want out of life than to have my husband, his parents, and my parents all professing Yeshua as Savior and Lord? God is so good."

Sylvia ventured to ask a question, "Okay, you guys say what you think about this. Alvin and I will find an Orthodox synagogue close by us in Port Jefferson and begin regular attendance. After we have had a perfect record of attendance and involvement in the activities of the synagogue, we will ask the rabbi to endorse us for aliyah. Oops! I just thought of something. The name Sondheim may put us at a disadvantage with the Israeli government, if they have found out how the Ministry of the Interior broke their own law in affirming the citizenship of Alvin's parents."

Alvin squeezed his wife's hand, "No worries, beautiful wife. We have the same God that Papa Sam and Mama Anna do. He will hear our prayers, too, and we can do it. What is that verse I love so much from Zechariah? Say it with me, 'It's not by might nor power, but by My Spirit, says the Lord.'"[66]

The next day, Thanksgiving Day, was truly a time of thanksgiving in every sense of the word. After a light breakfast, Gloria directed everyone into the living room where she led them in songs of thanksgiving and praise. She eagerly played the piano that was Jeff's inheritance, rejoicing that it would have a new home in Israel next summer. Jeff begged Gloria to sing and play the song from Felix Mendelssohn's oratorio, *Elijah*, "Lift Thine Eyes." He announced, "Family, Dad is proud to be a descendant of the famous composer, Felix Mendelssohn, and so am I. Settle back in your seats, and enjoy hearing Gloria perform this song by Mendelssohn that is filled with marvelous promises from God, based on Psalm 121." Gloria sang:

> "*Lift thine eyes,*
> *O lift thine eyes to the mountains,*
> *whence cometh help.*
> *Thy help cometh from the Lord, the Maker of heaven and earth.*
> *He hath said, thy foot shall not be moved.*
> *Thy Keeper will never slumber.*"

"Gloria, you sound like an angel," gushed Jeff. "And the music is angelic, too. I wish it had the full Psalm. I love the last verses – 'Behold, He who keeps Israel will neither slumber nor sleep.... Yahweh shall preserve you from all evil; He shall preserve your soul. Yahweh shall preserve your going out and your coming in from this time forth, and even forevermore.' And that will be on my lips as we leave America and fly to Israel."

Leah was busy in the kitchen with Jetty for the lavish Thanksgiving meal. Everyone was enjoying conversation when they were called into the dining room. "I want my husband to say thanks over the meal and whatever the Lord puts on his heart."

Mr. Quentin gave thanks with great emotion for the many blessings all of them enjoyed, including the lavish meal before them and for the hands of Leah and Jetty who prepared it. He praised HaShem for His wonderful attributes and for forming the modern nation of Israel, and then closed with a petition for guiding them in making aliyah. "In Yeshua's name. Amen."

After the meal Jetty was called into the dining room. Jeff told his mother to stand beside Jetty, and then thunderous applause erupted. Jeff thanked their cooks for "the preparation and serving of the most delicious Southern food anywhere."

Mr. Quentin directed the family to the living room. "Get ready for a program. My wife insisted that I recite some history about America that you may not know. So, I have been studying and found out some amazing things."

CHAPTER TWENTY-EIGHT

AMERICAN HEBREW ROOTS

Mr. Quentin asked Gloria to lead them in singing the first verse of "America, the Beautiful" and then sing as a solo the second verse. This would help to emphasize what he was about to share with them. A feeling of patriotism surged in every heart as they sang and especially as they listened to Gloria's beautiful voice on the second verse: "O beautiful for pilgrim feet whose stern impassioned stress, a thoroughfare for freedom beat across the wilderness. America, America, God mend thine every flaw. Confirm thy soul in self-control, thy liberty in law."[67]

Alvin stood up. He felt strongly about the importance of Thanksgiving. His daughter's beautiful singing had brought back memories. "Gloria, that was so beautiful. I wish your grandparents could have heard you sing today. Patriotic songs are their favorites of all the holiday songs. One year when we were gathered for Thanksgiving, we sang several of them – 'My Country Tis of Thee,' 'The Star-Spangled Banner,' 'God Bless America,' but 'America the Beautiful' was their favorite. I would watch them sing the words with the deepest conviction. I asked my father why he was so emotional about that song, and he said his deep love for America was because the American army liberated him and Anna, as well as his parents from the Nazi concentration camp. He and Anna were only twelve years old. That was in 1945, and they had suffered the horrors of that place since 1942, three long years. Anna's parents died, but his parents, my grandparents, Isaac and Ruth Sondheim, survived. Then Papa Sam described what it felt like when his family, along with Mama Anna, first saw the Statue of Liberty in the New York Harbor as their ship came to shore in a free country. He said, 'Oh, America, the Beautiful. We knew that truly God had shed His grace on her, and we began our new lives with joy and gratitude bursting from our hearts!'"

Mr. Quentin held a book in his hands. "Thanks, Alvin, for sharing. I think we all know that America has historically been a refuge for the Jewish people fleeing persecution, but I will share with you some little-known facts about America's Hebrew roots. Let me read from this classic book by Marvin R. Wilson, *Our Father Abraham: Jewish Roots of the Christian Faith* – 'The Puritans came to America deeply rooted in Hebraic tradition. Most bore Hebrew names. The Pilgrim fathers considered themselves as the children of Israel fleeing Egypt (England), crossing the Red Sea (the Atlantic Ocean), and emerging from this Exodus to their own promised land (New England). The Pilgrims thought of themselves as 'all the children of Abraham' and thus under the covenant of Abraham.... The seeds of liberty for the American Church... came from the Hebrews themselves, whose sacred Writings inspired the Puritans.... William Bradford (1590-1657)... Governor of Plymouth Colony for more than three decades.... stated that he studied Hebrew so that when he died he might be able to speak in the 'most ancient language, the Holy Tongue in which God and the angels spake.'"

Leah was ecstatic. "Isn't that fantastic? And I want to add that Yeshua also spoke Hebrew in His everyday language. Scholars always said He spoke in Aramaic, but more recent scholarship has shown that, although people knew Aramaic from living in Babylon, they spoke Hebrew in their daily lives in the first century. It's proven in the Bible by the sign that Pilate had written and placed on the cross above Yeshua's head. It read 'Jesus of Nazareth, King of the Jews,' and it was written in Hebrew, Greek, and Latin – not in Aramaic. Those were the common languages that the people could read. I found that fact in John 19:19-20. The religious leaders wanted Pilate to change it, but he refused. That spoke volumes to me. It's important to know Hebrew, and I am so glad that Jeffrey and I have been seriously learning the language." Gloria and Jeff wholeheartedly agreed.

"Let me continue," said Mr. Quentin. "I am still quoting Marvin Wilson: 'Early American educators insisted that Hebrew be center stage in the realm of higher education. Harvard University has the distinction of being the oldest institution of higher learning in America, founded in 1636, just sixteen years after the Pilgrims landed the Mayflower at Plymouth, and the school was named for a Puritan minister, John Harvard. Hebrew had been an obligatory study from the foundation of the college.' This part of the book impressed me: 'Rabbi Judah Monis was the first Jew to receive a college degree in America, and it was from Harvard College. He said, 'I think the more acquainted the ministers of the gospel are with the Hebrew tongue, and so with the Old Testament, the better able they will be to understand the New Testament and so to preach…' In 1735 Monis published his Hebrew grammar studies, the first Hebrew grammar to be printed in the New World…. Yale and Dartmouth colleges also emphasized Hebrew studies. In 1777, immediately after the establishment of this nation, Ezra Stiles, president of Yale, declared that study of the Hebrew language was 'essential to a gentleman's education.' He reasoned to himself, 'Isn't it [Hebrew] the language I am sure to hear first in heaven?'"

Jeffrey continued, "I got something else interesting from another book, *Jews, God, and History* by Max I. Dimont.[68] He said there was a proposal that Hebrew be made the official language of the colonies, and John Cotton wanted to adopt the Mosaic Code as the basis for the laws of Massachusetts! Now what do you think of that, young people?"

Jeff answered, "I have to admit I did not know how important the study of Hebrew is. But my sweet wife certainly did, and in the beginning of our relationship she started teaching it to me. Now I can say 'I love you' to the Lord and to my wife in Hebrew! As you, our parents, know, Gloria and I are studying Hebrew on Monday nights at the college with our friend, Dror Mizrachi. He is an Israeli. He came to MSU to get his graduate degree in history and also to search for his family roots. Dror found his long-lost grandmother! It was done with Pete's help, and now Dror and Mrs. Goldberg are going back to Israel about the same time we are. Dror's mother is so excited to be reunited with her mother after many years. I will tell you more later, but please do continue this interesting program, Dad."

"That is wonderful news. Leah and I talk about it a lot, how you and Gloria get involved in so many exciting things, lives are changed, and you see miracles. We are looking forward to living in Israel with you and participating in those type things. But let me continue. Sad to say, and I will quote Wilson, 'At the start of the twentieth century, Hebrew was dropped from course offerings at these universities.'[69] It's not surprising, is it? Abandoning Christianity's Jewish roots has had bad consequences. The first colleges in America which were established to educate preachers, have now become bastions of anti-God philosophies. It grieves Leah and me."

Leah urged her husband, "Honey, we want to know how Thanksgiving is specifically connected to our American Jewish roots. Keep sharing."

"Yes, well let's look at the Feast of Tabernacles, called 'Sukkot' in Hebrew. God instructed the Israelites to appear before Him yearly in Jerusalem and bring offerings. It was a harvest festival and commemorated the time the Israelites wandered in the wilderness for forty years, living in booths, also called tabernacles. You can read about it in Leviticus 23:33-36, 39-43. The American Pilgrim fathers were most likely inspired by the biblical account of Sukkot by which to pattern the holiday of Thanksgiving. Both Sukkot and Thanksgiving are in the fall, and both are about gathering the harvest and giving thanks. But there's something funny about the connection between the two holidays: They both involve a Hebrew word, *hodu*, which means 'turkey.' But it's also the word for the country of India. And *hodu* additionally means to **give thanks**! In English, we call that tasty roast bird a turkey, thinking that it originated from the nation of Turkey. But Israelis call it *hodu*, thinking that it came from India! Either way, *hodu* is very much on the menu at Thanksgiving."[70]

Everyone laughed. "Oh, what an education we are getting here today!" exclaimed Gloria. "Folks you won't believe it, but I know a Hebrew song with the word *hodu* all through it. It's based on Psalm 136. I have got to teach it to you. The English words are, 'Give thanks to the Lord, for He is good, and His mercy endures forever.' I will play the piano and sing it for you. Then maybe you can sing with me the second time around. The melody is very soothing. I hope it doesn't put you to sleep. But it really blesses me and helps me to worship Yahweh."

Gloria played and sang in a gentle manner – "'*Hodu l'Adonai ki tov, ki leolam chasdo, Hodu l'Adonai ki tov, ki leolam chasdo. Hodu, hodu, hodu, hodu, hodu l'Adonai ki tov. Hodu, hodu, hodu, hodu, hodu l'Adonai ki tov.*' Now here's the song in English: '*Give thanks to the Lord for He is good, and His mercy endures forever. Give thanks to the Lord, for He is go-o-od, and His mercy endures forever. Oh give thanks, give thanks, Oh give thanks, give thanks, Oh give thanks to the Lord for He is good. Oh give thanks, give thanks, Oh give thanks, give thanks, Oh give thanks to the Lord for He is good.*'"[71]

Jeff led everyone in a rousing cheer for Gloria and for the Lord. And Sylvia complimented her daughter. "Gloria, you did almost put me to sleep, but I loved it. It felt like the Lord was in a rocking chair holding me, and He rocked me and sang a lullaby to me. I never knew Hebrew could be so lovely. Alvin and I need to do like the rest of you and undertake a serious study of the language. You have convinced me how important it is. You know what? Being Jewish is really special. I am just now beginning to understand that at this late age, and I am so sorry that in the past I was not proud of my heritage. But today, my heart is truly full of thanksgiving."

Gloria said, "Everyone, I say we give Miss Leah and Mr. Jeffrey a big 'thank you' and a round of applause for the fabulous food, both for our bodies and our souls. But wait, I have to say this. The word 'thank you' in Hebrew is 'toda,' with the accent on the last syllable. And 'toda' is related to the verb *hoda*, 'to thank.' We just sang it in the plural form, 'hodu.' And this is interesting - both the names, Judah, pronounced 'Yehuda,' and the name Jewish, pronounced 'Yehudi,' come from this verb *hoda*. These names mean 'giving thanks,' or 'thanksgiving.' What could be more appropriate for **Jewish** people than to give thanks in Hebrew? So follow me. I will say 'thank you' and 'thank you very much,' first in Hebrew and then in English. Let's hear it loud for Jeff's parents: 'Toda! Thank you! Toda rabbah! Thank you very much!'"

Everyone clapped enthusiastically, then sat back down. In a few minutes one by one, they began to yawn. Mr. Quentin suggested they hold hands in a circle and conclude with individual prayers of thanksgiving, going around the circle. After that, he said, it was nap time, and then Jeff would be in charge of some entertainment for the next stage of their celebration.

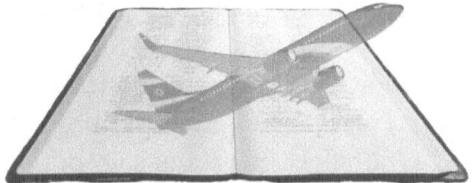

CHAPTER TWENTY-NINE

CONCERT PREVIEW

At 3:30 the doorbell rang. Jeff and Gloria went to the door and welcomed Pete, Sarah, Dror, and Grace. Jeff shouted up the stairs, "Mom and Dad, Mr. Alvin, and Miss Sylvia, come and welcome your guests."

The Quentins and Sondheims were awakened out of a sound sleep. Leah was the only one who knew ahead of time that they would have additional guests. She hurried down the stairs to welcome them. "What a treat. Come on in. It is so good to see you again, Pete and Sarah." Mr. Quentin and the Sondheims were right behind Leah and warmly welcomed the Carsons.

Jeff quickly introduced Dror and Grace, took their coats, and then led everyone to the living room. They all sat down except for Dror who stood beside the piano. Jeff nodded to him.

"Ladies and gentlemen, welcome to a Christmas Holiday Concert in Jerusalem, starring Gloria Sondheim Quentin from the USA." Dror sat down at the piano and began to play a simulated drum roll followed by a simulated trumpet fanfare. The Quentins and the Sondheims were elated at this surprise concert.

Jeff explained, "You all have heard the good news that Edsel Gruber, the man who arranged Gloria's musical debut in Europe over a year ago, has now secured a concert appearance for her in Jerusalem on the two nights of December 23rd and 24th. Gloria received the finalized concert program last Monday, and she is now prepared to give you a preview. This little woman has been practicing her fingers to the bone as well as stretching her vocal cords to the limit. We are indebted to Dror for his hard work preparing the piano accompaniments for her vocal numbers. Mrs. Pagani wanted to be here for this concert preview today, but she had other plans. Take it away, Gloria!"

Gloria took a deep bow and sat down on the piano bench. Every ear perked up when she began to play "Miniature Overture from *The Nutcracker Suite, Opus 71a*," arranged for piano solo in 1891, by the composer himself, Peter Ilyich Tchaikovsky. This was well known music to them, and so was the next number from the Suite, the famous "Dance of the Sugar Plum Fairy." At its conclusion Gloria stood, and the audience clapped enthusiastically.

Next on the program was a crowd pleaser that would display the pianistic skill of Dror as well as the beautiful voice of Gloria – "Sleigh Ride" by Leroy Anderson.[72] Dror introduced the song with some interesting background information. "'Sleigh Ride' received its premiere on May 4, 1948, with Arthur Fiedler conducting the Boston Pops Orchestra at Symphony Hall in Boston. According to Conductor Keith Lockhart, 'Sleigh Ride' is the Pops' signature work. For the performance in Jerusalem I contacted some music friends, and they will secure a trumpet player to do the horse whinny and a percussionist to do the whipcrack."[73]

At the conclusion of "Sleigh Ride," Sylvia was on her feet, shouting, "Beautiful! My favorite Christmas song, and the best I have ever heard." The others continued to applaud. Gloria and Dror took numerous bows.

Dror announced the next vocal numbers, all from Handel's *Messiah* – "'Then shall the eyes of the blind be opened, and the ears of the deaf unstopped; He shall feed His flock like a shepherd, and He shall gather the lambs with His arm; and Come unto Him, all ye that labour and are heavy laden, and He shall give you rest.' Gloria will start with a Recitative, which is like an announcement that describes the miracles the Messiah will do. The ending shows his tender care as a Shepherd who will give His people rest."

Jeff was deeply affected by Gloria's singing. *She has never sung more beautifully or with more passion. I feel the anointing of the Holy Spirit so strong. I hope Gloria will not be overcome and fall to the floor. Oh, my, she is crying. She is feeling the pain of our people. I know it. Open their hearts when she sings in Jerusalem, Yahweh. Cut them to the core. Give them a vision of Yeshua, their own Messiah, as Gloria sings words from both the Old Testament and the New Testament.*

Dror and Gloria took their bows, but there was no applause. All were crying. Dror paused before announcing the next number. He also had cried inwardly, but he didn't want anyone to know his heart was touched. Grace wanted so badly to hold him and tell him how his playing had moved her. Dror struggled to keep his composure. After a few minutes, he explained that the University Singers, a women's ensemble, would do three holiday numbers, which he was not familiar with. He read the titles from the program. Raising his eyebrows, he couldn't help but comment that these must be obscure pieces and would serve as an academic concession to the faculty and musically elite members of the audience. He laughed.

Jeff replied, "Well, that's just great. Their academic songs will provide a contrast to the heartwarming performances of you and Gloria." Everyone agreed.

Dror resumed his role as master of ceremonies. "Gloria will end the concert with two more selections from the *Messiah* – 'I know that my Redeemer liveth, and that He shall stand at the latter day upon the earth.' Then this final number is going to require a lot of practice with the University Orchestra and Chorus, featuring Gloria on the piano for the timeless, much-loved 'Hallelujah Chorus!'" Sylvia was sitting on the edge of her seat.

Before she played, Gloria explained that the words to the "Hallelujah Chorus," like the other numbers from the *Messiah*, would have the full text and Scripture references printed on an insert in the program. "These Jewish people will hear the gospel mostly from

225

their own Hebrew Scriptures. I am so excited. And it may come as a surprise to them that the words of 'I know that my Redeemer liveth' are out of the Book of Job in their own Tanach."

Pete exclaimed, "Amen! And the Christian tourists, being familiar with the *Messiah*, will no doubt be inspired to pray for their blindness and deafness to the gospel to be removed when you sing the words, 'And the eyes of the blind shall be opened, and the ears of the deaf unstopped.'"

Dror squirmed in his seat. Grace silently prayed for him to open his heart to God's Word.

Gloria came down hard on the piano keys for the opening bars of the "Hallelujah Chorus" and continued at maximum volume for almost the entire piece. She felt strength pouring into her arms and hands and was amazed to have far surpassed her own expectations in performing this difficult music. When she arose to take her bows, she was overcome with emotion. Jeff saw she was about to fall and quickly encircled her in his arms, both laughing.

"Honey, you don't need the University Orchestra and Chorus. What I heard must have been heavenly instruments and angelic voices added to your piano, because it was magnificent and completely satisfying." All agreed with Jeff.

The whole family crowded around Gloria and Dror, congratulating them. But Dror backed off. "No need to congratulate me. I won't even be there. I promised Grace to go with her to Charlottesville to spend Christmas with her parents. We hope to go on a sleigh ride and enjoy 'walking in a winter wonderland,' as they say. But don't worry, all the piano accompanists at Hebrew University are a lot better than me."

The family was shocked. Alvin knew what they were all feeling and decided to be their spokesman. "Dror, you **must** be Gloria's accompanist. I will fly you and Grace to Jerusalem and back free of charge. You could return to Charlottesville on Christmas Day, if that agrees with Grace's parents. Sylvia and I weren't sure about attending, but after hearing this preview, we are sure. We are going!"

226

Grace spoke up. "Let me answer for Dror. All the time this concert preview was going on, I was thinking how badly I want to be present in Jerusalem to hear it. I have been turning it over and over in my mind. That is a fantastic offer from you, Mr. Sondheim. I think I can get my parents to understand how much it would mean to me."

Dror whispered to Grace, "We need to talk. I don't want to upset your parents."

Gloria admitted, "Mrs. Pagani has worked hard with Dror on these accompaniments, knowing all the time he would not be my accompanist in Jerusalem. But if she could have heard him today, I believe she would feel the same as all of you, dear family. Also, Grace could room with Mrs. Pagani, and she would have a companion, cutting her hotel expense almost in half. Mr. Gruber is paying for our hotel rooms for the nights of the rehearsals and performances, but that is all. He will be sharing in the profits from the concert, about fifteen percent of ticket sales, according to Mrs. Pagani, but after paying for our lodging and airfare, he won't come away with a lot extra, I fear. We need to pray for a large audience."

Dror had made up his mind. "Well, if I make the trip with Grace, leaving at the same time Gloria and Jeff are leaving, we would still have quite a few days to spend with Grace's parents after Christmas. And on the extra days in Israel before the rehearsals I would like to take Grace to Tel Aviv to meet my family. It's not for the purpose of free lodging and food, but, nevertheless, it really would help my pocketbook." He looked at Grace and grinned.

Pete interjected, "Things have a way of working out, don't they? Sarah and I already have a trip planned to New York to visit Chaya, Max, and our little niece Estelle. But who knows? We still might be able to join you in Jerusalem."

"We will be lifting up a multitude of prayers for the success of the concert, Gloria and Dror, and we expect a 'play-by-play account' of those miraculous nights," Sarah added.

Dror's mind was racing, trying to comprehend the magnitude of taking his beloved Grace to meet his parents. He was thinking that they should be invited to the concert. If they accepted, they could provide transportation for the four of them from Tel Aviv to Jerusalem for the rehearsals and performances. He knew his dad enjoyed being in Jerusalem that time of year, and money was no object, as far as hotel rooms. Also, he was excited for them to hear him play and Gloria sing. "I want to say that we must have an encore prepared, Gloria. Have you thought about what it could be? I am sure you will get at least one encore."

"Oh, yes! A classic Christmas song is flooding my mind right now. I think by the time the audience drinks in the 'Hallelujah Chorus,' they will be ready for 'O Holy Night.' Just to think, I would be singing it on Christmas Eve, the very time that Christians celebrate the birth, the incarnation of Yeshua, the Son of God! And Jerusalem is so close to Bethlehem, some of the audience would have already gone there before the concert on the 24th and some earlier on the 23rd," Gloria exclaimed.

"Yes, 'O Holy Night' is a classic among Christians, but I don't know it very well, even though I have heard it before. But don't worry. Mrs. Pagani will get a copy for me, and I will get right on it, practicing as much as it takes," promised Dror.

228

CHAPTER THIRTY

TEL AVIV

TEL AVIV, ISRAEL
TUESDAY, DECEMBER 14

"**A**re you sure this taxi cab driver isn't trying to kill us?" whispered Grace. "This is worse than a roller coaster. Please make him slow down, Dror. I'm so scared I may have a heart attack!"

Dror drew Grace closer and comforted her. Talking softly, he said, "Oh, I didn't realize he was going fast. This is normal in Tel Aviv. Trust me, he will get us there safely. I can't even remember an accident involving a taxi as long as I have lived here." Dror decided since this may be the last opportunity for a while to enjoy intimacy with his beautiful girl, he would take full advantage of it. He pressed close against her, breathed in her tantalizing perfume, nuzzled her neck, and kissed her soft cheek. It was only minutes to his house, and Ima would be watching them like a hawk. Abba was more tolerant, but Ima had issued a stern warning that he better keep his relationship with Grace at a friendship level. She could not accept a Christian daughter-in-law, and that was final, she had decreed.

"Well, we're almost there, Grace. My neighborhood is called Neve Tzedek. It may be the first Jewish neighborhood that built up outside the Jaffa walls, so it's historic, and it is an expensive area. There are only three of us, so we didn't need a big house. Although our house is small, it's beautiful. The neighborhood is peaceful with quaint houses, good restaurants, and you can walk to the beach, the Carmel market and the Tachana shopping area in just a few minutes. I know you have toured Israel with the church, but you may not have seen many sites in Tel Aviv and Jaffa. So after we get over the jet lag, I would like to take you to Independence Hall and Old Jaffa, where you can see the Church of St. Peter, Simon the Tanner's House, Jaffa Port, and the history of Jonah. But be prepared to see very worldly people in my home city. After all, it is regarded as the 'gay capital of the Middle East' with an annual Gay Pride Parade. The saying in Israel is, 'If you want to **play**, go to Tel Aviv. If you want to **pay**, go to Haifa, and if you want to **pray**, go to Jerusalem.'" The taxi stopped. Dror got the suitcases out of the trunk.

Grace tried not to flinch. "Israel is quite a diverse place, I see. Do you mind saying the reason your parents wanted to live here in Tel Aviv?"

"Well, Abba is a businessman. He didn't want to live in Haifa, even though that is the business and industry center of Israel, but he chose Tel Aviv for its proximity to the airport. He does a lot of traveling. You know the government of Israel was established here before it was moved to Jerusalem. This is the place that our first Prime Minister, Ben Gurion, declared Israel to be a nation on May 14, 1948. Of course, you have already learned that from the Holy Rollers. By the way, I have to confide in you that I have never felt comfortable with that name for their association, doing the Lord's work, as they say."

"It seems to fit them, in my opinion. Brrr! It's getting cold out here on the sidewalk, Dror. People are looking at us, standing here with our suitcases. Is there a reason you haven't taken me inside your house yet?"

"I was hoping I would see Abba drive up, and I could introduce you before we go in the house. Grace, please forgive Ima if she is not very friendly to you. She has always had her heart set on my finding a 'nice Jewish girl.' That's the way she puts it."

"Don't tell me you have never dated anyone that wasn't Jewish, at least before you met me," worried Grace. "Oh, don't answer that. Mrs. Mizrachi will either like me, or she won't. I can't change who I am. I have been praying that God would give me favor with your parents. Dror, I do love you, and I know I will love your parents. Let's go inside."

Dror decided to ring the doorbell and not barge in. It would give him a few more minutes to prepare himself to introduce Grace. All of a sudden he began to perspire and be short of breath. *Get a grip, Dror. What's the worst that can happen? Ima could refuse to let Grace in the house. And in that case, we can get two rooms in a hotel. But Abba will pitch a fit, and Ima will come get us and apologize. Quit worrying, Dror. Ima is going to love Grace. She has to. Why in the world am I being so paranoid? This is not like me. I can't wait to get this coat off. I am burning up!*

Devorah opened the door with a big smile, and Dror introduced Grace. Devorah responded, "Bruchim habayim l'bayit shelanu, Grace veh b'nee! I am so glad to finally meet you. Dror did not exaggerate your beauty. Benyamin and I are honored you will be staying with us a few days, and we look forward to going to the concert in Jerusalem that Dror has told us so much about. Come, come, I will show you to your room. It has been redecorated for my mother, and we are overjoyed she is making aliyah next year. I think it will be comfortable for you."

Dror reached out to hug his Ima, and he held on for dear life. "Ima, please forgive me. I feel so hot, and I need to go lie down. All of a sudden I feel terrible. My head is killing me. I don't know what's wrong. Maybe it's the flu, but it's gotta be something else because a few minutes ago I started itching."

Devorah felt his forehead. "Yes, you definitely have a fever. And I see you have a rash on your neck. Excuse me, Grace. I will tend to Dror. Just make yourself at home." Devorah reached in the chest of drawers in Dror's room and pulled out some winter pajamas. "Here, Dror, put these on. I will check your temperature and get you some water and Cartia for your fever."

Grace went right to her room and got on her knees. "Oh, Father, please heal Dror. And show his parents what to do. Lord, we were very close in the taxi. Please don't let me get sick, too. As You know, we need to be in Jerusalem for the concert rehearsals next week. I ask You to rebuke Satan. He is trying to stop this concert which may open the eyes of the Jews attending it. Thank You, Father, for causing Mrs. Mizrachi to like me. I can see you have given me favor with her. Now, please direct my every word and action here in this home. Bless both of Dror's parents, and take control of this situation. In Jesus' name. Amen."

Devorah opened Grace's door, bringing her a lemonade, and realized she had interrupted her prayer. "Slicha! I didn't mean to interrupt you."

"Oh, that's fine, Mrs. Mizrachi. I was just finishing my prayer for Dror and for all of us. If Dror had to be sick, what better place than in his home with the care of his mother and not on the airplane, the terminal, or the taxi."

"My goodness, what an optimist you are, Grace. I should be optimistic, too, because I am a volunteer at the hospital and am friends with the best doctors. Not only that, but my next-door neighbor Shira is a registered nurse, and she happens to be having some time off. I am going to call her and ask her to take a look at Dror. While you are waiting, you can give yourself a tour of the house. There is reading material everywhere, and if you desire, you can 'raid the cookie jar,' as the expression is." Devorah smiled at Grace.

"Uh, Mrs. Mizrachi, I hope your reading material is in English. I need to tell you that I do not read or speak Hebrew. I only know a few phrases and words that Dror taught me. Also, Gloria, the one Dror is accompanying for the concert, has taught me a little, and so has her husband Jeff. Could you tell me what the words, *b'nee* and *slicha* mean? I do know that *bruchim habaim habayit shelanu* means 'welcome to our home.'"

"You darling girl. Your Hebrew is 'cute!' I was welcoming Dror as 'my son' – *b'nee,* and *slicha* means 'excuse me.'"

Grace reached out and hugged Devorah. "I have to hug you. I barely know you, but I already love you. And please go ahead and call your neighbor."

Devorah was surprised but accepted this display of affection. "I was about to tell you that Dror's fever is 101 degrees, so I gave him two tablets of Cartia – that's aspirin. I will call Shira. You can go see Dror, but don't stay long. He needs to rest a lot. And make sure he keeps drinking water."

Grace was at Dror's bedside when Shira came in the room with Devorah. An introduction was quickly made, and Grace stood in a corner of the room while Shira examined Dror. After she questioned him about symptoms, when he first noticed them, and probed his body, she said, "Which airline brought you here?"

"El Al from New York," Grace answered.

With authority Shira said, "We need to get Dror to the hospital as quickly as possible."

Dror cried out, "Where is Abba? I am not going until he gets here!"

Devorah answered, "Son, I just talked to him, and he is almost home, but I will call and tell him to meet us at the hospital."

Grace and Shira were in the emergency waiting room while Devorah was with Dror in the exam room, awaiting a specialist. The waiting room doors swung open, and Shira jumped up to meet Benyamin Mizrachi. "Praise HaShem you are here. We almost couldn't get Dror to leave the house without you. When I examined him at your home I saw this was very serious, and there was no time to waste. I will take you back to the exam room, but wait just a minute. I want to introduce you to Dror's girlfriend from Mississippi State University. They just arrived this morning."

Grace heard the words "very serious" and "no time to waste." She couldn't stop the tears from rolling down her cheeks, but she reached out her hand to Mr. Mizrachi and smiled, "I am Grace Thomas from Charlottesville, Virginia, and I flew with Dror here from the airport in Columbus, Mississippi. Dror has told me so much about you, Mr. Mizrachi. I am very glad to meet you and your wife."

Benyamin noticed Grace's tears and forced himself to take a minute to give her a warm welcome. "And I also am very glad to meet you, Grace. Dror has described you perfectly – beautiful and gentle. I must hurry now, but Devorah said you had prayed for Dror to be healed and for all of us. I want you to know that I believe in prayer, and I thank you."

Shira led Benyamin back to the exam room and then returned to Grace. She felt strongly that although her usual response would be to stay continually with Dror, she must stay with Dror's beloved girlfriend now. Devorah had already told her that Grace was a Gentile and a Christian. She and Benyamin were grieved when Dror expressed a wish to marry this girl. Taking Grace's hand, Shira spoke softly, "Grace, I am very grateful to know that you have prayed for Dror's healing. I also am a strong believer in prayer. First of all, let me assure you that Dror's sickness is probably not contagious, so don't worry about yourself or any of us."

"Thanks for telling me, Shira, but that is not my concern at all. I was jarred to hear you tell Mr. Mizrachi that Dror's illness is 'very serious,' and there is 'no time to waste.' You have to tell me what you think is wrong. I can take it, if it's bad news. I believe in miracles. I will fight for Dror, and I will call all my believing friends. They will fight in prayer also, and I know Dror will be healed!"

"I pray I am wrong, but Dror's symptoms are almost identical to the symptoms of two people who died in this hospital only three months ago. Somehow they had contracted the West Nile Virus."[74]

Grace felt like yelling, "No, he will live, not die!" Although she restrained herself from a public outburst, she couldn't stop herself from falling into Shira's arms and sobbing. "Shira, you believe in prayer. Please go in there and lay hands on Dror and pray for HaShem to heal him, to heal him supernaturally. I know they won't let me go in there, or I would do it myself."

Shira paused. She wanted to be sure she heard from the Holy Spirit. Was this His plan? What would be the ramifications, whether Dror was healed or wasn't healed? She waited to hear. She would not rush something this important.

"Shira, I know you don't believe that Jesus is the Messiah, and normally I would not talk about Him around you or Dror's parents, but this is an emergency. I have seen miracles happen when the prayer is made **in His name**. Is there any way you can get me to Dror's bedside?"

Shira grinned. "Well, that's my answer. I have been waiting on the Holy Spirit to show me what to do. I have to admit that I have a selfish motive in wanting you to pray instead of me. You are wearing a cross, and even without it you just look like a Christian. The doctors and nurses would expect you to pray in Jesus' name, but my job here may be in jeopardy if it's obvious that I am a Messianic Jew."

Grace couldn't stop a low-key squeal. "Praise the Lord, you are a Messianic Jew! This is awesome news. The minute the words were out of your mouth, it seems that the Holy Spirit told me that we both could go to Dror, and the personnel won't stop me, even though I am not a family member. I feel the boldness right now to lay hands on Dror and pray for his complete healing. You can also lay hands on him, but 'in a medical way.'" Grace chuckled. "I will pray out loud, and you can pray silently. Wait. The Lord just reminded me of His Word – 'if two of you agree on earth concerning anything that they ask, it will be done for them by My Father in heaven.'[75] Shira, there are two of us. It's a sure thing. What is the Holy Spirit saying to you now?"

"I am reminded that the Lord gently leads, but the devil pushes. Let us not rush. The Lord God is setting this up. I believe

He wants you to call your believing friends and ask for their prayers, not only for Dror's healing, but for a shield of protection against any persecution that may ensue when Yeshua's name is uttered."

"Wait a minute, Shira. What if it turns out not to be the deadly West Nile Virus but only the flu or a sinus infection? I don't want to expose you to persecution unnecessarily. On the other hand, whatever illness it is, Dror simply must be in Jerusalem to play the piano for Gloria to sing in the 'Holiday Concert.' The rehearsals begin a week from today. If God decides to heal him with a long recovery process, Dror may not get to be the accompanist. How much time will normal recovery take if it's the West Nile Virus?"

"As I already said, God is setting this up, so you must 'cool your jets,' sweet Grace. All I know right now is that you are supposed to call your friends to pray. While you are doing that, I will go back and see if there is a diagnosis yet," advised Shira.

Grace made a call to Pastor James and Miss Celeste and said to get Mrs. Goldberg on the phone with them. She described what had happened to Dror and told them to alert the whole church to pray and to call Miss Lizzie first. She realized she had called right before they would be retiring for the night, due to the time difference, and she thanked the Lord for that. Then she called Gloria. She and Jeff had just gotten settled in their hotel room and were about to take a nap. They prayed with Grace on the phone and said for her to call them back when she knew the diagnosis and had a full report from the doctor. Grace couldn't leave Pete and Sarah out, so she called them, too, even though they would eventually be notified by Pastor. Suddenly, she felt a deep peace fill her whole being. It was like the Father was cradling her in His arms. His Word came into her mind – "The eternal God is your refuge, and underneath are the everlasting arms; He will thrust out the enemy from before you, and will say, 'Destroy!'"[76] *Yes, Yeshua, right now You are destroying Dror's enemy, that virus!* Grace declared within herself.

CHAPTER THIRTY-ONE

DREADED
DIAGNOSIS

W hen Shira returned to the waiting room, Grace was fast asleep, looking like a kitten curled up on the hard sofa. "Grace, wake up. I am glad I didn't hurry back to you, because you really needed a nap…. Are you fully awake? …. Listen to me. I have talked with several doctors. They gave Dror tests and examined him thoroughly. He told them he had a memory of something biting him in the JFK Airport while you were waiting for the El Al flight. Dr. Rothschild, a specialist in viruses, said he was the one who attended the two people who were hospitalized for the West Nile Virus and died back in September. This virus can be transmitted by a mosquito bite but also by diseased birds and geese, which was the case for several people last year in Israel. It so happens there was an outbreak of the West Nile Virus in New York City between August and October of this year. More than 66 people were infected, and six died. It was the first time the West Nile Virus had been detected in the Western Hemisphere, said Dr. Rothschild. It was found that many of the patients had been exposed to a breeding ground for mosquitos in a Queens neighborhood, so the city instituted mosquito-control measures rapidly."[77]

"You mean that is definitely the sickness Dror has, the West Nile Virus?" asked Grace.

"That is the official diagnosis. They are keeping Dror in an intensive care unit. So far he does not have any alarming symptoms, but they could develop suddenly, and there is actually no treatment, just rest and intravenous fluids," answered Shira, sadly. "The worst that can happen is encephalitis, which is inflammation of the brain, or meningitis which is caused by inflammation of tissues that affect the brain and run down the spinal cord. Neck stiffness could progress to paralysis, and there could even be seizures. The patient could begin to hallucinate. Oh, my goodness! I didn't need to tell you all that. Dror could possibly have a light case, something like the flu. That may be all there is to it. Please don't be fearful. I just felt like I was obligated to give you this information, so you can pray more effectively. We believers have to stand on the Word of God, even if it appears contrary to evidence. I have learned that as a nurse. Believe me, I have seen hopeless cases make a startling recovery." Shira took Grace's hand and squeezed it.

Grace felt she needed to make a declaration, so she stood up. "My God says this to me: 'Fear not, for I am with you; be not dismayed, for I am your God.' I will not fear. I will claim God's promises of healing and pray for Dror. But I need Gloria and Jeff here. I know the hospital limits the number of people who can go in ICU, so they could stay in the waiting room and pray at the exact time that you and I go in to lay hands on and pray for Dror. I will call them now."

"Go ahead and call them. As a nurse, I can stay in the unit in addition to visitors, so I will go keep watch with Devorah and Benyamin. It's less than an hour from Jerusalem to Tel Aviv. If they leave right away, they should be here around 4:30 or 5:00 p.m."

"Grace, we're here. Wake up, sweetie. I know you are getting over the jet lag, which Jeff and I have yet to do." Grace didn't move, and Gloria couldn't bear to shake her awake. She looked so peaceful. "Oh, well, Jeff, we might as well join Grace in dreamland. Here are two sofas by her. Let's lie down."

"Should we really do that? I thought we came here to pray for Dror," argued Jeff.

"Yes, we did, but God's timing is perfect, and I believe the prayers of all our friends back home are preparing the way for us. I have heard people say they can feel when others are praying for them. That has never happened to me before, but I think it's happening now. Evidently, Grace has fallen asleep because of feeling those prayers. Honey, our bodies are craving sleep. We've got a battle ahead. Strangely enough, there are only a handful of people in the waiting room. Let's crash," begged Gloria.

The three had been sleeping peacefully for about an hour when Shira walked in. Devorah and Benyamin were following her. Shira gently shook them, and they sat up.

Grace stood and saw Jeff and Gloria were beside her. "Oh, forgive me, Mr. and Mrs. Mizrachi. I felt so sure that Dror is going to be all right that I relaxed and fell asleep. My friends, Jeff and Gloria Quentin, arrived from Jerusalem after I fell asleep, and I haven't even greeted them. I hope you understand that the jet lag is responsible for our behavior." Grace couldn't help but laugh. She didn't feel one bit guilty, but she hoped Dror's parents wouldn't disapprove of her and her friends. "Please meet Jeff and Gloria Quentin from Starkville, Mississippi. Gloria is the one that Dror will be accompanying for the 'Holiday Concert' in Jerusalem on December 23rd and 24th. All three of you are invited. I had a preview of the concert at Jeff's parents' house during Thanksgiving, and I can tell you the music is absolutely magnificent."

Benyamin cleared his throat as he reached to shake hands with Jeff and Gloria. "We are so glad to meet you. Dror speaks very highly of you both. Thank you for the invitation, Grace, and I know the music is wonderful, but I'm afraid Dror will need a substitute pianist. With an illness as serious as the West Nile Virus, there is no way he will be fully recovered by then." Devorah agreed.

Shira stood slightly behind the Mizrachis and put her finger to her lips. Grace knew she should not insist that Dror would be healed in time. *Lord, help me not to get in the flesh, but keep me attuned to Your Spirit. I want to say and do only what You direct.*

239

Devorah stepped forward. "Grace, Jeff, and Gloria, I know you are trying to get over jet lag, but I also know you have not had a meal since you arrived in Israel. At least, I'm sure Grace hasn't. I think it would do us all good to leave this hospital and go to a nice restaurant for a good meal and relaxing conversation. In fact, Dror told me to do that. He said he could get well a lot quicker if he didn't have to worry about us worrying about him. That's my son, always putting others ahead of himself. Well, what do you say? And I am including you, too, Shira." The decision to go eat was unanimous.

"What delicious food," said Gloria. "Jeff and I really like a lot of vegetables and fruit with a moderate amount of meat, so this meal hits the spot. We're trying to be in maximum health, preparing for aliyah. Of course, both of us have a weakness for sweets. The blueberry cobbler was very tasty."

"Yeah, Mr. Mizrachi, it was a blessing to have you order for us, and we appreciate the American dishes alongside the Israeli ones. Eggplant is something I never eat, but the eggplant casserole was really good. I think I will live now!" laughed Jeff.

Grace had been quiet during the meal. Gloria was sitting by her, so Grace squeezed her hand, then slipped both her hands under the table in a praying position. She subtly elbowed Gloria, who caught on, and together they silently prayed for Dror.

Devorah couldn't help but be aware of the good looks of these three college people, as well as their poise and good manners. But her focus was on Grace, and she intended to find out as much as she could about this girl who had a hook in her son's heart. "Grace, please tell us all about yourself, why you enrolled at Mississippi State University, what your major is, and what career you hope to pursue after graduation. Not being Jewish, I guess you have no plans to immigrate to Israel along with your Jewish friends."

"Oh, no, Mrs. Mizrachi, I will certainly miss Jeff and Gloria, as well as Pete and Sarah. And, of course, I will miss Dror, but he has promised to visit me in the USA often. I have been studying interior design, following in my mother's footsteps, and I plan to return home to Charlottesville, Virginia, after graduation. My mother wants to groom me to take over her decorating business eventually. I have to tell you that I think your house is very, very beautiful. Whoever decorated it did an excellent job. Almost everything about it suits my own tastes."

"That's so nice of you to say, Grace." Devorah was relieved to hear about Grace's plans after graduation and wondered if Dror had decided against proposing marriage to her. As she pondered this, Benyamin's phone rang, and he reached for it. She could see his face cloud over.

"It's the hospital. I have to take this call, of course. I will put it on speaker, so you all can hear."

Dr. Rothschild spoke in his usual professional voice, but Grace detected a note of fear. "I hate to interrupt your dinner, but you must return to the hospital immediately. Dror is having hallucinations, and that is a bad sign. His brain is certainly being affected by the virus and could lead to paralysis." The doctor didn't even say 'goodbye.' Everyone at the table was stabbed with fear, everyone except Jeff.

CHAPTER THIRTY-TWO

HALLUCINATION?

D r. Rothschild was in the waiting room as the Mizrachis, Quentins, Shira, and Grace came in the door. "Come on back to ICU with me. All of you can come. The nurses and I have tried our best to bring Dror back to reality, but his hallucination persists. He seems to be living in some kind of mystical drama. I will admit it is quite interesting the things he is saying, and the movements he is making, but it doesn't make any sense. He has had stiffness in his neck, and the rash has spread. We continue to give him strong medication for the pain in his head. I fear the inflammation of his brain is increasing, and he may not be with us much longer. We have tried everything we know to do, so we want you all to see if you can bring him back to reality. If you can, then he's still got a chance because it would prove that his brain is still functioning normally. Otherwise, it's only a matter of a few hours, and his loved ones need to be with him." They entered Dror's room. "I will leave your friend and my nurse, Shira, here with Dror. He may respond to the ones closest to him." Dr. Rothschild left the room.

Jeff felt like the Lord was telling him to take the lead. "Let's just observe Dror for a few minutes, please. I think I know what is happening."

Devorah and Benyamin looked at Jeff incredulously. The others fully agreed and waited. Dror was sitting up in bed. He spoke unintelligibly and made strange gestures.

Grace and Shira nodded to each other. It's now or never, thought Grace, as she went around to the far side of the bed, and Shira moved opposite her on the near side. Together they laid their hands on Dror's head and heart. Grace looked into Dror's face which was beaming with love and joy. She was encouraged to simply pray in acknowledgment of what the Lord was doing in their presence. "Dear Yahweh, God of Abraham, Isaac, and Jacob, and the God and Father of my Lord, Yeshua HaMashiach..." She could hear Devorah and Benyamin gasp, but she continued. "I thank You for Your great plan of salvation that was carried out on the cross when Your Suffering Servant bore our griefs and carried our sorrows. He was wounded for our transgressions and bruised for our iniquities. The chastisement for our peace was upon Him, and by His stripes we are healed. We receive this great promise now for Dror Mizrachi. His sins are forgiven and his body is healed. We praise You and thank You for this miracle today. In the name of Yeshua the Messiah."

At that moment, Dror opened his eyes and looked around the room. He was fully awake and extended his arms to his parents. "I am well, Ima and Abba! I heard Grace praying, and I say 'Amen' to that prayer. I want you to be happy for me that I know that Jesus, Yeshua, is really our Messiah, and He has saved me and healed me today. Please call Savta. She experienced this, and she will be overjoyed to know her grandson is now part of the Shepherd's flock like she is." Dror got out of bed and embraced his parents.

Benyamin and Devorah were in a state of shock. They tried to get Dror to get back in bed, but he refused. Benyamin said, "Son, the doctor told us you were hallucinating, and that was an indication that your brain was inflamed, and you may not live much longer. He even let all of us come in here because he thought your death was imminent. When we walked in this room, you were acting very strangely. You were seeing things we couldn't see and talking out of your head. It was like you were living out a drama of some kind. Do you remember any of that?"

"Yes, I do. I want to tell all of you what I experienced. I think the Lord said that Jeff has experienced this kind of thing and could affirm my experience as authentic, not crazy, and not a hallucination."

Jeff responded, "Yes, the Lord has spoken to me in two dreams over the past months. They were vivid, and both gave me direction in my life. The first one concerned my father starting a food business in Israel, which would give Gloria and me income when we move here. We found out we are not qualified to make aliyah, because we believe that Yeshua is the Messiah. We are Messianic Jews, so we have to get a work permit and have it renewed every year. We were shocked to find out that every type of Jew, even atheists, can make aliyah, but a Jew who believes in Jesus is considered to have changed religions and is no longer Jewish. Gloria and I know we are more Jewish than ever. We have a Jewish Messiah, for cryin' out loud! Anyway, what I dreamed came to pass. My parents think they can make aliyah, but whether or not they qualify, they will still open up a food business in Israel."

Devorah interrupted. "Yes, we know something about that because Shira and her husband Aharon are Messianic Jews, and they told us that a lot of their friends have encountered obstacles to making aliyah." Shira was nodding her head.

Jeff continued, "The second dream involved our search for your mother, Mrs. Mizrachi. In the dream, I saw a city with casinos. The city sign stood out – Vicksburg. Soon after the dream, we found out that our friend Pete's sister Elinor and her friend Julie were there. They had been kidnapped, and the F.B.I. and the Jackson police rescued them. From what they told us we knew your mother, Susannah Goldberg, was still in the casino. We went back, but she had already left. We searched for her in Jackson and found her, as you know."

Gloria added to the discussion. "Your mother, Mrs. Mizrachi, had a vision. It happened when Elinor and Julie were with her in an upstairs room of the casino. She told them she was going to get them out of there, even if she lost her job. Then Elinor prayed for the three of them, and they fell to the floor and lay there for a good while unconscious. Later, Mrs. Goldberg said at that time she had a vision of her dancing in Israel, and she knew she would be going there."

Devorah and Benyamin looked at each other. Their faces showed bewilderment.

Jeff looked intently at Dror, trying to discern what the Lord may be doing in his life right at the moment. "Dror, would you like to relate what has just happened to you? If it is not a hallucination, would you describe it as a vision? I think a vision is sort of like a waking dream, but I am not well-versed in these supernatural things. Anyway, it could be that God has given you this experience to share with us here today for His own purposes. I am eager to hear you tell about it. But before you do, I have to say the Scripture that comes to my mind is Acts 2. It was the Day of Pentecost, called Shavuot in Hebrew. Jews had gathered for the feast in Jerusalem, when the Holy Spirit was poured out on Jesus' disciples like He had promised them. Peter stood up to preach, and he quoted the prophet Joel. I can't recite it, but basically he said that in the last days God would pour out His Spirit on all people, men and women. The old men would have dreams, and the young men would have visions. Men and women would prophesy. Then he gave some of the signs in the heavens that would occur before the Messiah returns to earth. He ended his words from Joel by saying, 'Everyone who calls upon the name of the Lord will be saved.' So, anyway, Dror, you are a young man, and this vision you had, if indeed it was a vision, could have something to do with God's message to us for the times we are living in. Go ahead and share."

"Okay, I will tell you, but you've gotta promise you won't laugh at me. I admit it's kind of weird. But get this, I just realized that the Scripture you quoted, Jeff, must be the same scene I was in the middle of. Now that's amazing. I was walking along in a crowd of people, lots and lots of people, who were going to a tall, imposing building. Maybe that was the temple, and yes, it had to be Jerusalem, although it didn't look like it looks today. But pictures I have seen of ancient Jerusalem and the temple in the days of King Herod and the Roman occupation, that's what I was seeing. I said to the people around me, 'Quit pushing. Give me some room.' I guess that's why the doctor and nurses thought I was talking out of my head. There was a group of people coming toward us from the direction of the temple, I guess about 120 people maybe. It was the strangest thing. It looked like their heads had fire on top. I figured they were going to the mikvot – that's what Christians call baptismal pools – to douse their heads with water. The crowd I was in started backing up to give them room. Someone said, 'They are going to the southern steps of the temple. Their heads are still on fire!' I was transfixed, gazing at them, and then they began to jabber really loud, words streaming out of their mouths. A woman in the crowd yelled out, 'I hear my language. They are talking about God doing miracles.' The man next to me started speaking French. I said, 'What are they saying?' He answered, 'One of those people on the steps is speaking French, and she is telling about God's love and forgiving terrible sinners!' This went on probably thirty minutes, and the crowd was really worked up. Some were shouting, 'Hallelujah!' Next, everything suddenly quieted down, and a tall man who looked like he had greater authority than the High Priest started speaking and explaining what was happening with the fire on their heads and the different languages coming out of their mouths – it was what the prophet Joel said would happen at the end of days."

Jeff interjected what Gloria, Grace, and Shira were also thinking. "Dr. Rothschild was right about you 'living out a mystical drama,' except that it wasn't a mystical drama, but a real historical event. You are describing the scene in the second chapter of Acts."

"Well, that must be in the New Testament, which I haven't read. Let me go on, and you can tell me, Jeff, if I went back in time and was reliving that chapter. Next I saw an evil-looking man in the crowd raise his fist to the spokesman who looked like an authoritative rabbi. This evil-looking man accused that group of drunkenness. I said to a woman standing by me, 'Who is that rabbi?' She answered, 'It's Peter, an Apostle of Yeshua HaMashiach.' Well, Peter got that man told. That's when he quoted Joel and also David from the Psalms to prove that everything that was happening that day on Shavuot was real and was a fulfillment of prophecy that the Messiah would die and then be raised from the dead. Things got scary when Peter pointed his finger at the crowd and accused them, or rather us, of crucifying Jesus! But then he shocked me by saying it was God's plan all along. The only way people could be forgiven of their sins was for Jesus to die in their place, or rather our place. Lots of people started asking Peter, 'How can we be saved?' It was hitting me hard, because Peter had just accused me of putting the sinless Messiah to death. I cried out like the other people, cut to the core, that I had done such a thing. Peter answered the question and I remember his words: 'Repent, and let every one of you be baptized in the name of Jesus Christ for the remission of sins; and you shall receive the gift of the Holy Spirit. For the promise is to you and to your children, and to all who are afar off, as many as the Lord our God will call.'[78] I yelled out, 'I repent. I need to be saved.' The last thing I remember is walking down into one of the pools of water at the bottom of the southern steps, going under and then coming up, feeling light as a feather. The person in the water beside me said, 'I am clean, I am clean. I have a brand new life.' I reached over and hugged that man and agreed I felt the same way. Then I woke up and saw Grace and Shira standing beside me and praying. A heaviness and a darkness left my head in a whooshing sound, and I felt something like oil running down my spine. Then I saw all your beautiful faces staring at me. I have never felt such joy in my life!"

CHAPTER THIRTY-THREE

DOCTOR
ROTHSCHILD

Shira told the others she had to report to Dr. Rothschild. As she turned to leave she asked Grace to follow her. Outside the door, Shira grabbed Grace's hand. "Let's pray, but don't give the appearance of praying. Just make it look like we are discussing the patient's case. Keep your eyes open and pray softly."

"Lord, I am about to explode with joy. You have just answered our prayers for Dror's healing in such a dramatic way, that it is almost unbelievable. Thank You, Yahweh, for performing a miracle. Now Shira must be wise as a serpent and harmless as a dove in her report to Dr. Rothschild. Put the words in her mouth. Give her favor with the doctor. Lord, may Your will be done, whether it involves persecution or not. May You be glorified in this miracle. If Shira loses her job, supply her with a better one. Oh, Lord, cause this obviously supernatural work to be credited to You and to the believing prayers of Your children. In the mighty name of Yeshua. Amen."

When Grace went back in the room, Dror had center stage, speaking from his heart about all the ways the Lord had prepared him for the display of God's mighty power in this dramatic healing. "Ima and Abba, last June, I met Gloria and Jeff and their friends Pete and Sarah. Looking back on our encounter in the restaurant that night, I can see the Lord setting up that meeting, as well as all the events that have happened since. They needed me to teach them

Hebrew and advise them about aliyah, and while that was going on, I was being exposed to the genuine Christian lifestyle. The way these two couples lived was very attractive to me, but I never let on how impressed I was with their character, good morals, purpose in life, and genuine love for God. Then I met Grace, and those qualities were displayed in her life also. Because I was attracted to her romantically, I squelched my disdain for Christianity and attended church with her. A woman named Miss Lizzie who offended me at first became someone I admired for her powerful prayer life. I would have eventually come to believe that Yeshua is the Messiah over a long period of time as I continued interaction with these people. But the supernatural events that began happening speeded up my understanding of spiritual things and made me jealous. For instance, Savta came out of a horrible experience in sex trafficking, and the hand of God was evident throughout her rescue and subsequent rebirth in the Messiah."

Devorah cried out. "What? You told me about her rescue right after it happened, and Jeff just now said she worked in a gambling casino, but you didn't say the words, 'sex-trafficking!' How in the world did she get into that? Since her rescue, has she been fully rehabilitated?"

Dror didn't have a chance to answer. Dr. Rothschild entered the room with Shira and another nurse who held a notebook. Dror was sitting on the side of the bed. Everyone moved to the periphery of the room as the Doctor began to probe Dror's body thoroughly. Nurse Miriam wrote everything the doctor called out. "Mr. Mizrachi, it appears that you have recovered, but sometimes the external symptoms will leave while the disease is still progressing internally. I am arranging for you to have extensive tests. This is needed not only for you but for future patients, as we still have much to learn about the West Nile Virus. You must remain in the hospital for a full week in order for us to make an extensive evaluation of your case. The virus outbreak in New York a few months ago, as well as the case of my two patients who died from the virus, provided much information with which we would like to compare your case." The doctor turned to Nurse Miriam and told her she should type an official documentation of Dror's case thus far.

Dror felt the Holy Spirit anointing him as he opened his mouth to speak. Everyone in the room, including Dror, stood in amazement at the words pouring forth from him. It was obviously some language they didn't know, but as they looked at each other in awe, they couldn't help but notice Dr. Rothschild's mouth drop open and tears coming in his eyes. The more Dror spoke, the more moved the doctor seemed to be. Finally, Dror was quiet, and everyone's attention was turned to the doctor.

When Dr. Rothschild regained his composure, he looked directly at Dror and asked, "How do you know the Austro-Bavarian language? You just spoke it beautifully, and I have not heard it spoken in years."

"Oh, Doctor, I thought it was gibberish, and I am embarrassed, but I couldn't stop myself. You say it is a real language? I have never heard of Austro-Bavarian. What did I say?"

"Please, if you don't mind, I would like to talk to you privately. Would everyone leave, please? You can come back in about thirty minutes."

Dror suddenly realized that the West Nile Virus had not caused him to be in a Tel Aviv hospital, but it was really the Lord God who had brought him here for His own purposes, and part of the divine plan must have to do with Dr. Rothschild. Dror could feel the Holy Spirit moving in him, letting him know that this conversation was very important. He prayed that he would have the right answers for the questions the doctor would ask.

Dr. Rothschild struggled to speak, getting his emotions under control. "I believe you when you say that you don't know the Austro-Bavarian language. It is not in common usage today, so I have to conclude that what just happened is supernatural. That leads me to understand your healing is also supernatural. No doubt your family and friends here have prayed fervently for your healing. Not many people know that I pray for my patients because outwardly I am not religious. I am a secular Jew who is in the medical field because of my heritage from the Austrian branch of the Rothschild family. I am sure you have heard some of the conspiracy theories about the wealthy Ashkenazi Jewish Rothschilds, famous international bankers originating from Frankfurt, Germany in the late eighteenth century. We are supposed to be taking over the world!"

"Yes sir, I heard that the Rothschilds were part of the Illuminati, but I have never believed all that stuff. The thing I'm thankful for about your family is your part in the formation of a homeland for the Jews in Palestine under the British Mandate. I am an ardent Zionist, so I know that on November 2, 1917, Britain's Foreign Secretary, Arthur James Balfour, wrote an important letter to Britain's most illustrious Jewish citizen, Baron Lionel Walter Rothschild, expressing the British government's support for a Jewish homeland in Palestine. The letter would eventually become known as the Balfour Declaration."[79] After World War I, the British were charged with securing this homeland for the Jews.

"I am glad you know that, Dror, because I am proud of that and also the many positive contributions our family has made, not only in finance and Zionist causes, but in the arts, medicine, and in other fields. I would like you to call me by my first name, Salomon. This family name goes back to the founder of the Austrian branch of the Rothschild family.[80]

"Thank you for telling me your first name and about the history of your family. Now I must know what I said to you in the Austro-Bavarian language. It seemed very personal. It was a message from God. I am sure of that because it was like the vision I had – and it was not a hallucination. My vision came right out of Scripture, and people were speaking in languages they had never learned, just like me today. But people hearing them could understand in their own languages what they said. The crowd was from many different countries and had come to Jerusalem for the Feast of Shavuot. The message was from God Himself, telling of His wonderful works."

The doctor's eyebrows were raised. "I have never heard of this, and I read the Tanach daily. Do you know where it is found in the Tanach?"

"Salomon, please don't discredit me and my experience when I tell you. If you will get a Brit Hadasha, you can read the whole story in the Book of Acts, Chapter Two, but Jeff said it's good to also read Chapter One leading up to it. I plan to do that."

"I do have a Brit Hadasha, and I will read it. In my field we have to check out as many sources as possible, even if we have a prejudice against them. Okay, your message has greatly helped me not to lose hope, so it is only right that I translate it for you. This is what you said: 'Salomon, you are forgiven for aborting that baby. Your wife's barrenness is not My punishment. Avigail will bear you a child next year. You are to name him Jedidiah.'" The doctor broke down and cried unashamedly.

Dror felt the holiness of the moment and remained silent. He wanted so badly to hug Salomon, but he only patted his shoulder and sat there in awe, pondering all that had happened.

Dr. Salomon came in Dror's room with a big smile on his face. "Young man, I want to thank you for agreeing to remain in the hospital three days until we could make those tests. You passed them, of course. You may even be healthier than you were before you got sick! You were admitted on Tuesday, December 14th, and today you will be discharged as Shabbat will soon begin at sundown. I could have discharged you the next day after you were healed, but I had several reasons not to. You have been so patient. I have personally enjoyed our visits and discussion of your spiritual journey. Because of you I am determined to read the Brit Hadasha all the way through. I must say that the second chapter of Acts has made an impact on me. My nurse Shira has finally told me why she glows all the time. Like you, she is a Messianic Jew. I have now given her permission to pray openly for my patients in the name of Yeshua. Well, you must call your parents and your girlfriend Grace and tell them to come pick you up."

"Before I go, Doctor, I want to ask you if you documented my healing as an answer to prayer. I am not denying that I received the best medical care available, but you and I both know that my healing was supernatural and an answer to prayer."

"Yes, I wrote in your case file that your healing was a miracle, and I quoted our first Prime Minister, David Ben-Gurion, who said, 'In Israel, in order to be a realist, you must believe in miracles.'"[81]

Dror couldn't resist embracing his new friend, Salomon Rothschild. "And remember my invitation to attend the Holiday Concert at the International Convention Center in Jerusalem. The two performances are next week on Thursday and Friday. I will have Mr. Edsel Gruber, Gloria's concert manager, to mail you and your wife free tickets. I am not trying to brag, but you will see that my piano playing won't show any trace of brain damage!" Dror laughed.

"I can assure you we will be there. My wife is a pianist, too, so it will be quite a treat for her." Dr. Rothschild gave Dror a firm handshake and went out the door.

Dror called his parents to come pick him up. A half-hour later he took his discharge papers to the desk, and his parents and Grace were waiting for him. As they got in the car, Devorah began to describe the Shabbat dinner they would soon be enjoying.

CHAPTER THIRTY-FOUR

GOD'S
PREVENTION
AND PROTECTION

BACKSTAGE AT CONCERT HALL
FIRST REHEARSAL, TUESDAY

"This piano teacher has never been more proud of her students!" exclaimed Mrs. Pagani. "Dror, if you need a piano scholarship at Hebrew University, just say the word. Gloria's scholarship in voice and piano came through, and I bet I could get you one, too. You can continue being her accompanist for many concerts in the future. Of course, you will soon have your master's degree in history at MSU, but why not also pursue a master's degree in music? Whatever your vocational goals are, you would have extra income from your skills as an accompanist. That guy out there, playing for the University Singers, is not nearly as good as you are." Mrs. Pagani left to find the restroom.

Gloria looked at Dror, knowing what satisfaction that compliment brought him. He had already told her when he saw the final concert program that the accompanist, Peter Strauss, was the man who stole Ginna away from him. Gloria observed Peter at the piano and scanned the faces of the singers onstage. "Dror, which one of the singers is Ginna? Is it the redheaded one on the back row center? She is beautiful."

Dror struggled with emotions that had been dormant in him for a long time. "Yes, she's the one. Her vocal capacity is amazing, but somehow it seems her heart is not in the words she is singing. I noticed her staring at me from the first row as I accompanied you on 'Sleigh Ride.' I couldn't believe it when she winked. Of course, Peter was sitting beside her. I don't know if they are married or not, but I thought they were headed in that direction. She has no business tantalizing me."

Gloria looked intently at Dror. "Have you told Grace about her?"

"No, I haven't. It didn't seem important until now. I have been looking at Grace and Jeff sitting out there. While I was playing 'He Shall Feed His Flock' for you, I noticed Grace was forming a kiss with her lips and then blowing it to me. My heart jumped, and I almost lost my place in the music. I love her so much. I want to be with her all the time. I feel incomplete without her."

Gloria was thoughtful. "You know what, that makes me think of God's creation of Eve from Adam's rib. She was inside of him, and God took her out of him. That made them both incomplete. Now I know what it means when it says, 'For this reason a man shall leave his father and mother and be **joined** to his wife, and the two shall become one flesh.'[82] It's like the two have magnets that attract each other. '**For this reason**' they have to come back together and be **one** to be complete. And God knows which particular ones are meant for each other. Dror, you have found your bashert!"[83]

"My heart jumped again when you said that, Gloria! I'm surprised you know that Yiddish word, but you got it right. It's a match made in heaven."

"Well, do you remember what I told you that night you came for your first piano lesson with me? You revealed to me how Ginna broke your heart. She jilted you. Then I gave you a message I was certain came from the Lord. I said, 'God has already reserved someone for you, someone who has never loved or been loved by any man. She will give you her whole heart, and you can trust her. God will use her to heal your wounded heart. You will love her, and together you will make beautiful music.'"

"Gloria, I have to say I had forgotten that, but it has happened. Being with Grace caused me to completely forget Ginna. And seeing that hussy again tonight made me wonder why I ever loved her."

"Can't you see, Dror, that God was protecting you? He was preventing you from making a big mistake. It caused you pain, but it would have been more painful to be married to a girl like Ginna. I don't want to judge her, but I can't help but sense that she has selfish ambition. Peter Strauss may be the next casualty in her climbing the ladder of success."

"Gloria, I am slow, but I am fully awake now. I know what I have to do. I am going to ask Grace to marry me. I am going to do it on Christmas Eve. Then, courtesy of your father, we will be flying to Charlottesville on Christmas Day to announce our engagement to Mr. and Mrs. Thomas."

Gloria began to laugh. "So, you are following in the footsteps of Jeff and me, making your announcement and setting off fireworks in the Thomas household! We didn't do it correctly, but the customary way is for the future groom to first ask the father of his future wife for her hand in marriage and after he is given approval, then he proposes to her." Dror grinned and shrugged his shoulders.

The University Singers, followed by Peter Strauss, left the stage. It was time for Gloria and Dror to rehearse the last numbers, including a possible encore, "Cantique de Noel (O Holy Night)" by Adolphe Adam. After an outstanding performance of the "Hallelujah Chorus," the orchestra and chorus filed out. Gloria arose from the piano, and she and Dror began "Cantique de Noel." All the singers and orchestra members were leaving the auditorium, but the unfamiliar music Gloria was singing was so beautiful that it caused most of them to sit down and listen. Unfortunately, only a few minutes into the song, they realized it was all about the birth of Christ, and loud groans expressed their distaste. They quickly left the auditorium.

Mr. Gruber pondered asking Gloria for a different encore, but the thought came to him that the many Christian tourists in the audience would greatly enjoy this song. He knew it was the favorite of all Christmas songs for Christians. He approached Gloria and Jeff backstage. "My dear protégé, you must sing for the two performances exactly like you did tonight. I have no criticisms or corrections. The encore was well done. Please ignore the response of the members of the university orchestra and the singers. Thank you for modeling the two gowns Bianca picked out for you. You were stunning. I want to know how you like the rooms I reserved for all of you at the brand new David Citadel Hotel. Its location in the center of Jerusalem on King David Street and close to the entrance of the Old City makes it the perfect place for hosting VIPs like you," chuckled Mr. Gruber. "You have the opportunity of rubbing elbows with global political leaders, business moguls and celebrities. I hear that this hotel is competing with the nearby King David Hotel and the new Waldorf Astoria for the title of 'Jerusalem's flagship hotel.'[84] Nothing but the best for my musical stars."

"Mr. Gruber, we have a marvelous view of the Old City walls from our windows. Jeff and I can see David's Citadel at Jaffa Gate. Wow! You outdid yourself. And I am praying hard that the ticket receipts will enable you to pay all your expenses and have lots of money left over. You are one amazing man, and I love you so much." Gloria gave her smiling benefactor a warm hug.

Dror reached out to shake Mr. Gruber's hand. "I love my room and view, too, Mr. Gruber. The location right across from the International Convention Center couldn't be better. Thank you for allowing my parents to reimburse you for our suite of rooms. Grace told me she enjoys rooming with Mrs. Pagani, and she had many accolades for the accommodations."

♥ ♥ ♥ ♥ ♥

DAVID CITADEL HOTEL, JERUSALEM
THURSDAY AFTER THE FIRST PERFORMANCE

"My prima donna wife, come here and let me congratulate you the way I longed to do it backstage but couldn't because of so many of your worshipers surrounding you," pleaded Jeff, as he reached out for Gloria.

Gloria replied over her shoulder as she hurried to the bathroom. "Jeff, I can't now. Nature calls."

Jeff waited as the minutes ticked by. Impatiently, he called at the bathroom door, "Gloria, are you all right?" There was no answer. "Gloria! Answer me! Are you sick?" Still no answer.

Jeff banged on the door, louder and louder, calling Gloria to open the door. Finally, he got a running start and kicked the door in. Gloria was lying on the floor with a peaceful expression on her face. He bent over her to make sure she was breathing, and she was. She appeared to be asleep. He took her pulse, and it was normal. She didn't have a fever. He decided to pray out loud. "Dear Lord, please show me what is going on. Is Gloria in a trance, or is she sick? Please wake her up. I confess I am worried. Show me what to do."

Jeff couldn't hear from God, so he shook Gloria hard until she woke up.

"Oh, my wonderful husband. Please hold me close. I am so weak. I could hear you calling me, but I couldn't make myself respond. I feel at peace, but why am I so weak, so drained? I was supposed to meet with some government leaders tonight after the concert. Mr. Gruber arranged it. They approached me backstage right before my performance and asked for a meeting at 10:30 tonight in a private room here at the hotel. They didn't look like government leaders. They were dressed like ultra-orthodox Jews. I think they said they were from the Yad L'Achim, which means 'hand of the brothers.'[85] They adhere to Haredi Judaism, they said. Anyway, they told me not to bring anyone with me, only Mr. Gruber. I was about to tell you, when I had to go to the bathroom. I thought I was going to throw up. But I didn't. And then I fainted, I guess."

Jeff was puzzled. "That is the weirdest thing. Let's see, it is now 10:15. I think I am hearing the Spirit say not to let you meet them. Is Mr. Gruber coming to our room to get you?"

"Yes, he should be here any minute. But, Jeff, I feel so very weak. I don't think I can even walk there. Maybe we should call Mr. Gruber and tell him not to come."

"Okay, I am dialing him now…. Hello, Mr. Gruber. Gloria said she couldn't make that meeting tonight. All of a sudden she felt so weak she fainted. Maybe you could arrange another time to meet……. Whaaat? You don't know anything about it? But Gloria said…"

Gloria took the phone and questioned Mr. Gruber thoroughly. In a few minutes, she said goodbye and looked at Jeff, incredulously. "He said he saw those strange-looking men backstage, but he did not talk to them. Oh, Jeff, they lied to me! They wanted me to come alone to meet them. What in the world are they trying to do?"

"I don't know, but what I do know is that God made you weak and made you faint so you couldn't go meet with them! Before I alert hotel security I want to search on the internet and see what kind of organization Yad L'Achim is."

"Yes, Jeff, do both those things, but first, let us get down on our knees, thank Him for anointing the concert with His Spirit, and worship Him. After I finished the encore I wanted so badly to lift my hands in worship to our King of kings and Lord of lords. Let's do it now, and then we must ask Him what is happening and how we should respond to it." Gloria immediately fell to her knees and began to sing from her heart 'My Tribute' by Andrae Crouch[86] – "*How can I say thanks for the things You have done for me, things so undeserved, yet You gave to prove Your love for me? The voices of a million angels could not express my gratitude. All that I am or ever hope to be, I owe it all to Thee. To God be the glory, to God be the glory, to God be the glory for the things He has done. With His blood He has saved me, with His power He has raised me. To God be the glory for the things He has done. Just let me live my life, let it be pleasing, Lord, to Thee, and if I gain any praise, let it go to Calvary….*"

Gloria and Jeff prayed a long time, until they felt complete peace. Then Jeff found information about the Yad L'Chim on the internet. "Babe, you are definitely a threat to the kingdom of darkness, and its lackeys have come looking for you to stop your powerful witness for Yeshua among His own people at the concert. The primary purpose of these extremists is to block the Jewish people from hearing the gospel or to cause them not to respond out of fear. They are called counter-missionaries. Witnessing in Israel that Yeshua is the Messiah is called proselytizing. It is not illegal, technically, unless a minor is targeted without parental consent. Nevertheless, this group hates what they call 'missionaries' and has been known to vandalize Messianic congregations and persecute individual Jewish believers. They can be pretty violent sometimes. I praise God that He prevented you from meeting with them. God has shown Himself to be your Protector."

A big smile spread over Gloria's face. "Then I am blessed, indeed! Jesus said so in His Sermon on the Mount – 'Blessed are you when they revile and persecute you, and say all kinds of evil against you falsely for My sake. Rejoice and be exceedingly glad, for great is your reward in heaven, for so they persecuted the prophets who were before you.'[87] Hey, Jeff, that makes me a prophet."

"Okay, babe, you're a prophet, or rather a prophetess, but I already knew that. What I didn't remember is the persecution that goes along with it. Besides being your husband, now I have to be your body guard." Jeff paused with a fresh realization. "And what a beautiful body I will be guarding. Oh, my, and just to think you belong to me. However, the Bible says, if it comes down to it, I will have to lay down my life for you. And how grateful should you be, little wife? Come here right now. These body-guard arms are longing to hold you. I have not had my quota of kisses since you have been rehearsing and performing, you gorgeous woman." Jeff's voice was filled with passionate desire.

"Jeff, I am only too glad to fill the quota, but first, you better call hotel security and also alert the security guards for the concert tomorrow night. We need to warn Mr. Gruber and Dror, too."

Jeff was mumbling under his breath as he dialed the number – *Doesn't this husband's needs ever get priority?*

CHAPTER THIRTY-FIVE

CHRISTMAS EVE
BLESSINGS

The parking lot of the International Convention Center in Jerusalem was completely full, and latecomers to the concert had to look for parking places elsewhere. Mr. Gruber was in the lobby early and was so excited he thought he might have a heart attack, watching formally-dressed concertgoers lining up to get in the Ussishkin Auditorium. *This is the pinnacle of my career, and I know You did it, God. Never could I have pulled off a concert of this magnitude in my own strength. I promise You I will serve You the rest of my life. Thank You for introducing me to these fine young people. They continually inspire me and cause me to want Your glory more than my own. I only ask that tonight may fulfill Your purposes in Your Holy City in the midst of Your chosen people, the Jews. Forgive me for all the times I have made jokes about them and have regarded them as Christ killers and as greedy, unscrupulous people. Thank You for teaching me how wonderful they are, and how much they have contributed to the good of all people. I am a beneficiary of the blessings of Abraham. Last of all, I request that Gloria sing better than ever before and that Dror play magnificently. Oh, and one more thing, God, please bless my dear Bianca, bless Jeff, bless Grace, and bless all their families, especially the ones attending tonight. In Jesus' name I pray, Amen.*

Gloria and Jeff were about to leave the hotel for the convention center when Jeff's phone rang. "Hey, it's you, Pete! Yes, you're coming through loud and clear, bro. It is so good to hear your voice. Are you having a great time at Chaya and Max's house? I know Sarah is enjoying her little one-year-old niece Estelle.... What? You were planning to leave there in time to be here tonight and surprise us? That is really great.... I didn't get that. Say it again, the reason you didn't come.... No, you can't mean it! That's wonderful news, but what about our plan to leave next June? Wait a minute, Pete. I need to put this phone on speaker, so Gloria can hear. Okay, now go ahead. Talk slower. You certainly are excited. I can't quite make out your words."

Gloria took the phone. "Well, I can. I hear you saying that Sarah has morning sickness, and you can't fly this far. Sarah is pregnant! You guys are having a baby! You beat us!" Gloria broke down crying and then laughing.

Pete and Sarah both got on the phone. Sarah spoke loudly, "Yes, we are overjoyed. Chaya took me to the doctor on Wednesday to confirm it, but I already had given myself a pregnancy test. Don't worry one bit. I will still be able to make the move to Israel with you in June like we have planned all along. The doctor said the baby would most likely be born the end of August. I am four weeks pregnant now, and he advised I not travel overseas to your concert. But when we move to Israel, flying will be no danger to me or the baby at six months and two weeks of pregnancy. And if we could leave at the end of May instead of on June 13th, it would be even better."

Gloria and Jeff replied simultaneously, "Maybe we can." Jeff added, "We gotta help a new mother. Hey, an idea popped into my head. Will the baby be a holy roller, too?"

Gloria suddenly realized she would be onstage playing the opening number of the concert in only thirty minutes. "Pray for me, Pete and Sarah. Jeff and I need to leave right now to get to the concert on time." Gloria turned the phone off, grabbed her purse, and pushed Jeff out the door.

As they walked in the lobby, Jeff saw Dr. Rothschild. Dror had instructed him to look up the doctor and tell him and his wife to meet them backstage after the concert. Jeff knew he needed to escort Gloria to the stage, and they had not a minute to spare, so in passing, he said, "Dr. Rothschild, I must get Gloria to the stage quickly. Dror told me to find you and tell you to come backstage immediately after the concert." Salomon and his wife Avigail nodded to Jeff and Gloria. Gloria blew them a kiss.

Mr. Gruber came out in front of the curtain promptly at seven o'clock and gave a hearty welcome, interspersed with a few Hebrew and Yiddish words. "Erev tov. Bruchim habaim. I am Edsel Gruber from New York City. They said I was 'meshuganah' when I booked concerts for an American teenage girl in Vienna, Budapest, and Prague in the summer of last year. I had the newspapers put her name in headlines, and hundreds of people came out of curiosity to the first concert in Vienna. They were amazed. The reputation of Gloria Sondheim as a spectacular vocalist and pianist preceded her to the next concert in Budapest. The house was packed, and the audience never stopped applauding and begging for more encores until Miss Sondheim sang a beautiful spiritual song that touched their hearts. Finally, they were satisfied and left the concert hall in a state of reverence. The tour ended in Prague with an avalanche of applause and cries for more encores. So, tonight you can judge for yourself after you hear Mrs. Gloria Sondheim Quentin play the piano and sing in our Holiday Concert – was I meshuganah or not? One of your own, an Israeli who learned to play the piano at Hebrew University, Dror Mizrachi, will accompany Mrs. Quentin. And the Hebrew University Singers, accompanied by Peter Strauss, will be featured in the middle of the program. The University Chorus and Orchestra will accompany Mrs. Quentin on the final number. Sit back and enjoy!"

Jeff's heart burst with pride as Gloria gave a flawless piano performance of "Miniature Overture" and "Dance of the Sugar Plum Fairy" from Tchaikovsky's famous *Nutcracker Suite*. The audience clapped politely, but Jeff could hear a few gasps when Gloria came to the front of the stage to take her bows. He could hardly catch his breath, drinking in her beauty so exquisitely displayed in her red velvet gown and with what appeared to be a stunning diamond necklace and drop earrings. He realized he had never seen them before and was in awe.

After the performance of "Sleigh Ride" with a trumpet player and a percussionist positioned close to the piano, the audience stood and applauded vigorously. Gloria took Dror's hand, and they both bowed to whistles and shouts of affirmation in Hebrew, as well as enthusiastic applause. Gloria brought the trumpet player and percussionist to the front of the stage to bow along with them.

It was a lengthy applause, and Gloria enjoyed it. She realized there may not be such a great reception for the next sacred numbers from the *Messiah*. It may even seem anti-climactic to the audience, although the Christians in attendance would love it. Gloria prayed silently for the hearts of the Jewish people to be open. For this final performance, she was sure she heard the Spirit tell her to introduce these numbers with the story of how the *Messiah* was written. *Lord, please help me to tell it well, and please give me favor with Mr. Gruber and his approval for departing from the printed program.*

Gloria began, "I must tell you how this greatest of all musical works, the *Messiah*, was written. I will be singing three numbers from it now, and at the end of the program I will sing another one and end by playing the piano, along with the Hebrew University Chorus and Orchestra, for the well-known 'Hallelujah Chorus.' Please notice that all the words are printed in your program insert. This is a true story about the composer of the *Messiah*. George Frederic Handel was a German man living in London. He mainly composed operas, but his operas began to fail, and so did his health. He went bankrupt. In 1741, he was asked by a charity in Dublin to write something for a charity performance. Handel was depressed, thinking that this would be his final work. But a turning point came, when his friend, Charles Jennens, Jr., gave him a libretto, the words, for an oratorio. It was an assembly of Bible verses, focused on the Messiah, both from the Tanakh and Brit Hadasha. Handel set about writing the music to fit the words and finished with two and a half hours of music. But it is obvious that HaShem wrote the music **through** him, because it certainly was a miracle that he composed it in only twenty-four days, during which time he barely ate or drank or got any sleep! When he finally completed the last of it, the 'Hallelujah Chorus,' his servant opened the door and saw him crying. Handel shouted out, 'I did think I did see all Heaven before me, and the great God Himself!' At its London premiere, King George was so moved by the 'Hallelujah Chorus' that he spontaneously rose from his seat. The entire audience followed his example and, for the past 250-plus years, audiences have continued to do the same."[88]

Gloria began to sing, but she was so emotional about singing the gospel that she could not stop the tremor in her voice. "Then shall the eyes of the blind be opened, and the ears of the deaf unstopped. Then shall the lame man leap as an hart, and the tongue of the dumb shall sing.... He shall feed His flock like a shepherd.... Come unto Me, ye that labor...."

Jeff looked around and saw people in the audience crying. He surprised himself that tears were also flowing down his own cheeks, and looking over at Grace, he saw it was happening to her, too. *HaShem, you are here, You are here, touching the hearts of Your people. Gloria's voice is not as beautiful as it usually is, but it doesn't matter. You are using her anyway. Yes, Lord, receive the glory. It is all Yours.*

There was a disturbance coming from the far left of the auditorium, close to the stage entrance. Jeff saw someone throw something on the stage from that direction. He leaned over to Grace. "Look at that! It's a tomato. Oh, no! It hit Gloria on the arm." Jeff moved quickly toward the man dressed in black with a black hat who was trying to go backstage. A security guard tackled him. Another guard grabbed two other men who were also about to throw what turned out to be rotten tomatoes.

Jeff heard a woman cry out, "It's the Yad L'Achim. They vandalized our church this summer!"

The concert had come to a standstill. Edsel Gruber had the curtain drawn, and he came out to the front of the stage. "Do not be alarmed, friends. Those musically illiterate people will have to spend a night in jail. Of all people, you Israelis know what it is like to be unjustly attacked. I say we encourage our performers with an extra round of applause. They will be right back with you to complete the beautiful music from the Messiah and to add one more song before the University Singers come out for their numbers."

Edsel hurried backstage and asked Gloria and Dror what they could possibly perform to recover the good mood of the audience. Mrs. Pagani was seated beside them and without hesitation urged them to perform "He That Keepeth Israel" from Psalm 121, composed by Adolphe Schlosser. Mr. Menotti, Gloria's voice teacher, had advised Mrs. Pagani that this number should be done for an encore, so Gloria and Dror had it ready. They heartily agreed because it emphasized God's special care for Israel. He was always watching over them and never slept. His ears were always open to their prayers.

The curtain opened. Dror and Gloria came to the front of the stage and were greeted with thunderous applause. Dror introduced the song. "Fellow Israelis and tourists, after we complete the performance of 'Come Unto Me' from the Messiah, it is our deep honor to present this faith-building song about HaShem's special love and care for His chosen people and the nation of Israel. The title is 'He that Keepeth Israel,' and it is based on Psalm 121."

Before the concert that night, Dror had talked with his parents about having a celebration in their suite of rooms after the concert, at which time he would propose to Grace. Devorah and Benyamin were not surprised at all. They both had given up their prejudice against Christianity after seeing Dror's supernatural healing. And they had welcomed Grace into their hearts. Dror would invite twelve people besides his parents to witness his proposal to Grace and enjoy refreshments. He planned that everyone would not know they were coming to an engagement party. The invitation would be for an after-concert celebration. His mother said she would arrange for the food. Dror had asked his dad to sell him a diamond ring from the small pouch of jewels that he always carried inside his coat.

As he and Gloria had resumed their performance of "Come Unto Me," Dror realized that the only time guests could be invited was during the three numbers the University Singers would perform following the song, "He That Keepeth Israel." There would be no intermission. The invitations had to be given out while the University Singers were performing. As soon as the heartwarming applause after their extra number ended, he enlisted Gloria to help him carry out his plan. He pulled out a memo pad and pen inside his coat and wrote party invitations on several sheets of paper. He asked Gloria to get Jeff's attention and tell him to pass them out discreetly. Dror wrote the names of the guests on another sheet of paper – Dr. Salomon and Avigail Rothschild, Alvin and Sylvia Sondheim, Sam and Anna Sondheim, Edsel Gruber, Bianca Pagani, Shira and Aharon Shapiro, and, of course, Grace. They all were seated on the first two rows. From backstage at the edge of the curtain Gloria peeped out at Jeff and curled her finger in a "come here" motion. Jeff went backstage. Gloria whispered to Jeff to pass out the invitations.

The University Singers finished their numbers. The audience applauded politely as the Singers left the stage and returned to their seats in the auditorium. Gloria and Dror re-appeared on the stage, and Gloria was dressed in a shining royal blue gown with a beautiful pearl necklace and earrings. Delicate, sequined Stars of David adorned her shimmering gown. The audience came alive. Gloria's voice reached amazing heights in her performance of "I Know that My Redeemer Liveth" from Handel's *Messiah*. The audience began applauding the words of Job in the middle of the song, but when the song neared its conclusion, you could have heard a pin drop. Jeff asked the Lord if this was good or bad. Did they like it? Then he realized the words were all about the resurrection of Yeshua, which would be scandalous to the religious Jews – "For now is Christ risen from the dead, the firstfruits of them that sleep" – and this phrase was repeated over and over. After the last note was sung Jeff looked around the auditorium, and many were not applauding at all, but there were groups scattered throughout the auditorium who were applauding vigorously. Then he understood the contrast between the Christian tourists who fully accepted this truth and the Jewish people who were blinded to it. A heartfelt prayer rose up to heaven from his inner being.

The final number on the program was the famed "Hallelujah Chorus" from the *Messiah*. The University Orchestra had already assembled in the orchestra pit immediately after the University Singers had left the stage. Now the large Chorus was filling the risers and most of the stage as the piano was positioned toward the center. Gloria sat down at the piano, got comfortable, then nodded to the Conductor. Her fingers came down hard on the keys. The singers, the orchestra, and the piano had equal volume. *How could it be?* thought Jeff. *The piano is not overpowered at all. Only You, Yahweh, could make this perfect balance.* Jeff was almost jarred out of his seat with the sheer volume of the glorious music. His arms were covered with chill bumps, and his heart was about to explode out of his chest. *Oh, Yahweh! This is surely a foretaste of heaven. Handel must have felt this power and beauty, multiplied ten times over as he composed this. Please don't let me faint. I can feel your Holy Spirit charging through my body like an electric shock. Oh, I love it! Thank You, God. May You receive all the glory, ALL the glory!!*

CHAPTER THIRTY-SIX

TWO VERY
DIFFERENT
ANNOUNCEMENTS

Dror stood in the hall outside his hotel room and greeted his guests as they arrived all together. In case not everyone had met, he made introductions and thanked each one for coming. "Welcome, friends. It is time to celebrate our two successful concert performances on Christmas Eve in the Holy City. Gloria and I have already had plenty of applause, but now I want us to applaud my parents, Benyamin and Devorah Mizrachi, for hosting this party in their suite of rooms. My mom has provided the refreshments." Cheers, whistles, and applause filled the air. Everyone was in a celebratory mood. Grace held on tightly to Dror's arm as she looking adoringly into his face.

Jeff got the attention of the guests. "All of us are thankful to you, Mr. and Mrs. Mizrachi, for your gracious hospitality. You are certainly very supportive parents, having been here throughout the two rehearsals and two performances and now hosting us tonight. I pray HaShem will greatly reward you. And I also want to thank Gloria's grandparents, Sam and Anna Sondheim, for making the trip from Katzrin to be present for the two performances. Gloria and I are looking forward to traveling back with them and enjoying their hospitality until we fly back to Columbus five days from now. Thanks are due to Gloria's parents, Alvin and Sylvia Sondheim of New York, for coming to support their daughter in the highlight of her music career thus far. I love my in-laws, Mr. Alvin and Miss

Sylvia. And Dror could not have performed in these two concerts had it not been for his doctor and nurse in Tel Aviv, Dr. Salomon Rothschild and Shira Shapiro. However, they know, and we all know that HaShem is the real Healer, and through the power and the name of Yeshua the Messiah, Dror was healed of the West Nile Virus."

The second round of applause had intensified. Jeff continued, "We owe a debt of gratitude to Mrs. Bianca Paganini for her excellent piano teaching for both Gloria and Dror. And, of course, Mr. Edsel Gruber arranged this whole thing. Let's give a shout out to them!"

Dror quieted the guests. "Let us recognize Avigail Rothschild, my doctor's wife, and Aharon Shapiro, my nurse's husband. We are so glad you are a part of our special group tonight. Now there is one person here who has not been applauded so far. I have saved the best till last. But before I do this, I want to thank Jeff Quentin, whom I admire greatly, for being the leader of our group. What he has just done in recognizing and thanking everyone is natural for him. Even though Gloria is a shining star, Jeff is not standing in her shadow. He is also a shining star, and let's show our appreciation for Jeff now."

Gloria shouted above the applause, "Jeff is the wind beneath my wings, and he is the leader of our ministry group, the Holy Rollers. If you want to know about that, just ask me later."

Dror resumed his speech. "Okay, I know everyone is ready for some refreshments, but there is something more important that is about to take place first. Please find a seat, and be comfortable. I have an announcement, and it involves the most beautiful and wonderful woman in the room, Grace Thomas." Dror took Grace's hand and led her to the center of the room. The guests seated behind them got up and walked to the other side of the room, facing Dror and Grace. Dror pulled Grace close beside him. She was trembling. He looked down into her eyes that were brimming with tears. It was like liquid love pouring on him, and his heart was greatly moved. "I feel like we are standing on holy ground, but I must get down on my knees now."

Grace's body began to shake. Dror quickly reached into his pocket for the little box, opened it, and held it up to Grace. "Grace, you are truly the best thing that has ever happened to me. After I dated you the second time I knew I would never find another woman to whom I could give my whole heart but you. My heart is on fire with love for you, Grace. I want you for my wife. I cannot live without you. Will you marry me?"

Grace began to sob and could hardly get the words out. Finally, she answered, "I love you the same way you described how you love me. It's so hard to believe this is actually happening. I loved you the minute I first met you. And my answer is YES! I will be your wife!"

Dror slid the diamond ring on Grace's finger, then enveloped her in his arms and kissed her passionately. Hand in hand, they turned to face their guests. With her face wreathed in smiles, Grace extended her hands to everyone in the room. "You all are invited to our wedding, whenever and wherever it is." Another round of applause filled the room.

Benyamin Mizrachi invited everyone to toast the engaged couple with some special wine he bought for the occasion. The refreshment table had to be resupplied after a half hour had gone by. All were in a jovial mood, and no one thought about retiring for the night.

Jeff's phone rang. He retreated to the nearest bedroom and answered. It was Pete, calling from Chaya and Max's house in Stony Brook, Long Island, to tell him that he heard from the Botanical Gardens Café in Jerusalem where he had applied for a security job. He was very excited that he got the job, especially since it was close to the Givat Ram campus of the Academy of Music and Dance where Gloria would have her music classes. "Pete, that is perfect! Gloria and I have scouted the area around the Academy and found a good neighborhood that has reasonably priced apartments. It's called Rasko. Maybe the four of us could find places to rent in that neighborhood. I need to talk to Dad about his progress on finding a location for the food business. I saw Mr. Alvin and him talking when we first got here for Gloria's rehearsals. It's possible they will team up with their distribution and catering businesses. Sarah will surely be needed as a bookkeeper. Wouldn't it be something if mine and Gloria's parents could also find apartments close to ours? But to change the subject, guess what happened a few minutes ago?"

Pete didn't care how much the phone bill would be. He had the speaker turned on for Sarah to hear. She was sitting right by him, taking it all in. "Tell us everything. I really miss y'all, and Sarah does, too."

"Well, we now have two candidates for admission in our Holy Rollers ministry," Jeff teased. He waited for Pete to figure it out.

"You mean Dror finally popped the question? Hallelujah! He and Grace are a perfect match. After he got born again in the hospital, evidently the Spirit took over and worked fast to open his eyes to his bashert." Sarah was squealing with delight in the background.

"Yes, it was a romantic scene. Dror's parents agreed for him to use their suite of rooms at the hotel for an after-concert celebration. He invited his doctor and wife, Gloria's parents and grandparents, Mr. Gruber, Mrs. Pagani, and a nurse and her husband who are his Tel Aviv neighbors. Grace didn't know what was about to happen until Dror made an announcement. Then he got on his knees and proposed, giving her the biggest diamond you ever saw! She could hardly talk for sobbing, but she finally got the words out – YES! And they are flying out to Charlottesville, Virginia, tomorrow to visit Mr. and Mrs. Thomas and ask for their blessing. Y'all better pray. I hear they are prejudiced against Jews, and when they are told that Dror wants to take his bride to live in Israel, they may expire on the spot!"

Pete started to laugh but stopped himself. "Oh, this is serious. I didn't mean to laugh. I can see we must call Miss Lizzie to help us pray this thing through. But with her swat team on this case you know the Thomases will yield to the persuasive power of the Holy Spirit."

"Right, and that reminds me that I need to put in a call to Pastor and Miss Celeste and Mrs. Goldberg. Wait a minute, we shouldn't tell them yet. It's best they first hear it from Dror. Oh, what rejoicing there will be about this good news. Hmmm. I guess he told them about his miracle healing from the West Nile Virus. That man has been so lovesick, he probably forgot. I'll find out. Anyway, I better get back to the party. You never know what our God will do next, and I don't want to miss anything. Love you and Sarah, and we will see you on December 30th."

When Jeff returned to the party, Mr. Gruber was speaking and had everyone spellbound. "Yes, my eye for talent has served me well over the years, and I was confirmed once again in this final concert. The applause came in waves of ever-increasing volume, and it seemed that there would be no end to the demand for more encores. You witnessed it. We could see that the Christian pilgrims outnumbered the Israelis in their hearty response after 'Cantique Noel' with its obvious message of the birth of Christ. After the negative response from the members of the orchestra and chorus in our final rehearsal, I had considered asking Gloria to substitute another song for 'Cantique Noel.' It must have been God who dissuaded me from doing that. The applause meter went the highest on the 'Hallelujah Chorus,' but that song came in second, I would say. Mrs. Pagani and I put our heads together to come up with additional encores, but we ran out of ideas. Dror's suggestion that Gloria sing 'Days of Elijah' was a genius idea. Gloria didn't even know that he had brought the music and could play it, but she was delighted to sing it and hoped it would be the final encore. Don't you all agree that it was the absolute icing on the cake?"

Everyone agreed that the words about the coming of the Messiah were very exciting, and it got even more exciting when someone in the back of the auditorium blew the shofar during the chorus – "Behold He comes, riding on the clouds, shining like the sun at the trumpet call! Lift your voice. It's the year of Jubilee, and out of Zion's hill salvation comes!"[89] Mr. Gruber said, "Gloria told me she loved the spontaneity of the shofar blowing. None of us could find the person who did it. We wanted to thank him, or maybe it was a her. It made the hairs on my arms rise!"

Mr. Gruber paused as several had to share their responses to the shofar blowing. Then he called for their attention and made his announcement. "Friends, something else wonderful happened tonight. At the conclusion of the concert Giovanni Galante of Hebrew University Academy of Music and Dance came backstage and sat me down to talk. He is the University's program manager for the holiday season, but he also arranges foreign concerts for out-standing music students. He was so inspired by Gloria and Dror's performance that he proposed a concert tour for them, accompa-nied by a small orchestra and singers' ensemble in Europe in the spring, even though they would not be at the University in Israel until later. I told him that since Gloria and her husband would be very busy in their senior year in college until their move to Israel next summer, it did not seem feasible for them or for Dror. Nev-ertheless, I said I would talk to our musical stars and see if a short concert tour could be arranged. Gloria's first concerts in Europe took place during her spring break, so perhaps it is possible that Gloria and Dror may want to accept this offer."

Jeff clenched his fists. This did not sit well with him at all. He looked at Gloria to see if she was tempted. He noticed Grace looking at Dror. Her face had a trace of anxiety, but Gloria's face was beaming.

♥ ♥ ♥ ♥ ♥

Jeff and Gloria had put on their night clothes and were sitting upright in the bed. "Every bone in my body is crying out for ten hours of sleep," said Gloria as she yawned.

"Well, you deserve those ten hours after all the effort you put into the rehearsals and performances. It's interesting that per-formers who are not big names only get a small percentage of the ticket receipts, but I guess the applause and numerous accolades are sufficient for you music people," replied Jeff, acidly. "Oh, and let me add – concert offers all over the country."

Gloria sensed resentment in Jeff's voice. "I take it that you are not happy about the concert tour in Europe next spring that Mr. Gruber offered Dror and me. I hope you don't think that my husband would not be going with me."

"Well, why should I go? Do you want me to sing a duet with you or turn pages for Dror at the piano?" replied Jeff, sarcastically. "Grace and I could pray together for your success. Is that my role, following you around like a puppy dog? Dear prima donna, had you even thought of what my plans might be next spring?"

"Jeff! I didn't say I would accept the offer. Have you assumed that I would?"

"Of course, you will, and Dror will, too. Everyone knows that musicians have huge egos," Jeff spit out. His voice was edged with anger. "Well, you said you needed sleep. Maybe you should consider that I need sleep, too. Good night." Jeff turned off the light, pulled up the covers, and turned his back to Gloria.

"Laila tov to you, too," said Gloria, sorrowfully. Soon she could hear Jeff quietly snoring. Her pillow was wet with tears. After a half-hearted prayer and an hour of sleeplessness, she finally fell asleep.

CHAPTER THIRTY-SEVEN

HE BINDS UP THE BROKENHEARTED

Gloria rubbed her eyes. Sunlight was streaming in the hotel window, and she realized they forgot to pull the drapes the night before. She stretched and raised her arms in praise to God. Then she threw her legs off her side of the bed and sat there, letting the memory of the glorious music wash over her. "Boker tov, Abba. Toda rabbah for an excellent night's sleep. It's just what I needed. You are so good to me. I loved singing and playing the piano in the concerts. Toda rabbah for giving me this fabulous opportunity to shine for You. I hope it brought You pleasure, Abba. I admit it brought me pleasure to hear such enthusiastic applause. I asked You to make me a blessing, and You did! Oh, thank You for Dror's magnificent playing. There couldn't have been a better accompanist. And thank You for my wonderful husband who has been a great support and a protector."

Gloria was fully awake now and looked over at Jeff. But Jeff wasn't there. Now she remembered the argument they had the night before. She bounded out of bed, calling for him, knocking on the bathroom door. Looking around, she did not see his suitcase or shoes or one article of his clothing, and his toiletries were not in the bathroom. She gasped. "He's packed and gone! Jeff is gone! Where is he, Father? This has never happened before. When we have had arguments, we have always quickly forgiven each other and made up." Then she broke down and cried. Distraught, she knew she had to look for him. *I will get dressed and go down to the desk. Maybe he has left a message for me. Could there have been some emergency? It's ten o'clock.* As she started to go out, she saw a sheet of paper lying on the floor in front of the door. Sitting down in a chair, she anxiously read:

> "*I got a call from my parents to come get them at Ben Gurion Airport. They made a last minute decision to fly to Jerusalem in time to see us before we leave. Dad wanted me to help him complete the arrangements to rent a building for Quentin Food Services. You go ahead with your parents and grandparents to Katzrin. I'm sure you won't miss me. I will be waiting for you at the airport next Thursday at noon on the 30th. I have the tickets and will meet you at the check-in desk. You don't need me. Just get a taxi or ask your parents to drive you to Tel Aviv. --- Jeff*

> "*P.S. Dror and Grace were in the lobby earlier when I came down to get coffee. They were leaving for an early flight to Virginia. Dror said to tell you to keep the diamond necklace and earrings. They are a gift from Mr. and Mrs. Mizrachi in appreciation for all you have done for Dror in advancing his musical education and performing experience. Also, Grace said to tell you 'Merry Christmas.'*"

Gloria's heart was broken. *He should have waked me up and told me. He always kisses me goodbye. But he wrote a note to avoid seeing me, evidently. He didn't even say he would miss me. He always signs his notes with 'I love you,' but not this time. Why is he treating me so coldly? I have to talk to somebody. Grace could counsel me, but she is leaving. Dear Father, please bring us back together. I love Jeff. I will give up my musical career entirely if that is what it takes. Tell me what to do.* She threw herself on the bed and cried. *Oh, goodness, I better call Mom and get my ride to Katzrin. I hope they haven't already left.* Gloria couldn't get either her parents or grandparents on the phone. She was alarmed. *Maybe they are in the dining room having breakfast. I must hurry down.*

Gloria pasted a smile on her face as she greeted her parents and grandparents in the dining room. But she had forgotten that her red eyes would be a contradiction to the smile. "Boker tov, Mom and Dad and Papa Sam and Mama Anna."

Sylvia pulled Gloria down in the chair beside her. "What's wrong, Gloria? Where is Jeff?"

Steadying her voice, Gloria answered, "He had to leave quickly for the airport to pick up his parents. They couldn't be here for the concerts because Mr. Jeffrey was tying up loose ends with his business in Tupelo in preparation for the final arrangements to launch his new food business in Jerusalem. They got a flight at the last minute while Jeff was still here. You know that they are making aliyah in the spring before we move to Israel next June. Jeff told me to go on with you all to Katzrin and meet him back at the airport for our flight home on the 30th."

Sylvia's face was marked with worry. "What a disappointment that Jeff won't be with us in Katzrin. But maybe he and his parents will have a slice of time available to come up and visit before the 30th. At Thanksgiving, Alvin and I really bonded with Jeffrey and Leah. I want to pursue our friendship, especially in view of the fact we are all going to live together in Israel."

Papa Sam was very quiet and thoughtful as the others talked. The food was served, and while they ate, the conversation centered on the concerts, the response of the two audiences, the attack of the Yad L'Achim, Dror's proposal to Grace, and Mr. Gruber's startling announcement. Gloria participated in the conversation until Mr. Gruber's announcement was brought up. Papa Sam noticed that she flinched, and her eyes were cast down. He began to seek the Lord for understanding and what he might do. It was clear to him that Gloria was wounded.

Alvin wasn't aware that Gloria was troubled and blurted out, "What did Jeff say about you and Dror going on tour in Europe next spring during your school break?"

Gloria began to cough and couldn't seem to stop. She drank a full glass of water. As she continued coughing, she excused herself to go to the restroom. After a few minutes she returned to the table and said, "I am ready to travel with you all to Katzrin as soon as I complete my packing. I will be back down in less than twenty minutes."

Papa Sam met Gloria at the elevator as she returned with her suitcases. "Merry Christmas, my darling granddaughter! Chag sameach!"

Alvin had already contacted the valet parking garage for their rental car to be brought out in front of the hotel. "Oh, Gloria, you have a lot of luggage. I guess you had to pack those gorgeous concert gowns and all the accessories in these overstuffed bags. No problem. The rest of us packed light, but we will have to sit tight," he chuckled. He could see that Gloria was anxious to leave, so he took it on himself to quickly direct the seating arrangement and make sure every piece of luggage was stowed away in the large trunk.

Gloria was seated by Mama Anna on one side and her mother on the other side in the back seat. Both did their share of 'mothering' with love pats and tender words during the trip north. Papa Sam continued his silence as he prayed for discernment and wisdom.

♥ ♥ ♥ ♥ ♥

SUNDAY MORNING, DECEMBER 26
KATZRIN, GOLAN HEIGHTS, ISRAEL

After breakfast Papa Sam directed everyone into the living room. "We are going to have a worship service today. Yesterday was Shabbat, but was mostly spent in traveling, so we missed our usual time for worship at the synagogue. Gloria, I know this is the day that you and Jeff attend the Adaton Baptist Church and also teach a Jewish roots class. I have heard about what a blessing it is to the congregation when you play the piano and sing in the worship service on occasion. I will open our service, but I would like for you to sing a favorite hymn of mine, 'The Love of God.'"[90]

Gloria felt like crying. "I'm sorry, Papa Sam, but I need to rest my voice. I hope you understand. The two rehearsals and two concerts back to back gave my vocal cords a real workout. As a matter of fact, all of a sudden I feel completely exhausted. It must be a delayed reaction. Please excuse me, everyone, but I need to go to my room and rest. I'm sure I'll be back to normal after a good nap." Gloria controlled her emotions until she had closed the bedroom door.

The family looked at each other, knowing something was wrong. But they went on with their worship service. Papa Sam opened the service with a heartfelt prayer, including a petition for his precious granddaughter.

Gloria knelt at her bed and poured out her heart in silent prayer. *Father, 'The Love of God' was the song I sang to Jeff right after we first met. I remember we were just talking, and before I knew it I was singing that song to him and feeling such love as I sang it. He stared at me like he was spellbound. Then he reached up and kissed me on the lips, such a sweet, innocent kiss, like you would kiss a child. Our hearts were bound together right at that moment. It felt holy. I can't ever sing it again until Jeff comes back to me.* Gloria let the tears flow freely as she prayed over and over, "Dear Father, please bring Jeff back to me."

Mama Anna heard the Spirit telling her what to do. She hated to leave the worship service, so she waited for about fifteen minutes, then went to Gloria's room. As she opened the door she saw Gloria still kneeling at her bed and quietly crying.

Scripture poured into Mama Anna's mind, words from God that would bypass Gloria's emotions and reach her spirit – life changing, powerful words – and she began to repeat them as she knelt beside her. "Yeshua is here in this room, and He is saying this to you, Gloria: 'The Spirit of the Lord Yahweh is upon Me, because Yahweh has anointed Me to preach good tidings to the poor; He has sent Me to heal the brokenhearted…' 'Yahweh is close to the brokenhearted and saves those who are crushed in spirit.' 'He heals the brokenhearted and binds up their wounds.'[91] You must put the Father first in all your affections, child. He promised to meet all your needs by His riches in glory in Messiah Yeshua."[92]

"Mama Anna, my need is for Jeff to forgive me for disappointing him and for me to forgive him for treating me so coldly and accusing me of something that's not true." Gloria recounted the whole conversation she and Jeff had after Dror and Grace's party, concerning Mr. Gruber's announcement.

"And were you tempted with worldly fame, Gloria? Answer me honestly."

"Not really, Mama Anna, certainly not at the cost of my marriage. I do have to admit that all the adulation and applause did please me immensely. I wanted Jeff to share in my happiness. He always had supported me until that moment when Mr. Gruber gave Dror and me the offer of a concert tour. He jumped to the conclusion that I was going to accept it, but I would never have done that without Jeff's approval. Why didn't he know that, and why did he accuse me falsely?"

"Listen to me, Gloria. When you are on the mountaintop, everything is rosy, but there's the valley below waiting for you. You have to prepare for it. It even happened to Yeshua. Remember when he fed the 5,000, and the people were going to take Him by force to make Him their king?[93] He sent the crowds away, as well as His disciples, and went up on the mountain to pray. He was tempted by the crowd's desire to make Him king, and He had a spiritual struggle that night to keep from yielding to the temptation. What Yeshua did is our model. We should be on our guard when Satan tempts us with power and fame. He will try to make us fall from the top of the mountain. You weren't prepared. You didn't notice how Jeff was reacting to your glory. I know you wanted the glory to go to God, but at the moment, you were enjoying it for yourself."

"Oh, that hurts, Mama Anna. Maybe you are right, and Jeff saw it before I did."

"As for glory, did you know that Yeshua wants you to have glory along with Him? That was part of His high priestly prayer in the Garden of Gethsemane. He said, 'And the glory which You gave Me I have given them, that they may be one just as We are one… that the world may know that You have sent Me, and have loved them as You have loved Me.'[94] See the purpose of His glory that He shared with us? It is to make us one, and it's that unity that will attract the world."

"But it had the opposite effect on Jeff and me. Our oneness has been destroyed."

"No, child. The world was bestowing glory on you. Now your challenge is to glorify God in your restoration as Jeff's wife. Remember marriage is a picture of the Messiah and His bride. When you two were joined together as one, you promised it would be for better or worse and till death would part you. Why don't you call him? I will leave the room. I know the Holy Spirit will give you exactly what to say. Let me pray for you before I leave."

As Mama Anna prayed for her, Gloria felt a literal 'binding up' of her broken heart. It was like the healing oil she had read about in her Bible reading for the day from Psalm 133. Gloria sank down on the bed, limp and completely immersed in the Holy Spirit. *Mama Anna is quoting that very same Scripture in her prayer for me, Abba. How could she have possibly known? I feel Your healing of my broken heart, Abba. I love Your Word – 'Behold how good and how pleasant it is for brethren to dwell together in unity. It is like the precious oil upon the head, running down on the beard, the beard of Aaron, running down on the edge of his garments. It is like the dew of Hermon, descending upon the mountains of Zion; for there Yahweh commanded the blessing— life forevermore.'*

Anna quietly slipped out the door as her granddaughter was soaking up God's blessing.

CHAPTER THIRTY-EIGHT

RESTORATION

G loria fell asleep after Mama Anna prayed for her. She dreamed she was flying high like an eagle, but suddenly the winds that had kept her aloft quieted down. She plummeted to the earth. Her arms were damaged, and she cried, believing she would never fly again. But a tall handsome man bent over her. He healed her arms and sent her flying again. When she awoke, a song was forming in her mind. She was excited, knowing God had given her a message for Jeff. She picked up her cellphone and dialed his number. *Please, God, cause him to answer. Let him have time to talk to me.*

"Hello, Gloria. I see your name on the display. I really don't have time to talk now."

"Honey, I promise not to keep you long, but this song says everything I feel about you in the situation we have been in. Don't think I am using this to change your mind about anything. In fact, you have been right. Could you listen to me sing it? It came out of a dream God gave me."

Jeff felt his heart stirred a little, but his mind tried to take control. *What trick is she going to pull now? She knows how much her singing affects me. God, may Your will be done in our relationship. I think You have been telling me we need to be apart a while. If not, let me know after I hear this song. In Jesus' name.* "Okay, Gloria. I am going back in my room at the Dan Panorama. Dad said he wasn't in a big hurry."

"I am not going to sing all of this song. It's a secular song, and you already know it. It doesn't perfectly describe our relationship, but still it does express how I feel about you. Well, here it is. *'It must have been cold there in my shadow, to never have sunlight on your face. You were content to let me shine, that's your way. You always walked a step behind. So I was the one with all the glory, while you were the one with all the strength. A handsome face without a name for so long. A beautiful smile to hide the pain. Did you ever know that you're my hero, and everything I would like to be? I can fly higher than an eagle, 'cause you are the wind beneath my wings. It might have appeared to go unnoticed, but I've got it all here in my heart. I want you to know I know the truth, of course I know it. I would be nothing without you....'"[95]*

Jeff was silent a few seconds. Gloria was praying his cold heart was thawing. *My heart is bursting with love for you, you big ox. Can't you see I don't even have a life without you?* "Jeff, I meant every word of that. Please be patient with me. Since I last saw you, our song has been going over and over in my mind. I can't forget how you gently kissed my lips right after I sang it to you that night on the campus, and we had only known each other a few days. But I knew you were the only man I would ever love. Is it all right if I sing it to you now? Papa Sam asked me to sing it at our worship service this morning, but I was hurting so bad I couldn't sing it. Since then Yeshua has healed my broken heart, and this song with its background story expresses what I know we have had together and what I pray we will soon recover."

Jeff was hesitant. *Is she manipulating me? Is this Your way, God, of making me humble down to Gloria's agenda in order to make me have a servant's heart? I thought the wife was to submit to her husband, not the other way around. I know she's talking about that hymn, 'The Love of God,' and I do want to hear it. Please, God, take control of our marriage. I still love Gloria, but she needs to see my need for respect and trust that I will lead our family right.* "Okay, go ahead and sing it. And then I've got to go with Dad. We have a business to set up so we can have a steady income."

Gloria felt the anointing of the Holy Spirit as she sang the hymn passionately. She repeated the ending and sang with all her heart. "....*Could we with ink the ocean fill, and were the skies of parchment made, were every stalk on earth a quill, and every man a scribe by trade, to write the love of God above would drain the ocean dry. Nor could the scroll contain the whole, though stretched from sky to sky. O love of God, how rich and pure! How measureless and strong! It shall forevermore endure the saints' and angels' song.*" Gloria had done all she could do. God had to do the rest.

"Babe, that was beautiful, as usual. You are my favorite singer. We can talk about what happened on Christmas Eve, if you want to, but right now I have to be with Mom and Dad. They are going to make aliyah, probably around the time we have our spring break. I may need to come back over here and help them get settled."

"Oh, I see," was all Gloria could get out. That was just one more reason that she and Dror could not go to Europe on a concert tour during their spring break, although the only reason she needed was Jeff's disapproval. "Well, before I hang up, I want to pass along to your parents what my mother said yesterday. She said that she and my dad really bonded with your parents on Thanksgiving when we were together in Tupelo. She was hoping Mr. Jeffrey and Miss Leah would come up to Katzrin before the 30th, so we can all be together again."

"I will speak to them about that. It may be possible. Actually, we could talk about where we are going to live in Jerusalem. You had expressed a strong desire to live in the Old City in the Christ Church Guesthouses, until we toured the Rasko neighborhood. And now I know you agree that Rasko is ideal in location, price, and everything else for our entire families and the Carsons to live there together. I already showed it to Dad, and he liked it. Anyway, I may see you before the 30th, but I can't be sure. Bye now."

After she ended the call Gloria poured out a prayer of thanks to God. Her hopes were renewed for the restoration of her marriage.

When Jeff got off the phone, he let out a heavy sigh. His cold heart was melting, and he wanted to be with Gloria as soon as possible. But he didn't want her to know how eager he was. His dad would go along with whatever plan he put forth. He decided he would find a honeymoon cabin on the Golan Heights and rent it for two nights. Maybe he and his dad could conclude their business dealings the next day, and he could take Gloria to a romantic spot for Tuesday and Wednesday nights. They would make it to the airport on Thursday and fly out. It would be a new start for them. His parents could enjoy some time in Katzrin with Gloria's family before they flew home. Faith filled Jeff's heart as he prayed this plan would work. Then he searched the internet for honeymoon cabins.

Leah and Jeffrey arrived in Katzrin on Tuesday morning. Papa Sam was preparing the most delicious kosher Jewish lunch he had ever prepared, and the only person he would allow in the kitchen was Alvin. Mama Anna and Sylvia greeted their guests and ushered Jeffrey and Leah into the living room. Jeff came on a separate rental car about a half hour later, and Gloria greeted him. She had dressed in the most alluring dress she had with her, and her hair and makeup were flawless. The fragrance she chose was Jeff's favorite. Jeff swept her up in his arms and told her how gorgeous she looked. The game plan was on. All had been informed that Jeff and Gloria would be spending two days and nights in a romantic getaway on the Golan Heights. Gloria took time to visit briefly with Jeff's parents before Jeff took her luggage and stowed it in the trunk along with his. There were heartfelt hugs and kisses all around. Mama Anna was beaming as she kept waving goodbye until Jeff and Gloria were out of sight.

The Sea of Galilee sparkled like diamonds in the sun, and the happy couple was enthralled with its beauty. Jeff drove part way up the mountain overlooking the Kinneret, which was the Israelis' name for it. "Do you like this location, babe?"

"Oh, yes, Jeff, I love it! I hope we will have time to take a boat out on the water. But I am leaving the activities strictly up to you. I trust you completely to plan everything. Your wife is at your disposal. I want to please you in every way."

"That is music to my ears, and I do have some plans. On our first honeymoon we barely knew what marriage was about, but now that we have had a year and a half of experience, this second honeymoon should be more satisfying. I am looking forward to these two nights with you in complete privacy. No interruptions. No concerts. No telephone calls. No classes. No working in the kitchen. No working in the office. No going to church. And let me repeat – no concerts and certainly no rehearsals! Do you get my drift?"

"Yes, I do, and I am in complete agreement. From the top of my head to the tip of my toes I am thrilled beyond words."

Jeff grinned. "It's true that words and songs help in a relationship." Jeff winked. "But actions speak louder than words. And I'm ready for some wordless romance." Jeff reached over and tickled Gloria.

"Stop, you wolf. Wait until we get inside, please," laughed Gloria.

CHAPTER THIRTY-NINE

ROMANCE

Gloria got the coffee brewing and the table set for breakfast, then went to wake up Jeff with a song. "*Arise, shine, for thy light has come. Arise, shine, for thy light has come. And the glory of the Lord is risen, the glory of the Lord is come, the glory of the Lord is risen upon thee.*"[96]

Jeff reached his arms out to Gloria and tried to pull her down to the bed. She pulled back. "Oh, no you don't, you overactive lover. There should be moderation in all things. And talk about wordless romance, have you had your quota of kisses now? I am ready for some conversation. Come on, get out of bed, and let's eat breakfast. It was in the refrigerator, and all I had to do was warm it. I love this place."

Jeff shocked Gloria when he suddenly bounded out of bed and chased her around the kitchen. "The answer to your question is no, I have not had my quota of romantic kisses. Just one more kiss, and I will come to the table for conversation."

"Okay, just one now." Gloria reached up and kissed Jeff on the cheek. "Absence, meaning absence of kisses, makes the heart grow fonder. Also abstinence increases desire. Haven't you heard that?"

"I march to the beat of a different drummer, little wife. And only you can tame the heart of this savage beast."

"Jeff, this is getting corny. Come on, let's eat breakfast and act normal, okay? To increase your enjoyment, I say we eat, have some conversation, brush our teeth, and get dressed, and then do whatever you have planned." Gloria winked.

"Yes, dear, said the hen-pecked husband." Jeff chuckled. "This food is pretty good, and I love the hot coffee. I'm ready to talk now. What do you want to talk about? I'm done with serious subjects. There is time enough for that when I get home and have to put my nose to the grindstone again."

"Well, the first subject I want to talk about is Dror and Grace. You got to see them last Saturday, and I didn't. I wonder how things are going up in Charlottesville with Mr. and Mrs. Thomas, if they like Dror, and if they consented to the marriage. That was sweet of Grace to wish me a merry Christmas. Isn't it amazing that it's easy to forget Christmas in Israel because they don't celebrate it? I didn't let them forget it at the concert though, did I? Just right out in the open I sang about the birth of Christ in that encore number, 'O Holy Night.'"

"Gloria, I have to be honest. You just touched a sore spot. Your song was fabulous, but I got tired of seeing you holding Dror's hand and bowing after almost every song. I was sitting by Grace, and she didn't give off any jealous vibes, but it occurred to me that she might feel intimidated, since she isn't musical. I'm not sure she can even carry a tune. It keeps me from feeling musically worthless to know I am a descendant of Felix Mendelssohn, but I have to keep reminding myself not to be jealous. Then when Mr. Gruber put forth that proposal for you and Dror to go on a foreign concert tour **together**, I lost it!"

Gloria got up from the table and went over to Jeff, wrapping her arms around him. "Honey, Dror can't hold a feather to you. You are the most gorgeous and desirable man I have ever come in contact with. I consider myself highly favored to have won your love. Dror is my friend and an outstanding accompanist, but I have never been attracted to him romantically. I have eyes, and I can see that he is very handsome, but it doesn't move me. Anyway, I wish you had given me a chance to say that I couldn't go on that tour.

We are too close to moving to Israel, and my focus is on you and our move, as well as our life together with our friends and family and people at Adaton Baptist Church. But let me add that I have learned something through this experience. I confess to you now that I did love the applause and adulation, and it was about to steal my heart. Mama Anna helped me to see that it was a genuine temptation for me to pursue worldly goals. I learned the hard way. I thought I had lost you, and that woke me up. Oh, Jeff, please forgive me for hurting you so badly. You have always been very supportive of everything I do, the music, the teaching at church, everything."

"Babe, come here. Let me hold you. I love you so much, I ache. I have been acting like a fool. I hardened my heart, because I couldn't stand the hurt. But you melted it when you sang to me over the phone, and now love is pouring out of me like a river. I can't get enough of loving you, and it's not just the physical loving I'm talking about. I admire you, and I adore you. I want to be your earthly protector, provider, and shield. I do support your musical career. I trust you to make the right decisions, so you will keep all areas of your life balanced."

"Jeff, you are massaging my heart. It broke that night after the concert, but your words and the love in your eyes and in your touch have completed my healing. How in the world could I ever deserve a man like you? The glory I felt in the concerts can never match the glory I feel now in our oneness as man and wife. You know what, it's almost like a storybook romance. Jewish people are fascinating anyway, and our taking up residency in the Jewish nation is just a miracle story. Of course, we are one with our Gentile friends, Pete and Grace, as well as all of Adaton Baptist. And God has commissioned us and the Carsons and maybe the Mizrachis to teach the church about our Jewish roots and to win Jews and Gentiles to a saving faith in Yeshua the Messiah. We have to keep the main thing the main thing and make God proud of us."

"Right, Gloria. What we are doing in making aliyah is the 'the main thing.' The last few days I have been squeezing in some study of what the prophets say about Jews returning to their homeland from the four corners of the earth. From the notes I took when you taught our class a while back, this verse really stood out for me: 'Hear the word of Yahweh, O nations, and declare it in the coastlands afar off, and say, 'He who scattered Israel will gather him, and keep him as a shepherd does his flock.''[97] I checked on the population of Jews in Israel this year, and it is 4,882,000.[98] These numbers have been growing every year, especially since 1949. God has been gathering His people to come home. But they better get ready to add eight more Jews – you and me, our parents, Sarah, and Susanna. We have been scattered, or dispersed, and have been living in the 'Diaspora,' but now we are going home! Didn't you feel it, Gloria, when we first visited Israel? I felt like I had gone back to my roots."

"Yes, darling. I felt the same way. And now the time has come for us to return home. Listen to this: 'The Lord is building up Jerusalem…'[99] He 'will arise and have mercy on Zion; for the time to favor her, yes, the set time, has come…. When Yahweh shall build up Zion; He shall appear in His glory.'[100] Just think, we are helping Him build up Jerusalem. And wouldn't it be something if we are still alive and living there when Jerusalem is sufficiently built up, and Yeshua appears, when He comes back?"

"You said it! There is no doubt in my mind whatsoever that our prophetic destiny is to move to the land of our inheritance, Israel. I bought this little book in Jerusalem, *Let My People Go! by* Tom Hess.[101] He lists 700 verses from Scripture where God promises the land of Canaan to His chosen people and commands or encourages them to return to the land of Israel which He gave to them, or rather, us, as an everlasting possession. The sheer number of the verses, possibly more verses on this subject than any other subject in the Bible, tells you what is closest to God's heart. Now I know Yeshua died for all people and loves us all equally, Jews and Gentiles. But I also know He chose the Jewish people through whom He would give us the Scriptures and, most importantly, the Messiah. In the Book of Ezekiel I have learned that His mighty power in restoring the Jewish people to their land and then to Himself will cause the whole world to acknowledge that He is God! Ezekiel ends quite a few chapters with this phrase, '**Then** they shall know that I am Yahweh.'"[102]

"Honey, have you considered that we are soon going to be living in the Middle East which is a hotbed of conflict between the Arabs and the Jews, between the descendants of Abraham's sons, Isaac and Ishmael? I am glad you got that book by Tom Hess. I also have a new book I bought in Jerusalem – *Prophetic Destinies* by Derek Prince. I have it right here. Let me quote this part: 'Here are two main spiritual forces that meet in conflict over the Middle East: on the one hand, the grace of God working toward Israel's restoration; and on the other hand, the deceitful strategies of Satan, who is opposing this process by every means in his power.' He goes on to say that Satan is obscuring the truth in the Bible and creating confusion which is causing the church to misunderstand God's purposes for Israel. He says, 'The battle for Israel is, in fact, the battle for truth.'" [103]

"Sweet wife, in this battle we know how to put on the armor of God and wield the 'sword of the Spirit, which is the Word of God.' Yeshua is sending us out to show in our lives and to speak His specific word that Yeshua, their Messiah and our Messiah, is 'the Way, the Truth, and the Life.' You can do this in your singing. I will have an audience among our food business customers. Oh, how exciting! Regardless of what the Ministry of the Interior says, you and I are making aliyah. We are bona fide Jews who know our Messiah and know that the land of Israel is our inheritance. You and I and our group are fulfilling our **prophetic destinies**. Glory to God!"

"Thank you, Jeff, for having serious conversation with me, but do you mind if we return to our purpose for coming to this honeymoon cabin? We only have one more night. Remember that I said after breakfast and some conversation, we would do all you have planned." Gloria held out her arms to Jeff.

With a gleam in his eye, Jeff picked up his wife and carried her outside. As he turned around and carried her back inside, he smothered her with kisses. "Over the threshold we go, my awesome wife of eighteen short months. Let's see if this second honeymoon can surpass the first one."

EPILOGUE

D ror and Grace were married at Adaton Baptist Church with her parents' full approval. The date was set for Friday night at the beginning of the MSU spring break in March. Mrs. Thomas provided beautiful dresses and tuxedos for the wedding party. She brought in a team to decorate the church and a team to cater the reception which was held at Sessions Manor. Mr. Thomas invited his Washington political friends and provided airfare and lodging for them. Grace asked Gloria to be in charge of the music and also to be her matron of honor. Dror's father, Benyamin Mizrachi, would be his best man. Jeff, Pete and Sarah were in the wedding party, as well as Shira and Aharon Shapiro from Tel Aviv.

Dr. Salomon Rothschild was given the special honor of blessing Dror and Grace with the Aaronic benediction in Hebrew and English at the close of the ceremony. Avigail Rothschild stood beside him. Her formal dress revealed a shapely figure with a little 'baby bump.' She couldn't have been more beautiful. At the rehearsal dinner the night before, Salomon and Dror brought each other up to date since they had last seen each other at the concert. The doctor expressed his deep gratitude to Dror for introducing him to a supernatural God who loved him, forgave him, and sent His Son to die for him. He said that Avigail became pregnant within two weeks after Dror prophesied to him in the Austro-Bavarian language. "Dror, we are naming this baby Jedidiah, just like

HaShem said to. If we have another baby boy, we are naming him Dror." Dror became so emotional, he could hardly speak.

At the wedding reception Walter and Jenny stood with the Thomases and the Mizrachis, parents of the newlyweds, to welcome everyone to Sessions Manor. Jenny was glowing, dressed in a beautiful maternity dress her mother had made. Walter was continually at her side, smiling broadly, as they moved about the room, having conversations with friends. Gloria said, "Jenny, you are even prettier in your maternity dress than you were in your wedding dress."

"Gloria, you said it would happen, and it was only about six weeks after you made that prophecy that I got pregnant. Walter is treating me like a queen. And just to think, if you and Sarah had not continued to care about me, even though I was so hateful and wicked, I might never have been saved. And now I could not love Jesus more. Walter and I are living the abundant life He promised."

Gloria hugged Jenny, "We were all lost before Jesus saved us. Keep shining for him, Jenny. I hope we are still here when you give birth. Jeff and I will be praying for the three of you, rest assured."

After the reception was over, Dror and Grace boarded the plane at the Golden Triangle Airport for Aspen, Colorado. The newlyweds had enjoyed the snow in Charlottesville, Virginia, so much during the Christmas break that they decided to spend their honeymoon in another winter wonderland, high enough in the mountains to have snow in the spring. That evening Dror and Grace's parents, the Shapiros, and the Rothchilds were taken to the airport by the Holy Rollers, Pastor, Celeste, and Susannah. Their parting embraces were heartfelt, and the Thomases made Pastor and Celeste promise they would come and visit soon. Susannah and her daughter Devorah kept up a steady stream of conversation in the airport lobby and continued to give warm hugs up to a few minutes before departure. That night Jeffrey and Leah hosted a dinner at Harvey's in Columbus for Lars and Elsa Carson, Jeff, Gloria, Pete, and Sarah, and then drove home to Tupelo.

The Holy Rollers continued their ministry in area churches, teaching about the Jewish roots of the church and testifying about the blessings of visiting Israel and walking where Jesus walked. After Dror and Grace returned from their honeymoon, they took up residence in Dror's apartment. When classes started back, they joined the Holy Rollers in ministry, taking a turn teaching the Jewish Roots class at Adaton. Dror became a supplier for his father's Israeli business. Jeff made room at the Distribution Center for Mizrachi Jewelry of the Golden Triangle. Grace helped him take calls, visited stores with him, and even modeled the jewelry. Due to time constraints Dror quit his job of writing articles for the Journal of the Southern Jewish Historical Society. He continued to take piano lessons from Mrs. Pagani and accompany Gloria for her voice recitals on campus, as well as her solos at Adaton and in other churches. He completed all the requirements for a Master of Arts degree in history of the U.S. South. Grace completed her Bachelor of Science degree in interior design.

Jeffrey and Leah booked their connecting flight to Israel through New York in April, joining Alvin and Sylvia in making aliyah. Jeffrey had turned over the operation of his wholesale grocery business in Tupelo to a long-time trusted employee at the beginning of the year. He and Leah would have a steady income from the home office and could take the time necessary to build up their new business in Israel. They had their piano shipped to Israel, and it would be moved into Jeff and Gloria's apartment when they arrived in June. Thanks to Sam and Anna's advice, Alvin and Sylvia, as well as Jeffrey and Leah, bought furniture and appliances after they got to Israel. As olim, they were entitled to fifty per cent off their purchases to set up housekeeping. There were many other perks for them as new immigrants. Sam and Anna had known a family who had their furniture shipped from America, and none of it would fit in their Israeli apartment. Even the bed was too big, so it was obvious that buying furniture and appliances needed to be done after they got to Israel. They would have to go to the ulpan to learn Hebrew, and they had mixed feelings about it. It was a big commitment and a lot of work, but they did want to learn the language. After all, they would be living in Israel the rest of their lives, and they still considered themselves young. All four of them were in their mid-forties.

Dror had an Israeli passport, but the others who were moving to Israel in June had obtained work visas, except for Gloria, who had obtained a music scholarship and student visa. Being believers in Yeshua had made them ineligible for aliyah and the benefits of citizenship. Dror and Grace had decided to live in Jerusalem in the Rasko neighborhood with Jeff and Gloria and both their parents and Pete and Sarah. First, however, they would help Dror's grandmother get moved into his house in Tel Aviv. Susannah was overjoyed that she would be living with her daughter Devorah and her son-in-law Benyamin.

Benyamin Mizrachi had taken it on himself to direct the flight plan. He would bear the expense, but he would be reimbursed after everyone was settled in.

June 13, 2000, finally arrived. Jeff had turned over the Quentin Distribution Center in Starkville to Walter Sessions. Jeff had completed his Bachelor of Science degree in business administration. Gloria had completed her Bachelor of Arts degree in piano and voice. Sarah had completed her Bachelor of Science degree in accounting, and Pete had received his Bachelor of Arts degree in criminal justice.

Since furniture, appliances, and vehicles had to be purchased after the Quentins, Carsons, and Mizrachis got to Israel, they would not need to ship very much, so a few days before June 13th, the six of them consolidated their belongings, excluding clothing and essentials, into the smallest container they could purchase and ship. They would take with them the maximum number of suitcases allowed by the airline, each with clothes and personal items. The shipped container would arrive in Israel several weeks after they landed. They had prayed God would lead them to the right company, and they felt confident the one they chose could be trusted. The price quote was reasonable and included warehousing and customs fees.

This group of seven people was accompanied to the airport by Lars and Elsa Carson and their entire family, Pastor Jeff and Celeste James, many members of Adaton Baptist Church, Walter and Jenny Sessions, Gary and Priscilla Grayson, and Mrs. Pagani. Grace's parents had flown in to the Golden Triangle Airport for the sendoff and would spend two nights with Celeste and Pastor Jeff before they returned to North Carolina.

Before entering the terminal Pastor James directed everyone to make a circle around the seven people moving to Israel. He anointed each one with oil. Everyone laid hands on the travelers or on the nearest person. Pastor James led the prayer, asking God for His guidance, protection, and blessing. Loud "amens" went up in agreement.

Gloria couldn't suppress her good news any longer. As soon as they had checked in and gone to the gate and were seated, Gloria stood in front of the group and said, "Dearest friends and my husband, I want to say that there are not seven of us moving to Israel. There is an eighth person here today."

Jeff interrupted, "Well, of course there is. Sarah is carrying hers and Pete's baby."

Gloria resumed her announcement, "Oh, that's right. I miscounted. There is a ninth person going to Israel with us." She looked at Jeff with a huge smile on her face.

"What, babe? You're not saying that..."

"Yes, honey, you will be a father in eight months!"

There was an uproar in the airport. Jeff's jaw dropped, and he couldn't get out a word for a few seconds. "Oh, our baby is the ninth person! Gloria, you didn't tell me. But's it's okay. I'm not mad at you. I guess you haven't known it yourself very long."

"That's right, honey. I wanted to be sure before I told you, and I was only sure this morning. I didn't have time to go to the doctor, but the pregnancy test is positive. I am so happy. And I promise I will not have morning sickness on the flight. I promise the baby will be safe. I know it, I know it."

"Don't get hysterical, babe. I know everything will be all right, too. Let's praise the Lord! How can He keep blessing us so much? It's crazy, I know, but I feel like naming the baby after Him. Oh, Gloria, let's name him Joshua. That is really 'Yeshua' in Hebrew."

Pete laughed. "Have you ever known a girl to be named Joshua?" Everybody joined in the laughter and congratulations to Gloria and Jeff.

Gloria exclaimed, "If it's a boy, Joshua, and if it's a girl, she will be named Miriam, which is Mary's Hebrew name. Sarah, us new mothers have got a lot to talk about, don't we?"

Celeste chuckled. "Those babies are stowaways! I should have sneaked on this flight, too. But I have a unique role to play today. As the only Jewish person left behind to say it in Hebrew, I want to wish you seven people and two babies in the womb, 'Nesiya tovah!' Wonderful journey!" Celeste gave Susannah one more passionate hug. "Mother, I love you so much, and I am really going to miss you. When you start dancing in Israel, please send me pictures and videos. You will be the talk of Tel Aviv!"

Elinor and Julie took Susannah off to the side. They had a gift for her, an exotic scarf. Susannah drew them close and thanked them. "Girls, I want you to know that God used you to change my life. First of all, I felt a love and acceptance from you that was a brand new feeling for me. When you prayed, and we all fell to the floor unconscious, I had a beautiful vision of my dancing in Israel. This scarf you have given me is perfect. I can already imagine how it will look on me when I am fulfilling that vision. How could you have known? Well, surely the Lord revealed it to you. Please think about visiting me in Tel Aviv some day when Lars and Elsa go to Jerusalem to visit Pete and Sarah." The girls reached up and hugged Mrs. Goldberg and promised they would visit. Susannah was at a loss for words, but just nodded her head with tears in her eyes.

Mrs. Pagani had to speak to Gloria. "My protégé, I am thrilled beyond words that you are making your home in the Holy City. Only recently have I come to understand that the center of the music world is not in Europe. It is not in New York. It is in Jerusalem. As I said, this is new knowledge for me, but I have learned a lot from the Bible study I have been attending. King David, who wrote most of the Psalms, also created musical instruments, and they were used primarily in the temple for the worship of God. He started out worshiping God as a boy shepherd, playing his harp and creating beautiful songs. I also want to say that when you sang arias from Handel's *Messiah* and told how he wrote it at the Christmas concert last year, I felt the Lord speaking to me that He had used me in a mighty way to teach you piano and help you on your way to your destiny in Jerusalem. He clearly said to me, 'I love you.' At that moment I gave my heart to Him." Mrs. Pagani broke down and cried.

Gloria wrapped her teacher in her arms. "Mrs. Pagani, we want you to visit us as often as you can. Yes, God has used you to change my life as a performer of His music, and I deeply thank you. And you have greatly blessed me with what you just said."

All the Carsons and Julie crowded around Pete and Sarah and gave them kisses and hugs. Jenny walked over to Sarah, carrying her baby son. "Please, let's keep in touch constantly. Maybe Walter and I can fly over to see you after your baby is born. Being a mother to little Seth is the greatest thing that has happened to me besides marrying Walter. If our next baby is a girl, I am going to name her Sarah after you." Sarah reached out to Jenny and the baby and wouldn't let go for several minutes.

As the spokesman for the travelers, Jeff called for everyone's attention. "Dear friends and family, let me give you thanks for all the love and support you have shown us, culminating in this glorious sendoff. I speak on behalf of Gloria, Pete, Sarah, Dror, Grace, Mrs. Goldberg, and myself. I heard from my parents this morning, and Gloria also got a call from her parents, telling us that they have been lifting us up to God's throne of grace for a safe journey to Israel. They are already sowing seeds of the gospel, and they are praying we will begin doing the same thing, even on the airplane. I told them about the special prayer meeting we had at Adaton last night with the entire church attending. And that when we had hands laid on us, the Holy Spirit almost knocked us out! So, thank you again. The seven of us feel equipped and ready to fulfill our prophetic destinies in the land of Israel. Toda rabbah, you wonderful people! Shalom!"

Members of Adaton Baptist with Miss Lizzie and her ladies at the forefront raced up to each of the seven and pinned flowers on them. Elsa pressed a little snack bag of homemade goodies into each one's hand. Then Gary and Priscilla distributed confetti to throw on the travelers as they lined up to board the plane. Shouts of "Shalom!" and "Nesiya tovah!" reverberated through the terminal.

Jeff waited till the plane leveled off, and everyone quieted down. Then he whispered in Gloria's ear, "I didn't forget, adorable wife. It's June 13th. Happy anniversary. You have given me the two happiest years of my life. 'Marital bliss' is too trite to describe what I have had with you. I had rather say, 'marital ecstasy.'" Jeff gave Gloria a gentle kiss on the lips, the same way he kissed her the first time they met, and then handed her an envelope.

Gloria looked deep into Jeff's eyes, savoring the kiss. "I knew you wouldn't forget, honey. I don't know what is inside that envelope, and we also don't know what is inside me, a girl or a boy, but I do know that our Lord continues to increase our love day by day. I was going to wait until we arrive in Israel, but I can't wait. I have to tell you now. Mom and Dad are planning an anniversary party for us and also for Pete and Sarah in our new apartment in Jerusalem. Mom had our piano tuned, and I am going to play and sing to you, 'The Love of God,' in remembrance of that night you first kissed me."

"That's all the anniversary gift I want, precious girl. Well, I can't wait for you to read what I wrote you, so give me that envelope. I have to read it to you now. It's what I feel for you, the same as King Solomon felt about his beloved bride." Jeff opened the envelope and read, 'Rise up, my love, my fair one, and come away! O my dove, in the clefts of the rock, in the secret places of the cliff, let me see your face, let me hear your voice; for your voice is sweet, and your face is lovely.'[104] I mean it, Gloria. Now you finish reading. The rest of my gift is a poem, the first I ever wrote. I had to copy it two times, because my tears kept wetting the pages."

Gloria was overwhelmed with Jeff's love. "Jeff, my heart is racing so fast, and I feel such passionate love for you. What Solomon said reminds me of our honeymoon and how we read that very passage together right before we truly did 'rise up and come away' with Jesus on the plane to Israel! And now I'm the one crying! I can't put it into words how much I admire, trust, and long to fully express my love to you. Jeff. Let us just sit here and bask in the unfathomable love of Jesus that caused Him to give us to each other. It is our divine destiny to be loved by Him and to be loved by each other. What an honor that He would send us to take up residence in the Holy Land where He lived, died, rose again, and where He is returning soon!"

ALEPH-BET
THE HEBREW ALPHABET (SQUARE LETTERS)

Letter	Name	English	Value	Signification
א	Aleph	'	1	Ox
בּ בּ	Bet/Vet	b	2	House
ג	Gimel	g	3	Camel
ד	Dalet	d	4	Door
ה	He	h	5	Latticewindow
ו	Vav	v	6	Hook
ז	Zayin	z	7	Weapon
ח	Chet	ch	8	Fence
ט	Tet	t	9	Snake
י	Yod	y	10	Hand
כּ כ	Kaph/Khaph	k	20	Bent Hand
ל	Lamed	l	30	Ox-Goad
מ	Mem	m	40	Water
נ	Nun	n	50	Fish
ס	Samech	s	60	Prop
ע	Ayin	'	70	Eye
פּ פ	Pe/Fe	p	80	Mouth
צ	Tsade	ts	90	Fish Hook
ק	Qoph	q	100	Back of Head
ר	Resh	r	200	Head
שׂ	Sin	s	300	Tooth
שׁ	Shin	sh	—	''
ת	Tav	th	400	Cross

Hebrew is written and read from right to left.

HEBREW VOCABULARY

1. שָׁלוֹם!
   Shalom!
   (Hello, goodbye, peace)

2. בּוֹקֶר טוֹב.
   Bóker tov.
   (Good morning.)

3. אַבָּא
   ábba
   (father)

4. תּוֹדָה
   todá
   (thank you)

5. אָלֶף־בֵּית עִבְרִי
   álefbait ivrí (Hebrew alphabet)

6. אֲנִי
   Ah-ní' (I)

7. אַתָּה
   ah-tah' (you-m.)

8. אַתְּ
   aht (you-f.)

9. הוּא
   hoo (he)

10. הִיא
    hee (she)

11. כֵּן
    Ken (yes)

12. לֹא
    lo (no)

13. מִי
    mi (who)

14. אִמָּא
    íma (mother)

15. אִמָּא וְאַבָּא
    íma veh ábba
    (mother and father)

וָ, וְ
vah, veh
(and)

16. בְּבַקָשָׁה
    bevakashá (please, you're welcome)

הַ
ha
(the)

17. יֵשׁוּעַ הַמָשִׁיחַ
    Yeshúa HaMashíach
    (Jesus the Messiah or Jesus Christ)

18. הָאֱלֹהִים הוּא אַהֲבָה.
    HaElohím hu aháva.
    (God is love.)

In the Hebrew transliteration, the vowel A is pronounced AH as in 'father.' E is pronounced EH or A, as in 'pet' or 'hey.' I is pronounced E as in 'submarine.' O is pronounced as a 'long O' as in 'home.' U is pronounced OO, as in 'super.'

GLOSSARY

Abba – father or daddy

Aliyah – "going up," immigrating to Israel – only Jews can "make aliyah"

Ani ohevet otcha – I love you (female to male)

Ani ohev otakh – I love you (male to female)

Balagan – a big confusion

Baruch Ata, Adonai Eloheynu, Melech HaOlam, hamotzi lechem min haaretz.

(Blessed art Thou, O Lord our God, King of the Universe, who brings forth bread from the earth.)

Baruch haba – welcome (singular)

Bashert – Yiddish word, meaning "fate" or "destiny," a perfect match for marriage

Bayit shelanu – our home

Bemah – stage in the synagogue

Bereshit – Genesis (literally "in the beginning")

Boker tov – good morning

B'nee – my son

B'seder – fine, all right – literally "in order"

Brit Hadasha – New Testament

Bruchim habayim – welcome (plural)

Chag sameach – Happy holiday, literally "joyous festival"

Chutzpah – cheeky nerve

Erev tov – good evening

Goy – Gentile

Glossary

Goyim – Gentiles, the same word as nations
Hadash – new
Hava – love
Haverim – friends
Hodu – give thanks (also the word for turkey)
Hora – national folk dance of Israel
Ima - mother
Ivrit – Hebrew
Kehilah – faith community, congregation
Ken – yes
L' – to
L'Chaim – to life (a toast)
Laila tov – good night
Lecha, lecha! – Get going!
Lo – no
Mazel tov! – Congratulations! (literally, "good luck")
Mevin – understand
Min – from
Moreh - teacher
Meshuganah – Yiddish word, meaning "crazy"
Nesiyah tovah – good journey
Oleh – immigrant, masculine (olah – feminine)
Olim – immigrants (plural)
Oy vey! – Yiddish, expressing grief, frustration, pain, or exasperation
Ruach HaKodesh – Holy Spirit
Saba – grandfather
Savta – grandmother
Savlanut – patience
Shalom shalom – perfect peace
Shalu – ask for (pray)
Shema – creed of Judaism, named for the first word: "Hear (Sh'ma) O
    Israel, the Lord our God, the Lord is One" (Deut. 6:4).
Slicha – excuse me
Talmidim – students (disciples)
Tanach – Old Testament (Torah-Neviim-Ketuvim = TNK, acronym
    for Torah-Prophets-Writings)
Toda – thank you
Toda rabbah – thank you very much or many thanks

Torah – Hebrew for "instruction" – the first five books of the Bible, also called "Pentateuch"

V' or veh – and

Yafah – beautiful

Yaldah – girl

Yehudi – Jew

Yehudim - Jews

Yerushalayim – Jerusalem

Yeshua Ha Mashiach – Jesus the Messiah

Yisrael - Israel

Yofi – great (used as interjection)

END NOTES

1   "Aliyah" in Hebrew means "going up," immigrating to Israel.

2   *Shock Absorption: A Survival Guide for Living in Israel* by Esther Rivka, © 1990 (Burnet, TX: Shock Absorption).

3   See Hebrew alphabet at end of the book.

4   Dick Mills and David Michael, *Messiah and His Hebrew Alphabet* (Orange, CA: Dick Mills Ministries, 1994).

5   1 Sam. 16:7.

6   "Shepherd Boy" by Ray Bolz and Steve Millikan, © 1989, Musicascap and Sonworshippersascap. Video: https://youtu.be/mkNhPboI-5Y.

7   "Shalu Shalom Yerushalayim," Messianic Jewish song - https://youtu.be/apnUUm6NC2g

8   Eph. 2: 11-18.

9   Rom. 11: 25-27.

10 Matt. 5:35; Psa. 48:2.

11 "Open your mouth wide, and I will fill it," (Psa. 81:10).

12 *Spirit Filled Life Bible,* New King James Version, Gen. Ed. Jack W. Hayford, ©1991 (Nashville: Thomas Nelson Publishers), p. 1334.

13 Isa. 55: 11.

14 Num. 6:24-26.

15 Matt. 9: 20-22.

16 Mills and Michael, *Messiah and His Hebrew Alphabet*, p. 83.

17 Ramon Bennett, *When Day and Night Cease* (Jerusalem: Arm of Salvation ©1996, Dist. Shekinah Books, Citrus Heights, CA), p. 110.

18 Mark 10:18.

19 Gal. 5:22.

20 "Up to Jerusalem" by Paul Wilbur - https://youtu.be/U7XCU-aBOzQ

21 Isa. 49:22.

22 Isa. 55:8-9.

23 1 Kings 13: 1-6.

24 2 Kings 23: 15-16.

25 1 Peter 2:2

26 Heb. 5:14.

27 Zech. 12:10.

28 Jer. 32:27.

29 Heb. 2:10.

30 Text of "Jerusalem Documentary," Barry & Batya Segal, *Sh'ma Yisrael, Messianic Praise* - cassette tape (Jerusalem: Greetings from Jerusalem Ltd., 1994 Kingsway ThankYou Music).

31 Acts 2:17.

32 "Shoo-Fly Pie and Apple Pan Dowdy" by Sammy Gallop and Guy Wood, ©1945, https://www.lyrics.com/lyric/3299883/Dinah+Shore

33 Ima, pronounced Eema, means "Mother."

34 Linda Alexander, *The Unpromised Land: the Struggle of Messianic Jews, Gary & Shirley Beresford* (Baltimore: Lederer Messianic Publications, 1994) p. 183.

35 Ibid, p. 187.

36 Ibid, p. 168.

37 John 11: 47-48.

38 "Morning in My Heart" by A.H. Ackley, © 1933. Homer A. Rodeheaver, renewed 1961, Word Music. https://hymnary.org/text/all_the_darkness_of_the_night

[39] The U.S. Attorney's Office, Southern District of Mississippi, January 15, 2000 - https://www.justice.gov/usao-sdms/pr/three-jackson-residents-plead-guilty-human-trafficking

[40] Gen. 41:32.

[41] Zech. 4:6.

[42] Psa. 97:10 (NIV).

[43] 2 Cor. 6:14.

[44] Psalm 121: 7-8.

[45] Luke 23: 42-43.

[46] https://comfortoneanother.com/2020/07/28/the-9th-of-av-jewish-tragedies-a-2020-update/

[47] Isa. 40: 1-2.

[48] Matt. 5:4.

[49] Rev. 22:16.

[50] Mal. 4:2.

[51] Matt. 11:28-30 (NLT).

[52] Zech. 7: 1-10.

[53] Isa. 58: 1-7.

[54] Lev. 23:27.

[55] Isa. 43: 25.

[56] 2 Sam. 23:1.

[57] Job 42: 10.

[58] 2 Sam. 6: 16-23.

[59] Neh. 8: 9-10.

[60] Isa. 1:18.

[61] Isa. 55: 12.

[62] Gen. 28: 10-17.

[63] 2 Cor. 5:17.

[64] Luke 4:9.

[65] Rom. 8:11.

[66] Zech. 4:6.

[67] Words by Katharine Lee Bates, composed in 1893. Music by Samuel A. Ward, composed in 1892. Music and words were published in 1910 and entitled, "America, the Beautiful." Both composers were inspired by America's beauty and history.

[68] Max I. Dimont, *Jews, God, and History*, 1962, 2004.

69 Marvin R. Wilson, *Father Abraham: Jewish Roots of the Christian Faith* (Grand Rapids: William B. Eerdmans Publishing Co., 1989), pp 127-131.

70 https://www.oneforisrael.org/holidays/was-thanksgiving-based-on-sukkot-the-feast-of-tabernacles/

71 "Hodu L'Adonai Ki Tov" by Barry & Batya Segal - https://youtu.be/15zBF3VL2H0

72 "Sleigh Ride" by Leroy Anderson, ©1948 Woodbury Music Co. Lyrics by Mitchell Parrish.

73 http://leroyanderson.com/sleigh-ride.php

74 Two people in Tel Aviv and one person in Eilat contracted the West Nile Virus in September 1999. https://www.researchgate.net/publication/11560694_West_Nile_fever_in_Israel_1999-2000_From_geese_to_humans

75 Matt. 18:19.

76 Deut. 33:27.

77 "The Outbreak of West Nile Virus Infection in the New York City Area in 1999" - https://www.nejm.org/doi/full/10.1056/nejm200106143442401. Also, https://www.ncbi.nlm.nih.gov/pmc/articles/PMC1127855/

78 Acts 2: 38-39.

79 https://www.history.com/this-day-in-history/the-balfour-declaration

80 https://en.wikipedia.org/wiki/Rothschild_banking_family_of_Austria

81 https://israelmyglory.org/article/the-man-who-believed-in-miracles/

82 Gen. 2:5.

83 In Yiddish, this perfect match is called 'bashert,' a word meaning *fate* or ***destiny***. https://www.jewishvirtuallibrary.org/marriage-in-judaism

84 https://en.wikipedia.org/wiki/David_Citadel_Hotel

85 https://en.wikipedia.org/wiki/Yad_L%27Achim

86 "My Tribute" by Andrae Crouch, ©1971.

87 Matt. 5: 11-12.

88 https://www.breakpoint.org/the-story-behind-handels-messiah/

89 "Days of Elijah" by Robin Mark, © 1994

90 "The Love of God" by Frederic Lehman - https://
    hymnstudiesblog.wordpress.com/2017/11/20/the-love-of-
    god-is-greater-far/ and also https://israelmyglory.org/article/
    the-love-of-god-is-greater-far/
91 Isai. 61:1; Psa. 34:18 (NIV); Psa. 147:3.
92 Phil. 4:19.
93 John 6:15.
94 John 17:22-23.
95 "Wind Beneath My Wings" by Larry Enley and Jeff Silbar, first
    recorded by Roger Whitaker in 1983 and made famous in the
    soundtrack for the movie, "Beaches," with Bette Midler in 1989.
96 Isa. 60:1 (King James Version).
97 Jer. 31:10.
98 http://www.ajcarchives.org/AJC_DATA/Files/2000_13_WJP.pdf
99 Psa. 147:2.
100 Psa. 102:13, 16 (KJV).
101 Tom Hess, *Let My People Go!* (Jerusalem: Progressive Vision
    International, 1997).
102 Ezek. 35:15; 36: 38; 38:23. https://www.esv.org/resources/esv-
    global-study-bible/global-message-of-ezekiel/
103 Derek Prince, *Prophetic Destinies* (Altamonte Springs, FL: Creation
    House, Strang Communications Company) ©1992, p.12.
104 Song of Solomon 2:13-14

ALSO BY NANCY PETREY

Jewish Roots Journey

Why Christians Should Care About Their Jewish Roots

Habitation of Honey

The Honeycomb Is Waiting

Letting My Light Shine

www.energiondirect.com

Get other volumes in this trilogy, or the whole set!

https://www.energiondirect.com/product/family-secrets-trilogy-group/

Also by Nancy Petrey for Amazon Kindle:
https://amzn.to/2J5AI3B